"Full of actio...
table tale tha... Silver City

"Hot rom...
and powe...
now that ...

—Night Owl Romance Reviews

You get great suspense, vivid characters, and a world that just pops off the pages . . . Not to be missed."

—*Night Owl Romance Reviews*

"Gritty danger and red-hot sensuality make this book and series smoking!"

—*Romantic Times*

"Deliciously sexy and intriguingly original."

—*USA Today* bestselling author Angela Knight

"Sizzling suspense and sexy magic are sure to propel this hot new series onto the charts. Bast is a talent to watch, and her magical world is one to revisit." —*Romantic Times*

"A sensual feast sure to sate even the most finicky of palates. Richly drawn, dynamic characters dictate the direction of this fascinating story. You can't miss with Anya."

—*A Romance Review*

"Fast-paced, edgy suspense . . . The paranormal elements are fresh and original. This reader was immediately drawn into the story from the opening abduction, and obsessively read straight through to the dramatic final altercation. Bravo, Ms. Bast; *Witch Fire* is sure to be a fan favorite."

—*ParaNormal Romance Reviews*

"A fabulously written ultimate romance. Anya Bast tells a really passionate story and leaves you wanting more . . . The elemental witch series will be a fantastic read."

—*The Romance Readers Connection*

"A terrific romantic fantasy starring two volatile lead characters . . . The relationship between fire and air [makes] the tale a blast to read."

—*The Best Reviews*

# WICKED
# ENCHANTMENT

## ANYA BAST

BERKLEY SENSATION, NEW YORK

**THE BERKLEY PUBLISHING GROUP**
**Published by the Penguin Group**
**Penguin Group (USA) Inc.**
**375 Hudson Street, New York, New York 10014, USA**

Penguin Group (Canada), 90 Eglinton Avenue East, Suite 700, Toronto, Ontario M4P 2Y3, Canada
(a division of Pearson Penguin Canada Inc.)
Penguin Books Ltd., 80 Strand, London WC2R 0RL, England
Penguin Group Ireland, 25 St. Stephen's Green, Dublin 2, Ireland (a division of Penguin Books Ltd.)
Penguin Group (Australia), 250 Camberwell Road, Camberwell, Victoria 3124, Australia
(a division of Pearson Australia Group Pty. Ltd.)
Penguin Books India Pvt. Ltd., 11 Community Centre, Panchsheel Park, New Delhi—110 017, India
Penguin Group (NZ), 67 Apollo Drive, Rosedale, North Shore 0632, New Zealand
(a division of Pearson New Zealand Ltd.)
Penguin Books (South Africa) (Pty.) Ltd., 24 Sturdee Avenue, Rosebank, Johannesburg 2196,
South Africa

Penguin Books Ltd., Registered Offices: 80 Strand, London WC2R 0RL, England

This is a work of fiction. Names, characters, places, and incidents either are the product of the author's imagination or are used fictitiously, and any resemblance to actual persons, living or dead, business establishments, events, or locales is entirely coincidental. The publisher does not have any control over and does not assume any responsibility for author or third-party websites or their content.

WICKED ENCHANTMENT

A Berkley Sensation Book / published by arrangement with the author

PRINTING HISTORY
Berkley Sensation mass-market edition / January 2010

Copyright © 2010 by Anya Bast
Excerpt from *Cruel Enchantment* copyright © 2010 by Anya Bast
Cover design by Rita Frangie
Cover art by Tony Mauro
Interior text design by Kristin del Rosario

ISBN: 978-0-425-23201-9

BERKLEY® SENSATION
Berkley Sensation Books are published by The Berkley Publishing Group,
a division of Penguin Group (USA) Inc.,
375 Hudson Street, New York, New York 10014.
BERKLEY® SENSATION and the "B" design are trademarks of Penguin Group (USA) Inc.

PRINTED IN THE UNITED STATES OF AMERICA

10  9  8  7  6  5  4  3  2  1

*This book is dedicated to my husband and my daughter
for filling every day with love, laughter, and support.
I cherish even the everyday domestic annoyances.
I am lost without you.*

# ACKNOWLEDGMENTS

Thanks to Lauren Dane and Jody Wallace for giving me their proofing skills and opinions when I desperately needed them.

Thanks to Brenda Maxfield for always being my sounding board and for listening to me prattle on about my stories and characters.

Major appreciation to Axel de Roy, the brilliant artist who created the interactive map of Piefferburg that can be found on my website. I have loved your art for the last fifteen years, just about the same amount of time I've been married to your good friend.

And an extra thanks to my husband for not only putting up with me when I'm stressed and/or deadline-frenzied, but for suggesting the brilliant name of *Faemous* for the human media coverage of the Seelie Court.

# ONE

"SEX incarnate," the women and men around her whispered. "Half incubus."

Aislinn didn't know if it was true, but she did know the man was Unseelie in a Seelie Court. That didn't happen very often, so she stared just like everyone else as he passed down the corridor.

Dressed head to toe in black, wearing Doc Martens, a pair of faded jeans, and a long coat over a thin crewneck sweater that defined his muscular chest, he seemed to possess every inch of the hallway he tread. He walked with such confidence it gave the illusion he took up more space than was physically possible. Seelie nobles shrank in his wake though they tried to stand firm and proud. Not even the most powerful ones were immune. Others postured and drew up straighter, offering challenge to some imaginary threat in their midst. Not even the gold and rose–bedecked Imperial Guard seemed immune from his passing, as if they sensed a marauder in their midst.

And maybe this man was a marauder.

No one knew anything about him other than that the dark

magick running through his Unseelie veins was both lethal and sexual in nature. The court buzzed with the news of his arrival and his meeting with the Summer Queen, High Royal of the Seelie Tuatha Dé Danann.

According to gossip, Gabriel Cionaodh Marcus Mac Braire had been welcomed past the threshold of the gleaming rose quartz tower of the Seelie Court because he was petitioning the Summer Queen for permanent residence, a subject that had received a huge amount of attention from Seelie nobles. Predictably, most of the people against it were men.

Gabriel, it was said, held Seelie blood in his veins, but the incubus Unseelie part of him overshadowed it. The rumors went that he was catnip to females and—when his special brand of magick was wielded at full force between the sheets—he possessed the power to enslave a woman. The afflicted female would become addicted to him. She'd stop eating and sleeping, wanting nothing more than his touch, until she finally died from longing and self-neglect.

Just the thought made Aislinn shudder, yet it didn't seem to deter his female admirers. Maybe that was because no one had ever heard of any woman who'd suffered that fate. If this man could use sex like a deadly weapon, apparently he never did.

Yet some kind of sexual magick did seem to pour from him. Something intangible, subtle, and seductive.

Watching him now, so self-assured and beautiful, Aislinn could see the allure. His long black coat melded with his shoulder-length dark hair until she wasn't sure where one began and the other ended. A gorgeous fallen angel whose every movement promised a night filled with the darkest, most dangerous erotic pleasure? There was nothing to find uninteresting. Even herself, jaded and pride pricked by "love" as she currently was, could see the attraction.

That attraction, of course, was the stock-in-trade of an incubus and Gabriel was at least half, if court gossip was to be believed. But for all his dark beauty and lethal charm, and despite that odd, subtle magick, he didn't entice Aislinn. To her, he screamed danger. Perhaps that was because of the very humbling public breakup she'd just endured. All men, *especially* attractive ones, looked like trouble to her now.

"Wow," said her friend Carina, coming to stand beside her. "I see what everyone was talking about. He's really . . ." She trailed off, her eyebrows rising into her ebony hairline.

"He's really what?" Carina's husband growled, coming up from behind them to twine his arms around his wife's waist.

"Really potent," Carina answered. "That man's magick is so strong that even standing in his wake a woman feels a little intoxicated, but it's false." She turned and embraced Drem. "My attraction to you is completely real." Her voice, low and honey soft, convinced everyone within hearing range of her honesty.

"Do *you* think he's 'potent,' Aislinn?" Drem asked, curving his thin lips into a teasing smile.

She watched the man disappear through the ornate gold and rose double doors leading into the throne room at the end of the hallway. The last thing she saw was the trailing edge of his coat. Behind him scurried a cameraman and a slick, well-heeled commentator from *Faemous*, the annoying human twenty-four-hour "news" coverage of the Seelie Court that the Summer Queen found so amusing. "A woman would have to be dead not to see his virility, but if he's got any special sex magick, it's not affecting me."

Drem shifted his green eyes from her to stare at the end of the hallway where the man had disappeared. "So detached and cool, Aislinn?"

She shrugged. "He doesn't make me hot."

"You're the only one," Carina muttered. Her husband gave her a playful swat on her butt for punishment. She gasped in surprise and then laughed. "Look over there. He's the reason no men are making you hot right now."

Aislinn followed Carina's gaze to see Kendal in all his glittering blond glory. He stood with a couple of friends—people who used to be *her* friends—in the meet-and-greet area to socialize outside the court doors.

Ugh.

Kendal locked gazes with her, but Aislinn merely looked away as though she hadn't noticed him. She'd wasted too much time on him already. She could hardly believe she'd ever thought she'd loved him. Kendal was a social climber, nothing more. He'd used her to further his position at court, for the prestige of dating one of the queen's favorites, and then tossed her aside. It had worked for him, too. That was the truly galling part.

"I have nothing to say to him," Aislinn said in the coolest tone she could manage.

Carina stared at him, her jaw set. "Well, I do." She began to walk across the corridor toward him.

Aislinn caught her hand and squeezed. "No, please, don't. Thank you for being furious with him on my account, but that's what he wants. The attention feeds his ego and Kendal doesn't deserve it."

"I can tell you what that weasel *is* deserving of."

Aislinn laughed. "You're a good friend, Carina."

The doors at the end of the corridor opened and a male hobgoblin court attendant stepped out, dressed in the gold and rose livery of the Rose Tower. "The queen requests the presence of Aislinn Christiana Guinevere Finvarra."

Aislinn frowned and stilled, looking toward the doors at the end of the corridor through which Gabriel Cionaodh Marcus Mac Braire had recently disappeared. Why would the queen wish to see her?

Carina pushed her forward, breaking her momentary paralysis. Aislinn moved down the corridor amid the hush of voices around her. She'd grown used to being the topic of court gossip lately. The Seelie nobles didn't have much to do besides get into each other's business. Magick wasn't a valuable commodity here, practiced and perfected, like it was in the Unseelie Court.

She entered the throne room and the heavy double doors closed behind her with a loud thump. Caoilainn Elspeth Muirgheal, the High Royal of the Seelie Tuatha Dé Danann, sat on her throne. Gabriel stood before her, his back to Aislinn. The

Imperial Guard, men and women of less pure Seelie Tuatha Dé blood, lined the room, all standing at attention in their gleaming gold and rose helms and hauberks.

It always gave her shivers to stand in the throne room before the queen. Arched ceilings hand-painted with frescoes of the battle of Cath Maige Tuired, depicting the Sídhe taking over Ireland from the Firbolg, who were humans in their less evolved and more animalistic form, instilled a sense of awe in all who entered. Gold-veined marble floors stretched under her shoes, reaching to rose quartz pillars and walls. It was a cold place despite the warm colors, full of power, designed to intimidate and control.

The Unseelie, Gabriel, seemed utterly unaffected. In fact, the way he stood—feet slightly apart, head held high, and a small, secretive smile playing over his lips—made him seem almost insolent.

The *Faemous* film crew had been allowed within. They stood near a far wall, the light of the camera trained on the Summer Queen and Gabriel. Though now the camera turned to record Aislinn's entrance. The silver-haired female commentator—Aislinn thought her name was Holly something— whispered into her mike, describing the goings-on.

Ignoring the film crew, as she always did, she halted near the incubus, yet kept a good distance. The last thing she was going to do was fawn like most women. Out of the corner of her eye, she saw him do a slow upward appraisal of her, the kind men do when they're clearly wondering what a woman looks like without her clothes. He wasn't even trying to hide it. Maybe he was so arrogantly presumptuous that he felt he didn't have to.

Aislinn was seriously beginning to dislike this man.

She curtsied deeply to the queen, difficult in her tight Rock & Republic jeans. If she had known she was going to be called into court, she would have worn something a little looser . . . and a bit more formal. Today she was wearing a gray V-neck sweater and wedge-heeled black boots with her jeans. She'd twisted her hair up and only dashed on makeup. This was not an event she'd planned for.

The queen, as always, was dressed in heavy brocade, silk, and lace. Today her color theme was a rich burgundy and cream, her skirts pooling at her feet like a bloody ocean. The royal's long pale hair was done up in a series of intricate braids and heavy ruby jewelry glittered at her ears and nestled at the base of her slender, pale throat. She wore no makeup because she didn't need it. Her beauty was flawless and chilly. Her style, as ever, old-fashioned. It worked for her.

Caoilainn Elspeth Muirgheal gestured with a slim hand, the light catching on her many rings. "Aislinn, please meet Gabriel Mac Braire. He is petitioning the Seelie Court for residency, in case you hadn't already heard. It seems word has spread through court about it. I am still considering his case. As you know, we don't often grant such requests."

Yes, but there were precedents. Take Ronan Quinn, for example. He was a part-blood druid and Unseelie mage. He'd successfully petitioned the Summer Queen for residency in the Rose Tower over thirty years ago because he'd fallen in love with Bella, Aislinn's best friend. Not long after his residency had been granted Ronan lost Bella and consequently fell into a state of reckless despondency that had lasted for decades. Last year he'd pulled some mysterious job for the Phaendir that had nearly gotten him beheaded by the Summer Queen. In the end, Ronan had retained his life and won Bella back—but both had been banished from the Rose Tower as punishment for Ronan's transgressions. Aislinn didn't know where they were now.

She missed Bella every single day. Bella had been the only one to know her deepest and darkest secrets. Without her presence, she felt utterly alone.

That entire story aside, Ronan Quinn was one example of an Unseelie male who'd managed to find a place in the Rose. Gabriel, like Ronan, was exceedingly good-looking. That would weigh heavily in his favor. The queen couldn't resist a virile, highly magicked man.

"He'll be staying here for the next week and I have decided you shall be his guide and general helpmeet while he's here."

"Me?" Aislinn blinked. "Why me?" The question came out of her mouth before she could think it through and she instantly regretted it. One did not question Caoilainn Elspeth Muirgheal; one simply obeyed.

The Summer Queen lifted a pale, perfectly arched brow. "Why *not* you?"

"With all respect due you, my queen, I think—"

"Do you have a problem with my judgment?"

Oh, this was getting more and more dangerous with every word the queen uttered. The room had chilled a bit, too, a result of the Seelie Royal's mood affecting her magick. Aislinn shivered. "No, my queen."

Gabriel glanced over at her with a mocking smile playing on his sensual, luscious lips.

Nope, she didn't like him one bit even if he did have sensual, luscious lips.

"That's a good answer, Aislinn. Do you have a problem with Gabriel? Most women would kill to spend time with him." The queen gestured airily with one hand. "I thought I was doing you a favor after your . . . unfortunate incident with Kendal."

Oh, sweet lady Danu. Aislinn gritted her teeth before answering. "I don't have a problem with him, my queen."

The queen clapped her hands together, making Aislinn jump. "Good, that's all settled then. You're both dismissed."

Aislinn turned immediately and walked out of the throne room, Gabriel following. She didn't like having him behind her. It made her feel like a gazelle being stalked by a lion. He'd soon find out this gazelle had fight. There was no way she was going to lie down and show him her vulnerable, soft stomach . . . or any other part of her body.

They exited into a corridor thronged with curious onlookers. Carina, partway down the hall with Drem, made a move to walk to Aislinn, but Aislinn held up a hand to stop her. All eyes were on her and Gabriel. She didn't want to linger here and she really didn't want anyone listening in on their conversation and using it to weave rumor. They could watch *Faemous* for the juicy details, just like everyone else.

Falling into step beside her, Gabriel surveyed the scene and ran a hand over his stubble-dusted, clefted chin. "Is it always like this over here?" His voice, deep and low, reminded her of dark chocolate.

"Like what?" she snapped in annoyance.

He encompassed the corridor with a sweep of his hand as they made their way down. "All the Seelie nobles standing around and gossiping." He glanced at her stern expression and sobered. "Never mind. Forget I mentioned it."

"Insulting my home is not a good way to start things off, Mac Braire."

"Call me Gabriel, and I wasn't insulting it. I was making an observation. I want this to be my home, too, remember? That's why I'm here."

"Sounded like an insult to me," she muttered, hightailing it away from the clumps of Seelie nobles doing exactly what he'd just accused them of. Although he walked faster than she did. She had to fight to keep up with the strides of his longer legs.

"I apologize."

"How does the Shadow King feel about your defection from the Black? He can't be very happy."

Gabriel gave a low laugh. "He's not. I'm taking a huge gamble. If the Summer Queen rejects me and I lose the protection of the Seelie Court, I may lose my head, too."

"You don't seem all that nervous about it."

"I don't live my life in fear. Anyway, I've lived so long that I'm a thrill seeker. Anything to break up the monotony. Anything for change, Aislinn."

The way he pronounced her name sent a shiver down her spine. He rolled it on his tongue like a French kiss, smooth and sweet as melting candy.

It made her miss a step and deepened her annoyance.

She picked up her pace and matched his strides once more. "Listen, I don't know why the queen selected me for this job, but the last thing I want to do right now is babysit you." Ouch. That had been harsh. She winced as the words echoed through her head. He hadn't done anything to her and she wasn't sure why she was feeling so hostile. It had to be because of her recent breakup with Kendal. Gabriel reminded her of him.

Every man reminded her of him.

She still felt so raw and vulnerable. She needed time alone to lick her wounds and heal. The last thing she wanted was to be forced into spending time with an obvious woman-izer who could wield sex as a weapon. Literally. Perhaps she was using this man as a scapegoat for her wounded pride and broken heart. If so, that was wrong . . . yet she couldn't seem to help herself.

He halted, hand on her elbow. "Whoa. Look, Aislinn, if you feel so strongly about it, I'm sure I can find someone else to 'babysit' me."

She winced again, turning to face him. She was being a bitch and needed to rein it in. Regret pinched her and she opened her mouth to apologize.

"It's too bad you don't want to spend time with me, though, since I have news of Bella and Ronan. They've been anxious to get back into contact with you."

*Danu.* Bella and Ronan? So they were at the Unseelie Court, after all. Aislinn had assumed they'd gone there, but wasn't sure whether or not the Shadow King had allowed them residence in the Black Tower.

The Seelie Court was called the Rose Tower because it was constructed of rose quartz. The Unseelie Court was re-ferred to as the Black Tower because—never to be out-done—it was made from black quartz. The delivery of large quantities of each had been allowed by human society and the Phaendir, and magick had been employed to make it us-able as a construction material.

Gabriel walked ahead of her, intending to leave her in the dust. Damn the man! He'd tossed that last bit out, and then left, to punish her. He knew she'd chase him. Clearly her first impulse to dislike the man had been dead-on.

"Hey." She took a couple of running steps to catch up with him. "I'm sorry. I've been unfair to you. You're all alone and could clearly use a friend"—although she was sure

he'd end up with plenty of "friends" here soon enough—
"and someone to show you around. Let's start over."

He stopped, turned toward her, and lifted a dark brow.
"Ah, so you do want to know about Bella and Ronan."

"No." She shook her head. "I mean, yes, but I didn't say
that just to have news of them. This is about me being fair
and giving you the benefit of the doubt."

"Benefit of the doubt? What movie about me have you
made in your head, sweet Aislinn? And without even knowing me."

"That you're a dangerous, arrogant, superficial man with
piles of discarded, heartbroken female bodies on each side of
the path you tread."

They'd stopped in a large open area where a huge fountain, in the shape of a swan, flowed into a pool. There were
fewer people here. For a moment all was silent except for the
sound of running water and the clicking heels of the few
passersby.

He studied her with hard, glittering, dark blue eyes. "Your
honesty is very refreshing. I'm sorry that's your first impression of me. Perhaps I can change it."

"Maybe you can."

"A little too honest, that's my first impression of you." He
narrowed his eyes. "And perhaps a bit jaded about men at the
moment." He loosely shrugged one shoulder. "Just a guess."

Good guess. Time to change the subject. "Why do you
wish to change courts anyway?"

"I'm surprised a pure-blood Seelie Tuatha Dé would ask
such a question. I thought everyone here believed the Rose
Tower superior in all ways. There should be no question why
I wish to defect from the Black."

Aislinn didn't understand the twist to his words. It was
almost—but not quite—mockery. An odd attitude to have
when he seemed to want to join those he mocked for the rest
of his very long life.

"Apparently Bella and Ronan have gone to the Unseelie
Court. It can't be that bad."

Gabriel smiled. "Well, there's no *Faemous* film crew

there." No. Apparently the film crew the Shadow King had allowed in years ago had been eaten. "And the nobles aren't as . . . prissy."

She raised her eyebrows. "Prissy?"

He nodded. "The Unseelie Court is darker and you have to watch your step."

"So I've heard. Magick cast, blood spilled."

"Sometimes. The magick is stronger, more violent, and held in higher regard. You know that. The laws are different there and you have to be careful. You don't want to make enemies of some of them."

Fear niggled. "How are Bella and Ronan?"

"Good. They've adjusted to life in the Black. They said to tell you they're fine, but Bella misses you. They say to tell you they're happy."

She studied him for lies. It was what she wanted to hear, of course, and Gabriel seemed the type to tell you what you wanted to hear. But she *so* wanted to believe what he'd said. She'd lost more than one night's sleep worrying about her friends. The memory of watching them walk away into Piefferburg Square on Yule Eve, forever banished from Seelie by the Summer Queen, still made her heart ache.

Though the crime that Ronan had committed—taking work from the Phaendir—normally would have held the punishment of death. He'd been lucky. They both had. The Phaendir, a guild of powerful immortal druids, were the sworn enemy of the Sídhe—Seelie and Unseelie alike. Enemy of *all* the fae races.

There was good reason.

The Phaendir, with the full support of the humans, had created and controlled the borders of Piefferburg with powerful warding. They called it a "resettlement area."

Piefferburg's inhabitants called it prison.

If one wanted to be philosophical about it, the fate of the fae was poetic punishment for the horrible fae race wars of the early 1600s that had decimated their population and left them easy prey to their common enemy, the Phaendir. The wars had forced the fae from the underground, and the humans had panicked in the face of the truth—the fae were real.

On top of the wars, a mysterious sickness called Watt syndrome had also befallen them. Some thought the illness had been created by the Phaendir. However it had come about, the result was the same—it had further weakened them.

The two events had been a perfect storm of misfortune, leading to their downfall. When the fae had been at their most vulnerable, the Phaendir had allied with the humans to imprison them in an area of what had then been the New World, founded by a human named Jules Piefferburg.

These days the sects of fae who'd warred in the 1600s had reached an uneasy peace. They were united against the Phaendir because the old human saying was true—the enemy of my enemy is my friend.

Aislinn cleared her throat against a sudden rush of emotion. Bella had been the only one in the court who'd carried the weight of Aislinn's secret. Really, Bella had been more of a sister than a friend. "Come with me. I'll give you a tour before dinner."

"Sounds good."

They walked the length and breadth of the Rose Tower, which was enormous and completely self-sufficient. She showed him all the floors and how they were graduated in terms of court ranking. The higher floors, the floors closest to the queen's penthouse apartment, were where the purest-blood Seelie Tuatha Dé resided. She showed him the courtyard in the solarium where the families with children lived so they could have yards to play in. The school. The restaurants on premise where the nobles dined. The ballroom, the numerous gathering areas, and the banquet halls.

Most of the residents never really left the building for much beyond shopping or to have a night of dining out. Some of the more adventurous slummed it at a few of Piefferburg's nightclubs, but the Summer Queen discouraged the Seelie Tuatha Dé from mixing with the trooping fae—those fae who didn't belong to either court and weren't wildings or water dwelling.

While social contact with the troop was discouraged, unchaperoned and unapproved contact with the Unseelie Tuatha Dé was strictly forbidden. Aislinn suspected more of the illicit sort went on than was widely known. After all, she suspected her own mother of it. There was no other way to explain away certain ... oddities ... in Aislinn's magickal abilities.

She and Gabriel ended up at her front door. A good thing, since she wanted her slippers, a cup of hot cocoa, and her own company for the rest of the evening.

Gabriel grabbed her hand before she could snatch it away. "Thank you for spending time with me today," he murmured in Old Maejian, the words rolling soft and smooth like good whiskey from his tongue. He bent to kiss her hand in the old custom, his gaze fastened on hers. At the last moment, he flipped her hand palm up and laid his lips to her wrist. All the while his thumb stroked her palm back and forth.

That callused rasp in conjunction with his warm, silky lips sent shivers through her. Made her think about his hands and lips on other parts of her body, which made her think of his long, muscled length naked against her between the sheets of her bed.

In a sweaty tangle.

Limbs entwined ...

*Bad incubus.* She snatched her hand back.

He stood for a moment, bent over, hand and lips still in kissing position. Then he grinned in a half-mocking, half-mischievous way, straightened, and walked down the corridor, all sex wrapped in black and adorned with a swagger.

She supposed the Summer Queen thought spending time with Gabriel would be good for her after her breakup with Kendal. A little meaningless fling to get her back on the dating horse? But she did not do meaningless flings.

And she was definitely unappreciative of being saddled with a man like Gabriel Mac Braire.

Sweet Danu, what had the queen thrown her into?

# TWO

AISLINN shifted uneasily, watching Gabriel come toward her in the ballroom. A hundred other men in the room were dressed in the same style of black wool tuxedo, but none of them wore it like the incubus. His hair was pulled back at his nape, revealing the almost brutally perfect bones of his face and accentuating the deep blue of his eyes.

"Sweet Danu," Aislinn murmured, taking a sip of her champagne. She jumped, startled, as Carina came up on her side.

"Oh, my goddess," Carina said, gazing hungrily over the rim of her glass. "Look, he's coming over here." She made a low growling sound. "There's something about a man from the dark side, isn't there?"

"No, there's not."

"I'm so jealous you get to be his guide."

"You're not the only one. Think of Drem."

"Drem doesn't care how much I drool over other men as long as I come home to him."

As he cut through the crowd, people seemed to move out of his way by pure instinct. It was odd the way the men seemed to sidestep him. Even the women did, though they might take an appreciative look at him while they moved aside. Was it because he was Unseelie? Was it because he was incubus? Neither explanation seemed right to her, but she couldn't put her finger on the threat he seemed to unconsciously exude.

Somewhere deep within, Aislinn also had the subtle impulse to get out of his way, despite his attractiveness, and it had nothing to do with the fact that she wanted nothing to do with men at the moment. She pointedly looked away from him as he approached.

"Aislinn," Gabriel greeted as he came to stand near them. "Carina. You both look beautiful tonight."

"Thank you," answered Carina with a simpering smile. Aislinn rolled her eyes.

He motioned with his hands at the thronged room. "So, is this a special occasion?"

"You know well that this is a common event," Aislinn answered. "We discussed it this afternoon."

"Yes, that's right. Weekly, right?"

"Periodically." Gabriel was ever so lightly mocking again. "Would you like to dance, Aislinn?"

She hesitated, jaw locking.

"Sure she would," Carina answered, slipping Aislinn's champagne glass from her fingers and giving her a "helpful" push forward.

Gabriel slipped his hand around her waist and led her toward the dance floor of the glittering ballroom, where couples already swirled to the traditional music of the Seelie Tuatha Dé Sídhe. They had all danced to the same melodies a millennium ago. These days they were just more refined.

His hand was large, imposingly so, and possessive on her waist as he led her into the crush. He took her hand in his and pulled her much closer than she wanted, though the proximity was proper for the dance. Her breasts swelled above the bodice of her dove gray gown, making her feel naked all of a sudden.

She cleared her throat and tried to get comfortable in his arms. The problem was that she actually *was* comfortable in his arms. He made her feel safe in a way she didn't want to examine too closely.

"How are you enjoying the Rose Tower so far?" That was a nice, distant question and she'd even sounded polite. Score point one for her.

"It's nice and the women are friendly. Not the men, though."

She gave a short laugh. "That can't be anything odd for you, an incubus. The men feel threatened."

"Not in the Black Tower."

She made a scoffing sound. "I find that hard to believe."

"I missed you today," Gabriel said, his voice low and soft near her ear.

She'd been gone all afternoon. "I was volunteering in the *ceantar láir*. There's a center there for—"

"Homeless fae. Yes, I know of it." He smiled a little. "Close your mouth."

She realized she'd been gaping and snapped her mouth shut. It was hard to believe he knew of the shelter. Aislinn couldn't think of one Seelie who did. "Sorry. I volunteer there once a week preparing and serving meals."

"The queen can't like that much."

"She's fine with it," Aislinn said defensively. In actuality, the queen suffered Aislinn's "hobby," as she called it, badly.

He gave her a look of doubtfulness. "She allows you to rub elbows with down-and-out goblins, boggarts, skillywiddens, and red caps?"

"She's very compassionate."

He laughed.

"She can be," Aislinn amended, "sometimes. Anyway, I don't need to defend myself or her to you."

"Then why are you?"

"Because you're making me." Her voice was a low, annoyed hiss. Gah! This man brought out the worst in her and she just couldn't control it.

"I would never make you do anything you didn't want to do, sweetness," he murmured over her head, looking out over the crowd. The words seemed laden with innuendo.

"The Seelie Court is about more than just balls, clothes, and shallow gossip. We are an honorable tower. Our men and women believe in chivalry and integrity. We operate with a respectable code of ethics here."

"Relax, Aislinn. The last thing I wanted to do was rile my tour guide."

"I'm not your tour guide," she snapped.

"No, you're my dance partner and a very good one, too." A slight note of wonder threaded his voice.

Aislinn blinked and looked around, realizing all eyes were on them. Her voice had been strained and stiff while she spoke to him, but her body hadn't been . . . at all. In fact, she'd shamelessly melted against him and let him lead her into an intricate dance pattern that had all the ballroom admiring them.

She glared at him. "You did that on purpose."

Unperturbed, he only shrugged a shoulder. "I can't make you do anything some part of you doesn't want to do."

Annoyance flashed. She pressed her lips into a thin line to control it. "I still don't understand why you want to come to the Rose, Gabriel. You seem to hold this court and even the queen in contempt." She stared up at him for a long moment as if she could read his mind. "What game are you playing?"

"You caught me. I'm actually here on a top-secret mission for the Shadow King, with orders to target you. I compelled the Summer Queen to help me get closer to you and I'm using my charms as an incubus to seduce you to the Black for nefarious purposes."

She rolled her eyes. "I'm serious, Gabriel. What makes you want to be here?"

He spun and then dipped her. His mouth came down close to hers. "I'm bored, sweetness, and you're the perfect cure." He held her that way for a heartbeat, their lips almost touching. Around them people clapped.

He righted her and she hurried away, returning to Carina's side to retrieve her drink. She needed that drink, lots of them. Gabriel melted back into the crowd.

"He likes you," said Carina.

"What? Well, yes, maybe. He likes me in the way he likes all women: as possible fodder for a night in his bed."

"No, I mean he really likes you. I can see it in his body language. Remember? That's my magick. I can tell truth from lie when I watch someone move and Gabriel likes you a lot. I would even say, *admires* you."

Aislinn's cheeks heated. "Not possible. I've given him nothing to admire. I've been awful to him, a total shrew."

"I don't know." Carina shrugged and took a sip of champagne. "I'm just telling you how I see it. He admires something about you and, while he might like them, it's not your boobs." She cast a pointed look at Aislinn's cleavage, which was particularly showy tonight.

Aislinn blew out a hard breath. "No way. The only person that man likes is himself."

UNDER a sky littered with a million chips of starlight, Gabriel made his way through Piefferburg Square to the dark half, the collar of his shirt loosened and a partly empty champagne bottle in one hand. On the Seelie side all the bright and shining roamed, along with the occasional troop passersby, those fae who belonged to neither court and simply lived as citizens of their fair resettlement area—or prison, as most regarded it.

The middle of the square, where the much-maligned and abused statue of Jules Piefferburg stood, crafted from charmed iron—giving them all an eternal fuck-you with its presence—lay in a twilight area where both the courts almost touched. Here you began to see some of the more monstrous examples of the darker side of Fae.

There were the tall, spindly goblins who appeared so frail but were actually incredibly strong and vicious when prompted to be. Some of them lived and served in the Black Tower, but most lived in Goblin Town, a distance away from Piefferburg Square. There were the poweries, huge, hulking men and women also known as red caps, who needed to kill periodically to survive—luckily, "periodically" was every few hundred years, and they kept their restorative murdering to their own kind in elaborate gladiator-like tournaments that all the fae turned out to see. There were alps, tiny, squat German fae who sat on the chests of their victims and caused nightmares bad enough to cause permanent psychological damage. There were the crossbreeds, too—large brutish hunchbacks that twisted the mind a bit and shorter elflike creatures with postnasal drip. The Unseelie took in all, no matter their appearance.

There were plenty of the nonmonstrous in the Black, too. The Unseelie Tuatha Dé Danann, men and women who looked just like Gabriel but who, unlike their shining Seelie counterparts, could kill or maim with their magick. They were perhaps the most dangerous of all the members of the Black Tower. Deceptively deadly at times.

After spending a day at the Seelie Court with all its glittering pretensions, Gabriel knew he preferred monsters and mayhem to gilt and gossip.

He couldn't wait to get home.

He waded further into the darkness of the other half of Piefferburg Square, under the shadow of the tall black crystal tower that mirrored the Seelie Court's rose one. The doors opened for him immediately and he entered the black marble foyer.

"Gabriel," said Hinkley, chief adviser to the Shadow King and majordomo of the Black Tower. He was a thin, balding, knobby man with a permanent stoop. He peered up at Gabriel through wire-rimmed glasses perched on his long, crooked nose. "He's been asking for you. You said you'd return much earlier than this."

There could only be one *he* Hinkley could be referring to.

Gabriel handed him his now-empty champagne bottle and strode past him, making Hinkley's short legs work to catch up. "I couldn't get here any quicker without raising suspicion. I spent almost all yesterday and this evening with

Aislinn Christiana Guinevere Finvarra. There was a ball tonight I couldn't get away from until now." He shrugged and
grabbed a shiny red apple from a bowl of fruit near a sofa. "I
was working." He snapped out a bite.

"So I trust she's already under your spell?" asked Hinkley
with his brows raised in a smarmy way that made Gabriel
shudder for any female he might turn his attentions toward.
"I'm sure you'll have the matter put to rest within a couple
nights' time."

Hardly.

When Gabriel had first arrived at the Rose yesterday, he'd
seen Aislinn as he'd passed her in the corridor on his way to
see the Summer Queen. She'd watched him with cool gray
eyes set in a heart-shaped face. The coolness and detachment
in her gaze and on her face was the first thing he'd noticed
about her—coolness wasn't usually a quality most females
displayed where he was concerned. The second thing he'd
noticed was how attractive she was. What the Shadow King
had sent him to do wouldn't be a hardship at all. For once.

No, Gabriel would love seducing sweet, luscious Aislinn
Finvarra of the beautiful silver blond hair and succulent,
small, curvy body. In fact, he couldn't wait. But it looked
like he'd have to wait, for he'd noticed something else about
Aislinn—she was not affected by his particular "charm."

Not at all.

Out of all the women the Shadow King had ordered him
to seduce to the dark side, it was the one woman who seemed
immune to him.

Normally women weren't much of a challenge for him,
but sometimes he found one who could resist him. It had
never troubled him much; after all, there was always a willing one nearby and Gabriel wasn't all that picky. As long
as they were pretty and adventurous in bed they'd do. But he
had to seduce this unwilling one if he was to stay in the
Shadow King's favor.

And Gabriel very much wanted to stay in the Shadow
King's favor.

He enjoyed high status in the Black, a nice apartment, good food, and other little perks. He had no family fortune to fall back on, coming, as he did, from abject poverty and a dark, twisted history of doing what he had to do in order to survive. The king asked little of him to maintain his high status. He couldn't fail the royal in this.

In addition to the coolness and detachment, Aislinn, out of all the Seelie who'd watched him enter their tower, was the only one who hadn't looked at him with some kind of combination of fear and lust on her face. The fear made sense and he was used to seeing it—even from the Unseelie. He was sex and death all in one package.

Even if most didn't sense the death consciously, it was there. And it didn't come from his capacity to create sexual addiction in women, either. It was true he could do that, though not to the point where they'd die from want of him. That sort of power had died out in his line long ago, though it was in Gabriel's best interests not to reveal that secret. Creating sexual addiction in those who came to his bed was *not* a desirable thing—it made his lovers needy and clingy and that was something he couldn't abide.

No, the intangible threat of death that people sensed came from something far more powerful. Something only a handful of trusted Unseelie knew about.

Gabriel turned down the corridor toward the Shadow King's quarters and Hinkley scurried to keep up. The floor and walls here were made of black marble veined through with silver. Framed pictures of some of the historical battles between the Rose and Black adorned the walls above small tables with vases of orchids or bowls of fruit or candy. Those battles had occurred back before the Great Sweep had compelled them all into Piefferburg and the fae courts had been forced into an uneasy peace.

This was the floor where the Shadow King and his advisers lived. Not many of the other Unseelie had cause to be here, so all was silent save for the click of his and Hinkley's shoes on the floor.

His thoughts turned to Aislinn and he had a moment of uncharacteristic discomfort. "I may need more time with the woman than we thought."

Hinkley made a choking sound. "You don't have long. For whatever reason, the Shadow King is most obsessed with bringing this woman over. I don't think I've ever seen him this impatient."

Gabriel stifled a yawn and set to undoing the cuff links on his tux. "I'll get the job done."

They came to the double doors that led to the king's quarters. The Unseelie Court had both daytime and nighttime fae. It was active around the clock, as opposed to the mostly daytime Seelie Court. The king was a night dweller, which meant Gabriel wasn't waking His Majesty from slumber. Even if he were it wouldn't matter. The Shadow King didn't sit on his throne like a half-dead statue the way the Summer Queen did. He moved, fought, danced, laughed, and cavorted with his people.

Though one could never mistake the Shadow King for one of them. Imbued with the power of the Shadow Amulet, he was far more powerful than any of them could imagine. The amulet gave the Shadow Royal eternal agelessness and the ability to call and control the goblin army. You didn't want to cross him, and you never wanted to disappoint him. When the Shadow King decided you needed to be punished, his ways of doing so were legend. Magickal torture was torture like none could imagine.

That was why Gabriel didn't want to fail in the task he'd been set. Not even the king's favorites were immune to his anger. On the contrary, he expected more of them.

The doors opened by themselves as he approached—a handy little bit of magick—and Hinkley fell back, allowing Gabriel to enter on his own. No one was in the waiting room and the doors to the apartment were open, so he walked into the spacious foyer of the residence and passed into the living room.

The room was modern, done in shining silvers and whites. It was a cold room for a friendly king. Gabriel didn't like it, no matter the lushness of the décor and the obvious signs of wealth that were displayed. The term "Shadow King" was not apt, in Gabriel's opinion, not when shadows were so dark and chilly.

Aodh Críostóir Ruadhán O'Dubhuir, also known as the Shadow King, stood at the huge window that overlooked Piefferburg Square, a short glass filled with amber liquid in his hand. The long hair that cascaded down his back started out silver blond at the roots—his natural color. From there it faded into dyed hues of orange, then rose, ending at the tips in fiery red. He was many centuries old, but because of the Shadow Amulet, he didn't look a day over thirty-two. The amulet was a part of him, literally. Once donned by its rightful owner, the heavy necklace sank into the flesh and imbued the royal with magick, leaving only a tattooed image on the neck and upper chest to mark its physical presence.

The Shadow King didn't acknowledge Gabriel as he entered the room, but Gabriel knew he was aware of his presence.

The crystal-knobbed fighting staff that was his favored weapon—a weapon he'd practiced with against Gabriel many times in the sparring room—leaned up against the wall beside him. And Barthe, an ogre, a wilding creature of limited cognitive power, lurked silently in the corner, his small black eyes fastened on him from a doughy face.

There were only a clutch of ogres left after Watt syndrome had ripped through the race. Most of them lived in close-knit family clans, residing in caves in the Boundary Lands. Typically ogres disdained contact with the rest of Piefferburg, but Barthe was a rare one who wanted interaction with others. In fact, he'd bound himself in service to the king. The beast acted like a pit bull of sorts, protecting his master.

Towering over seven feet, Barthe was built like a mega linebacker with a narrow waist, huge muscular arms, and broad shoulders. His fleshy face was closer to that of a boar than a man, with small white tusks that couldn't be underestimated in battle. His body was covered in fine black hair. He walked upright, was deadly and brutal in a fight, and loved his king more than his own life. Barthe was capable of only limited communication, but Gabriel understood that his clan had rejected him for choosing service to the Unseelie king over them.

Gabriel collapsed into a pearl-colored armchair and slouched. As the king's favorite, he enjoyed certain allowances. Plus, he was exhausted. Having to work the Seelie Court by day and get himself over to the Unseelie after midnight was going to take its toll.

"You did not report to me last night," the king stated without turning, then took a long drink.

"I had nothing to report and lots of work to do."

"But I trust you have something to report now. Have you seen her?"

Gabriel knew he meant Aislinn, not the Summer Queen. "I've done more than just see her. I managed to tie myself to her, by convincing Caoilainn Elspeth Muirgheal that she was my preferred choice for court guide during my stay. Once I discovered Aislinn's recent breakup, it wasn't difficult to convince the queen the pairing would be beneficial for Aislinn. The queen seemed amenable to helping one of her favorites. So now I have an excuse to seek her out and spend time with her."

The Shadow King had no queen and the Summer Queen no king. They'd lived for centuries that way and there was some speculation that relations had not always been so icy between them. Gabriel had always wondered at the look the Shadow King got on his face whenever Caoilainn Elspeth Muirgheal was mentioned. Right now Gabriel couldn't see the king's face, but his shoulders had tightened the moment her name had wafted to his ears, the bloodred-tipped ends of his hair shifting over his shoulders.

"And?"

"And did Aislinn come to my bed, fall in mad, passionate love with me, and ask to do anything I wished of her?" He smiled. "No."

The king turned. His eternally handsome, pale face was set in grim lines. His light blue eyes snapped with irritation. "Why not? I thought you'd have the job done in no time. I thought she'd swoon at your feet like all the other women and this would be no trouble at all. I was surprised *and displeased* you didn't have her with you tonight. Don't tell me I have to send someone else to fetch her."

*Someone else.* Gabriel knew what that meant and it was nothing good . . . for Aislinn, anyway. Gabriel wasn't sure what the Shadow King wanted with Aislinn Christiana Guinevere Finvarra of the long silver blond hair and gray eyes, but he didn't think the king meant her bodily harm. Still, the "someone else" the king was referring to would not be as pleasant on the eyes or as gentle as he would be and would likely frighten her.

Gabriel shifted in his seat and sighed. "Let's try it my way first. I haven't failed yet; I just need a few more days. You've gone a long time without this woman's presence in your court. You can spare another week or so, right?" He paused. "But I need to know why she's so important to you."

Aodh regarded him silently for a long moment. "She's a distant relation. I don't have many of those, so I intend to lavish upon her all she deserves. Please, don't fail me in this, Gabriel. This means more to me than I can say. I don't have many—any—relations."

Gabriel raised an eyebrow. There was a slight resemblance in the chin and the hair color was right, otherwise he would never have guessed they were blood relations. Aodh had the light blue eyes of icy water or a husky. Aislinn's were gray like gunmetal or stormy skies. Close, but no cigar. "You can count on me, my king."

The king took another drink and then turned back to the window. "Good. Now leave and do your duty. I can hear the souls calling."

Gabriel could hear them, too. What was more, he could feel them pulling at him. If he let his work go too long, they would start screaming and clawing at the inside of his psyche. It was time to do what he'd been born to do. He couldn't escape it. Gabriel didn't want to escape it. It was his sacred duty.

He stood. "I'll return to give you a progress report after I've actually made some progress." But the king had already tuned him out and stood deep in thought at the window once again. Gabriel showed himself out.

He didn't stop at his apartment. There was nothing there for him anyway. No family. No romantic entanglements. Gabriel didn't even keep any servants, preferring total solitude within his walls. No pets. Not many friends, though the ones he had were close.

Admirers and lovers he had, sure, but they were the nighttime kind, for sex only. Relations between them were warm . . . burning, but the actual friendship was cool.

That's the way he liked it.

And if once in a while he became lonely, well, that was the cost of the secret he kept—the secret he wouldn't trade for anything because it gave him a reason to exist. It gave him a purpose and a way to serve his people in a meaningful way. Take away his duty here in the Black Tower and he would fade to nothingness.

He moved through the dark marble hallways and past carved wooden doors. In places, water streamed down the stone faces of the walls or fires burned in the fireplaces of the myriad small sitting areas of the tower.

The architects had done a good job with the place and there was nowhere else Gabriel wanted to call home. He'd been there when the tower had first been designed and constructed. As a child he watched every day from the square as it went up, hope burning in his chest that he would someday live behind its walls with his kind. Back then it had been the only hope he'd had. It had kept him alive in the first harsh years after Piefferburg had been formed. He'd had no one back then, and he had learned it was better to stand on your own than to rely on anyone else.

He slipped through a secret door in the west wing and mounted the winding stairs that would lead him to the roof of the Black Tower. The twisting cool gray stone was like something out of a human child's faery tale. Once in a while a gargoyle head—placed there by the builders and imbued with spells of protection—jutted from the rocky walls. Small shelved alcoves held hand-carved wooden statues depicting

famous Unseelie fae. Gabriel made this climb every night—
had for more than a century—and knew each of them by
name, as well as their stories.

When he reached the top of the winding staircase he found
Aeric Killian Riordan O'Malley, also known as The Blacksmith. Leaning in the doorway leading out onto the roof, Aeric
crossed his brawny arms across his chest and lifted a dark
blond brow. "You're late and the souls are restless. We almost
left without you."

Aeric, long ago and in another world for the fae, had been a
blacksmith with an ability to forge magickal weapons that
had given a whole new dimension to the battles in which
they'd been wielded. These days there wasn't much call for
magicked battle weapons, though Aeric still found work here
and there, making charmed restraints and the occasional illegal
charmed club or sword. Now Aeric was a part of Gabriel's
host and one of his best friends.

Some called it "the Furious Host," but Gabriel thought
they were only mildly annoyed. Probably more so than usual
since he'd been making them wait.

"I've been busy. I'm doing something for the Shadow
King over in the Rose," Gabriel said, reaching the door.

"The Rose?" Aeric pushed off the door frame and fell into
step beside him. His longish, dark blond hair was tied at the
nape of his neck and he wore a pair of battered jeans, steel-
toed boots, and a T-shirt that strained over his chest. He
wasn't a blacksmith anymore, but he still had the build of
one. "What's it like over there?"

"Boring." Except for Aislinn. She was a spitfire. Normally he'd tell Aeric all about it, but Aodh wanted it under
wraps. "Are the rest of them here?"

"Yeah. We've been waiting for the last hour." His voice
came out an angry, low growl. Aeric had a temper that was
infamous in the Black Tower.

Emerging onto the roof, he saw the rest of his host reclining
on the shiny black quartz top of the tower. The mystic horses
roamed aimless. There were six of the Netherworld horses
tonight, which meant a healthy amount of souls to reap. Abas-

tor was Gabriel's black quarterhorse and the only mount that appeared nightly. A headstrong horse only Gabriel could control, Abastor led the hunt. The sleek black Netherworld hounds, Blix and Taliesin, also roamed, sniffing what there was to sniff when they weren't tracking needy souls throughout the city.

Melia, a petite, redheaded battle fae, lounged on the roof near her husband, Aelfdane. Aelfdane was much taller than his tiny spouse, stick thin, and had long blond hair that hung to the small of his back. Aelfdane had a gentle, almost effeminate air about him in the way all the Twyleth Teg did, but that gentleness was as deceptive as Melia's size. They were both deadly in a fight. To boot, Aelfdane's magick was giving sickness on a whim. Not someone you wanted to piss off.

Bran sat at the card table playing solitaire. There was nothing unusual about that. Bran was a mystery to most of them. His skill lay in managing animals—controlling and directing creatures like the waterhorses and phookas in the Boundary Lands and even the host's mystic hounds. Blix and Taliesin adored him. Bran's pet crow, Lex, perched nearby, watching everything with his fathomless black eyes. Bran didn't look up as Gabriel approached, lost in his own world. He seemed to communicate well with fae animals, but not so well with anything or anyone else.

All of them had been handpicked by unknown forces to be his posse, the Furious Host. Every night they formed the Wild Hunt, the group that tales had been told of in almost every culture of almost every land since time had begun. Every night they met here and did their sacred duty.

Every night, they rode.

Melia and Aelfdane's heads popped up as he strode past them. "Okay, let's go gather souls."

# THREE

AISLINN gasped and came awake, her white silk sheets a tangle around her legs. She sat up, breathing hard, trying to push away the remnants of the dream that clung to her like a spiderweb. Clutching the soft sheet to her chest, she shuddered.

It had been a prophetic dream, like other ones she'd had from time to time. There was no mistaking the difference in it, the clearer quality and sense of utter and total reality. That was what made them so terrifying: they seemed real and were usually horrific.

This one had been more horrific than most.

With a heavy sense of foreboding clinging to her, she slid from the bedding and found her slippers and bathrobe. She made her way out to the kitchen in the semidarkness and poured herself a tall glass of cold water with shaking hands. The rim of the water jug trembled on the lip of the glass, nearly making her slosh liquid everywhere.

It was times like these when she hated living alone, when she regretted not keeping a servant like just about everyone else in the Rose. She'd almost taken on Lolly, her friend Bella's house hobgoblin, when Bella had been banished, just because Lolly felt like part of the family. But Lolly had found employment elsewhere and it was just as well. Because nights like these were also the reason Aislinn couldn't allow anyone to live with her, not even someone she could trust like Lolly.

Taking her glass to the couch in the living room, she stood at the window that overlooked Piefferburg Square and took a long, cool swallow, trying not to recall her dream. Of course, that was fruitless. She could probably kiss sleep good-bye for the night.

The ability she had to occasionally see the future was a fae skill that had been passed down by her forebears. It was a common and respectable Sídhe trait and part of what made her Seelie. But she wasn't *just* Seelie. Her bloodline was—at least so far as was documented—*pure* Tuatha Dé. One needed such a pedigree to be a part of the highest echelons of the Seelie Court.

Her mother was incredibly proud of her family's social standing. In fact, their family's place in the Rose was the only thing she really cared about.

Aislinn's mother didn't know that her daughter possessed another skill besides prophetic dreaming. A much darker one. An ability that would put her on the other side of Piefferburg Square, with the monsters. It was the reason she couldn't have anyone living with her. They might notice her odd behavior as she dealt with her ability and tell the queen about it.

Aislinn could communicate with the dead.

She could see them and talk to them when no one else could. Souls sought her out for exactly that reason. She suspected she could also summon and influence the dead, though she'd never tried it. It just didn't seem right to use those who came to her for aid as guinea pigs. Even so, she could feel the ability in the center of her. She simply *knew* she had it. Calling and controlling spirits from the Netherworld was magick that lay in the realm of the necromancer.

And that was certainly *not* a respectable Seelie ability.

It had started when she was young, but Aislinn had learned to conceal her skills quickly. If anyone in the Rose knew that Aislinn had Unseelie magick, she'd be exiled and her mother would be disgraced. So she'd grown up squelching and denying it, even though there had been a part of her that had been intensely fascinated by her ability.

A dangerous part of her still was.

Aislinn would love the chance to find a teacher, one who could help her wield her ability more effectively, increase her talent. The fact that she wanted to develop her necromancy instead of suppress it was a secret she couldn't reveal—not even to Bella, whom she'd told about her dark magick. Anyway, even if there were any other necromancers, they all dwelt on the dark side of the square.

She watched the Wild Hunt lift off from the top of the Black Tower. As one of the highest-ranking Seelie nobles, she enjoyed a beautiful, lavishly furnished apartment with a wonderful view. If she was up late, she often caught a glimpse of the Wild Hunt taking off to do its work for the night—gather the souls of those fae who had passed on during the twenty-four hours since their last ride.

Those fae who died outside Piefferburg's walls—and there were still some out there, those who'd managed to evade the Great Sweep by the Phaendir in the mid-1600s—were never collected. They wandered aimlessly for an eternity, growing angrier with their fate and dangerous to humans. Aislinn knew that because she could feel them pulling at her from beyond the warding that guarded Piefferburg's borders. They called to her through the strong magick the Phaendir had imprisoned them in. Their cries were muffled but audible.

Humans thought the fae were immortal, but that wasn't quite right. The Seelie and Unseelie royals were immortal because of the magick bestowed on them by the court artifacts. The Unseelie Royal wore an amulet and the Seelie Royal wore a ring, each piece of jewelry bestowing on them eternal life—freedom from disease or age. They could still be killed, however. They weren't granted immunity from mortal wounds.

The fae, most breeds, were immortal by human standards but not by exact definition. They were simply very long-lived, the aging process slowing to a crawl once a fae hit twenty-five. But the fae races still fell prey to accidents, illness, and, eventually, age, just like any human. Watt syndrome had taken an especially large toll and still stole away a fae here and there within the limits of Piefferburg. The only fae races that were not long-lived were the goblins and their lesser nightmarish offshoot species, the hobgoblins. Their life span ranged only to around a hundred years.

She watched the Wild Hunt sail off into the darkness on phantom horses and with hounds at their side to sniff out the needy spirits. Did the Lord of the Wild Hunt hear the lost ones beyond the warding of Piefferburg, too? Could he feel all those departed fae yanking his psychic chain and demanding help he could never give like she did?

In an odd way, she felt more kinship with the mysterious Lord of the Wild Hunt than with anyone at Seelie Court . . . at least since Bella had gone.

No one knew who the Lord of the Wild Hunt was. His identity, and that of his host, was closely guarded. Too bad, since she'd like to meet him sometime, no matter that he resided in the Black.

But then she *would* meet him, wouldn't she? And soon. Her dream had told her that much. She'd meet him when he came for her soul. Her dreams always foretold someone's death.

This time it had been hers.

She closed her eyes against the swelling memory of the dream, the glass of water slipping from her fingers and crashing to the thick fawn carpeting at her feet.

Hands. So many hands, grasping, yanking.

They'd pulled at her, caught in her hair, her clothes, bruising her limbs. Below and behind her a murky darkness had spread. Before her and in front of her had been lighter, like she'd been submerged in water and was looking toward the surface of the lake. The owners of the grabbing hands had been moaning and purring in her ear to give up, let go, and allow them to carry her soul over the twilight threshold of life and death to the Netherworld. To death. She hadn't been able to resist them. She'd been so tired, so weak.

She was going to die soon and Gabriel Cionaodh Marcus Mac Braire, somehow, someway, would be the catalyst.

THE man stood flickering in the image his soul took to the living—gray and softly glowing. A shimmering silver cord rippled and pulsed from his back, reaching to the Netherworld, where his place already waited for him. All he needed was for the Wild Hunt to show him the way. The elderly fae's expression was a mixture of sorrow and pain as he gazed down at his still-living wife, who lay sleeping in bed beside his motionless and silent body. The wife probably wouldn't realize her husband had passed until morning.

Gabriel regretted her discovery and her impending grief, but this was the natural pattern for all living things. No one was immune. He was only a ferryman, imbued by some unknown cosmic force with the ability to escort the departed to the afterlife.

Only himself and his host could see fae spirits. He guessed there were probably a few others beyond his circle with the ability, but he'd never met any. Gabriel wasn't sure if his skill extended to human souls. He'd been born outside Piefferburg, but he'd been a child and not yet Lord of the Wild Hunt during those few, short years of freedom. Since he'd probably die in Piefferburg, he'd probably never know.

The torch of the Wild Hunt had passed to him nearly two hundred years ago. In those two hundred years Gabriel had seen every type of soul there was to see. Some left their life with a peace and acceptance that was beautiful to behold. Some were angry and fought to stay earthbound. Some did remain earthbound.

But most of them were simply sad to leave those they

loved and were reluctant to sever their attachments. Sometimes it was hard to get souls to take that final ride with him, a ride that would usher them forward to their next life—whatever that was. Gabriel wasn't privy to the secrets of the world that lay beyond this one, despite his job servicing it.

His host waiting outside, Gabriel reached out a hand to the soul. "It's time to go now."

The man looked at him, then turned away and knelt at his wife's side. Clearly he needed some time to say good-bye. Gabriel was always willing to give it. If the man's wife woke while Gabriel was in the room, all she would see were shadows. All she would hear were murmurs and whispers. Magick protected the hunt's true identity and had since the dawn of time.

Though she would perceive the Wild Hunt, the woman would not be able to see her husband. She would probably presume that the Wild Hunt had killed him. The trooping fae, who lacked the gentle spirituality of the wilding fae and the knowledge of the nobles, believed that the hunt was evil.

Gabriel gave the man until dawn began to edge slowly over the horizon. "Come. Your life is done here and another is waiting for you. Your wife will grieve you, but her journey on earth isn't finished yet."

The man ignored him, gripping his wife's hand like he would never let go.

Most of the souls he collected seemed to understand that it was time to leave. Some did not. He kept track of every soul he couldn't collect, returning periodically to see if he could entice them into passing. Fae souls didn't have magick anymore, but they could still hurt others if they wanted to badly enough. A powerful enough necromancer could even make them into weapons and kill people with them. Luckily there were no necromancers in Piefferburg.

The man finally moved away from his wife and toward Gabriel. Silently, they walked out of the small house in the *ceantar láir* and back to the waiting host. They had a full collection tonight. Five other souls were mounted on the horses.

Once the man was secure on a jet-black mare, the hounds led them off once more, toward one last soul to retrieve.

"NOT again," Aislinn mumbled and turned over, pulling the blanket over her head. It was almost dawn and she'd finally managed to fall back to sleep after convincing herself that the dream she'd had was just a dream and not prophetic.

It was a lie she *had* to believe. She couldn't function any other way. How could she look Gabriel in the eye thinking anything else? How could she do the job that the Summer Queen had given her believing Gabriel was somehow a trigger for the events that would lead to her death?

Finally, after she'd managed to divert her mind from the grasping hands, she'd fallen back to sleep. Now she was awake again and someone was watching her, looming over the side of her bed. It was a feeling she was familiar with . . . one she selfishly wanted to ignore right now.

*A soft whisper.*
*Shuffling feet.*
*The psychic press of a soul in need.*

Aislinn rolled back over and confronted the soul that stood at her bedside. She sat up and her breath came out in a shocked whisper. "Elena?" She was one of her mother's friends. The cord that anchored her in the Netherworld shimmered a soft peach color. "No. That's impossible. You're too young to die."

"I'm already dead, dear. Watt syndrome," Elena whispered in that gentle, breezy way that souls spoke in. "It lay dormant in me for close to a century then finally sank its claws in."

Watt syndrome was a fae-specific illness that was mostly under control . . . but not quite. It had decimated the fae races, both during the years of the Great Sweep and in the preceding years when Piefferburg had been newly born. Those left behind after the illness had burned through were either naturally immune or had developed immunity to it. The disease itself was magickal in origin—which was why most believed the Phaendir had created it—but no countermeasure for the illness had been developed, not for a lack of effort. Watt syndrome still claimed victims occasionally, even after so many years.

Apparently Elena had been one of them.

Aislinn had noticed Elena had often kept to her apartment lately and hadn't been participating in the social events that dominated the Rose Tower calendar. She'd seemed grayish in color, had lost weight, and seemed tired most of the time. Elena had said she'd simply had some sort of bug.

Mostly it was souls whom Aislinn hadn't known in real life who came to her, ones who had no one close to them in life—no family, no friends. They simply wanted someone to see them, talk to them, ease their fear of the unknown. Sometimes they had a message to pass on to those they left behind, messages that she tried to deliver without endangering her secret.

A dark shadow appeared in the corner of the room, diametrically opposite the rising sun from the other direction. Aislinn blinked. More shadows appeared behind the first. There were a total of five indistinguishable forms near her door now.

She sat all the way up with a jerk of surprise.

The Lord of the Wild Hunt and his host? It had to be. They'd come to collect Elena.

*Lady*.

Never in her entire life had she been with a soul when the Wild Hunt came to collect him or her. She'd wondered about the odds of that, considering how many souls sought her out in the dead of night. Yet it had never happened. Secretly, she'd longed for it. She'd wanted a single glimpse of the group of people in all of Piefferburg who might understand her gift.

Suddenly a horrible thought occurred. She looked down at herself to make sure she wasn't out of her body and ready to be collected herself. No. She was still corporeal. The prophetic dream that she was going to die soon hadn't come true . . . yet.

Elena gazed at the hunt, her ageless face unlined and serene. "They're here for me."

Aislinn clutched her blankets to her and stared. She'd watched the Wild Hunt take off from the top of the Unseelie Court so many times; it was hard to believe they were standing in her bedroom.

The first tall and broad shadow—the Lord of the Wild Hunt—stepped forward and an unintelligible whisper echoed through the room. All the hair on the back of Aislinn's neck stood up. The furious host appeared as little more than shadowy smudges.

"I'm coming in a moment," Elena said in answer to the whisper, then turned her head back to Aislinn. "I felt your ability as soon as I passed," she said. "I was drawn to it immediately. It was a comfort to know I could come to you. No matter that it's Unseelie dark, don't let your skill languish, Aislinn. It's a gift."

"I-I won't." She wished she didn't have to.

"Tell your mother she was always a good friend to me and I'll miss her."

"I will." Aislinn paused, steadied her voice, and said, "Good-bye Elena. Good travels."

But Elena was already crossing the room toward the large shadow's outstretched hand. Together they left the room, the other shadows forming a procession behind her.

Aislinn leapt from the bed, grabbed her robe, and ran to the window in the living room. A few minutes later and the host lifted off from the roof, clearly laden with many collected souls on the backs of horses. Together the host flew off into the pinkish dawn, then seemed to explode in a glittery sunburst.

Then there were just the shadows, horses and hounds. The souls were gone. The Wild Hunt headed back to the Unseelie Court.

# FOUR

ONCE back on the roof of the Black Tower, Gabriel slid off Abastor and stared into the dawn-lightened sky behind the Rose Tower, his jaw clenched.

Aislinn. That had been Aislinn they'd just seen. And she'd clearly been able to see and talk to the soul they'd been there to collect.

"You okay?" asked Aeric beside him.

Gabriel blinked, trying to wrap his mind around the situation. "Yeah."

"That was pretty amazing, wasn't it?"

"Wow. Someone in the Rose who can see souls." Melia slid from her mount with Aelfdane's help. "She's got Unseelie blood. That woman shouldn't even be there. I can't imagine how alone she must feel, having to conceal a secret that big every day."

The Shadow King had said Aislinn was a relation; so of course she was displaced Unseelie. That part wasn't what had shocked him so much. In almost two hundred years of leading the Wild Hunt, Gabriel had never come upon someone who could communicate with souls. Tonight, he had. And that person happened to be *Aislinn*, the woman he'd only just met, the woman he'd been tasked with luring to the Black of her own free will.

The odds had to be infinitesimal, which meant it hadn't happened by chance. Gabriel didn't believe in coincidence, but he couldn't discern the reason for this.

One thing was for certain: Aislinn didn't belong in the Rose Tower. Even aside from the Shadow King's demand she defect from the Rose and come to the Black, her people were the Unseelie, not those fancy imbeciles across the square.

No matter how this had happened tonight, whether it had been a result of pure chance or the work of a higher power, he'd been given a gift.

Since his charm as an incubus didn't seem to be working, he could use this new information to tempt Aislinn to the Black.


WAS it possible she was a necromancer?

Gabriel slouched in one of Aislinn's armchairs and watched her from across the room. It didn't seem likely. Hells, it seemed impossible. Yet the skill to communicate with souls usually went hand in hand with the power to call and control them. And there were necromancers in the Shadow King's line-age, though the king had called Aislinn a "distant" relation and the necromancers of his line were direct—the power run-ning through the maternal side of his family. Perhaps Aislinn wasn't as "distant" as the king had claimed.

But why would he lie?

Necromancers were powerful, dangerous Unseelie. As Lord of the Wild Hunt, Gabriel had the ability to call the sluagh—the horde of unforgiven dead from the Netherworld—but he lacked the ability to direct and control them. A necro-mancer couldn't call the sluagh, but she could control them. It was sort of a cosmic safeguard since the sluagh were capable of such utter destruction.

A necromancer played yin to the Lord of the Wild Hunt's yang.

Even without the sluagh, a necromancer could wreak complete chaos, with the ability to call any soul she wished from the Netherworld, command the soul to take corporeal form, and then use it as a weapon if enough emotion could be engendered in that soul.

Gabriel frowned and rubbed his chin, deep in thought. In the kitchen, where Aislinn puttered, doing what Danu only knew what, she hummed to herself—a light, pretty little ditty. He tried to imagine her commanding an army of the unforgiven dead.

Nah, Aislinn wasn't a necromancer.

His lower lip twitched in a brief smile. She may not be a lightweight shallow ball of fluff like the rest of the women in this court, but she was no magickal heavyweight, either. *No.* No way could she wield power over the dead.

She must be what the Shadow King said she was—a distant relation. Perhaps she had a breath of the talent inherent in his direct line, but only a breath. Just enough to let her communicate with souls.

A cupboard door in the kitchen slammed. She was stalling. For the first time in his life a woman was actually *stalling* to put off attending a social function with him.

She entered the living room, the skirt of her long gold gown swinging with her movement. Her long silver blond hair was swept up in a chignon at the very attractive nape of her neck, a sensitive part of the body for most women. He wondered what kinds of sounds she'd make if he gently nipped her there. She wore a minimal amount of makeup, just enough to accentuate her liquid silver-gray eyes and her rosebud of a mouth. Her lower lip was much fuller than the upper, made a man want to suck on it. She wore little jewelry, too. Just two diamond earrings and a matching gem in the hollow of her throat.

"I'm ready," she announced, slipping on the two elbow-length white gloves that were sitting on the counter. Gabriel detected a note of resignation in her voice.

"Really? Are you sure you don't want to organize the cabinets? Alphabetize your soup cans, perhaps? Maybe go through your refrigerator and throw out all the past-date food? It's okay, I can wait."

"Very funny."

Still slumped in the chair, he spread his hands. "I promise I won't bite you, Aislinn. You don't have to keep stalling."

She raised a brow and cocked a hip. "Don't flatter yourself. Listen, Gabriel, I'm not afraid of much, especially not you. I'm just not looking forward to this party, but not because I'm going with you. If the queen hadn't entrusted me with the job of introducing you around, I wouldn't be going at all."

"What would you be doing?"

"I'd stay at home, make a nice dinner, have a bath, and go to bed early." She paused. "That might sound boring to you, but to me it's the perfect evening. I didn't sleep well last night and I'm really tired. Plus, I woke this morning to find a dear friend of my family had died from Watt syndrome during the night. I'm not feeling festive."

Yes, he knew all too well she'd woken up pretty early. Knew all about the friend of the family's death, too.

"Okay, I'll be honest, Aislinn, I'd rather have a quiet night, too." Gabriel's job was Aislinn, not being introduced around at court. "How about we skip the ball and make dinner here. I'm a pretty good cook. You can go take a bath and I'll prepare a meal. I won't stay late and you can go to bed early. That way we can get to know each other a little better and I can change this horrible opinion you have of me. What do you say?"

She hesitated, blinked a couple of times, and looked ready to bolt. "I don't have a horrible opinion of you. It's just—"

He held up his hands. "Your honor is totally safe with me, Aislinn. Lock the bathroom door if you want. I just want to be friends."

Lie. He wanted to sleep with her. Seduce her and betray her. Lure her into his bed and then to the Unseelie Court. He wanted to hand her over to the Shadow King, whose purposes were murky.

His conscience flickered.

But this was his job. And he'd known the Shadow King for many years. No matter what the stories were, he was not a bad man. He was not an unjust ruler. Gabriel didn't know what his king wanted with her, but he felt in his heart it wasn't to harm her. After all, she was a relative.

The plan was for Gabriel to get under her skin, make her care about him . . . addict her to him sexually, if he could. Then, at the end of his stay here, he would decide the Rose Tower wasn't for him and return to the Unseelie Court, throwing himself on the mercy of the Shadow King. He planned to convince Aislinn to come with him—tell her that he couldn't live without her and that the Shadow King would let him live if he saw he'd finally fallen in love.

And now he had the added leverage of knowing the monumental secret she was keeping.

Gods, he was a cold fucking bastard. Sometimes he even surprised himself.

Maybe it was better if they went to the party and surrounded themselves with other people. Maybe it was better if they didn't get to know each other, better that this stopped now. He could go back to the Unseelie Court and tell the Shadow King—

"All right." Aislinn stripped her gloves off and kicked away her stilettos. "Sounds good to me, but I don't know what you'll find to make for dinner. I don't have much food in the house. I live mostly on oatmeal and yogurt."

Gabriel's stomach sank. Suddenly he wasn't sure this was such a good idea. But he was in it up to his eyebrows now. "I'll find something."

She gave him a shaky smile, hesitated and looked as if she might say something. Instead, she walked into her bedroom.

He stared at the closed door for a long moment, still slumped in his chair. The decision had been made and he needed to get back on task. He couldn't ask for a better situation than this.

All he needed was his head in the game. He loosened his tie and got up to build a fire in the fireplace. Feeding it with small bits of kindling, he coaxed it into a blaze—just the method he planned to use with Aislinn. That done, he ventured into the kitchen.

She'd been right when she'd said there wasn't much food in the house. He managed to find some linguine in the cabinet, and some cauliflower that was nearly bad, olives, raisins, a little garlic and onion, nuts, and a small can of tomato paste from the rest of the kitchen. Anyone else looking at that collection wouldn't believe they could create something delicious with it, but Gabriel knew he could. He'd watched his mother get by on almost nothing when he was a child, watched her creativity with limited resources, and had never forgotten the lesson. She'd always been able to create something wonderful from scraps.

With the odd assortment of ingredients he cooked up a sweet and salty pasta dish along with a salad. Finding a bottle of red wine, he popped it open and poured a couple of glasses. By the time she was out of her bath, he had the table set and dinner ready.

Seduction, phase one, in place.

"Wow."

He looked up at the sound of her voice and his breath caught. She stood at the entrance of her formal dining room and surveyed the two places he'd set at the end of her polished mahogany table, using the fine china and crystal he'd found in her breakfront. Her gown was gone, replaced by a soft-looking pair of jersey pants and a dark sweater. Her feet were bare and her toenails painted in seashell pink, just like her fingernails. Her face was clean of makeup and her hair was freed from its chignon, falling freshly washed and still damp past her shoulders. She seemed completely at ease dressed this way and a bit younger.

Without the armor she wore around the court, she was even more gorgeous.

He cleared his throat and looked away, clamping down on his impulse to go to her. He knew that if he pulled her against him, kissed her, and stroked her soft skin, she would eventually relent. She might fight him at first, but he knew with the dark and erotic certainty of the incubus blood in his veins that he could push her past that stage, make her give in to him. It would be so sweet. He could draw her back to her bedroom, spread her out on her mattress, and strip those clothes off her. He could draw his lips and hands over her body, kissing, sucking, and petting her until she was incoherent with want—until the only sounds she could make were moans and entreaties for more.

His body clenched at the fantasy unfurling in his mind.

"It smells great and I'm famished."

Gabriel had to force his vocal cords into action. "Bath all right?" He wasn't going to think about her bare body slick with water and droplets of moisture. He was already having trouble controlling his erection—a thing that rarely happened.

"Wonderful." She settled herself at her plate and he served her some of the pasta from a pretty blue and yellow ceramic bowl. Aislinn was one of the highest born of the Seelie fae and she had the best of everything. When he took her to the Unseelie Court with him, she'd be giving all that up, though considering her blood ties and previous social rank, Gabriel was sure that the Shadow King would clothe and house her appropriately.

Probably. His conscience flickered again.

He sat down beside her and served himself as she tasted his meal. She closed her eyes and sighed. "This is great, Gabriel. I can't believe you just whipped this up in the twenty minutes I took to take a bath."

"At three hundred and sixty-five years old, I've had lots of practice."

"The Summer Queen mentioned you were a child during the Great Sweep and that you were only seven when the humans and the Phaendir created Piefferburg." She took a sip of wine. "She even said that you suffered from Watt syndrome as a boy and still had it when you were first imprisoned here."

"Yes. My mother had it, too. I was very sick and almost died, but managed to fight through. Now I'm immune. Unfortunately my mother wasn't. She died from it during the first year of Piefferburg's creation."

"I'm sorry."

"Thanks, but it was a long time ago."

"Still, it's never easy to lose a parent. It doesn't matter how long ago it was."

"True."

"What was Piefferburg like back then?"

Gabriel took a steadying sip of wine as memory he ordinarily tried to avoid swelled. He remembered hastily constructed wooden shanties that leaked when it rained. Remembered how cold it was at night and how dangerously freezing the winters were. Remembered moldy potatoes and dirty, parasite-ridden water. Remembered his mother lying on a narrow mattress with no one to take care of her but a scrawny seven-year-old boy who was also wasting away from the disease. He remembered his mother dying alone one afternoon while he'd gone out to scavenge for food. When he'd returned empty-handed, her eyes had been open, dull, and sunken into a gray face.

He remembered the years after his mother died, when he'd been left alone with all the other captured fae who were struggling to find a foothold in their new reality. In those early years, after his mother died, he'd been forced to do so many unsavory things to survive. Things in back alleys for fae with bad breath, greasy hair, and grasping hands. He'd been forced to use his magick in ways he didn't want to think of now, yet the memories dwelt like tiny demons in the corners of his mind, taking small, bloody bites.

He took another long drink of his wine. "It was a living hell for some of us."

"For all those who weren't Seelie, you mean?"

He nodded and said nothing more. Bitterness still crept up into the back of his throat remembering the years of the Great Sweep. How the Phaendir had hunted them down, rounded them up, and forcibly transported them from all over the world to Piefferburg. It had been so easy with the sickness on them all and because the fae races had been fragmented as a result of the wars.

The combination of events had spelled doom for all the fae. The wars and the illness had outed them to humankind, who panicked in the face of legend becoming truth. Intimidated by fae magick, they were easily influenced by the Phaendir, who told them to strike while the fae were weak.

So many fae had died on the ships; many more succumbed during their resettlement in the fledging Piefferburg, which had been so starved for resources. No food. No shelter. No medicine. No heat. Not even clean drinking water.

The early days had been very hard for all but the Seelie, who'd been kept like royalty on the backs of all the other fae. The troop believed the Seelie were a shining symbol of the greatness of their kind and supported them, no matter the cost to the rest.

He leveled his gaze at her. "Yes, that's what I mean."

It was an effort to keep the edge from his voice. It wasn't Aislinn's fault that the Seelie had caused the other fae to suffer at the time of Piefferburg's birth. She hadn't even been alive back then. It had taken Piefferburg years to get on its feet, build an economy, and suffer through the inferno that had been Watt syndrome, an illness Gabriel believed was Phaendir born.

"Your mother was Seelie, correct? Your father Unseelie?"

"My mother was troop. She had Seelie blood, but it was mixed with wilding fae, not pure enough for the Rose." His jaw locked for a moment. "My father was an Unseelie noble, one hundred percent incubus."

"And your father," she said softly, "did he die of Watt syndrome, too?"

His jaw locked. "No," he forced out. He hadn't had to speak of these things in a long time. They were wounds still fresh, even though they were centuries old.

"Is he here in Piefferburg then?" She took another bite of her dinner, unaware she drew blood from him with every question she asked. It was an innocent enough query from a

Seelie lady who'd known no hardship in her pampered life filled with people who adored her.

His hand tightened on his fork and he forced himself to relax his grip. "No, he never made it to Piefferburg." A good thing for his father, since Gabriel would have killed him once he was old enough and strong enough to do it. As a child he'd been powerless against the bastard who'd sired him.

She nearly dropped her fork and looked up at him. "You mean he's still alive? He evaded the Great Sweep?"

"Yes, but the way he lived his life, he's probably dead by now."

She studied him with eyes keener than he was comfortable with. Most likely she was weighing his words and the tone in which he spoke. She was probably wondering why his father had chosen freedom in the world over his family, or at least why he hadn't tried to stop the Phaendir from taking his wife and child. Those were questions he didn't want to answer. Fortunately, Aislinn had enough sense not to ask them.

She turned her attention back to her plate. "What did your mother do for a living?"

His lips twitched. "She was a whore."

Her hand shook.

"It's okay. I'm not ashamed. My mother did what she had to do to take care of us. She was a strong woman, a good woman, who did the best she could with the bad breaks life gave her." He paused. "I have more of my mother in me than I do my father. I'm happy to be able to say that."

She raised her gaze. "I would never judge a woman in a position like hers, in that time of history, alone and with a child to take care of. History has not been easy on us, on any of us."

"I would debate that the Seelie have had a rough time."

Her eyes snapped suddenly cold. "Why? We're the ones who have lost the most, even if eventually we regained it. The Seelie are the ones who ruled the British Isles after wresting control from the Firbolg and the Formorians, and then lost control to the Milesians when the Phaendir allied with them. It was the *Seelie* who had to negotiate for all the other fae races when that happened. If not for the hard choices we had to make, the fae might have been wiped from the planet. So don't tell me the Seelie haven't sacrificed just like all the rest of the fae."

The Milesians, simply a human tribe, had found a friend in the Phaendir and used charmed iron weapons in battle against the fae. With the Phaendir's aid, they'd defeated the ruling Seelie Tuatha Dé. But since the fae could really never be killed off, they were forced to make a solemn promise to disappear from the sight and knowledge of humans. They'd gone underground. Sometimes literally, in the case of some wilding fae and the goblins, but mostly they'd just faded into anonymity, eventually becoming only the stuff of myth and legend to the humans. At least until the wars and Watt had outed them.

Gabriel sensed a disagreement in the air, but he just couldn't leave it alone. He smiled, but he knew it was cold. "I think it's interesting how so much of Seelie court life is based on illusion."

"What do you mean?"

"The Seelie believe they're better than all other kinds of fae because they ruled over all of us before the Unseelie organized and came to equal power. They think they're entitled to the support they receive from the troop. They believe the Unseelie are all horrible bloodthirsty monsters, when they're not—"

"They're not?" She raised her eyebrows.

He spread his hands. "You're making my point for me. Not all of us are. I'm not, am I?"

"I don't know you well enough to make that judgment." She blinked innocently and took another bite of pasta.

She was viciously honest. He liked that about her. The Seelie were known for their ability to dissemble, but she seemed to lack talent at that dubious art. She was also very intelligent. He wasn't a bloodthirsty monster, but he wasn't exactly harmless, either.

He dropped his eyelids a little, leaned in, and lowered his voice. "Sweetness, I want you to know me much better."

Her eyes widened a little and she blinked. Good. It was time she got the hint that no matter what he might tell her, his intentions toward her were hardly honorable. Sensual, erotic, and most certainly sweaty—but never honorable.

He leaned back in his chair. "To finish my point, the troop believe that the Seelie are worthy of their support, that the Seelie are the last vestige of beauty, nobility, and power that the fae have. The troop think of the Seelie as royalty and want to keep them on a pedestal to adore."

She bristled. "It's the way things have been for millennia. It's how fae culture is constructed."

"Yes, but that doesn't make it a good thing. How can it be when it's all based on powerful false belief and illusion? I find it fascinating."

"You're saying the Seelie are just like any other fae, not the original genetic source from which all other fae spring, and therefore aren't entitled to special treatment."

With heavy-lidded eyes, he studied her angry face. She was even more attractive when she was riled. He should piss her off more often. "I subscribe to the belief that the Unseelie and Seelie were created at the same time. Dark and light to balance each other. That the troop and the wilding fae sprang from genetic combinations between the two."

She set her fork down and pressed her lips together before speaking. "You seem a little biased against the Seelie for someone who is petitioning to join the Rose."

"Not at all. My criticism of both the courts is equally scathing."

"I understand you're placed quite highly in the Black Tower. Seems like you must be comfortable there. I can't really believe you want to give all that up just because you're bored."

He took a sip of wine. "Maybe I want to explore my mother's Seelie Sídhe blood a bit, at least the little of it that she had. And I never lied about being bored, Aislinn. You'll see. You tend to search for more exciting stimulus at such an advanced age, even if it means defecting one court for another."

"You're not exactly elderly." She raised an eyebrow. "I'm sure most women think you're very . . . very . . ."

"Very?"

"Virile." Her cheeks turned a bit rosy.

He grinned. "And what about you? Do *you* think I'm virile?"

The rosy blush in her cheeks turned to red anger. "I'm done with men for a very long time, so you can get that thought right out of your head—and off your face, too."

He'd let her hold on to that lie for just a little while longer.

"Yes, the gossip of your breakup with Kendal is all over the Seelie Court."

"I don't want to talk about it."

"Fine, but I do want to say one thing. Kendal is an idiot. Every time I see him, I want to punch him. He never deserved you." Gabriel leaned forward. "If you let one miserable man spoil all your future chances for love, that's stupid on your part."

She gave a short burst of unexpected laughter. "Thanks for that bit of advice I never asked for."

His lips twitched. "Anytime."

"You may not be as bad as I thought, Gabriel."

"I'm glad you're finally coming to that conclusion. I can't help what I am, Aislinn. I'm half incubus and while I can control my magick to some extent, most of it comes naturally to me. It's a part of who I am. Believe me, it's not always easy. It's got its downside."

Lie number two. Occasionally it was tiresome fending off the advances of someone he wasn't attracted to, but overall his magick was one of the better kinds to have, in his opinion. He never spent a night alone unless he wanted to. Of course, there was the stray person here and there who seemed unaffected by his charm. Like sweet miss Aislinn. But that only made things more interesting.

"Other than being pure-bloodline Tuatha Dé, what magick do you possess?" He couldn't wait to hear her answer this question. Time to put her in an uncomfortable position. He leaned back and drained the last of the wine in his glass.

She cleared her throat and—was it his imagination?—did she go pale? How fascinating. "I have the power of prediction. I dream things that come true sometimes. Mostly I dream of people's deaths."

"That's dark." The words, of course, were calculated on his part.

She flinched. "It has its darker moments. It's not an uncommon sort of magick for a Seelie to have, however. It's not a magick that can kill or maim."

"Did you dream the death of your family's friend?"

"No." Her gaze dropped into her lap. "My gift is unpredictable that way. I dreamed of someone else's death last night."

"Someone you know?"

She looked up, a wry smile flickering over her luscious mouth. "Yes, intimately."

"I'm sorry. But you know death is a part of living. We might exist on this earth for centuries on end, but eventually we'll all be collected by the Wild Hunt."

Flinch again. Maybe having her first encounter with the Wild Hunt had thrown her a little. "True, but it's still a sad thing."

Gabriel shook his head. "Not always. Sad for those we leave behind, maybe. But I believe our souls pass into another life. There is no death, only change. You've seen the Wild Hunt in action, I'm sure, flying through the night. If nothing comes after death, there would be no reason for them to do what they do."

She smiled. "It's a nice idea. I hope you're right."

"I think I am right." He surveyed the wreck of their dinner. "I'll let you get some sleep, Aislinn, and see you tomorrow.

You've had a long day and you're grieving. I don't want to impose any longer." He rose from the table.

"Wait."

He paused.

She smiled and pushed her index finger along the top of the smooth table. "Stay a little longer, just for a drink. I feel like I've treated you so badly."

Gabriel gazed down at the top of her head, trying to get a handle on another rush of impulse. He wanted to stay. Suddenly, he needed to stay. Stay and have that drink, lean in at some point, ease the glass from her hand, and lick the leftover droplets from her lips.

That dark voice inside him, the incubus, whispered, *You can make her want you. You can make her beg.*

He knew he could seduce her this very night if he wanted to. All he had to do was get close to her, get her to allow him to kiss her, touch her. He could make her sigh in need for his body, whimper in desire. If only he could get his lips and hands on her. His cock stiffened at the thought and he had to grip the edge of the table to keep from trying it all on her right this very moment.

Gods, he was beginning to want this woman so very badly. He was starting to lose control and he *never* did that. This woman was dangerous to him, dangerous ambrosia. At some point the lure would become too strong and he would sample her.

But it was too early.

It wasn't just her body he was trying to seduce, although that would definitely be part of it. He had to seduce her heart and mind, too. That was the tricky part and the thing he had so little practice in—no practice, to be truthful.

Even though he fumbled in the face of developing this deeper relationship with her, he knew he had to take this slowly. He had to wait. He had to allow her to come to him. She needed to warm to him a bit more, open to him more.

He simply needed *more* from her.

Once she took the bait, then he could set the hook.

Even though it killed him to do it, he leaned over and

kissed the top of her head. "No, you need to go to bed, Ais-linn. I don't want to keep you up any longer. Tomorrow night we can have a drink."

She smiled. "All right."

Tomorrow night they would have that drink, and hope-fully a little more.

# FIVE

***

GIDEON watched at least twenty black vultures circle the spires of the church near the spindly and reaching white branches of the tree the birds roosted in. This place was a famous roost for vultures, and watchers came from all over to see them. The place where the birds rested their heads at night was above the Church of Labrai's cemetery, very fitting . . . for a nightmare.

His gaze listed to the left, the way it always did, toward the massive wall that separated Piefferburg from humanity. Spanning hundreds of miles in diameter, to the Atlantic on both ends, and sunken twenty feet into the earth, those massive walls weren't what kept the fae in. That work was done by the invisible warding that the Phaendir reinforced day and night, keeping the evil contained and away from the rest of the populace of the earth. He and his people made such huge sacrifices for humans, but did they appreciate it? No. They only took their efforts for granted.

Labrai, the one and true God, would smite them all when he came down to punish the sinners, the magicked, and the nonbelievers. Then the Phaendir would be raised up to the heavens and rewarded for their toil and hardships.

He moved his hand, allowing the light yellow curtain of his office in the Phaendir's headquarters to fall back in place, showing black shapes circling lazily in a piss-colored sky.

"Brother Gideon."

He turned to find the tall, black-haired figure of Brother Maddoc, his boss, standing in the doorway. "Yes, Brother Maddoc?"

"I had a report that you'd made some cell phone calls into Piefferburg. They were magick-laced?" Brother Maddoc's eyes were narrowed.

They were always at odds, he and Maddoc. They wanted different things for the Phaendir and, ultimately, for the fae. That difference in their agendas could be trying on their relationship.

Gideon answered with the ease of the innocent. He'd always been good at lying. He hooked his hands behind his back and met Maddoc's eyes. "Indeed. I needed to relay information to Brother Rhys about the incoming film crew from *Faemous*. The patrol searched them before they entered, but I still suspected they might be carrying in HFF propaganda and wanted Brother Rhys to keep a close eye on them."

Emily, Maddoc's personal assistant, came up on Maddoc's side. Her shoulder-length red hair was twisted up behind her head and secured with a claw clip today and she wasn't wearing her contact lenses. A pair of tortoiseshell glasses perched on the end of her small, cute nose.

His composure slipping a bit, Gideon shuffled his feet and glanced at the warm brown carpeting of his office.

Emily slipped a sheaf of papers into Maddoc's hand, their fingers brushing just a little longer than necessary. She glanced at Gideon and then eased away.

Maddoc studied the papers, frowning, while Gideon fumed. Maddoc was fucking her. He just knew it. His fingers clenched at his sides, fingernails digging into his palms. Maddoc had everything Gideon was supposed to have—the power, the prestige, the respect, the title.

And, now, the woman.

Rightfully, it was all Gideon's. *He* was the one with the better plan for the future, and he had plenty of backers in the Phaendir to prove it. More every day.

Maddoc made a mumbling response to Gideon's answer and shuffled away, nose buried in the papers. Abruptly, he turned back. "I forgot to tell you that we may have a lead on the Book of Bindings. The archivist has been tracking the trail of possession to a fae family, name of Finvarra. Seen the name in your research? They're apparently an affluent and well-connected Seelie bloodline."

*Oh, be careful, man. Danger.* He frowned. "It doesn't ring a bell, but I'll look through my notes." He gave him a pleasant smile.

"Thank you. If we can locate a document with information on who is still living in that family, we may be able to deduce which of them has the book. I don't need to tell you that this is of the utmost importance."

Gee, finding the Book of Bindings, the book that held the spell to obliterate the warding around Piefferburg was of the utmost importance? What a revelation.

Gideon smiled and bowed his head. "Of course, Brother Maddoc." When he lifted his head back up, the imbecile was gone. He stared at the spot where Maddoc had been standing a moment ago, feeling the burn of magick through his veins and spearing the spot as though he could light the former occupant on fire with his hatred alone. His body shook with it, his face flaming and his eyes popping.

His time would come.

From the heart of the building, a gong sounded. Three short bursts of resonating sound that immediately wiped away the lust and rage that had entered his body in the last couple of minutes. Leaving all the work he had to do lying on his desk, he entered a small room that adjoined his office. Every member of the highest echelons of the Phaendir had their own, private chamber where they could worship. The lower slobs had a communal room.

After lighting the six candles on the small wooden table

near the entrance, he closed the door and carefully disrobed, hanging his suit from a peg on the opposite wall so he wouldn't get blood on it. Then he removed his socks and shoes and placed them near the doorway.

Taking the leather cat-o'-nine-tails from its peg, he knelt before the table with the candles, closed his eyes, and lifted it. Pretty, sleek cat that bestowed pain and joy in equal measure.

The blows rained down on his back, steady and soothing, motions he'd made every day and millions of times. His back was a mass of white, mottled scar tissue. Each lash of the cat-o'-nine-tails flayed skin from his scarred back. Blood flowed ichorlike and hot down his skin, trickled down his back, trailed over his buttocks and in between his thighs. The scent of coppery heat filled the small space.

His eyeballs rolled back into his head as the pain entered the place between discomfort and pleasure, a sweet hot edge he walked every day. His voice droned out of him with the sure rhythm of words written into his soul and uttered five hundred times a day.

My burning desire is relentless.
It cannot be controlled.
Use me, Labrai. Control me.
Break me down and re-create me in Your reflection.
Make me worthy to be Your vessel.
Make my hands to do Your work.
Help me cleanse the world of evil.
Help me cleanse the world of the fae.

GABRIEL was standing too close to Aislinn in the crush. So close she could smell his skin. So close the heat of him radiated from his body and warmed her. Gods, so close it was making her lightheaded.

*No.* She couldn't do this, couldn't think these things.

She closed her eyes for a moment and searched for a handle on her reactions. She was not going to do this. She was *not*. Not with this man. Because whether or not he believed his natural form of magick was a burden, he was still sex on legs and a natural womanizer. He was the last man on earth she needed to feel even a flicker of an attraction for right now. No matter whether it was artificial or not.

Carina had cornered her as soon as she'd walked into the banquet with Gabriel at her side. As he'd located their seats in the massive Seelie Court dining room, Carina had pulled Aislinn aside and placed a very bad little bug in her ear.

"Don't feel bad if you end up sleeping with him," she'd whispered. "Think of him as your rebound man. I'm sure Gabriel wouldn't mind being used. That's sort of his job, isn't it? At the very least, he's hardly looking for a commitment, right?"

It was the same thing a tiny—very tiny—dark voice in the back of her brain had been whispering to her since last night. Although not quite in those terms. It was a little brutal to assume that Gabriel was some sort of natural whore that any woman could use and then toss away like a Kleenex. She didn't think of anyone in such cavalier terms.

Yet there was a part of her, a portion of her mind she tried to keep under lock and key, that wondered how Gabriel might be in bed—a man that old, that experienced, and with the magick inherent to his kind. It was the completely sexual part of her, the totally female part who noticed a man like Gabriel.

After all, she was a healthy woman. Any healthy woman would notice him.

Not even the weight of the prophetic dream she'd had seemed to be putting a damper on her attraction to him. She'd tried to talk sense into her libido several times. Gabriel was the man who would be the catalyst of her death. According to her dream, he wouldn't directly be the cause of it, but he would inadvertently have a major hand in bringing it about.

There was no denying fate. Aislinn believed that. Even if she cut and ran now, tried as hard as she could to distance herself from the catalyst, fate would have its way with her.

Aislinn hoped that she'd misinterpreted the dream somehow. Death was a symbol for change. *Danu*, even Gabriel had said as much at dinner. So perhaps Gabriel would be the catalyst for *change* in her life and not death in the literal sense. Dreams did use symbols, after all.

And the hands? Those grasping, pulling hands, drowning her in the lake of death? Well, okay, she hadn't found a palatable explanation for that yet.

After Carina had voiced Aislinn's own thoughts—in a harsher way—back at her, her friend had ensured Aislinn was seated next to Gabriel. They'd eaten dinner. Aislinn had done her duty, introducing him to all her friends, her mother, and her mother's friends. Her mother had regarded Gabriel like he was a bug, but Gabriel hadn't seemed to care.

Now dinner was over and the music had begun. Gabriel had asked her to dance.

And he was standing too close.

The last time they'd danced she'd been this close, but it had been different because she hadn't felt quite the same way toward him—such a jumbled mess of fear and desire. Maybe she'd finally become intoxicated by incubus magick, finally succumbing to whatever sexual power he wielded unknowingly.

Surely that had to be it. No way had she come to this on her own.

His hand was around her waist and he'd pulled her flush up against his chest. He was much taller than her, even in her stiletto heels, so her chin didn't quite fit over his shoulder. Instead she was forced to either lay her head on his upper chest or look up into his face, which seemed intimate since he liked to dip his face close to hers from time to time—lips almost touching.

Their hips were moving together with the music. Sway, thrust, sway. A little like sex.

Aislinn really wished she could stop thinking about sex. But as long as she could feel his muscled chest against hers and his cock pressing against her pelvis, that wasn't happening. He had an erection and she had probably caused it. The thought that she affected him that way brought a hard flush to her face and made something low in her stomach flutter and roll.

Tonight he wore a pair of black pants and a beautiful, probably very expensive, black shirt. Dark colors seemed to be his preference and they worked for him. They set off his eyes and accentuated the glossy fall of his hair. The sheer physical beauty of this man seemed to fit his special brand of magick, making him even more lethal to the women he encountered.

She was sure the Summer Queen would grant his petition. No one could deny the temptation of rich, sinful chocolate, and *that* was Gabriel Cionaodh Marcus Mac Braire.

She wondered about his father, a pure-blood incubus, wondered if Gabriel looked like him or more like his mother. She'd noticed the loathing in his voice when he spoke of his father so she hoped, for his sake, it was his mother he resembled. That conversation had revealed depth to Gabriel—depths she wanted to explore further.

Had that been when her attraction to him had grown deeper? Not a good thought because that would mean it was authentic and not just false fae magick.

She surveyed the rest of the throng. Dancers talked and laughed, twirled and swayed. Lovers rested heads on shoulders. Colors swirled as the women paraded like peacocks. It was like this so often at Seelie Court. This glittering world was consumed with the show—with thinness, wealth, social interaction, parties, and balls. It grew boring for Aislinn, but seemingly she was the only one who thought so.

*Faemous* crew circulated here and there, interviewing partygoers for the human world that purportedly found them so fascinating and frightening in equal measure.

Kendal had never thought the Rose boring, but he was a social climber, whereas Aislinn was not, much to her mother's chagrin. Of course, in hindsight, now she understood the only reason he'd ever been with her had been because of her name and her ranking. He'd never loved her. He'd only lied to her.

She was sick of liars and frauds. Sick of being used. Therefore, she could never bring herself to use Gabriel, no matter how tempting the prospect.

Not even if he wanted to be used.

She surveyed the throng, knowing she'd find Kendal. Indeed, there he was, over by the edge of the dance floor talking with Erianne and shooting her his trademark grin, the very one he'd used on her in the beginning. So Erianne was his new conquest. Fine. She wouldn't allow it to pinch her.

"What's wrong?" Gabriel asked, then spun her to the right to follow her gaze. He spun her back, making a scoffing sound. "Don't let that dick get you down. He's not worth it."

"Tell that to my heart," she said before she realized the words had slipped out.

"Did you love him? Really?" He frowned. "I can tell at a glance what kind of man he is." He paused and then growled, "Not the right kind for you."

"You can't tell that just by looking at him."

He turned her, took a longer look at Kendal over her shoulder, and then said, "He's weak and a user. Self-centered. He probably always talks about himself in a conversation. Am I right?" She nodded. "He's a putz."

"A putz?"

"Oh, yeah. Worthless."

She glanced around Gabriel's shoulder and saw that the putz in question had spotted them and was walking in their direction. "Oh, no. I don't want to talk to him," she said under her breath. "I haven't talked to him since the breakup and—"

Putting his hand at the small of her back, Gabriel dipped her . . . then he kissed her.

Aislinn's body stiffened, but she didn't fight him. To fight him in this position meant she'd probably fall on her ass in the middle of the dance floor. Gabriel held her there, suspended in air, his warm, broad hand on the small of her back, his strong arms holding her effortlessly.

And the man could kiss.

His lips skated across hers slowly at first, then he nipped at her lower lip before slanting his mouth across hers and coaxing her to open for him. His tongue swept within and brushed up along her tongue . . . slowly. So slowly. Up and down. Hot and wet. She'd had no idea until now that her mouth was an erogenous zone. Her stomach did a flutter and pulse. Time seemed to stop and Kendal left her mind completely.

His kiss reminded her of sex.

Her body heated and she shivered at the same time. Her muscles relaxed and the sounds of the ballroom receded to nothingness against the suddenly loud beat of her heart. A purr started in the back of her throat and she swallowed it forcibly. Gods, the man kissed like an . . . well, like an incubus.

His lips still on hers, he pulled her up to stand again, flush against his body. Although her knees were so weak, she wasn't sure she could. It didn't matter; he held her up . . . and still kissed her. They weren't even dancing anymore. His lips were sliding over hers and his tongue was skating along her tongue and there was nothing left but sensation. He took his time with her mouth, sucking on her lower lip and abrading it gently between his teeth, a thing that made places in her body much lower react. The hand he'd placed on her back found bare skin and stroked.

Someone cleared his throat beside her. Kendal? Aislinn could barely remember his name. Gabriel ignored him. He simply tightened his grip around her waist and turned her a little away from her conniving ex.

Kendal cleared his throat again. "Aislinn?"

Gabriel broke the kiss slowly, very slowly—dragging her lower lip once more through his teeth—before he raised his head.

She looked at Kendal, knowing her eyes were a little out of focus, her lips parted, swollen, and probably a bit red. She was completely unable to form words.

"Aislinn, you don't have to show off this way in front of me. Really, I've moved on. I couldn't care less who you're fucking these days." He flicked a glance at Gabriel. "Although I wouldn't touch Unseelie trash if I were you. You'll get a reputation."

His words threw a bucket of cold water on her warm lethargy, but Gabriel's reaction was faster. He gently extricated himself from her and loomed over Kendal, suddenly seeming twice the other man's size.

Kendal took a step back and Gabriel's hand reached out like lightning and fisted his shirt, making sure he couldn't flee. Kendal blinked, his face going pale.

Gabriel bared his teeth a moment before speaking. "You gave up your right to talk to her when you used her, then publicly dumped her in front of all the court. You should turn around right now and leave before I get angry."

"I have more of a right to talk to her than you do, incubus."

The entire court had gone breathless. The music was still playing but no one within eyesight was dancing or listening. Everyone was starting to form a circle around them, unable to resist the next bit of gossip.

Aislinn was sick of being gossiped about.

She stepped toward her old beau and Gabriel released Kendal's shirt, the pricey fabric now rumpled. "Kendal, if I didn't know any better, I'd say you were jealous."

His gaze flicked to her. "But you do know better."

"I know enough to call you an idiot for baiting a half Unseelie who possesses magick strong enough to kill." All Kendal could do was throw an illusion for a few seconds. Useless.

Kendal snorted. "What's he going to do, fuck me to death?"

Gabriel had been quiet for the whole exchange, but Aislinn suspected quiet from that man meant dangerous. The very air around him seemed to become thicker, as if something was growing, something violent. She didn't want to find out what it was.

She put her hand on Gabriel's arm. "Let's go. You took a rain check on a drink last night. I insist we have one together now."

"My magick works on men, too," Gabriel said, finally, "but I wouldn't touch you with someone else's dick."

Kendal looked ready to explode. Gabriel placed his hand on her lower back and guided her through the staring and snickering throng, out of the ballroom.

"Why did you do that?" she asked as soon as they were clear of the people. "Now he's going to be insufferable."

"Do what?" Gabriel answered smoothly, seeming completely unruffled. "Why did I kiss you or why did I say that?"

She stopped at the bottom of the curving red carpeted stairs that led up to her floor. "Both."

"The comment was to shock his ugly mouth into silence." He reached out and pulled her up against him. "The kiss was because I wanted it and he provided a great excuse for me to take it." His lips brushed hers very lightly, then he rocked back onto his heels.

She had to shake off the warmth from the light buss of his lips. "*Don't* use that magick on me."

"I didn't use even one tiny little bit of magick on you, Aislinn." He arched his brow. "I never have and I never will. I swear it. Whatever response you have to me, it's all you. It's all natural."

She stared at him a moment, trying to be angry, but seeing Kendal's face when he'd come up to them and seen her kissing Gabriel had been far too delicious. "I'm not some silly woman. I'm not going to fall right into your bed. You can just forget that." She pushed past him and mounted the stairs.

"I love a challenge, Aislinn," he called after her.

She almost missed a step.

# SIX

AISLINN ran her hand along the smooth rose marble of the corridor's wall, deep in thought. She was waiting for Carina. They had plans to go to a dress shop in downtown Piefferburg today. That was all her life was—an endless loop of teas, lunches, clothes, parties, and cocktails. Was it wrong that she wanted more?

Why was she the only one who did? There had to be more to life than this. She couldn't be the only one in the Rose who wondered what it might be.

Her friend Bella had yearned to travel. She had felt trapped at Seelie Court and wanted more than anything to see the rest of Piefferburg and beyond. Her friend had received her wish—not in the best of all possible ways—when she'd been banished from the Rose.

The fae lived long lives. There had to be more Seelie Tuatha Dé bored with the expectations placed on them to stay elevated on their pillars for the sake of the troop. If Aislinn wanted to work, she couldn't. If she wanted to develop her magickal skill, it wasn't allowed. If she wanted to go off for an afternoon to visit Goblin Town or the Boundary Lands or the Water Realm, that was forbidden. That was what Gabriel didn't understand. The Seelie were just as trapped by illusion as everyone else.

Or, at least, she was.

Her fingers slid along the wall until she eventually halted in front of a shadow. She turned her head and focused her eyes. Gabriel came into view.

"I watched you walk the entire length of the corridor. It's like you were sleepwalking. What's on your mind this morning, beautiful?"

*Beautiful.* He probably called every woman he knew beautiful.

"I don't know." The last thing she was going to do was spill her heart to this guy. "I was just thinking." She shrugged.

"Hmmm." He studied her. "Not just about new clothes, I would make a guess."

"What? How could you know that? I didn't tell you my plans for this morning."

Carina showed up at his arm. "I told him. I thought it would be fun if he came along."

Her gaze snapped to Gabriel. She had been hoping to escape him for a little while. He made her feel . . . well, he made her *feel*. She didn't want that now. She didn't want to feel attracted, compelled, interested . . . and maybe just a little bit crowded. But Aislinn understood Carina's game. She wanted to make a match between them. Her friend thought an affair with Gabriel would be a good thing—no matter how short and shallow.

Aislinn simply didn't want short and shallow.

She laughed. "Come on, Carina, Gabriel doesn't want to be dragged to the dress shop with us. I'm sure he'd rather spend time . . ." She eyed him from head to toe. Today he wore a pair of faded jeans that did nice things for his already nice butt and a navy sweater covering his broad chest. "Doing whatever it is he spends time doing."

"Nonsense." Carina hooked her arm with his. "I'm sure

he can't think of anything more interesting than spending time with one beautiful woman and a less-pretty married one."

"I enjoy spending time with gorgeous women and you definitely fall into that category, Carina," answered Gabriel with a smile.

Carina grinned at Aislinn. "I *really* like this man."

"Yes," Aislinn murmured. "So does everyone else, it seems."

"Except for Kendal," Carina answered. "Everyone's talking about what happened last night. That was some kiss and Kendal's reaction was classically jealous."

Aislinn sighed. "I noticed that, but it's not because he loves me. It's only because he loves himself." She turned her gaze to Gabriel. "So you're coming along, then?"

"I can hardly wait to go dress shopping."

"It takes a man who is very secure in his masculinity to say that," snickered Carina.

Together they walked to the entrance of the building that faced the streets of downtown Piefferburg. The hobgoblin servant at the double doors of the Rose Tower greeted them with an incline of his small, bald head. "Miss Finvarra, your car is here."

The three of them exited onto the street, where a cool, early spring breeze blew, and allowed the driver to usher them into the back of the limo she'd ordered to take them to the shop. The back of both the towers looked out on Piefferburg Square, where no cars were allowed, only pedestrian traffic. Along the edges of the huge cobblestone square were the most successful of troop businesses—some securities and law firms, a few cafés, and some retail shops.

In the center of the square was the charmed iron statue of Jules Piefferburg, founder of their prison. The statue could not be taken down because of its magick, but it could be altered and maligned, and usually it was . . . badly . . . profanely. Sometimes it was dressed up according to holiday or season, but usually in a way that disrespected the man it represented.

The only other notable landmark of Piefferburg Square was the clock tower on the north side, perfectly in between the two courts, like it was counting down to something.

The area around the front of the Rose Tower was the richest and poshest of downtown Piefferburg, complete with all the troop-run jewelry stores, clothing establishments, swanky restaurants, and coffee shops. Piefferburg and Piefferburg City had a thriving economy, though it still received much financial help from the world outside its borders and many shipments of supplies. Aislinn figured they were entitled to it, since they were keeping them in prison.

She understood the area around the Black Tower was also posh, except inclined toward the nightmarish portion of the fae troop. Aislinn was curious to see it, though she'd never say so out loud.

The car pulled away from the curb and started down the street. Troop passersby were dressed nicely in this part of town and paid very little attention to Seelie vehicles, which were commonplace here.

"You said Ronan and Bella are doing well," Aislinn said to Gabriel once they were moving, "but you didn't really elaborate. Can you?"

Gabriel gazed out the window as he spoke. She sat across from him in the back of the limo and Carina sat beside him. "They came to the Unseelie Court under the Summer Queen's banishment last winter. The Shadow King took them in immediately. Ronan was far more at ease in the Black Tower than Bella was, but it didn't take long for her to see it wasn't as bad a place as most Seelie believe it to be. They have an apartment there, have made friends, and seem to be happy. I believe they're trying to have children, may the powers that be allow it."

No fae could really *try* to have children. Fae fertility didn't work that way. Women couldn't use birth control to prevent a pregnancy, it never worked. Just as women couldn't time intercourse to increase the chance of conception. Pregnancy was at the whim of the Goddess Danu.

Aislinn blew out a slow breath. "I hope you're telling me the truth."

He turned his face from the window to study her. "Why would I lie?"

She looked him in the eye. "There's something about you I don't trust. Call it my intuition."

"Still? I think that's your ex talking, Aislinn. You don't truly believe I'd lie to you. Or perhaps you hold the same bias against me that Kendal does."

"Of course not. It's just that I don't understand why the Shadow King would take Ronan back so easily. I mean, he defected the Black for the Rose and then pulled that job for the Phaendir—he *worked* for the Phaendir, Gabriel— I'm surprised the Shadow King didn't kill him on the spot."

"He defected to the Rose for Bella, *for love*. The Shadow King understood that. He's not without a heart. Also, Ronan is a powerful mage, Aislinn. You'd be surprised how much currency you have in the Black if you possess strong magicks." He paused and his eyelids lowered halfway. Lazily, he asked, "Satisfied?"

"It sounds plausible enough."

"I'm happy you think so," he replied with a wry twist to his lips. "I aim to please you." The last words were spoken in a low, smooth voice and with a double entendre that made her lower stomach flip. She looked out the window at the stores they were passing.

The car reached the dress shop and let them out. The driver would return when they called for him. On their way into the small, high-class establishment, Carina squeezed Aislinn's upper arm and hissed, "Be nice!" Gabriel was already on his way inside.

"I'm honest and I always voice my feelings and opinions." She hesitated outside the door. "I can't pretend to be anything but what I am, Carina."

"Okay, but there's this little thing called tact. Try some, you'll like it."

* * *

GABRIEL was glad she was both honest and intuitive. For her sake it was better, though it was making his job much harder than he'd ever imagined it would be.

He watched her enter the store, having heard every word of their hushed conversation. It was good that she didn't trust him. Healthy. She shouldn't trust him. Gabriel liked her honesty, too. He knew where he stood with her. No guessing. And that was refreshing.

Aislinn was an intelligent person and insightful, too. Those two things, combined with her beauty and the mystery of her magick, made her intriguing to him on a level not many women were.

He genuinely liked her.

Too bad he was duping her.

An odd, heavy sensation filled his chest, wilting the smile he wore as he gazed at her. For some inexplicable reason his thought process had diminished his pleasure. What was this feeling? Aislinn breezed past him, touching the gowns hanging on the racks near the door of the small, crowded shop. His smile completely faded and the heavy weight grew as he watched her. Was this regret?

Gods . . . was it . . . *guilt*?

Carina hit him playfully on the shoulder. "You're frowning. What's wrong?"

He blinked and jerked, not sure how long he'd been standing there so annoyingly confused. "Where's the lingerie and let's see if we can get Aislinn into some," he growled and walked toward his prey.

"There's my boy," Carina purred.

Aislinn had stopped to finger the material of a dark red gown with a plunging neckline and back. It was sleeveless and had a long straight sheath skirt. Aislinn would be a knockout in that dress. It would set off her light skin tone, the silver blond fall of her subtly curling hair, and her beautiful light gray eyes.

"It's beautiful," he murmured as he imagined taking it off

her. She'd look even better swathed in nothing but moonlight. Or just his hands.

She flipped the tag up at him. "It's Valentino and it's twelve thousand dollars."

"You can't afford it?"

"Oh, yes, I can afford it," she said, moving to the next rack of gowns. "My family had money before Piefferburg was created." She flicked him a sour glance. "*We* don't live off the backs of the troop. However, I make it a point never to spend that much on any article of clothing for myself. It's too self-indulgent."

"I would spend that much in a heartbeat," murmured Carina, coming to stand beside Gabriel. She fingered the rich material of the dress, then wandered off toward the purses.

"Okay," answered Gabriel, pushing past Carina. "Then let *me* buy you something expensive and self-indulgent."

She turned and narrowed her eyes at him. "No."

"You have to let me. It's to show you my appreciation for being my guide this week."

She turned her back to him. "No, thank you. It's not necessary."

"Something slinky and sexy for your next lover, maybe?" He paused. "Who won't be me." Lie, lie, lie.

"No."

"Ah, that means you will be taking me as your next lover?"

A clerk came near. Aislinn smiled and waved her away. "Hardly."

"Good. We're agreed. Let me buy something for the next lucky man. You have no reason to say no and you'll offend me if you do, since I'm trying to repay you for your kindness."

She halted near a rack of designer shoes. "I haven't been very kind to you."

"All the more reason to relent and allow me to buy you a gift."

She ran her index finger down a pair of red Jimmy Choos. "I'll say yes just to get you to quit and let me shop. I have a feeling you won't stop until I give in to you."

*Oh, she was right about that.*

He flashed a smile and hoped it didn't look as predatory as he felt. "I'm nothing if not persistent."

"Believe me, I noticed." She turned and began to saunter away. "When I find something suitable, I'll let you know."

"It has to be lingerie and you have to let me see it on you before I buy it. You know, to make sure your next lover will approve."

Her steps faltered, but she only called airily over her shoulder, "Fine."

He blinked. He thought she'd howl at that string he'd attached.

Having no particular interest in women's clothing other than when he was taking it off someone, Gabriel watched Aislinn. She touched the gowns, examined their sizes and lengths, talked to the clerk about alterations, but she did it all with a dull look in her eyes. Whereas Carina seemed beatific in the shop, with her ability to buy new things to wear at court, Aislinn touched the garments with listless, roaming hands, as though searching for something that wasn't there, something she knew she'd never find between the four walls of the building. While all the time she kept glancing out the plate-glass window to the street and the passersby.

Aislinn Christiana Guinevere Finvarra of the Seelie Court, supposed purebred Tuatha Dé Danann, was bored. Bored with her life, yearning for more. That was another secret she kept from her peers. Add it to the pile.

She had to feel so lonely.

The heaviness that had settled in his chest earlier eased a bit. Luring her to the Unseelie Court was the best thing he could do for her. In the Black Tower she could develop her magick without fear of reprisal or banishment. A woman as intelligent and as interesting as Aislinn deserved that and more. She didn't deserve to be stifled and strangled in a toxic and delusionary environment like the Seelie Court.

She wouldn't be bored anymore. She wouldn't be alone. Sure, she'd hate him for what he'd done. This couldn't end any other way. But in the long run she'd be better off in Black with her own people.

"I think I found it."

Gabriel came back to himself, realizing she'd browsed over to the lingerie section. A distance away he could hear Carina nattering at one of the store clerks. He walked to Aislinn and saw she held a red satin and chiffon slip in her hands. It looked long and . . . fascinating. Sexy. Now *these* were the kind of clothes that men were interested in, at least for the couple of minutes a woman wore them before they became a heap on the floor of the bedroom.

His eyebrows rose. "Try it on."

She disappeared into the fitting room and reappeared a couple of minutes later. It covered her down to her ankles, yet still managed to be the sexiest thing he'd ever seen. The bodice cupped her breasts just perfectly, just the way he wanted to. His fingers curled as he imagined doing just that. The red looked incredible against her skin tone.

"Turn around." His voice came out just a tad hoarse and he realized he was clutching a silk gown off one of the racks hard enough to wrinkle.

She turned and he lost his breath. The back dipped down very far, all the way to the top of her beautifully rounded bottom. He wanted to run his lips over every inch of slender, flawless skin from the nape of her neck to the small of her back and then—

"Gabriel?" She'd turned around and was staring at him, frowning.

He cleared his throat. "It's beautiful on you. Your next lover will drool all over the carpet." He knew that for certain because he would be that man. No way was he allowing any other man to see her in that gown. Aislinn was his.

"I like it, too." She flipped her heavy hair over one shoulder, the silver locks curling around her breast and making him almost swallow his tongue, and turned this way and that in front of a nearby mirror. Her nipples were rock hard and pressing through the thin fabric of the gown. "I never wear stuff like this."

"You looked just as pretty in your sweater and pajama pants a couple of nights ago, but luxury is good once in a while." He turned and walked toward the shoes. She needed to put her clothes back on before he spontaneously combusted in the middle of the store. "You need a pair of pumps to go with it."

She laughed and said in a dry tone, "Yes, with fluffy feathers on them."

He picked out the fluffiest pair he could find while he kicked the plot for her seduction into high gear. Except this time it had nothing to do with the Shadow King and everything to do with his own desires.

# SEVEN

AISLINN was still shaking a little bit when they arrived back at the Rose Tower. Still shaking even though they'd spent the whole morning at the dress shop while Carina practically bought the place out. Still shaking even though afterward they'd lunched at O'Shea's, where they served traditional Tuatha Dé Danann dishes like roasted sea bass with capers and lamb cutlets with honey and apricots.

Gabriel affected her that way and it made her mad.

She was exhausted and well fed, but she couldn't shake the shivers she had from when Gabriel had watched her try on the lingerie. She'd done it thinking it wouldn't matter. He was never going to get into her pants, no matter how high he cranked up the charm. She'd told herself she wasn't at all attracted to him—or at least she could control her attraction—and teasing him a little bit would be fun.

The joke had been on her.

She thought she'd concealed her reaction well enough, but standing there in front of Gabriel in that very sexy swath of silk almost-nothing had completely and totally flipped every switch she had. Right now she hated herself for it, but she couldn't deny that the way his gaze had taken her in— like she was not just the most attractive woman he'd ever seen, but the *only* woman he'd ever seen—had heated her blood.

Which was stupid.

Gabriel Mac Braire probably looked at *every* woman that way. Most likely it was a practiced look, not at all genuine, perfected after centuries of womanizing. A consummate actor, he was skilled at seduction and she didn't buy for a minute he wasn't trying to seduce her.

Although it seemed that her body might be working against her mind in this aspect, since being partially clothed in front of him, wondering . . . *knowing* what had been going through his mind as he'd looked at her, had made her nipples hard and her body more aware than it had been in a very long time. Sex with Kendal hadn't been bad, but it hadn't been earth-shattering, either. Mostly, it had been average. All those memories with him were tainted now, anyway.

They reached the tower and entered amid the usual crowd of Seelie going here and there, preparing for the evening, standing in small clutches impeccably dressed and gossiping or talking to the people from *Faemous*.

She was home. Ugh.

"I would like to make dinner for you tonight, Aislinn. Although the catch is we'll probably miss the . . . what is it tonight?"

"Drinks in the common room," Carina answered.

Aislinn hesitated because the prospect of having an excuse to miss cocktails was very tempting. She could only beg off with headaches or fatigue so many times before people began to talk. But the lingerie . . . "I don't think—"

"I'm inviting Carina and Drem, too."

"Oh, lovely. Yes, we'll be there." Carina gave her a sidelong glance. "You, too, right, Aislinn?"

She sighed. As long as they wouldn't be alone. "Fine. Thank you. I think I'll go up to my apartment now and relax a little. See you at the dinner hour?"

They made their good-byes and one of the Rose Tower hobgoblin footmen followed Aislinn up to her place with all her packages. Carina would probably need five helpers.

She spent the afternoon cleaning up, drinking tea, and thinking. Restless, she put on some Nina Simone and prowled her apartment, poking in closets and organizing drawers until she wanted to scream. Close to twilight the skies clouded over and it began to rain. She found herself at her living room window, wrapped in a throw from the couch against the spring chill and looking out over Piefferburg Square. Raindrops splashed against the glass. Below her people scurried to get out of the rain, at least the ones lacking umbrellas or the magickal ability to shield themselves.

Raising her gaze, she hugged herself and stared at the Black Tower. Bella and Ronan were there now. What were they doing with their days? Surely life had to be much different. While she'd been shopping this morning, Gabriel had said they were studying their magick, developing it. She frowned, wondering what it would be like to have a meaningful purpose every day.

Must be nice.

The rain was coming down harder now, obscuring her vision, but she could just make out the roof where the Wild Hunt met every early morning.

She envied them, envied their role and responsibilities.

She envied Bella and Ronan, too. That was something she could never say out loud. Just thinking it made her fear the Summer Queen's wrath. The Seelie Tuatha Dé were supposedly *the chosen*, the special ones. They were privileged to reside within the walls of the Rose Tower and bear the title and bloodline of the goddess Danu. To even entertain the notion that the Unseelie might have some advantages over them was unthinkable.

But maybe having a job, any kind of job, would help her get out of this rut she'd entrenched herself in. Maybe it would help her to stop feeling so sorry for herself. She hated that she did right now. Loathed this edge of self-pity. She had a beautiful apartment, all the money she could want. What did she have to dislike about her life?

Her thoughts drifted to the book she'd found in her father's things when he died. She hadn't looked at it for years, hadn't dared. There was something about this time, on this rainy day as she contemplated her life and her recent encounter with the Wild Hunt, that made her want to risk taking another read.

A moment more of indecision and she was headed to her bedroom. She opened the safe she kept in her walk-in closet, pushed her inherited jewels to the side, and found the cloth-wrapped book she sought. Though she had no idea what the book was, her intuition had told her it was valuable and needed to be kept under lock and key. She took it into the living room and curled up on the couch with it in her lap, though this was not a novel to be enjoyed on a rainy afternoon. This book was all nonfiction.

About spell casting.

It was ancient, with a worn red leather cover and a locked portion at the back with a grooved indentation where she assumed an object must fit, acting like a key. Beyond that, she knew nothing about the tome—whether it was Seelie or Unseelie. It could even be Phaendir in origin; there were no identifying marks. The book contained page after page of spells written in Old Maejian. She had no idea what the locked portion might contain. That portion was smooth, seamless, sealed with some sort of magick to be released only when the key was placed into the grooves, she was certain.

She wasn't sure how her father had come to possess it and she wasn't sure she wanted to know. She didn't know what the Summer Queen would do to her if she knew Aislinn had it . . . she wasn't sure she wanted to know that, either.

Staring down at the gold material that wrapped it for a long moment, she remembered her father. Gods, she missed him so much. Her father had been the one to comfort her when she'd had nightmares as a child. He'd been the parent to allow her to cry on his shoulder when a boy she liked had hurt her feelings or during any number of other adolescent traumas. Her mother had always been the reserved one, the one pushing her to be stronger, better, *perfect*, while her father had just wanted her to be happy. He'd loved her unconditionally and with every fiber of himself.

As she'd loved him back.

Never in all her days could she imagine her happy, simple father with a drop of Unseelie blood or being involved in any dark political scandal or drama. Yet she'd found this book under a few loose floorboards in his bedroom after his death. He and her mother had been long since separated at the time of his demise, and it had fallen to her, the only child of their union, to manage his estate. Clearly it had been hidden there on purpose.

Slowly, she unwrapped the dark red book. The vellum pages were old and scrawled in a handwritten text that was charmed to withstand the test of time. The volume was written in the old tongue of the Tuatha Dé and was probably just as ancient. Old Maejian was a language the Unseelie learned in school for spell casting, but as a spoken language, for the most part, it was dead. Especially to the Seelie, who had no use for it.

Once the fae had been forced to disappear into human society—go underground—many of their old ways had died. They'd been required to integrate with humans in so many respects to survive—speaking human languages was just one way. Aislinn knew a little bit of Old Maejian, but most of what she'd learned had disappeared from disuse.

She opened the cover and frowned, trying to read the first page. That one was still unclear to her. Gabriel could probably read it just fine. He was probably fluent. She quashed a flicker of envy.

Spotting the velvet page marker she'd left in the book the last time she'd opened it, she flipped to that page. Here was a part she could decipher. She wasn't even certain how she could translate this particular spell; it just called to her. It spoke to the magick running through her veins. Turning on the light beside her, she read until her eyes crossed, searching for something. She just wasn't sure what, exactly.

Coming to a small bit of a spell, she murmured the words aloud.

Tuela mae argo naught
Tae ilium tohurst velliu oost
Sarque pae neaht ar ingram naught
Velliu mae silan vo archt

Power rose around her in swirling currents, so subtly at first she barely noticed it, then growing stronger fast. She gasped and snapped her mouth shut and the book a second later. The cover closed with a thump and the power fell away abruptly.

"What was that?" she breathed to the empty room as if she expected someone to answer. Dark had fallen outside but it still rained. Fat drops of it slid down her windows.

Swallowing hard, she looked down at the book. Raising that magick had felt good . . . *right*. She said the words again. Oddly, she'd memorized them. They fell from her lips effortlessly.

Maybe it was dumb. No, she *knew* it was dumb. Yet she couldn't stop herself.

The words came again. She didn't stop even though the magick warmed the air around her, made her ears pop. The spell poured like water through a winter-cold pipe, trickling at first, but as the pipe grew warmer, the words flowed faster . . . and magick flooded.

"Aislinn."

She gasped and looked up. The invaluable, ancient book slid from her lap and dropped to the floor.

"Papa?"

He stood before her, wavy and insubstantial as a ghost. A long, shimmering silver cord anchored him somewhere in the Netherworld. The image of her father blinked, confused. "Aislinn? What am I doing here?"

The magick faltered, making his hazy image waver and nearly disappear. She reached out and the word ripped from her, *"No!"*

Her father held a hand toward her, a look of longing on his face.

She stood and took a couple of steps toward him, the blanket falling from her shoulders. The magick was slipping away fast. Sweet Danu, no! "Papa, don't leave!"

"I love you, honey." His voice sounded so far away, getting farther. His image wavered and then faded completely.

She stumbled to the middle of the living room and went down on her knees where her father had just been. Seeing him again like that—even hazy, as if in a dream—had been like a punch to the solar plexus. She simply hadn't been prepared. Apparently the words she'd been saying had *called* him. She'd called someone to her from the Netherworld.

"Oh, Papa," she whispered. She held a fist to the ache in her chest, closing her eyes against a swell of deep grief that never completely went away.

Why had she called him? Because she'd been thinking of him? Was that how it worked?

But how had she done it and could she do it again? It felt good, natural, like a missing part of her had returned with the power that swelled around her.

Oh, Gods, she was a necromancer. There could be no other explanation. Her Unseelie blood was stronger than she'd ever imagined.

She wasn't sure how long she knelt on the carpet of the living room with the priceless book in a jumble not far away. The shock of seeing her father again eventually eased from her body and she stood, gathered the book, wrapped it up, and replaced it.

The euphoria of what she'd done eased into reality. She'd called her father this time and the magick had been weak, mostly due to her own ignorance, she was certain. That had been heartbreaking, but also fortunate. What would have happened if she'd summoned some other spirit to her? Perhaps someone malevolent? And what would have happened if she'd done that and somehow the magick had remained? She would have been left with a spirit in this realm that she couldn't control.

She was too untrained for this.

Gods, how stupid could she be? She pushed the book to the back of the safe, locked it, then leaned her head against the door and let out a shuddering sigh. She had no training for her skill and she never would; therefore, she had no business poking around in arts as dark as these.

Of course, Gabriel could probably help her.

He probably had some direction when it came to these things, could speak Old Maejian fluently and knew what to do with spells like these. He definitely wasn't afraid of the dark. He'd grown up surrounded by magickal arts like this and maybe could even use them responsibly.

"No." She said it out loud, just to make sure it penetrated her mind. "No way."

Then she remembered the dinner. Glancing at the clock, she saw she was late. She quickly changed her clothes, freshened up a bit, and made her way to Gabriel's temporary apartment on the fifth floor of the Rose Tower's annex. It was a place used to house guests. In the center was a lovely atrium with year-round flowering gardens, a fountain, and live birds.

"You're late," Gabriel said, opening the door.

She nearly lost her breath. He was dressed head to toe in black—black jeans, black boots, black cable-knit sweater. She couldn't even see his hair in all that shadow.

"I know. I'm sorry." She tipped her head to the side. "What is it with you and black?"

He stepped back and opened his arms, sweeping down his body. "You don't like it?"

"Oh," she answered, drawing a breath to steady herself and attempting a dry tone of voice, "I think it suits you just fine."

"I'll take that as a compliment."

The place was fairly small, but decorated richly. A one-bedroom apartment with a small kitchen and an intimate dining area, currently set for two. Two?

She turned. "Where are Carina and Drem?"

He spread his hands. "You're late." Shrug. Satisfied grin. "They already left."

Of course they did. Her jaw locked and her eyes narrowed. She was sure Carina had waited approximately two minutes after eight p.m. and then decided she'd waited too long and used it as an excuse to leave her alone with Gabriel.

"I made chicken cordon bleu with chocolate mousse for dessert," he said quickly. "Stay, Aislinn, please." He paused and his lips twisted in a self-effacing grin. "You know, you're the only woman I've ever had to beg to spend time with me."

Dinner did smell delicious. Her stomach rumbled despite the rich meal she'd had for lunch. "It's good for you," she replied with a smile. She turned and began inspecting the shelves of small statues that decorated the wall of the living room. They were all of famous Seelie Tuatha Dé throughout history. Putting Gabriel in this apartment must have been the queen's jab at the Unseelie Court.

Soon they were sitting down to a meal that was so delicious she lost herself in every bite. The chocolate mousse melted in her mouth. She ate it slowly, savoring each mouthful.

"Are you happy here, Aislinn?"

She paused with the spoon in her mouth. Carefully, she set it beside her scraped-empty dish and leaned back in her chair. "What kind of question is that?"

"A relevant one for someone who's considering a major life change. I am considering moving from one court to the other, remember?" He caught her gaze and held it for a long moment. "Today in the store you seemed bored. Were you just bored with shopping, or was it something more?"

She glanced away. He was too perceptive by half. Maybe he wasn't as self-absorbed as she'd thought. "That's a very personal question."

"I don't mean it that way. I'm simply asking if you're happy with your life here. It's much different from the Black and I'm weighing my decision to change. I'm doing this to stave off the boredom of a long life, but if my move here will only bring more stagnation I won't want to do it."

She sighed impatiently. "You've been here nearly a week, Gabriel. You've seen all there is to see. This is a social court, protected by the immense powers of our queen. Magick is not valued here as it is in the Black Tower and we're largely idle—favoring parties, balls, and shopping to actual work. The advantage here is that it's safe. As long as you are an accepted member of this court, you will always be taken care of and will want for nothing. You will always have the respect of the troop and be revered."

"I don't want parties, balls, and shopping to be the extent of the rest of my life. I don't care about being revered or taken care of. I take care of myself just fine and always have." He smiled. "And I don't like to shop."

"Okay, I'm speaking from a feminine perspective. The men do other things."

"Like what?"

She pressed her lips together. "Kendal spends a lot of time with the Fianna, though he doesn't get into as much trouble as they do. They play pool and go out in the fields to play saecarr." Saecarr was an ancient fae game that had been the inspiration for rugby, the sport humans played. "Sometimes they go to troop bars to smoke cigars and drink beer."

The Fianna were men descended from the original Fianna of legend, though these men also had the blood of the Tuatha Dé. Long ago they were hired swords, fighting for whatever king needed them to support his battles. Here in Piefferburg that tradition was long dead, leaving these men with little to do but get in trouble, a thing they did on a regular basis.

"Not a big fan of saecarr."

"Well, there you have it, Gabriel. I don't know what else to say. What you've seen is what you get here at Seelie Court. You should have known that before you came."

"You sound frustrated."

She shrugged one shoulder and looked down at the table. "Maybe you're not the only one who is looking for new experiences."

He said nothing.

Finally she looked up to find him staring at her, studying her with eyes far more perceptive than she'd ever imagined.

All of a sudden she felt naked sitting there beside him—emotionally naked, anyway.

She blinked. "What?"

"Maybe you should be considering a court move, not me."

She frowned and her spine straightened. "That's a stupid thing to say. Who would want to go to the Unseelie Court?" She realized only a second after she'd said it that it sounded like an insult to him. "I mean—I'm sorry—"

He shook his head. "They have truly brainwashed you, haven't they?"

"I didn't mean to offend you."

He held up a hand. "You didn't insult or offend me, but you don't know what you're saying. I wish I could take you to the Unseelie Court so you could see firsthand the bias and the lies you've been told your whole life." His eyes, so beautiful in their dark blue mystery, flashed dangerously, negating the easy tone he used with her. "Just because someone appears monstrous or has the ability to use magick to draw blood or kill doesn't make him a monster. That's something the Seelie have never understood."

She pushed away from the table and stood. "Clearly your sympathies lie with the Black Tower. I don't even know why you want to leave that half of the square." She paced away from the table, turning her back on him. "The way you talk, it's like you're still one of the Shadow King's subjects, heart, body, and soul."

"I lived there a long time, Aislinn. I went to the Shadow King in my late teens, after they'd established the Unseelie Court once Piefferburg was on its feet. Before then, I watched them build it bit by bit, standing out in the square every day and dreaming of the moment I could enter its halls. Once I did enter, I never left. Old habits die hard."

She turned. He was standing directly behind her. She hadn't even heard him stand up. "Sounds like you don't really want to leave."

A wry smile twisted his lips. "Maybe I don't."

"I'm worried about you."

"You're worried about me? I thought you didn't like me."

She smiled. "You grow on a person, Gabriel."

He raised an eyebrow. "Like a fungus?"

Her smile widened. "You're a different person than the one I assumed you were at first."

"Hmmm. I guess I'll take that as a compliment."

"You spoke a little Old Maejian to me on your first day here." She crossed her arms over her chest. "Do you only know enough to smooth-talk women or are you fluent?"

"Fluent." He sounded surprised by her question. "I was taught from the cradle. It's the language of magick."

She nodded, chewing her lower lip.

He said nothing for several moments, then: "I wish you would just come out and tell me what's on your mind, but I know you won't. I know you feel that you can't."

"What do you mean?"

"I know you're more than what people see, Aislinn. I know that somehow, in some way, you're special."

Maybe he had some other magick than sex magick. Maybe he was telepathic. How could he know? She walked toward the living room, fleeing him as much as she could. "Why are you saying that? You don't know anything about me."

"I see more than you think. Don't worry, your secret, whatever it is, is safe with me. But remember that if you want to confide in someone, I'm here, I'm willing, and I may just be the only person in the Rose Tower you can talk to."

"I don't trust you. Why would I confide in you?"

He raised an eyebrow and walked toward her, chasing her back into the living room. Suddenly the apartment felt way too small and far too hot. She had to stop herself from taking another retreating step away from him and she really had to stop herself from recalling the kiss they'd shared the other night.

"You shouldn't trust me." His gaze swept her from toe to head.

"Why? Because you're trying to seduce me? There's a newsflash. You intend to seduce every woman you see."

"No. Only the ones who are worth the effort, sweetness. You most certainly fall into that category."

"This conversation isn't making me want to spill my deepest, darkest secrets in your ear." Her tone was dry. It was a reflex against the unwanted reaction of her body—elevated breathing, heart pumping—as Gabriel took yet another step closer.

"Where sex is concerned, you definitely shouldn't trust me. Where magick and bloodlines are concerned, there, love, is where I am the most trustworthy person in this tower."

What did that mean? She opened her mouth to ask, but he dipped his head and kissed her. Lips pressed against hers, he walked her backward until she hit the wall. She pushed away from him a little and murmured against his lips, "Stop, Gabriel."

"I know I said I wouldn't—"

"Don't. *Don't you dare.*" Her voice trembled on the words. She would never forgive him if he used his magick on her. "No magick," she gasped, breaking the kiss. "You promised."

"I won't." He smiled slowly, showing white teeth and a whole bunch of arrogance. "I'm not using any magick but the old-fashioned kind. I don't have to." He put his mouth back on hers.

And suddenly she didn't want to get away. All the questions left her mind. She wanted his lips on hers more than anything, his hands on her, his—

He made her think very bad things.

Shivers rolled through her body and she grasped his shoulders as he parted her lips and slid his tongue inside. It was hot and rough against hers and brought to mind sweaty skin-on-skin things they could be doing instead.

Clearly being with a man for these past days had revved her libido.

Desperately she fought for control over it because the last thing she wanted to do tonight was fall into bed with Gabriel, although her body liked the idea. In fact, her body had practically gotten out pom-poms and was contemplating cartwheels.

He moved her more firmly against the wall and slid his hands to her hips, then around to the small of her back. There he found the hem of her shirt and pushed beneath it, rubbing his thumb against her warm skin back and forth. The motion was slow and methodical. It had nothing to do with sex directly, but that was all she could think of when he did it.

She could imagine how he'd be in bed, how focused and controlled, how single-minded in purpose. She'd had glances of bare parts of his body and she could imagine how he'd look, how he'd feel. Gods, sex with Gabriel was probably completely . . . addictive.

That thought, combined with the knowledge that somehow he would indirectly lead to her death, dampened her lust for him, but only for a few moments as other emotions welled up to take over. Deeper, far more dangerous emotions. To sleep with Gabriel would be like possessing part of his spirit, joining herself with him, if only for a short time.

She wanted that.

It had nothing to do with the sex itself, or the pleasure he could undoubtedly give her. Nothing to do with selfish need. She just wanted—needed—to be as close to him as she could. The thought was jarring, frightening. Never had she felt that way about Kendal or any other man she'd ever been with. There was something about Gabriel that drew her and it had nothing to do with sex or the fact that he was an incubus.

But the cost was too high.

She pushed him back with both hands. "I can't do this. You're too dangerous to me." She went for the door.

"Aislinn, don't leave."

She paused halfway between him and the exit.

He walked to her. "I have never used that power on any woman because it's a myth that I even can. A convenient misconception I use to my advantage, but a lie all the same. I can use magick during sex to create a mild addiction, but not anything that would kill a woman."

"No, that's not what I find dangerous about you," she said, pushing past him. "That's not what I'm afraid of."

"Then what's the problem?"

She couldn't tell him about her dream and she definitely couldn't tell him about her desire for closeness with him, this bizarre sensation in the center of her chest whenever he drew close to her and how she wanted—craved—more of it.

"I just need to go." She crashed out of his apartment, shut the door, and leaned against the wall just outside, letting the sound of rushing water and chirping birds calm her.

Dangerous. Yes, Gabriel was dangerous to her, but it was turning out that it was for different reasons than she ever would have imagined.

# EIGHT

GABRIEL found the Shadow King in the gardens of the Black Tower. The fae loved their wild places, even when the fae in question weren't wilding or water fae. All of them yearned for green spaces and growing things, it seemed. Even the Seelie, who were as far removed from their roots as any of them were, an ironic thing, considering they were supposed to be the true bloods—the direct line.

"Gabriel." The Shadow King turned from examining a beautiful pink and white orchid. "You wouldn't be here if you weren't making progress, so I trust you are?"

Birds tittered above and around. Moonlight filtered in through the glass ceiling of the space. It was moist and warm in here, redolent with the scent of green, growing things.

No one could say that the Unseelie were all about death. It simply wasn't true.

The Shadow King was growing impatient. Gabriel could read it in his body posture, the tone of his voice. Something like that could become unhealthy for him very fast.

"I am." He paused. "It's slower than I would like, but I'm winning her over."

At the same time, Aislinn was winning him over. She was prickly at first, too honest by half, and a little stuck up. But peel back that exterior and there was sweetness inside. Gabriel wanted more of that—more of the true her.

He could still taste her on his lips and feel her soft skin under his fingertips. It had hurt physically to have her run out after dinner. He still felt the ache of her rejection deep within. Never had a woman been able to resist him. Never had a woman pushed him away like that, with fear in her eyes. And, fittingly, it was the one woman in the world he actually wanted.

*Had to have.* And it had nothing to do with the demands of his liege anymore.

The Universe had a sense of humor, it seemed.

The Shadow King turned back to his flower. "I don't like to wait. You know that."

"She's strong willed and coming off a bad breakup with some useless Seelie Court fop. She's got good instincts, too." He smiled and touched a rose that quivered in the light breeze of the green space. "She doesn't trust me. It's necessary for me to work past all that in order to align her with my desires. I've never met a woman more stubborn than she is."

The Shadow King grumbled something intelligible. "Talk to . . . what is that woman's name? Her friend? Bella. Talk to Bella and Ronan. See if you can gain any insight that might help you woo Aislinn to the Black. I need her over here voluntarily and soon. I need her out of the Summer Queen's reach and under my control."

*Under my control.* Gabriel shifted uneasily. "If you told me specifically what you wanted Aislinn for, it might help me."

The Shadow King turned to face Gabriel, eyes squinting. "I've told you before, Gabriel. She's a relative of mine. I'm certain the magick running through her veins needs cultivation and training. She's wasted over there. Here we can groom her to take her proper place in the Black Tower hierarchy. I mean her no harm."

Gabriel inclined his head, regretting the moment he'd doubted his king's intentions. "I'll work as quickly as possible. My week in the Rose Tower is almost up as it is."

"Bring her here soon. I'm sick of having this issue open. Do your job and come home to us, Gabriel. I promise you will be rewarded." He turned back to his orchids, a clear dismissal.


GABRIEL sought out Bella and Ronan in one of the main gathering areas, when he didn't find them at home. The Unseelie Court didn't have as rigorous a formal social schedule as the Rose Tower, but there were still many places throughout the building where the Unseelie gathered.

Bella and Ronan were sitting near a decorative black marble waterfall and talking with Llewellyn, a tall, slender, dark-haired Twyleth Teg, when Gabriel found them. Llewellyn took one look at Gabriel, said good-bye, and left the room. Long ago Gabriel had slept with his sister, and Llewellyn had disliked him ever since. Not so his sister, Rhianwen.

"That guy knows how to hold a grudge," Gabriel commented, sitting down.

Bella eyed him. "Did the Summer Queen deny your petition already? I thought you were supposed to be at the Rose Tower."

"I'm still under consideration. I should have her final verdict the day after tomorrow." And by then he was supposed to have Aislinn convinced she wanted to come with him back to the Black Tower. Inwardly, he cursed.

Under that fear of failure was the bare desire not to leave her. The prospect of never seeing or talking to her again pinched him more than he wanted to examine.

"Why does the Shadow King allow you to come and go between the courts? Isn't he angry that you're trying to leave him for his rival's domain?" asked Ronan.

"The Shadow King and I have known each other a long

time. We have a special relationship. He's not taking my defection personally."

Bella blinked. "How odd. He doesn't strike me as the forgiving sort."

"None of the royals are, are they? Like I said, we have an unusual relationship."

Bella apparently accepted his lame explanation. She hadn't been here long enough to know any different, but Ronan eyed him with suspicion. "Have you seen Aislinn?" Ah, she was eager for news of her friend.

Gabriel nodded. "She's my guide. I'm spending a lot of time with her this week, actually. I've been getting to know her quite well, though she's a tough one now that Kendal dumped her. She's feeling a little vulnerable and sad." He laughed. "Doesn't like men much at the moment."

"Kendal broke up with her?" Bella breathed.

"Right in front of the entire court and the queen. It was pretty humiliating for her, but Kendal is an idiot. He didn't know what he had. She's better off without him."

Bella pursed her lips. "My sentiments exactly. I never liked him. I never thought he was good enough for her."

"Your instincts about him were right." He leaned forward. "What do your instincts about me say?"

Her eyes widened. "You? Oh, no, Gabriel. Don't ask me that." She sat back, shaking her head.

"The thing is, Bella, I like her. I like her a lot, but she's so hurt by this breakup that she won't allow another man close to her." He wasn't even lying. Not about any of it. Even if his intentions behind this information mining were slightly left of honorable.

"I'm sorry, Gabriel, but no way." She crossed her arms over her chest. "The last thing Aislinn needs in her life is an incubus like you. You'll sleep with her, break her heart, and leave her."

"I'm sick of everyone making judgments about me because of my magick. Just because I'm an incubus doesn't mean I'm incapable of a true relationship."

Bella raised an eyebrow. "Oh, really? I haven't been here

long, but I know your rep. When's the last time you had a serious relationship?"

She thought she had him there, but she didn't.

"Caitlin Aoife Catriona O'Murchadha. We were together for almost ten years and nearly were married. *She* broke *my* heart, Bella, and left me for her current husband."

"But how long ago was that?"

Damn. Now she had him.

"A while ago."

She blinked slowly. "Yes, *a while*. I've met Caitlin. She's been married to her husband for over a hundred years now."

"She has. We're friends now."

"That means nothing, Gabriel. It was such a long time ago. You can't exactly say you've got a good track record."

"So I'm picky." He spread his hands. "Why don't you just come out and tell me you don't think I'm good enough for her?"

"Bella doesn't think anyone is good enough for her best friend, Gabriel." Ronan finally broke in. "Don't take it personally."

"Let's let Aislinn be the judge of that. Let's allow her to make her own decisions." Gabriel leveled his gaze at Bella. "Help me to know her better. I want only the best for her. Believe that."

He truly did believe that coming to the Unseelie Court would be the best thing for her. She was stifled and strangled at the Seelie Court, unable to use her magick, which he suspected was strong. She was probably not a full-fledged necromancer—those were rare—but her abilities were unique and deserved to be tutored. That's exactly what the Shadow King wanted to do. Moving here would bring richness to her existence.

But the Summer Queen had such a strong hold on her people, had brainwashed them so well, that Aislinn would never imagine voluntarily moving courts.

Gabriel gathered his thoughts, leaned toward Bella, and cleared his throat. "I know that Aislinn is more than she seems. I know she has a secret much like the one you kept while you were in the Rose Tower."

Bella's eyes widened. "How could you know that?"

"I'm very perceptive." There was no way he could reveal his own secret—that he was Lord of the Wild Hunt. "How I know is not important, but she's playing a dangerous game. If I know, others could know. Others who are a threat to her. Dangerous game aside, she possesses magick not suited for her court and she yearns to develop it. She feels isolated and alone in the Rose, that she's got no real purpose in life. That's the vibe I'm getting, anyway." He paused and studied Bella. "Am I right?"

Bella chewed her lower lip, clearly debating how much of her friend's life she should share with him. She let out a slow breath. "You're right, Gabriel, she's got Unseelie blood and not just a little bit. I'll tell you because you know already. She's not sure where it comes from, but she suspects her father's side since she found a book—" She snapped her mouth shut. "She just suspects her father's side of the family."

"A book?"

"Look. I'm not going to spill all her secrets. She'll tell you about the book if she chooses."

"Fair enough."

"For the record, I think you're right, Gabriel. She's taking a big risk hiding the secret and I suspect she would like to develop her magick. You're going to have to approach the subject carefully, though, because to reveal you know what she's hiding will threaten her."

Yes, he'd seen that already.

"Still," Bella continued, "that's where you both have common ground. If you really care about Aislinn and want the best for her, if you truly want something more than a one-night stand with her, that's where you should start." She paused and drew a sharp breath. "I can't believe I'm helping you do this."

"You have my absolute word that I won't hurt your friend."

"That's good, because you know my magick, right, Gabriel? I'm not someone you want to piss off."

No, she wasn't. Bella had the ability to curse people. All she had to do was wish something bad happened to you and it would. Her husband was no slouch in the magick department, either. Ronan was a class A sorcerer, a mage with druid blood. Ronan had a brother here at court with much the same magick, though Niall was even more powerful, even darker. No one doubted Niall had a touch of Phaendir. People gave him a wide berth because of it.

"One more thing you might want to know about Aislinn," she said, fingering a sapphire drop pendant nestled in the hollow of her throat. She smiled. "Tomorrow is her birthday."

AISLINN opened the door at an insistent knock and found one of the Rose Tower footmen on the other side, holding a large white box wrapped with a red bow. Frowning, she took the box, thanked the footman, and closed the door. Once inside she laid it on her coffee table and stared at it.

There were only a couple of people who might send her a gift on her birthday. As a general rule, the fae didn't make much out of them. After all, they were such a long-lived race that birthday celebrations got old after a while. Her mother may have done it, though she hadn't sent her anything in several years. Bella would have done it for certain. Bella had sent her a gift every year on her birthday for all their lives. But Bella was gone now, so it couldn't be from her. Tears stung her eyes at the prick of pain the thought caused. Carina might have done it, but Aislinn doubted it. Kendal definitely wouldn't have sent anything. Her friends were more the superficial kind.

That left one last possibility.

There was only one way to find out. She untied the ribbon and let the velvet strand lay across the table. After she pulled off the top of the box and folded back the tissue paper, she found the gown from the shop, the too-expensive dark red

Valentino, along with a pair of gorgeous matching shoes. A card lay in the box, too.

*Happy birthday to a woman who is beautiful both inside and out. I hope to see you tonight. Gabriel.*

Tonight. She frowned. He must mean at the ball. She reached in and fingered the expensive material of the gown. It truly was gorgeous and she would never have bought it for herself. It touched her deeply that he'd done so for her.

She hadn't been planning to attend tonight. The first kiss they'd shared she'd been able to sweep under the carpet because he'd only kissed her to dig at Kendal. The second was impossible because he'd kissed her out of desire and pure desire only.

And she'd kissed him back that way and wanted more.

Her intention had been to avoid him until the queen made her final decision about his petition. If she accepted it, her stint as Seelie companion to the petitioner would be over and life would return to normal. If the queen denied Gabriel, he would return to the Unseelie Court to beg for his head and his former place back.

Aislinn would miss him. She'd even worry about him.

However, she had every reason to believe that the queen would allow him to stay, as long as he hadn't shot off his mouth about the Seelie within her hearing. He was far too colorful and beautiful a man to refuse. He was the type that was like candy to the Summer Queen.

Then he'd gone and bought her an expensive birthday present. Of more concern, he was growing on her. She actually liked him. She was attracted to him. There was no denying it. Even worse? Nightmarishly worse? She was developing *feelings* for him. Feelings that eclipsed the good sense she should have, to stay away from him because of her prophetic dream. Even if Gabriel wasn't going to do it intentionally, *somehow* he was going to lead to her death.

How stupid could she be?

Apparently since she'd met Gabriel her IQ had dropped a

bajillion points because despite what her good sense told her, she was putting on that gown, slipping into those shoes, and going down to the ball.

Willpower had never been her strong suit.

GABRIEL watched Aislinn come toward him, parting the crowd of fae around her like an ocean. The gown fit her perfectly, clinging to every luscious curve so closely it made him jealous. The dress was backless and if it dipped any farther than it did, all the men in the room would've been very happy instead of just teased beyond belief.

She'd done her light hair up on the top of her head, leaving her slender throat and the back of her neck bare. His fingers itched to caress her nape and free her hair so it fell down around her shoulders. The color of the dress set off her gray eyes and the shade of her skin.

The knowledge that it was the gown he'd bought for her that encased her body and rubbed against her skin aroused him beyond belief. It was erotic to watch the way she moved in the garment, knowing he'd held it in his hands that morning. Why he should be struck with this oddness now was a mystery. After all, he'd purchased many gowns for many women, yet this one was different.

Everything about Aislinn was different.

Gabriel had seen many women in his life, but Aislinn was by far the most beautiful. That beauty came from more than just her physical appearance. It came from her intelligence and her strong backbone. It came from her wit and her deep compassion for others. Hells, he even loved her stubborn streak and that far-too-honest mouth. He could think of lots of things to do with that mouth, too. . . .

The bottom line was that he wanted to get to know her even better.

For the first time in more years than he could remember, he wanted a relationship with a woman. Hells, he just wanted Aislinn, whatever way he could get her, for as long as he could have her.

Coldness washed through him, followed by a wave of warmth. This faint beginning of a deeper caring for a woman scared the hell out of him. He frowned. It wasn't like he was a sociopath; he cared about all the women he was involved with. He'd cared for Caitlin deeply.

But this was different. More involved or something. Honestly, he wasn't quite sure what this was yet. He only knew that he was in unfamiliar territory, and that watching her walk toward him right now made him happy.

"Hello," she said, looking up at him with a smile. Every person around them seemed to be watching, murmuring. Gabriel had no doubt they were admiring Aislinn. She was a knockout every night, but more so tonight.

And tonight, she was his. *His.* And no way was she escaping him.

Without a word, he pulled her forward into his arms and up against him. The movement was purely instinctual and completely impulsive. She gave a little cry of surprise but allowed him to drag her up against his body.

"Gabriel, Kendal isn't here tonight. You don't have to put on an act for him."

"Who's acting?" he growled. "You have a short memory. I tried this the other night, but you ran away from me, as I recall."

"I know. I'm sorry about that, I really am."

"I can forgive you, but you'll have to make it up to me."

Her cheeks colored a little and she licked her lips. His gaze ate up every movement. "Maybe I will."

"Tonight?"

"We'll see." She glanced around. "Everyone is watching us, Gabriel."

"There are other people in the room? I don't see anyone but you."

She ducked her head a little and smiled. "Thank you for the dress."

"Happy birthday." He turned her in time to the music and pressed his chest to her back. In one smooth movement, he pulled a necklace from his pocket and looped it around her throat, securing it in back.

She turned toward him, touching the sapphire pendant. "I know this necklace. This is Bella's."

"She asked me to give it to you for your birthday."

She looked up at him, a wet sheen in her eyes. "Thank you." She stroked the top of it with the pad of her index finger. "It means so much to have something of her. I miss her."

He took her into his arms and they began to dance. "I know. She misses you, too."

"But how did you get it?" She frowned. "I don't understand. Did she give it to you before you came to petition?"

He opened his mouth, intending to lie. To say, yes, that was exactly how he'd come to possess the necklace, but this curious thing happened. As he looked into her eyes, he became totally and utterly unable to force a lie through his lips.

Ah, there was that cold-warm rush of fear chased by contentment through his veins again. What the hell was that?

"Bella gave it to me last night, Aislinn." He paused, watching her jerk in surprise. "I can go back to the Unseelie Court when I choose and I have on several occasions since I came to petition the Summer Queen."

"How?"

"One day I hope I'll be able to tell you."

She shook her head. "I don't understand. Why can't you tell me now?"

"Let's just say that I have a good relationship with my king."

"Strong enough to withstand your attempted defection?"

Theoretically, it might be. The Shadow King didn't have the same vanity that the Summer Queen possessed. Ronan had gone from the Unseelie to the Seelie and back, though he was the only one who ever had. That situation had been different for a number of reasons, one of which involved Bella.

But mostly it had been because of the piece of the *bosca fadbh.*

That was the artifact Ronan had stolen for the Phaendir. He'd bought Bella's life and his freedom by giving it to the Summer Queen. The piece of the *bosca fadbh,* when combined with the other two pieces and used with a spell from the Book of Bindings, had the power to break the warding that imprisoned the fae in Piefferburg. Obtaining the other pieces was a long shot at best, but Gabriel had no doubt both the courts were trying. They might even be competing.

The Seelie and the Unseelie, the Summer Queen and the Shadow King, might war, they might hate each other—but there was one area in which they were united. All fae hated the Phaendir and most fae wanted out of Piefferburg. Almost everyone wanted the freedom to live in the world again.

The enemy of my enemy is my friend.

Gabriel knew firsthand that the Summer Queen and the Shadow King were already talking about combining forces to make a move on the Phaendir. It was only a question of time.

So when Ronan and Bella had shown up on the stairs of the Black Tower, refugees from the Seelie Court with no-where else to go, the Shadow King had had his fun, but there had been no doubt they would have a home there.

They needed Ronan.

They would need Bella, too, and Gabriel, along with many others, if they planned to make a move for the rest of the *bosca fadbh* and the Book of Bindings.

"I think my relationship with my king is strong enough to withstand an attempted defection, yes."

She looked at him sharply. "*My* king." She stopped moving, stepped back, and blinked. "You don't intend to stay here, do you? No matter how the Summer Queen rules."

He glanced around them at the rest of the dancing and conversing Seelie Court. "Can we talk about this later?"

She pressed her lips together and gave a curt nod.

"Good." He took her hand and whirled her out, around, and back against him.

She laughed out loud, the prettiest sound he could imagine. "You're a great dancer."

"Thanks." He stared down into her eyes and put everything he was thinking about doing to her into his gaze. "It's the second best thing I can do."

She swallowed hard and glanced away. "Yes, I can imagine

what the first thing is," she answered in her characteristically dry tone of voice.

"I'd be more than happy to show you."

"You have to know by now I'm not that easy."

"Easy things are generally not worth the time and trouble, sweetness."

"And you, Gabriel, you're just trouble."

"Not as much as you'd think. Anyway, I think you could use a little trouble in your life, the right kind of trouble, anyway. My kind of trouble." He growled the words and held her tight. Gods, he wanted her so badly. Having her body pressed against his, her hips to his, her breasts to his chest. It was driving him insane.

She stopped dancing and moved away, drawing a shaky breath. Could she be feeling it, too? "I think I need a drink."

A familiar figure caught Gabriel's eye. "Looks like Kendal decided to come after all." He was accompanied by his floozy of the moment.

"Correction, I think I need to get out of here."

What a great idea. "Then let's do it."

# NINE

SHE took him to her apartment with every intention of seducing him.

He wasn't staying here. She'd heard it in his voice and seen it on his face. Gabriel still swore allegiance to the Shadow King. Why he'd even come here at all was a mystery to her. Tomorrow, unless the Summer Queen had sensed Gabriel's distaste for the Rose, she would probably extend him an invitation.

He wouldn't accept.

By tomorrow he would be gone, back to the place where he'd come, and she'd never see him again. She assumed he'd already been to see the Shadow King about returning. That was likely how he'd obtained Bella's pendant. Just that morning she'd been thinking about how she'd miss Gabriel if he left. Now that it was a reality, she realized just how much.

Yes, he was polished in the womanizing department. He obviously loved them and had seduced many in his lifetime. Yet he wasn't cruel, misogynistic, or skanky about it. For as much as he enjoyed sleeping with women, he seemed to respect them just as much, even worship them. Yes, he was arrogant as all hell. But he was also witty and intelligent, caring in his own way, scarily insightful, and not as self-absorbed as she'd first assumed. He was fun to talk to and when he wasn't near she noted his absence.

Her heart felt a bit heavy at the prospect of losing another friend to the Unseelie Court.

"The Summer Queen will be very angry when she finds out you're declining her invitation to stay."

Gabriel turned from where he stood at her living room window, looking down at the square. She came to stand next to him. Night had fallen long ago and the sky was strewn with glittering stars. Across the square, the Black Tower stabbed upward.

He turned back to observe the square. "How do you know I intend to decline her invitation?"

"I just do."

He said nothing for several moments, letting her know that she was right. "If I were to stay, it would be for you."

At the beginning of the week she would have instantly believed that was a line, but now she felt he meant it. "But you won't."

"My heart is in the Unseelie Court, Aislinn. I know that now more than ever."

"You don't like it here because the focus of our lives is on the social."

"Aislinn, this place has no magick in it and magick is the core of who we are." He spoke with deep passion in his voice. "I'm surprised so many Seelie Tuatha Dé are happy with their lives here."

"Magick is the Summer Queen's domain within these walls. Not ours."

"And that's wrong." He turned toward her. "Magick is in our spirit, Aislinn. It's what we're made of—take it away and we're just like the humans; there's nothing left to make us different or special. Take away our strengths and we'll wither and die slowly as a people. Especially now. This is not the time to weaken ourselves."

She looked up at him. "You mean in the face of the Phaendir."

"That's one of the issues where the Shadow King disagrees most with the Summer Queen. She keeps her people pampered and distracted when she should be keeping them strong. She should be preparing them for battle."

She shook her head, looked out the window, and crossed her arms over her chest. "It's not true that the Summer Queen wants to keep us weak."

"She's vain, Aislinn, worried that someone in her court might turn up more powerful than she is. No woman is permitted to be as beautiful as she is. She desperately wants to be the focal point, the adored one. Most of all she wants to be the one you all need."

Suddenly Aislinn feared a knock at her door, the Imperial Guard coming to take Gabriel away for voicing heresy against the queen.

She snorted. "You're saying that Caoilainn Elspeth Muirgheal, the direct descendant of the original High Royal of the Tuatha Dé Danann, is insecure."

"Yes, that's what I'm saying."

Aislinn shook her head, but didn't deny it. What Gabriel said was true. It was just the kind of truth that no one really wanted to face.

Gabriel shrugged. "In the Black, magick is emphasized as important from birth. Formal education begins at five years old and is taught alongside a child's ABCs and one-two-threes. It's required we learn Old Maejian fluently. We all are encouraged to develop our skills and hone them, to be able to control them at all cost. Because the Unseelie can use magick to harm and to kill, it's not a safe place, but it's an interesting place." He flashed a smile at her. "Never boring."

"I can imagine."

"You can't, love. You can't imagine it. It's so different from here." He paused. "I think you'd like it. I think you would fit in there and be content. You would find a meaning and a purpose to your life that you lack here. I believe you would feel less alone."

She looked down at the square. Join the Unseelie? She had magick that could kill, if she truly was a necromancer . . . but live in the Black Tower? It was inconceivable. But if she was a necromancer, it was imperative she learn about her magick, that she understood it and could control it.

Gabriel had just opened a pathway she'd never believed she could take.

She frowned. "You don't think I fit in here?"

"No." His answer came fast. "I think you've made yourself try to fit the best you can out of a sense of self-preservation, but you don't belong here, Aislinn. Your magick is too strong and you're doing yourself a disservice by suffocating it. You have a secret, a dark one, like the one Bella was keeping. I can feel it in you."

A week before she might have been offended by the notion that the Seelie Court was anything less than perfect, but not now. She said nothing for a long moment. "How do you know so much about me?"

He turned her to face him and tipped her chin up, forcing her to look into his eyes. "I watch you. I'm interested in you. I want to know who you are inside and out. So I tune in and pay attention."

"You're very perceptive."

"Only because I wish to perceive every aspect of you, Aislinn."

A shiver ran through her. His eyes were a rich, warm blue and his voice a low, rolling seduction. She believed him.

The world seemed to shift under her feet. *She trusted him.* Her instincts screamed that she could. Maybe she couldn't before, but now something between them had altered and not just on her end. Gabriel had begun to genuinely care for her at some point and that had changed everything.

How nice it would be to have someone to confide in, to talk to, someone to understand who she was under the ball gowns and jewelry. Bella was the only one who knew the true Aislinn. How strange it was that Gabriel might also know the true her when she'd disliked him so much in the beginning.

There was so much more to Gabriel Cionaodh Marcus Mac Braire than first met the eye.

"And I don't mean only sexually," Gabriel added, his voice low and as smooth as warm chocolate, and probably just as bad for her health. "In case you were wondering."

She hadn't taken his comment that way when he'd uttered it, but now she did. A flush suffused her body. Images did, too. She'd brought him here with the intention of sleeping with him and she wasn't typically shy about sex. The fae, the ones who were so long-lived, rarely were about such things. Yet with Gabriel she'd developed a sudden case of bashfulness.

She turned away from the window and walked back into the living room.

"Aislinn?" he questioned from the window.

She turned. "Have you ever known any necromancers?"

He jerked and then went very still. "No. They're very rare. There has never been a necromancer in Piefferburg to my knowledge. The Shadow King's maternal line has them. We learn about those necromancers, among others, in school." He paused and turned back toward the window in a gesture that seemed almost too nonchalant. "Why do you ask?"

She frowned, trying to interpret the odd body language. "I'm curious about them." She wasn't going to give more until he did.

"I'll tell you anything you want to know."

She moved to pour them drinks. Gabriel liked his whiskey straight. She wanted a glass of red wine. "Then pick a necromancer and tell me everything."

He was still standing by the window. "Brigid Fada Erinne O'Dubhuir. She was—"

"A woman?" Her hand tensed on the bottle of whiskey.

"Yes. Necromancers are usually women. Didn't you know that?"

"No." Were her hands shaking?

He walked over and took the glass from her hand. His fingers brushed her slightly and it made her feel hot. "That's basic. It amazes me how sheltered the Summer Queen keeps you."

A tornado of defensive rebuttal rose up in her throat, but she just swallowed it down. He was right. There was no sense in denying it. She took a sip of her wine.

"Brigid Fada Erinne O'Dubhuir was the Shadow King's mother. She ruled the Unseelie before her son took over. She was very powerful, very feared, and was allied with the Lord of the Wild Hunt. He was her consort, in fact."

She sank down into a chair, her fingers tight around her wineglass. "So, she had control of the sluagh?"

He nodded and sat down on the couch. "The Lord of the Wild Hunt could call them, but it was Brigid who controlled and commanded them. As is the Shadow Royal's right, she also held the amulet that allowed her to command and control the goblin army. She was invincible." He smiled with that wry twist she was getting used to seeing him wear. "Or so everyone believed. Necromancy is one of the more feared abilities to have, the power to control the dead." He smiled ruefully over the rim of his glass. "Everyone is afraid of the dead, of dying. A person who lives alongside that ultimate change and is friends with it is terrifying to even the most powerful fae."

"And to you?"

"Death comes to us all." He looked down into his drink. "It doesn't scare me."

"What happened to this necromancer?"

"Someone killed Brigid Fada Erinne O'Dubhuir during the night, in her sleep. Someone she trusted, someone who could get past the Shadow Guard. The Lord of the Wild Hunt was found guilty of that crime and executed. They say he was jealous of her power. Necromancy is not an easy path to follow."

She pressed her lips together and looked down at the floor. Every fiber of her wanted to tell him her secret. She wanted so much to trust him and now she was feeling she could.

He downed the rest of his whiskey. "Aislinn, I know you want to tell me something. You can stop looking like all the answers to life's questions are somewhere on the tip of that beautiful shoe I bought you and tell me. I already told you I know you're more than you project, so why not just come out with it."

She plunged right in. "I think I have Unseelie blood. No. I *know* I have it." She looked up at him, but he didn't look shocked. Of course, why would he be? He was Unseelie, too. "I'm not sure where it comes from. My family is said to have blood straight from the veins of the original Seelie Tuatha Dé and the power I have . . . it's very dark. I seem to have"—she swallowed hard—"a lot of Unseelie in my DNA."

He laughed. "Look, don't say it the same way you'd say you had *troll* in your DNA. It's really not that bad."

"It's just that I wonder about my bloodline. How could it have Unseelie in it? I wonder who strayed, who lied, how it even happened."

"The Seelie and Unseelie mingle more than you might think. It's more of a shameful secret in the Rose than it is in the Black. Tell me about why you think you have Unseelie blood, Aislinn. What kind of dark power do you have?"

She leaned forward, excitement welling up in her. "Souls come to me. I can see them, talk to them. Sometimes I wake up in the middle of the night and they're there by my bedside, desperate for someone, anyone, to acknowledge their existence while they wait for the Wild Hunt." Now that she'd begun talking, she couldn't stop. She licked her lips and continued, unable to look at him while she spoke. She set her glass down on an end table and bolted up to pace. "It started when I was a child. I've never told anyone but Bella, not my mother or even my father. It got worse as I grew older because I never had any training, no way to control it."

"It's not an uncommon ability among the Unseelie."

She glanced at him. "I thought you said it was a rare talent."

"*Necromancy* is a rare talent, Aislinn; being sensitive to souls isn't. Necromancy is the ability to call souls from the Netherworld and control them, to make them do the summoner's bidding."

She stopped and turned toward him. "But I can call them."

That made him blink. "You can?"

"I found a—" She stopped and started again, not certain she should reveal the book to him. "There's a spell. I said the words the other night and a soul appeared. I did it accidently." She didn't want to reveal whose soul it had been.

"Under your command?"

"I hope not." She'd been excited at first, but now the thought turned her stomach, horrified her. "I don't know. The soul disappeared almost right away. I would never try to call and command a soul. It seems kind of . . . rude."

He blinked and then gave her a slow, sexy smile that made her stomach flutter. "If you really think that, you would make a good necromancer."

"So what do you think?" She gazed down at him, chewing her bottom lip. Suddenly she felt the way a human might feel awaiting final word from her doctor on a serious health issue.

Gabriel set his glass aside and rose. He stepped toward her. "I think you've got Unseelie blood, and I think it's possible you're a necromancer."

"What do I do about my ability?"

"What do you want to do about it? You have two choices, Aislinn. You can stay here and bury your ability for your entire life and try to keep your secret. You can shop and go to balls and gossip in the hallways. Or you can take a risk, change all that you know, and come to the Unseelie Court to live free, develop your skills, and gain a purpose to your life."

Live free. She'd never thought of it in those terms. Her face probably showed it, too. Clearly she had some thinking to do. She needed to figure out what her goals were and prioritize them. She also needed to come to terms with the lifetime of mistruths she'd been told about the Black Tower and those who lived within it.

"Know what else I think?" Gabriel said in a low voice. He stepped closer to her and hooked a tendril of hair that had fallen from her updo behind her ear. "I think you're strong, intelligent, and powerful. I think you're more courageous than you believe yourself to be and you'll make the decision that's the best one for you."

"I hope you're right."

"I have faith in you, Aislinn. Whether you stay here or choose to leave, you'll be just fine." He leaned forward and kissed her. This time it was soft, sweet—qualities she'd never imagined Gabriel possessed. His lips skated over hers, raising the hair along the back of her neck and goose bumps along her arms and legs. Her fingers curled into his shirt at his shoulders and she hung on for dear life.

Gods, his kisses did things to her that no man's touch had ever done. She didn't think it was his magick enchanting her. She hoped not. From the first she'd seemed immune to it; in fact, it had made her dislike him. But was it possible his natural powers of attraction were working on her now?

Yes, perhaps.

But she didn't care.

Gabriel broke the kiss and set his forehead to hers for a moment. "I'll see you tomorrow, Aislinn. You'll be there for the queen's verdict, right?" His voice was low and rough.

"Of course I'll be there. I'm your court companion." She licked her lips. "You sound like you're leaving."

He pulled away from her. "I am."

She lost her hold on his shoulders as he backed away and she felt the loss of the contact. Suddenly her apartment felt cooler and a little bit emptier. She reached out and touched his arm just as he turned away. "Don't go."

He faced her. "Aislinn, I know what will happen if I stay." His eyes flashed dark suddenly, like a thunderstorm passing through. "It wouldn't be right. The longer I stay the more I want you. I need to leave now before I do something I'll regret."

Shocked anger flashed through her veins. "Regret? You'd regret spending the night with me?"

"Not in that way." He tipped his head back and groaned. "Gods, not in the way you're thinking. I'd regret it for other reasons." He hesitated, then looked directly into her eyes. "I'd regret it would be the last time I could ever touch you."

"That's why I want you to stay. I know you'll be gone tomorrow, so give me tonight at least, Gabriel."

He shook his head. "Not like this, Aislinn." His voice had grown rougher. "Don't tempt me."

"I'm confused. I thought you wanted—"

He reached out and pulled her close. "Aislinn, I can't. I want you, but it's not a good idea. Not now."

His body pressed against hers took her breath away. She could feel that he was aroused. "I don't understand."

"Me, either."

Now she was getting angry again. "Stop being cryptic and talk to me."

"Maybe I will take a taste of you before I go, Aislinn," he murmured. "Just the flavor of you to keep on the back of my tongue. Something I can take back to the Black Tower with me. Something I can keep for a while and savor in my memories."

All her anger left her in a whoosh, along with her words and her ability to think. The way he looked at her, the intensity of his words, the low voice in which he uttered them— all of it combined to produce the most arousing, romantic thing that a man had ever said to her.

He moved her back toward the couch and kissed her again. This time it wasn't soft and it definitely wasn't sweet. This kiss brought to mind bare skin and smooth sheets, bodies fusing in passion.

His fingers skated down her bare back to the edge of the fabric just above her rear. "Ever since I bought this dress for you all I've been able to think about is taking it off."

"So do it," she murmured, her hand straying to the tie he wore and loosening it. "I won't complain."

Two little movements and the gown slipped off her shoulders to become a very expensive blood red puddle around her feet.

She wore the lingerie he'd bought her beneath it.

He backed up a little so he could take all of her in. His gaze swept her, heated and hungry. "You're gorgeous," he murmured. "You're the most beautiful thing I've ever laid eyes on."

She raised an eyebrow. "Gorgeous enough to convince

you to stay the night?" She kicked off her shoes, stepped away from the gown, and laid it over the arm of a nearby chair. She'd never owned something as beautiful as that dress and it meant even more to her because Gabriel had bought it for her.

Then she walked to him, confident that he enjoyed the look of her body, mostly undressed as it was, and removed his tie. She worked the buttons of his shirt free one by one and pulled the tails from his pants as he tangled his fingers through her hair, freeing it to fall over her shoulders.

She pushed his shirt off and took in the sight of his bare chest for a moment. He was any woman's idea of perfect male beauty—muscled and strong, broad shouldered, with rippling abs. The kind of body that made a woman feel safe. Once his arms came around her, Aislinn knew nothing in the world could hurt her. Admiring him, she skated her palms over his chest. His skin was warm—silk over steel. A small amount of dark hair adorned it, tapering down his abdomen and disappearing past the waistline of his pants.

Aislinn really wanted to follow that trail.

His hands gripped the material of her slip and fisted in the silk. With a hungry sound in the back of his throat, he pulled her toward him—flush up against all that lovely male chest—and he dragged the slip upward. Silk slithered over her skin, up farther and farther. The sensation of it combined with the look in his eyes made her body respond, her nipples going hard and her sex heating. The simple act of undressing her was pure foreplay. Finally, he drew the garment up and over her head and let it puddle to the floor, and she stood before him with only air and light to clothe her.

Making a low noise in his throat that sounded part appreciation and part torment, he kissed her, pushing her backward and down onto the couch. He knelt between her spread thighs, his hands slipping down over her breasts as his tongue speared into her mouth. Her nipples hardened against his palms and he petted them, exploring every ridge and valley with his masterful hands.

She shifted on the couch, pleasure coursing through her

and centering between her thighs with a need she wanted
assuaged. She moaned into his mouth and he moved—
cupping the back of her neck with one hand and dipping
lower with the other, over her abdomen to between her
thighs, where she so wanted him to touch her. He found all
the sensitive, secret places of her body and stroked, until she
wanted to purr like a cat.

Finding her pouting clit, he petted it with his thumb until
it bloomed beneath his touch. He dropped his head and his
hot, wet mouth closed over one nipple and then the other.
Giving each breast equal attention, he laved them with his
tongue until they were hard and rosy and Aislinn was a hot,
messy puddle of squirming need.

Her hands moved over his shoulders and back, but every
time she tried to unbutton his pants, he stopped her. She
made a sound of discontent and he shushed her. Yanking her
forward so her rear was just on the edge of the couch, he
covered her body with his, slanting his mouth over hers and
sliding his hand between her thighs once again. Suddenly she
couldn't remember why she'd been frustrated.

He kissed her hard, his tongue stabbing into her mouth
just as his fingers thrust in and out of her sex. The fabric of
his pants rasped against her inner thighs with their movement, reminding her that he was still clothed from the waist
down.

"Come on, Aislinn," he murmured against her lips as his
fingers speared in and out of her. "Come for me, love. I want
to hear you scream." He found her G-spot deep within and
stroked it.

Pleasure rose and increased with the power of an oncom-
ing train. He knew exactly how to touch her, just how much
pressure to use, just where and how to caress her. He wanted
to make her come, that was clear enough. He wanted it fast
and powerful.

It broke over her with a force she could never remember
experiencing, washing through every pore of her body and
mind, making her toes curl and her sex spasm around his
thrusting fingers. Her back arched and she cried out. She

could do nothing, think nothing. The only thing she could do was *feel*—and hold on through it as it went on and on.

"That's it, love. Good girl," he crooned to her.

Her neck arched as she moaned from the waves of it coursing through her, her head hitting the couch behind her. He nibbled her throat and breasts and whispered soft, dirty, almost unintelligible things to her, still stroking her sex, extending her orgasm as far as it would go.

Finally it eased away and she slumped backward under the force of it. "Gods," she whispered.

She reached for him, wanting more of him, wanting him naked and his body against hers, inside hers. But he pulled away and gathered her up in his arms, drawing her to the soft carpet of the floor and kissing her temple.

"Gabriel—" She felt so relaxed now, all the tension washed from her body by the stroke of his hands. Her limbs felt as insubstantial as the silk she'd worn that night.

"Shhh, look, Aislinn." He pointed out the window. The stars seemed especially bright. "Soon the Wild Hunt will ride."

She snuggled against him, enjoying the feel and scent of him and the afterglow of her orgasm. He felt so good against her, even half clothed. The sound of his breathing calmed her and the strength of his body made her feel safe.

Soon she drifted to sleep. When she woke, she was in her bed, sheets and comforter pulled over her. Her gown and lingerie were laid carefully over a chair in her bedroom and her shoes were on the floor near them.

Gabriel was nowhere to be found. If her body still didn't hold a delicious tremor of memory from their encounter, she would have thought she'd dreamed it all.

# TEN

GABRIEL inclined his head. "Thank you for your gracious invitation, Queen Caoilainn, but I decline. The Seelie Court isn't a good fit for me and I intend to return to the Black Tower." His words were blithe. Didn't he realize the danger he'd just put himself in?

For a moment Aislinn thought the Summer Queen's head would explode. The royal stared at Gabriel, her face flushing and her eyes going wide and shiny. Her fingers tightened on the heads of the carved rose quartz dragon armrests of her throne. The silver and gold tattoo from the ring she wore, giving her the power due a Seelie Royal, flashed for a moment in the light. Her entire body, slight though it was, seemed to vibrate with rage and the throne room filled with the power of her emotion, making Aislinn's ears pop.

"You dare to reject me and my court?" the queen bellowed. Even the hundreds of guards lining the walls of the throne room jerked in the face of her voice. The sound of clanking armor echoed from their mass flinch. "*You*, an

Unseelie degenerate, should be kissing my feet that I have allowed you entrance to the Rose Tower. *Guards!*"

The Imperial Guards all moved with a combined thumping sound of boots on marble floor. Every hair on the back of Aislinn's neck stood on end at the horrible sound. All of them had their hands on their swords. Visions of Gabriel's headless body hitting the floor, a pool of blood spilling from his neck, filled her mind's eye. It wouldn't be the first time Aislinn had seen such a sight. It was always horrible, but it would be unbearable if it was Gabriel.

"No!" The word jumped from Aislinn's throat before she could stop it. "No, please, just let him leave."

The Summer Queen's gaze swung to her like an owl that had just discovered a juicy mouse in the field. "Did you just tell me *no*? Me? Caoilainn Elspeth Muirgheal? Do you expect I'll obey you, Aislinn?"

Her stomach felt suddenly filled with cold gelatin. "If you harm him, I'll leave the Rose Tower forever." It wasn't much of a threat, but it was the only one she could make.

The queen laughed. It was a hollow, mirthless sound. "Is that supposed to scare me? Why would I care where you go, Aislinn?"

That's right; she didn't care where her people went because they were all just puppets anyway. The queen had ensured her people hadn't developed their magick, so they were really worthless to her in actuality. They were only here to populate the building, worship her, and uphold the tradition of the great Seelie Court of myth and history. More than ever, Aislinn could see that. Maybe she'd always known it on some level, but it had taken Gabriel to fully open her eyes. The truth was a cold swallow of bitter fruit and it turned her stomach.

"What's to stop me from keeping either of you from ever leaving this room?" the queen continued to Gabriel. "Alive, anyway."

Gabriel's voice boomed low and clear through the chamber. "Harm Aislinn or me and you will have a war on your hands. The Shadow King has claimed us both."

Aislinn jerked and looked over at Gabriel in alarm. This was news to her. He'd hinted at the possibility that the Shadow King would likely welcome her to the Black Tower, but he'd never come out and said that the Shadow King had *claimed* her. He'd never even told her he'd spoken to the Shadow King on her behalf.

Had he told the Shadow King about her Unseelie blood? About her ability? Was that why he'd left the night before? Was that why he hadn't wanted to make love to her? Could it be somehow related?

Or perhaps he thought the Summer Queen truly did mean to harm her and he was bluffing to get her out of the situation. Either way, the result was the same: she would have to leave the Rose Tower. She'd mulled the possibility, but she didn't want her decision to be forced. Not like this.

Gods.

For a moment all thought left her mind. It was only a sheet of white, blank—tabula rasa. She blinked stupidly, wondering how large a shift her life had just taken and whether it was a change for the better . . . or the worse. What would soon be written on that blankness?

Gabriel spoke again. "We belong—both of us—to the Shadow King. Harm us at your peril."

The queen stared hard at them both, her eyes narrowed and her fingers bone white. The guards had stopped moving once Aislinn had yelled no and the queen had entertained her, but their hands still rested on the handles of their swords. The cold jelly in Aislinn's stomach jiggled and made her nauseous.

"The Shadow King cannot have Aislinn Christiana Guinevere Finvarra. She's mine," the queen yelled, losing her frosty composure completely.

Aislinn jerked in surprise at the claim. A moment ago the queen had said she didn't care if she left the Rose and had threatened to kill her. Ah. Logic cut through her panicked confusion. The queen was only claiming her to thwart the Shadow King. Aislinn was only a pawn in their eternal struggle.

The queen pointed her finger at Gabriel. "You! Begone from the Rose Tower before I decide I don't care about a war. Guards, escort them out. Make sure Aislinn Christiana Guinevere Finvarra returns to her quarters and the Unseelie incubus exits the tower."

Five gold and rose–bedecked guards escorted them out of the throne room, armor clanking.

The corridor was thronged with onlookers as well as a *Faemous* film crew, but Aislinn paid them no attention. She gripped Gabriel's hand as the guards bustled them down the hallway amid a shush of wagging tongues and curious looks.

"Does the Shadow King really know about me?" she asked.

He glanced back at the guards and spoke in a hushed voice. "Come to the Black Tower. Not now, but later, when you can. Come to me there."

She swallowed hard and looked around at the building she'd known her whole life, the people she'd grown up with, the scents, the textures, the sounds. "That's a big decision to make."

"It's the *right* decision to make."

"Gabriel, I don't know. I can't just leave like this."

"Yes, you can. Don't be afraid." He pulled her forward by her upper arms and kissed her. Then he buried his nose in her hair and inhaled, as if he were trying to fill himself up with the scent of her and take it with him. "You know where I am, Aislinn. You won't be alone."

He dipped his head and gave her one last lingering kiss. Then he turned and walked down the corridor with the guards behind him . . . out of her life forever. Sorrow swelled within her as she watched him disappear from her sight.

All around her the Seelie who'd followed them down the corridor murmured. The commentator from *Faemous* pushed a mike into her face and asked a question she couldn't really hear through the roaring in her ears. She just pushed forward, away from all of them, and went up to her room as fast as she could, tears blurring her vision.

Her chest was empty and cold. She'd lost something important, something unique and special that she would never get back and would always remember. Maybe it was the possibility of pursuing her magick.

Or maybe it was Gabriel.

GABRIEL walked through Piefferburg Square in full daylight and without subterfuge for the first time in a week. He'd failed to bring Aislinn to the Unseelie Court and now faced the ire of the Shadow King.

But that was not what made ice form in the center of his chest. It was the loss of her. He would miss the scent of her, her presence, the sound of her voice and the feel of her skin.

He'd seen it in her eyes—she wasn't coming over to the Black. The Shadow King would be angry that he hadn't used his sexual magick to enchant her and possess her. He could have done that once she'd warmed to him. Last night had presented the perfect opportunity. He could have woven a dark spell of lust around her so strong that she would've followed him anywhere. The thought had occurred to him, but he hadn't been able to follow through.

Since he'd met Aislinn, he'd developed an annoyingly potent conscience.

He cared about her; therefore he hadn't been able to take her choices from her. He hadn't been able to manipulate her to his will, even though not doing so meant he risked his life.

Ultimately, it was better this way.

He would suffer the wrath of the Unseelie Royal, but he'd done right by Aislinn. That was the important thing. The only pity of the situation was that Aislinn hadn't done right by herself by choosing not to take a chance.

A cold wind blew his coat open and chilled him to the bone. He closed it, turning his collar up, and headed past the statue of Jules Piefferburg, which today was smeared with rotting fruit. One last glance up at the Rose Tower showed Aislinn silhouetted in her window, watching him. Alone. She was destined to remain that way.

He ripped his gaze away and stared straight ahead at the Black Tower, shaking her off him and gathering his armor back around himself. Some kind of spell had affected him at the Rose Tower, made him weak and vulnerable. He couldn't bring that back with him to the Unseelie; they would scent it in a minute and exploit it.

For a while Aislinn had transformed him into the man he might have been if his mother hadn't died when he was a boy, if he hadn't been left alone on the streets of the newly created Piefferburg, if his father hadn't been the man he'd been.

If.

But now that Aislinn was gone from his life all that history crashed back on him like a wave against rocks. He allowed it. He needed it. He needed the strength his experiences had given him, the mercilessness he'd been forced to acquire. He would need all that when he went to tell the Shadow King that he'd failed.

Bella tried to catch him as soon as he breezed into the Black Tower, but he waved her off. Niall Quinn, Ronan's brother, watched him from a corner of the foyer, an almost knowing smirk on his face. Aeric took one look at the glower on Gabriel's face and backed off immediately.

Hinkley hurried up to him. "The Shadow King demands your presence at once."

"Yes, I'm sure," Gabriel drawled.

"He's in a foul mood."

Gabriel turned the corridor leading to the Shadow King's chamber with Hinkley nipping at his heels. "That makes two of us."

The Shadow King *was* in a bad mood. That didn't bode well for Gabriel.

The royal sat in his office, behind a huge oak desk with legs carved in the image of satyrs. The Shadow King didn't sit on a throne surrounded by hundreds of gold and rose–bedecked guards as the Summer Queen did, but he was no less imposing from sheer reputation.

The Summer Queen wasn't the only royal known to cry *off with his head* upon occasion.

Barthe lurked in one corner, near the Shadow King's propped-up fighting staff. Two goblins stood in the other corner, far more deadly than a pretty Seelie Tuatha Dé with a sword. The Seelie Tuatha Dé guard would decapitate him, but a goblin would digest him. Neither death sounded good at the moment and he had a feeling he'd be threatened by both today.

"Where is she?" the Shadow King growled, coming to his feet behind his desk. His multicolored hair was tied at his nape today, the red tips touching the middle of his back. The bones of his face were thrown into sharp relief, giving him a brutal cast. The tattoo of the medallion embedded in his skin was visible at the open collar of his shirt.

"I have failed to lure Aislinn Christiana Guinevere Finvarra to the Black, my lord." There would be no sitting down and propping his feet up on the desk today. He needed to pay the king his respect since he was coming to him with a disappointment.

The Shadow King went silent and the temperature in the room dropped several degrees. There was a reason they called him *shadow*. That temperature drop was a bad sign of his temper. "How is it that you failed, Gabriel? Help me to understand."

"She was immune to my charms, my lord." No sense in telling him that eventually she hadn't been; he just hadn't wanted to manipulate her. "I gained secret information about her and attempted to use it to my favor, endeavoring to convince her that her life would improve if her dark magick was developed, but—"

"Dark magick? She knows about her abilities?" He went still and paled.

Gabriel frowned, wondering why that was an issue. "She told me she's sensitive to departed souls and believes she accidentally called one once. She thinks she may be a necromancer, but there's no basis I can see for it. She has a desire to develop her skills, so I encouraged her to come here so she could.

Since my power as an incubus was useless with her, I took that strategy. It failed."

The king turned his back to him and his body tensed. "I need her here, Gabriel. Her presence is essential to the retention of my throne. This isn't just some game I'm playing with the Summer Queen. Aislinn *is* a necromancer. This is life or death for me."

His voice had taken on a deadly quality that made Gabriel nervous, not for himself . . . but for Aislinn.

"What do you mean?"

"I mean having that woman come here of her own free will is vital to my placement on this throne. Her delivery to me is vital. Even more now that she knows what she is." The Shadow King turned. "If you can't bring her to me, I'll find someone who can." The words were dark, the tone he said them in even darker. "Of her own free will . . . or not."

Fear for Aislinn exploded through Gabriel, manifesting in acute anger. Suddenly he was thankful he'd failed in his task. Thankful that Aislinn was safe between rose quartz walls.

The Shadow King continued, "If she won't come to me willingly, I'll simply risk war with the Summer Queen and force her. I'll use the goblin army if I have to."

Gabriel took a menacing step toward the Shadow King and growled, "What do you want with her?" The two goblins stiffened at his threatening movement toward their king and Barthe snarled. No one talked to the Shadow King like that, not even Gabriel.

The Shadow King studied him with keen eyes. "Have you come to care for her, incubus?" He grunted. "Clearly you've become more of an encumbrance to my plans than a help." He shook his head. "I'm disappointed in you, Gabriel."

Gabriel took another step forward, putting his hands on the top of the desk and leaning toward him. "You're going to hurt her, aren't you?"

The Shadow King flicked his wrist at Barthe and the goblins. "I can tell you're going to interfere with my plans." The lanky gray goblins flanked Gabriel, growling and showing their teeth. Barthe came up behind him. "I thought *you* of all men wouldn't become ensnared by her. I thought you would be safe to send." He shook his head. "Such a pity."

Gabriel backed away from the goblins, but they had him in their unbreakable grip in a moment, claws digging into his flesh. He fought them, but they clamped down, making pain shoot up his arms. Any harder and they'd snap his bones. It didn't take much for a goblin to do that. They were tall and thin, but strong as hell.

"Lay a hand on her and I swear to the gods, I'll—"

"You'll what, pretty boy?" The Shadow King laughed. "You've got no threats to make, incubus. No lethal magick to call that doesn't involve fucking."

Wrong. He was Lord of the Wild Hunt. He had more power than any fae in the Unseelie Court, except for a necromancer. He had the power to call the sluagh—the army of unforgiven dead . . . he only lacked the ability to control them. Though Aislinn could. *Gods*.

It all came together.

*Danu*, what had he done?

"You killed your mother, didn't you?" Gabriel yelled. "It wasn't her consort who murdered her. It was her son! You murdered your own mother in her bed to obtain the Unseelie Throne, then implicated and executed the Lord of the Wild Hunt for it."

The Shadow King ignored him. "Take him away; put him in charmed iron until this is over. I don't want to lose you, Gabriel. I just want you out of my way for a while. You'll come to understand this is all for the best."

Barthe bore him back toward the door with the help of the goblins. He fought them as hard as he could, every muscle in his body straining forward, toward the royal. Gabriel wanted to rip his throat out.

"If you hurt, Aislinn," Gabriel roared, every muscle in his body fighting, "I will find a way to take you down. If you—"

"Oh, Gabriel. Stop. I *am* going to hurt her." The Shadow King smiled, showing sharp white teeth. "But only a little."

Gabriel wrenched free of the goblins' grip and threw one

punch that connected. Rotating, he threw another. Both goblins staggered backward, screeching.

Barthe grabbed Gabriel by the shoulders with a roar of anger and head-butted him. Pain screamed through Gabriel's head, followed by darkness.

# ELEVEN

AISLINN sat in her bed, covers around her ankles and her arms around her knees. The Valentino hung on a hanger near her closet. Rain pattered on her bedroom window, coming down from clouds as dark as her mood. It had been a week and the acute loss she'd felt had not dissipated.

The queen had been extra chilly to her—she could expect that treatment for the next fifty years at a minimum—and all the Seelie had some sort of comment to make, most especially Kendal. All of them thought she and Gabriel had been lovers.

That was fine. She wanted to remember Gabriel that way— as a lover.

All of them thought she'd been used and discarded by the Unseelie incubus, just like Kendal had used her. Two weeks ago she would've cared about the gossip, but not now. She had far more weighty issues on her heart.

Despite not sleeping with him, Aislinn had never been with a man who'd affected her so much. She'd never been with a man she'd missed as much after he was gone.

She gazed out the window, fingering Bella's sapphire pendant. If she wasn't such a coward, she'd get up and leave right now. Just leave this place and start over somewhere they'd appreciate her, somewhere she could develop her magick and be the person nature had intended—one with dark power. She could be with Bella and Ronan.

She could be with Gabriel.

So what if she'd be leaving everything she'd ever known? Wasn't it time she stretched her wings, discovered new things? Left fear behind her and forged new paths?

Yes, it was time.

What did she have here anyway? Her mother, who was one of the coldest people she knew; a woman who really only cared about one thing—her daughter's upward mobility at court. Since that mobility was officially downward these days, her mother probably didn't care if she was even still alive. There was Carina, but Bella had always been far closer to Aislinn's heart. She would miss Carina but she shared a shallow friendship with her, based on shopping and gossip.

Hollowness filled her body. Gods, she missed her father so much. Her thoughts strayed to the book in the safe. Her fingers itched to pull it out, utter the words, call him.

But it was selfish to want that. She shouldn't want it. Her father was . . . wherever he was, and she shouldn't call him back. He was where he was supposed to be, doing whatever it was they did in the Netherworld. It couldn't be right to call him.

Could it?

The frustrating part was that she simply didn't know and had no one to ask. No one here to confide in. Here, she could never be the person she was born to be. She would never meet her full potential magickally, never have a greater purpose for her life. She'd never truly fit in.

In the Black, she just might.

Never, ever, would that thought have occurred to her before she'd met Gabriel. He'd completely changed her life.

It didn't take her long to finally come to the decision she'd been toying with all week. All the same—even knowing somewhere deep within she would finally make the decision to leave—it felt impulsive. Reckless.

The hollow feeling in her stomach turning leaden, she packed a bag. Her money was in a bank in Piefferburg. She would always have that and could buy new clothes and items she needed once she relocated. So she took only the most valuable and sentimental things from her apartment. Jewelry, the gown and lingerie Gabriel had given her, photographs, and the book.

She wrote a note to Carina with the intention of slipping it under her door on the way out. No sense in allowing people to worry about her. Despite the queen's current displeasure with her, she wouldn't go to arms against the Black Tower if Aislinn defied her wishes and left the Rose for the Black. The note was just extra insurance—Aislinn needed the queen to know she'd left of her own free will and hadn't been taken. No one needed a fae war on their hands.

Taking one long last look at her former life, she closed the front door of her apartment and walked down the corridor toward a new one.

GIDEON concentrated on a small patch of the warding around Piefferburg, just the tiniest bit, not big enough for any of the Phaendir to notice. Collectively, the Phaendir maintained the power mesh warding in a pocket of their twilight subconscious mind, a pocket that was a hive mind—forming a seamless net that imprisoned the fae. Since Piefferburg had been created, this had been the way, power passing from father to son.

No female children had ever been born of Phaendir couplings with human or fae women, not since the dawn of their time. No muddy half-blood genetic messes, either. Phaendir blood ran strong and true, eclipsing weak human and fae DNA.

So it had been decreed by the one and true God, Labrai, just one more symbol that the Phaendir were the special ones, the chosen people.

The only exception were the two sons born of a Phaendir and wilding woman mating, Ronan and Niall Quinn. No one knew why those two men had turned out such an odd mix of fae and druid. No Phaendir wanted to examine it too closely. They hated that the two mages had certain skills beyond a Phaendir's scope, because didn't that make them superior in a way?

Gideon was the only one who wanted to examine it more closely. A lot more closely. If it were up to him, he'd kill them both and put an end to that bastard genetic line before either of them had a chance to procreate.

He leaned down and examined his work. Yes, this little rip and repair would go unnoticed. At least, he hoped so. Gideon knew he was taking a risk, but drastic times called for drastic measures. The space was only large enough to admit one man. One man at a time. If worse came to worst— and it was looking like it might—he would send more than one man in for the book.

But not himself.

He would never enter Piefferburg, but he would send his minions. Men he could trust and who were loyal to him. Men who supported the True Path—*his* vision for the future of the Phaendir. Men who believed Brother Maddoc coddled the fae, made their existence far too comfortable. Men who believed—as he did—that the fae shouldn't *exist* at all, comfortably or not.

Gideon knew he might be sending his minions to their death. Any Phaendir discovered within the territory of Piefferburg would be torn limb from limb and possibly digested if there were any goblins around. But sacrifices had to be made. In order for Gideon to gain control of the Phaendir, he needed to make Maddoc look incompetent. Finding the Book of Bindings before Maddoc did would make that happen. Gideon would take Maddoc's place, institute the True Path, and even get the girl—Emily.

He glanced up and down the warding, using his second sight to see past the haze of it to the other side. This part of the Piefferburg Boundary Lands was largely uninhabited. A distance away lay quiet brackish waterways where some water fae lived.

Feeling the thread of power pull on his body as he sewed the last bit of the hole up, loosely for future use, Gideon snapped off the tendrils with a few uttered words of Old Maejian and stepped back.

If those under his power did as they were told, he wouldn't have to use it. If he did, he felt sure he would emerge victorious.

Labrai loved him best among his peers. He would see him through.

IT was when she passed the statue of Jules Piefferburg, in that twilight area of Piefferburg Square, that things got dark.

Her footsteps faltered on the cobblestones just a little once she made it past that point. She may have cast a backward glance once or twice and cursed herself for not being stronger or more courageous. She didn't stop, though, not even when she passed a group of dark fae—a cluster composed of half-breed creatures who looked human, yet not quite—who stared at her hooded figure and her white hand clutching her suitcase and snickered as she passed. Not even when she glimpsed a bedraggled boggart covered in old newspaper sleeping against a wall, or passed by a beautiful and deadly Hu Hsien—a Chinese woman who could take the form of a fox with poisoned fangs—sipping a drink on the patio of a nocturnal café.

Gods, was she doing the right thing?

If she returned now, she could take back the note from Carina in the morning and no one would ever know she'd tried this. Things could go back the way they had been yesterday . . . the same way they'd been three weeks ago, five years . . . two decades . . .

She walked on.

The shiny black tower loomed above her as she reached the double front doors. Behind her the Rose Tower gleamed in the moonlight where the rain clouds had parted. It seemed miles away, not just on the other side of the square.

Tall gray goblins guarded the thick wooden doors of the Black Tower. One on each side. Her steps faltered once again and her heart rate ratcheted into the stratosphere. She'd seen them before, of course, just never so close. The goblins resided in Goblin Town, away from the rest of the fae because their culture was so alien. Mostly they kept to themselves, unless they were called to battle by the Shadow King—then they were ruthless, brutal killers who ate their enemy even while it screamed for mercy.

They peered at her curiously with slitted pig eyes as she approached. For all their tendency toward the unspeakable in battle, when they were given a set of rules they believed in, they would defend them to the death. They were loyal as well. For these reasons they made good guards as long as their liege was able to inspire them and hold their loyalty, a thing the Shadow King had been able to do for hundreds of years.

She halted before them and clutched the handle of her suitcase so hard her hand went bloodless. "I am Aislinn Christiana Guinevere Finvarra, formerly of the Seelie, come to seek audience with the Shadow King."

CARINA ripped through Aislinn's closet, pushing shoe boxes from shelves and pulling clothing from hangers. "Where is it? Where did you hide it, Aislinn?"

Gods, she'd waited too long to do this. The book was nowhere to be found. Maybe Aislinn had never had it and they had been wrong.

No, they were never wrong. It had to be here somewhere.

She pulled everything out of her drawers, then she checked under the bed and everywhere in the palatial bathroom.

Nothing.

Carina made a loud sound of frustration and slid down the bathroom wall to sit on the floor opposite the huge spa tub. Surely Aislinn hadn't put it in a safe somewhere. Aislinn would've had no idea of the book's worth so she wouldn't have bothered. *Danu*, they would have Carina's skin if she couldn't produce it. It was the one task they'd set for her and she'd managed to mess it up.

Worse, they'd have Drem's skin.

As soon as she'd picked up the note from beneath her door that morning, she'd known there was no hope of finding the book. She'd searched Aislinn's place three times and had never found it. Why should this time be any different? And now Aislinn was gone and Carina's hope of finding the book had gone with her.

She'd befriended Aislinn almost two years earlier. Even getting close to her had been difficult. Aislinn was more of an introvert than an extrovert and she didn't share much— not about her life, anyway. Plus, she'd had Bella, who had been Aislinn's confidant in all things—the position for which Carina had been competing.

When Bella had been banished from the Rose, Carina had thought she'd had a real shot. But her personality was the opposite of Aislinn's—loud where Aislinn was quiet and strong, outspoken where Aislinn was thoughtful and honest, more self-serving and shallow where Aislinn was compassionate. Carina knew her own shortcomings as well as her strengths. She and Aislinn had never quite meshed, never totally connected. She'd never managed to get close enough to Aislinn to coax her to tell her all her secrets . . . specifically the one about the book they thought she had.

She'd miscalculated. If she'd known then what she knew now, she would have skipped the soft stuff and gone straight for the hard core. But now it was too late to take another course. She was running out of time.

What would they do to her? What would they do to Drem?

A tear rolling down her cheek, she pushed up from the floor of the bathroom and went to gaze out the window in the living room. The Black Tower gleamed shiny and imposing in the bright midmorning sunlight. Aislinn was there chasing Gabriel right now, no doubt.

Never in all her days had Carina ever thought Aislinn would hare off to the Unseelie. What was in her head? She had everything a pure-blood Tuatha Dé Sídhe could want: a beautiful apartment, high social status, money. Why give all that up to go and live with monsters? It just didn't make any sense. It wasn't as though Aislinn had Unseelie blood in her. All her magick was white, harmless.

How could they hold Carina responsible for Aislinn's flighty, completely unpredictable behavior? How could she have known that Gabriel would turn down the Summer Queen's invitation? It was completely unheard of! It was even more amazing that the incubus had managed to keep his head after doing so.

Still staring at the tower in the distance, she pulled her cell phone from the pocket of her jeans and punched in the charmed, masked number she tried so very hard never to dial.

"Hello?" she queried once someone picked up.

Silence on the other end. Only breathing. Then, finally: "Why are you calling me?" His voice was a low, magick-laced rasp that made her backbone go cold and bowels want to let loose. She didn't know his name. She only knew he was high up in the Phaendir power structure, though not quite at the top.

She licked her lips and steeled herself. "Aislinn's gone. I've searched her apartment and . . . the book is nowhere to be found." She paused to gather her courage. "Maybe she never even had it."

"She has it."

"She went to the Black. Maybe she took it with her."

Silence.

Magick coursing from the other end of the line made her fingers and ear tingle. A low static sound filled her head. Her breath caught painfully in her throat as she wondered if this would be her end.

"S-sir?"

"I will give you one last opportunity to right this wrong. Find the book."

*Click.* The line went dead.

She lowered the cell to her side, marveling that it was

only the line that was dead. Drem! They'd threatened his life. It was how they'd snared her into this in the first place. Clutching the phone in her hand, she ran out of the apartment and back to her quarters, heart in her throat, straight into her husband's arms.

"Oh, thank you. *Danu*, thank you," she sobbed into the curve of Drem's collar. She held him tight, tight enough that no one could take him from her.

"What's wrong, my love?" Drem murmured into her ear. He stroked her hair and kissed her head, holding her close. "It's okay. I'm fine. I'm here."

She shivered and shook, unable to form words. Tears wet his shirt as she clung to him.

He pushed her back at arm's length to study her face. "Carina, tell me what's wrong."

"I-I love you, Drem." She wiped her cheeks and tried to smile. "I want you to know that I love you more than anyone in this world and I would do anything for you. *Anything*."

"Okay." He looked bewildered.

She melted into his arms and they sank to the carpeted floor, clinging to each other as if in rough seas.

Because they were.

Oh, how they were.

THE Shadow King was a very good-looking man. Pale like a winter moon, but his features were chiseled and handsome. His hair was striking in its length and in its graduation of color from silver-blond at his crown to bloodred at the tips. Amazing that he only looked to be in his early thirties. The Sídhe were a long-lived species, but they did age. By all accounts, the Shadow King was one of the oldest fae around, equaled in years to only a few of the wildings. The Shadow Amulet had given him immortality, locking his age in at whatever age he'd first put it on.

His creature, Barthe, was an Unseelie beast like she'd never before encountered. She couldn't keep her eyes off the hulking thing that stood so protectively near his liege. He seemed imbued with some Zen-like ability to remain perfectly and utterly still and quiet, but she didn't doubt for a moment that he was rapid and deadly when the object of his protection was threatened.

But Aodh Críostóir Ruadhán O'Dubhuir could take care of himself. It was said that when the Phaendir trapped him to put him in Piefferburg, he fought so hard he killed fifty of their men and tapped all their magickal resources. It took the Phaendir a month to recover. The Shadow King, like the Summer Queen, had many different kinds of magick—all of them lethal. His only equal was the Summer Queen herself, and because of that they remained immortal enemies, locked in an eternal cold war.

Aislinn had never met him in person, had never even glimpsed him from afar even though he'd lived across the square from her for her entire life. Unlike the Shadow King and unlike Gabriel, she'd been born in Piefferburg. Likely she would die in Piefferburg. The thought made her heart heavy, but it was something she'd reluctantly accepted long ago.

At the moment, the man in question was staring at her from across his living room. It had surprised her to be brought by the Black Tower majordomo, Hinkley, to the Shadow King's living area and not to a throne room. It appeared this royal did not stand on ceremony.

At least there were no goblins here. They gave Aislinn the heebies.

She hadn't had the luck of running into Bella or Ronan, and she acutely regretted not asking for Gabriel before coming to see the king.

There was something about the Shadow King that made her nervous, though she couldn't pinpoint exactly what it was. Her intuition again, telling her something her eyes could not see. Of course it made sense she was uneasy; she'd just drastically altered every aspect of her life.

"I am so glad you decided to come to us, Aislinn. Gabriel has told me so much about you." The Shadow King's hobgoblin servant arrived with a tray holding a flute of what appeared to be sparkling water and she took it gratefully. "I think with your skills, you'll be a real asset to the tower."

Her grip tightened on the glass. "So did Gabriel tell you about my . . . blood?"

"When he came to me to ask for forgiveness for his transgression, he mentioned you to me. He said there was more to you than met the eye and I should consider you an asset to the Unseelie Court if you decided to defect." He smiled, but the sight didn't reassure her. "And here you are."

"Here I am."

"I know you must feel out of your element right now, Aislinn. I realize what shaded truths are told about us in the Rose Tower." He spread his hands. "I don't care how the Summer Queen rules her people. The Seelie, most of them anyway, are of no value to me. However, it does prove to make the misplaced Unseelie nervous when they first arrive. That's an inconvenience."

"Misplaced Unseelie?"

He motioned to her glass. "Please, drink, Aislinn. Relax. By misplaced Unseelie, I mean people like yourself. Unseelie born into the Rose Tower and raised to believe they are Seelie. Unseelie keeping the truth of their dark gifts a secret."

She choked on her sip of water and coughed. It was the first time she'd ever been referred to as out-and-out Unseelie.

"We're happy to have you, Aislinn. Your blood is esteemed within these walls." He paused and smiled wolfishly. "In fact, I could hardly wait to get you here."

She blinked. Her vision was going a little blurry. Maybe it was exhaustion and stress. "What do you mean?" She set her glass down and touched her forehead. A horrible pounding pain had started in her temple as well.

"And you came of your own accord to boot. That was a treat. I feared I'd have to send some unsavory characters to fetch you. Looks like Gabriel didn't fail after all. He just brought you here in a way that was unorthodox for him . . . through honesty, well, mostly, anyway, and without the use of sex."

Her head snapped up. "You sent Gabriel to lie to me and seduce me to your court?"

"Actually, I sent him to fuck you, addict you to him, and lure you here. He failed."

Shock surged through her veins. "Why?"

The Shadow King took a few steps toward her, his pale brows rising into his hairline. "Why?"

She gasped as pain shot through her stomach. She rolled off the couch, to her hands and knees on the soft plush of the carpet. Glancing up at her glass on the end table, she put two and two together.

*Danu*, he'd poisoned her drink. Her vision was fading to black.

The Shadow King leaned forward and bared his teeth. "Because the Unseelie blood running through your veins is mine . . . *daughter*."

# TWELVE

GABRIEL sat on a charmed iron bench in a charmed iron cell wearing charmed iron cuffs and nursing a raging headache from where Barthe had used his big, hard head to knock him unconscious. Even days later the memory—and the bruise—of that hit lingered. He was surprised it hadn't cracked his skull. The beatings he'd received from his captors once he'd come to in his cell would have killed a human. As it was, they had knocked him out again for over a day.

Iron sickness, an illness the fae contracted when exposed for long periods to charmed metal, had long since set in. He was sweaty, though his extremities were ice-cold and he couldn't stop shivering. He'd heal the injuries from the beatings slower with the sickness on him.

His magick was obliterated in all this metal. His powers as an incubus neutralized. Ordinarily those wouldn't help him here, but his jailer was female.

Oh, the irony.

He also had no way to call the sluagh from here. Instead,

he was wrapped in charmed iron, rendered magickally impotent and fearing for Aislinn.

It had been about a week.

When the Shadow King wanted something, he got it. It was only a question of time before they got to Aislinn and either convinced her to come to the Black Tower of her own free will or took her by force.

Somehow, Aislinn was the Shadow King's direct descendant —*his daughter*. Since Aodh had said that Aislinn was both a necromancer and his relative, that meant she had inherited the magickal abilities of his family's maternal line. That could only mean she was the granddaughter of Brigid Fada Erinne O'Dubhuir.

The Shadow King feared Aislinn's strength. She was the heir to the Unseelie Throne and the king knew he could never hold his seat against her if she decided she wanted it. The only way to ensure he kept his throne was to kill her. He needed to do it before Aislinn learned how to wield her significant power.

The door to the cell opened and the one person he wanted least to see walked within. "Gabriel."

Gabriel spit on the floor near the Shadow King's expensively shod foot, narrowly missing the crystal-knobbed fighting staff he used as a walking stick.

Silence.

"I'd appreciate it if you would leave so I can rot in peace," said Gabriel in his iron sickness–ruined voice without looking up.

The Shadow King's shoes stepped back and the royal paced to the opposite side of the tiny cell. "Come now, Gabriel. I don't want you here any more than you want to be here."

He lifted his gaze and cemented it on the Shadow King's eyes. "Harm Aislinn and I'll find a way to destroy you. Count on it."

"Yes, you've mentioned that before, though I fail to see how you'd be able to keep your word." His gaze strayed to the charmed iron. "I think we have the better of you."

"I'll find a way," Gabriel ground out.

"I did what I had to do. You, of all people, should understand that sometimes you have to do unsavory things to survive. I know all about your teenage years in the back alleys of Piefferburg."

Gabriel didn't hear anything but the tense the Shadow King spoke in. *I did what I had to do.* Past tense. Aislinn, *past tense.*

Gabriel was up and running at the Shadow King before he even realized he'd moved. The cuffs snapped his arms back when he reached the end of the chain, like a dog on a leash. "What did you do to her, Aodh? I swear to the gods if you hurt her, I will make you pay."

The Shadow King blinked innocently at him. "There we go with the empty threats again. Gabriel, as I said, I did what I had to do. It's as simple as that. Now, please, forgive me and let's allow this to flow under the bridge. I need you exactly where you are—leading the Wild Hunt. I'm sorry you became so attached to this woman. It was . . . unfortunate."

"This woman?" Gabriel roared. "She is *your daughter.* She is *your blood.*" He refused to use past tense when speaking of her. He pulled on his chains, making them clank. Every square inch of his body throbbed. "If I ever get out of here, I'll take you off that throne you love so much."

"I intend to keep my throne," the Shadow King barked. "The woman came to the Black of her own free will. I have you to thank for that. She never would have come if not for the part you played."

Gabriel closed his eyes against a swell of nausea. *Gods, no.*

The Shadow King sighed and turned toward the door. "I'll give you a week to come to your senses. Aeric is covering you at the moment, but if you still feel this way when I return, I'll have to make his temporary position permanent and you know what that means."

Gabriel seethed and stared at the closed door, his chest rising and falling rapidly in his rage. The rage was good, better than the despair and grief that nibbled on the edges of his mind. If he gave in to the despair and grief he truly would be helpless, but rage was a tool he could use. He'd learned that as a child and it was a lesson he'd never forgotten.

Aislinn was dead and it was his fault.

He'd trusted where he shouldn't have. That was a lesson he'd learned as a boy, too—never trust. Yet he'd trusted the Shadow King not to harm her. Stupid, foolish man. It was his fault Aislinn had met her end; his fault one of the brightest lights in Piefferburg was now extinguished.

That odd feeling that he'd identified as guilt was now completely eclipsed—drowned—in a sensation he hadn't felt since he was a child—grief. It was an open wound in the middle of him and would cause him pain for the rest of his life.

Which, blessedly, wouldn't be very long.

## DRIFTING.

The pain in his wrists kept Gabriel from sleeping at night, that and his failure to find a way to escape. His mouth was dry, his head pounded, and his body felt drained of energy constantly as a result of the charmed iron touching his skin.

Shifting on the thin mattress of his bed, he allowed his arms to dangle suspended above his head by the chain. They were asleep, but it didn't matter. The dangerous despair had nibbled its way in and settled into the center of his bones. It gathered at the back of his throat like a poisonous berry he couldn't quite swallow.

Aislinn was dead and there was no way things could ever go back to the way they had been before. It didn't matter that the iron sickness had leached into every pore of his body or that he couldn't even feel the trail of blood snaking its way down his arms from his wrists.

For most of the night he'd drowsed, slipping in and out of awareness, the scent of blood and unwashed body caught in his nostrils. It was toward the edge of dawn that he heard the scuffle in the corridor.

Raised voices, shouting.

He made no move to sit up. There was no way to do that

without extreme pain and, anyway, likely it was only a prisoner uprising of some sort. His eyelids drifted downward and he wished whoever it was well. May they cause the prison guards hell.

*Drifting.*

"Gabriel."

He forced his too-heavy eyelids open to find Aeric staring at him. Licking his dry lips, he stared back. This had to be a hallucination. He'd finally gone over the edge of his sanity. There was no way anyone could break into the prison. With the possible exception of Ronan or his brother Niall, but it was Aeric looking at him now.

"Get up, Gabriel. We're getting you out of here." Aeric grinned and dangled a key in front of his eyes.

Gabriel grimaced and closed his eyes again. "Go away."

He wanted to dream of sweet Aislinn of the silver blond hair and gray eyes, of the sweet curves he could explore at his leisure in this place while her sighs and murmurs filled his ears. In his dreams she was warm and alive, laughing and dancing. Happy and in love with him. In his dreams he'd done things differently and she'd survived the insane Shadow King. Bells tinkled here and contentment reigned. They were together.

He liked his dreams.

Above him, the hallucination of Aeric growled, his light Irish brogue suddenly thicker. "You're getting up if I have to rip your arms off. We're risking our lives to get you out of this hole. Don't give up on me, man, or I will kick your ass."

"We're?" He opened his eyes to view his host blearily. All of them had come. Melia stood behind Aeric, and Aelfdane was guarding the cell door. Ah, and there was Ronan standing near Bran. And was that Niall over there? Maybe this wasn't a hallucination after all.

Aeric yanked him to a sitting position and unlocked his cuffs. Gabriel grunted in discomfort. "You didn't think we were just going to leave you in here, did you? I don't aspire to lead the hunt, my friend. That's your job." He gave his head a sharp shake. "I don't want it."

Pain shot through his arms and into his hands as the blood rushed back through. He made fists and gritted his teeth. The ache was good; at least it was something other than the bitter numbness that had been ruling him.

"Aislinn," he pushed out. "The Shadow King killed her and it's my fault. Just leave me here."

"She's still alive," said Ronan. "He's holding her in the dungeon."

Relief rushed through him so hard and so fast it made him light-headed. If Aislinn was still alive, there was a chance he could get to her, get her out of this mess, and make up for the wrongs he'd done her.

He had many more questions, but they'd have to wait. He couldn't help her if he was still locked up in here. Gabriel stood, listed to the side, but caught himself before he collapsed. "Let's get the fuck out of here."

"That's the Gabriel I know and love." Aeric went for the door, casting a grin over his shoulder. "Purely platonically, of course."

"You're not my type, either, sunshine," Gabriel rasped back at him.

He took a step forward and his knees almost buckled. The charmed iron on his skin had affected him badly.

"Whoa, big guy," said Ronan, catching and supporting him on one side while Bran got the other side.

He speared Ronan with his gaze. "You and Bella are sworn to secrecy with the knowledge I am Lord of the Wild Hunt and these fae are my host. Got it?"

Ronan nodded once tersely. "Now let's get out of here before they realize what's going on."

They all followed Aeric and Aelfdane out of the cell. The hallway was empty save for one fallen guard dressed in the gleaming silver and black armor of the Shadow Guard. Whether the man was dead or unconscious, Gabriel wasn't sure. They made their way down the corridor, finding more prone and bloody bodies. Aeric and the others had clearly made quick and clean work of them, but it was hardly surprising. The lot of them had a host of magickal defenses—and offenses—to use.

They managed to make their way out of the corridor and past the main doors of the prison before the alarm triggered. The alarm was silent, but magickal. It shivered through the molecules of their bodies as they ran down the hallway. Just as they turned a corner, additional guards spilled into the corridor, yelling and drawing their swords.

They turned back, only to see a horde of goblins rounding the opposite corner.

"Oh, fuck, we're trapped." Aeric had a firm hold on the obvious.

Gabriel listed to the side, caught himself against the wall, and cursed out loud in English and Old Maejian both. His fingers itched for a weapon. "We fight through them. It's our only chance."

And then they had no choice.

Gabriel targeted one of the Shadow Guard right off, coveting both a weapon and an immediate dissolution of the iron sickness. Summoning strength and balance from parts unknown, he rode a sudden adrenaline rush into battle. Grabbing the man's sword, he leveraged his superior upper-body strength and slammed the man into a nearby wall. Weapon in hand, he turned and met the next comer, as chaos exploded in the middle of the corridor.

He, his host, Niall, and Ronan fought back to back, battling their way through the ranks of the Shadow Guard and the goblins with a resolve their opponents lacked. That resolve made them stronger. They slashed with their swords, while the mages and Melia all uttered low spells in Old Maejian to make their blades land true and turn the tide of the fight in their favor.

When the last of the goblins had fallen and the Shadow Guard was long since done for, they ran for the tower stairs, knowing reinforcements were on the way. They went down the spiral stone staircase that would let them out into Piefferburg Square if they followed it all the way.

Gabriel stopped on a landing, his tortured and magick-muddled thought processes finally clearing up a little. He dropped his bloody sword to the stone floor with a clatter. "No! I can't leave the Black Tower. Not when Aislinn is still here and alive."

Aeric and Bran rounded on him, slack jawed.

"The whole Shadow Guard is after you," Melia said in her soft, dulcet voice, bright red hair tangled around her shoulders from their flight, blood marking her cheeks and clothes. "The king will call down the goblin army on your head. You *must* leave the Black Tower if you want to live to fight another day, Gabriel. We'll figure out the rest later."

*"No."* The word echoed up through the stairwell. He swayed against the cold, uneven rock wall and shook his head to try to get rid of the fuzziness. The adrenaline-fueled battle fury that had so recently filled him was waning fast, the iron sickness taking hold once again. "I won't leave without her." He paused and shook his head again. "I won't live without her."

Aeric leaned into his face, his dark brown eyes narrowing. "Who are you and what have you done with Gabriel Cionaodh Marcus Mac Braire?"

"No, he's right," Ronan said. "If he leaves the Black Tower he'll never get back in to help Aislinn, and that's what you want to do, isn't it?"

Gabriel blinked at the two Ronans in front of him, trying to get them to merge into one. "Yeah. It's the only thing that matters."

Melia rolled her eyes. "Fine, but I think you're an idiot, Gabriel. Just for the record." She turned and headed down the stairs. "Come with me."

"Where are we going?" Gabriel had big plans about rescuing Aislinn, but at the moment he wasn't sure how many more actual steps he could take without collapsing.

Aelfdane pulled him away from the wall. "She helped design and construct this tower. Of any of us, she knows best where to go right now."

Together they made their way down two more flights. On that landing, Melia touched something on the back of one of the craggy Unseelie statues in an alcove and part of the wall moved in and to the side, revealing a passageway.

None too soon, either, for above echoed the sound of the guards' boots on the stairs and shouting.

Once the wall closed behind them, blackness fisted them in the narrow tunnel. Bran uttered a spell in Old Maejian and light sparked to life around them. They were on a tiny landing with stairs leading up and down. Melia began to climb up and everyone followed. Gabriel hated going in the opposite direction of the dungeons. Every fiber of his body strained to go downward instead of upward.

Sense won out. He needed to go to ground right now and give himself some time, as little as possible, to regain his strength. Being wrapped in charmed iron for almost two weeks with nearly no food and water had almost killed him. Another couple of days like that and his life would surely have come to an end. He needed to be strong for Aislinn. If he went in now, impulsively, the way his body, heart, and mind were straining to do, all would be lost. He couldn't count on adrenaline and his willpower driving him any further. Physically, he was tapped out. He would die and so would she.

For once he had to be smart. For once he was going to have to trust others. He hated that. Even if it was his host with whom he was entrusting Aislinn's life. He would trust his own life to them, but not Aislinn's. No one was good enough to be trusted with her life.

Least of all, him.

Poor woman, he was all she had.

His muscles protesting every movement, he swayed now and again against the rough, cold walls on either side of him. Every step up was a battle, but he pushed past the iron sickness lingering in his body and forced himself up the stairs. Once in a while he felt Aelfdane and Aeric shove him forward a little, or brace him from falling.

Eventually they came to another small landing, this one with a wooden door. Bran's light revealed intricate spiderwebs covering it. Melia pushed it open. With a whine of unoiled hinges and long disuse, the opening revealed a large room with a fireplace, a cot, and some boxes.

Home, sweet home for the time being.

Gabriel took one step into the room and collapsed.

# THIRTEEN

AISLINN shifted restlessly on the slab she lay on, the fabric of her shift rasping against her skin. Charmed iron chains snaked their way over her body, holding her in place.

It was cold.

She could feel the chill of this place, wherever she was, right down to the center of her stomach. For the first couple of days all she'd done was shiver. Now she was too weak to shiver. She lacked the energy to do anything at all, not eat, not drink. She didn't even have enough energy to be terrified like any sane person. And maybe that meant she wasn't anymore . . . sane, that was.

In her iron sickness–laced haze all she could do was sleep, wake up, shift a little, and sleep again. Sometimes she heard voices talking low around her. Once in a while, in the distance, she could hear screaming or moaning. She wasn't always sure it wasn't herself screaming and moaning, but a careful analysis had rendered her almost certain the noises came from outside her head. Knowing she was not alone in her misery was an odd comfort. One she didn't want to examine too closely.

Thus her prophetic dream was realized.

There were no grabbing, pulling hands. No silver pool of a place between life and death. Maybe that was still coming. But surely she was going to die in this place, just as her dream had said she would.

And Gabriel had led her to it.

The voices around her had yielded a few clues to her predicament. She was in possession of four interesting facts. One, she was actually the Shadow King's daughter, gotten off her full-blooded Seelie Tuatha Dé mother in an illicit liaison. Two, Gabriel had been planted in the Rose Tower to lure her over to the dark side of her own free will. He'd done his job well. Was he laughing somewhere in the Black Tower now as a result of her demise? Three, the Shadow King meant to kill her. Four, the Shadow King didn't merely mean to kill her, he meant to obliterate her very soul—dismember it magickally and cast it to the four winds.

That was the holdup. That was why she wasn't dead yet.

Apparently she was, indeed, a powerful necromancer.

Apparently she was her father's daughter. The thought caused a burst of bitter laughter to rise in her throat like bile. It burned, made her smile. Then she rolled to the side and dry-heaved onto the slab.

Being a powerful necromancer would give her the ability to return from the dead and haunt the Shadow King for the rest of his immortal life. A thing that, if she knew how to do it, she most certainly would. That was why he was seeking for magickal ways to obliterate her soul.

Of course, she didn't have the first clue how to do anything as a necromancer, most certainly not how to return from the dead and haunt someone. For that matter, before now she'd meant the Shadow King no harm at all. She couldn't think of the first reason why he would want her dead. Did he think she was a threat to his throne?

She didn't want his throne. If she ever saw his throne, she would spit on it. But, then again, she never would see it. Never get a chance to spit on it. Instead she'd be dead, her soul obliterated.

* * *

IT was time.

A few hours of rest and a little food and water had made Gabriel feel a million times better.

While he'd rested, Ronan had chanted at him in Old Maejian and blown some bitter-smelling something in his face to prevent magickal tracking spells from gaining a grip. According to the mage, since Ronan and Bella's flight through the city evading the Imperial Guard, Ronan had been working nonstop on a powerful countermeasure to block tracking spells. Now Gabriel was tracking spell–proof. Aislinn would be, too, with Ronan's aid.

Ronan, Aelfdane, Niall, and Aeric remained with him. Bran and Melia had left an hour earlier to scout for him. He pushed up into a sitting position and paused, nearly retching.

Okay, maybe he only felt one or two times better, not a million.

It would have to be enough. He couldn't let any more time go by allowing Aislinn to be kept in the dungeon while the Shadow King's minions did the gods only knew what to her. He pushed up again, this time all the way to a standing position.

Across the room, Aeric, leaning against a wall, clapped. "Yes, I can see you're certainly in a condition to mount a rescue from the depths of the dungeons of the Black Tower. Shall I call down now and tell them you're coming or do you want to surprise them?"

Gabriel growled at him. His knees buckled and he caught himself with a palm to the wall before he could fall back onto the cot he'd been resting on. "I have no choice. It's a miracle she's still alive now. Who knows if she'll be breathing an hour from now?"

Aelfdane regarded him with cool blue eyes in the light of the myriad candles that lit the bare room. "Why do you care so much?"

Gabriel closed his eyes and leaned his head against the wall. "I care because I'm responsible for her situation. I told her to come to the Unseelie. Without my persuasion, she never would have defected from the Rose." He opened his eyes and found Ronan's gaze. "I told her she'd be safe here." He swallowed hard. "It's my responsibility to make this right."

Ronan shook his head at him. "It's partially guilt. I believe you on that score, Gabriel. But it's more than that, too. You love Aislinn, don't you?"

"Gabriel?" Aeric snorted. "Gabriel in love?"

"Why does that sound so impossible?" Gabriel challenged, leveling his gaze at his oldest friend. His voice came out a low, tortured rasp from the iron sickness.

"It sounds impossible because I've known you for two hundred years and your brand of caring for a woman extends only until after the bedding, maybe until sunrise if she's pretty enough."

"I know love when I see it," answered Ronan, a small smile playing on his mouth. "You may have duped her, but in the process you fell for her, too."

He wasn't sure what the knot of emotion in his stomach was exactly. Was it love? How could he know what love felt like when he hadn't loved anyone—not really, truly, and deeply—since his mother had died? That had been some 358 years ago. Even for a Sídhe, that was a long time.

Guilt, that was a new emotion. Now he knew what that felt like—*shit*. Guilt was definitely there in the knot, mixed up with other strange urges and desires—yearnings, really. For the scent of Aislinn's hair and the sensation of her skin against his. For the sound of her voice in his ear, whispering, laughing, arguing. Whatever. He just yearned for her presence. Needed it.

The Shadow King couldn't have her.

Aislinn was his to save, his to protect. His to kiss and talk to and tuck under the sheets and blankets of his bed. The thought of her gray eyes cold and dead, the idea that her voice might be silenced, her skin bloody and bruised—no.

The thought of having to collect her soul one night and help her to the other side—out of his life forever. They were not images and thoughts he could hold in his mind's eye and still hope to remain sane.

"I'm not going to stand around and debate my capacity for love with any of you," he snarled, pushing away from the wall. "I'm going to collect my woman, rub the king's nose in his shit, and get out of here."

"Oh, yeah, he's in love, all right. You're right, Ronan," snorted Aelfdane.

Gabriel stepped into the center of the small room and swung his head around to stab Aelfdane with a heavy stare of warning. "Does anyone know why the king is taking so long to kill her?"

"The only thing I know from one of the dungeon guards, who is a friend of mine," said Aeric, "is that the woman has been chained down there for almost a week, in charmed iron, while they debate methods to take her life."

"Debate methods to take her life?" echoed Aelfdane. "Why should it matter? Dead is dead."

"They don't just want to kill her. They want to destroy her soul, so that there's not even enough left for the Wild Hunt to collect. Destroy it so thoroughly that none of her remains, nothing to pass over to the Netherworld. It's a fate no fae should have to endure. Worse, even, than the death itself. He's denying her the afterlife and killing her soul."

"Why do they want to do that to her?" Aelfdane's voice came out bewildered. "What possible threat could she be to him that he would want to destroy her very soul?"

Aeric shrugged. "That's all he knows. The woman lives for as long as they take to find a way to completely destroy her. The Shadow King is very afraid of her."

"I know why," Gabriel ground out. He pushed a hand through his hair and told them what he knew about Aislinn, her bloodline and her necromancy. "Necromancers can come back from the Netherworld at will and harass their murderers. You can be sure that Brigid Fada Erinne O'Dubhuir, his mother, haunted him. That's probably how he learned the lesson."

The entire room went into a shocked silence once Gabriel was done speaking.

"Are you saying that Aodh murdered his own mother?" asked Aelfdane, finally.

"That's exactly what I'm saying," Gabriel answered.

The door opened with a whine and all the men in the room stiffened and readied themselves for what might come through it. It was only Melia and Bran.

Melia nodded at Gabriel and went to stand next to her man. "Nice to see you up. Feeling better?"

"Never mind that. What did you hear?" He staggered for the door and congratulated himself silently when he made it.

"You're welcome, Gabe. I love to stick my neck out for you and hope it doesn't get lopped from my shoulders."

Gabriel closed his eyes for a moment. "I appreciate all you have done for me, all of you, more than I can say and even more than I can ever repay. Thank you."

"Gabriel says thank you and nearly admits he's fallen in love all in one day. I think the world may be coming to an end," Aeric said.

Bran ignored them all. "We have good news. We spent the last hour spreading a rumor that you were seen fleeing through Piefferburg Square into the *ceantar dubh*. About twenty minutes ago a large dispatch of the Shadow Guard was sighted dispersing into that district of the city. I think the ruse worked. The king may now believe that you've left the Black Tower and are running for your life, leaving the woman behind."

"He's got no reason to think you'd stay for her. It's not exactly in your character," Melia interjected.

"True, such selfless behavior would hardly be expected from you. That impression is working in your favor right now," Bran responded.

Gabriel growled at them both.

Melia's voice lowered. "But there's bad news, too."

He stiffened. "Tell me."

"According to Aeric's friend, they've found a way to work the magick that will disperse her soul for eternity. Your time is limited."

He lurched for the door, fueled on a sudden burst of adrenaline.

Aeric stopped him with a hand to his chest. "You're not going anywhere without us."

"No." Gabriel shook his head. "Thank you, my friend, but I need to do this alone. Anyway, you and the rest of the host have to stay and lead the Wild Hunt in my absence. I can't risk you all being killed."

"You need a plan," Ronan said, coming up on his side.

"I have a plan," Gabriel snarled, picking up his bloody sword, which someone had propped by the door. "Go in, slaughter everyone, and take Aislinn out of there."

Ronan gave his head a sharp shake. "Not a good plan. Know any spells?"

He looked at Ronan. "My magick is innate: sex and death. I'm not a mage like you or Niall."

"You can still do some rudimentary spell casting. I've already set a spell to prevent tracking on you, but Aislinn will need one, too." He tucked a small bag and a slip of paper into Gabriel's pocket. "I have one more thing for you, and I think you'll like it. Once you get to the dungeon, say these words: *Tae soelle en bailian. Soot mael hai illium.* I've set everything else in place for you down there. It will help, you'll see."

Ronan said the spell in Old Maejian three times, making Gabriel repeat it until he'd memorized all the words.

"Okay, now you're as prepared as you can be." Ronan shook his head. "Aislinn is my wife's dearest friend and you're her only hope. We'll do all we can to help you. If you need to contact us, use this." He pressed a small disk into his hand. "Wet it and hold it up to the wind. Niall and I will know where to find you."

"Good luck," said Melia, going up onto her tiptoes and laying a kiss on his cheek. There were tears in her eyes. "Gods willing, you'll come back to us someday."

Aeric embraced him and clapped him on the back. "If you need me, call. You know how. Until then I'll keep the Wild Hunt for you."

"Thank you, my friend."

Then he lunged out the door and almost fell down the stairs. Gods help him and especially Aislinn. He was an unlikely hero and she deserved better.

He made his way down the narrow stairwell, into the bowels of the Black Tower. One of the benefits of being such an old fae was that he'd been a child when Piefferburg had been created and he'd lived in the Black Tower since he was eighteen years old. That meant he knew it well and could orient himself even in this secret space by glancing out the arrow-thin slits in the rock wall and glimpsing parts of the city beyond. He was in the northern section of the keep and if he kept making his way downward, eventually he would come upon the back entrance to the dungeons, exactly where he needed to be.

Finally, a little bit of luck.

Soon the slits became nonexistent, as did the meager bit of light. Rats scurried in the darkness, along with the scrape of claws of other even less savory fae creatures. He reached out his hands on either side, letting his fingers scrape the cold, naked rock, and stepped slowly down the stairs in the pitch blackness. It wouldn't help Aislinn if he tripped now, broke his 365-year-old neck, and was gnawed to the bone by the tiny gruesome monsters that lived here.

Finding one of the trip switches on the final landing that Melia had told him about, he pulled it and part of the wall opened. The light blinded him for a moment. When his pupils adjusted it was to find two astonished silver and black–clad Shadow Guards staring at him.

Gabriel reached out, grabbed them both by the shoulder, and slammed their heads together. They collapsed to the ground and Gabriel stepped over their bodies, feeling pretty pleased with himself . . . only to find twenty more Shadow Guards staring at him.

AISLINN lay on her side, gasping shallowly. Her eyes were wide open and unblinking as she watched water rivulets on the uneven stone wall seven feet from her face. It might be the last thing she ever saw. This scent of must, old blood, and sweat would probably be the last odors she ever smelled. Too bad it couldn't be something nice like cinnamon or honey.

The black mages had been swirling around her like a murder of crows all day, muttering to themselves. Their activity had taken on an urgency today that hadn't been there before. Something had happened. Perhaps they'd found a solution to their problem—a way to destroy her soul.

Aislinn was looking forward to an end to her misery, though a part of her still screamed for life. It was a tiny voice now, buried under the scrape of the charmed iron along her ice-cold skin, the rough rock of the slab she lay on, and the relentless battery of pain in her head and in her limbs.

Images from her childhood passed through her mind now and again, as if her subconscious was reviewing and releasing memories before she kicked off into eternal black. Not the Netherworld. She was being denied even that much.

She could see her father in her mind's eye—her real one— throwing light blue and pink balls of illusion into the air on her seventh birthday. Now she remembered the low, harsh conversations her parents used to have in the kitchen or behind their closed bedroom door. Had her father known she didn't carry his DNA? Had they been arguing about her mother's unfaithfulness? Aislinn would never know. So many questions would die with her today.

Perhaps that was the bitterest of all to swallow.

Sounds of battle met Aislinn's ear. It was far off, at the other end of the dank basement. A prisoner uprising, perhaps. They happened from time to time. Although this one seemed to give her captors pause. The crowlike mages paused in their muttering and their dark spell stirring. Their hooded heads bobbed up, faces turned toward the sound of yelling.

Somewhere in the distance, a man bellowed strange words in Old Maejian.

*"Tae soelle en bailian! Soot mael hai illium!"*

The words of power were laced with a spell. They tightened like a noose around her throat. Her eyes popped open even wider and she gasped. Terrified, she fought it, her body convulsing on the slab beneath her.

*Oh, Danu, not yet! I'm not ready yet!*

The mages stiffened, panicked, and yelled spell-strung words back into the dungeon, but it was too late for counter-measures. Even in her iron-sick delirium she knew that. Whoever it was, he'd taken the mages unawares. One by one, clutching the invisible threads around their throats, they dropped to the dirty floor of the dungeon.

She alone remained alive. Magick warred over her body, but the tendrils of the first spell were stuck tight around her neck, constricting harder and harder. Her will to live flared to brilliant life and she dredged up every tiny morsel of power she didn't know she had to fight.

*His* face appeared before her. His treacherous, lying lips formed her name but she couldn't hear anything but the rush of death loud in her ears. How unfair that *his* face would be the last one she ever saw.

Perfect, all-consuming rage was the last emotion she felt before every light inside her went out.

# FOURTEEN

GABRIEL collapsed against a far wall and slumped to the floor, hand tangling in his long, unwashed hair. She lay on the bed, moonlight slanting across her body and bleaching her hair even paler than its natural color.

The spell Ronan had given him had put all the occupants of the dungeon to sleep. The mage had laid the preparations beforehand somehow and given Gabriel the words to activate it. He'd even caught the Shadow King's personal mages before they'd had time to mount countermeasures. Unfortunately, the spell had also put Aislinn to sleep.

Maybe it was better that way. The look on her face when she'd seen him had not been a friendly one. That, coupled with the delirium of the iron sickness, probably would've had her fighting his rescue if she'd been conscious. He imagined she believed everything he'd said and done in the Rose had been a lie. He couldn't blame her for thinking that. He had lied to her. He had intended to do her wrong. At least, at first.

Not knowing how long everyone would stay asleep and not knowing when someone unaffected by the spell might enter the dungeon and raise an alarm, he'd ripped off the charmed iron chains as soon as he'd found a key and scooped her into his arms. Her body had been featherlight from almost a week of neglect and abuse. She'd been so cold it had given him pause—made him wonder for a moment if it was death and not sleep that she'd slipped into.

Getting out of the Black Tower hadn't been a picnic. He'd blown the antitracking spell into Aislinn's face and said the words to trigger it first thing, then kept to the shadows, walked on cat paws, held his breath, and asked the gods and the goddess Danu to see them through.

Once out, he'd taken them to a safe place, far from the Black Tower. He'd traveled on foot, walking in the alleys and the shadows, thankful that it was the dead of morning and almost no one but the guard had been out. Now he was exhausted, pushed way past what his iron-sick body could handle. His arms burned from carrying her because even though she was light and he was strong, he'd traveled a long way with no rest. The only thing that had kept him on his feet and moving was his will.

Now he could draw a breath. Now he could rest. They were safe, at least for the time being.

With his gaze, he traced her body in the moonlight. He'd covered her with as many blankets as he could find. Her dirty, tangled-silver blond hair hung over the side of the mattress, trailing onto the floor. Her face was still as a statue's, the light illuminating her dirt-smeared face. Despite the filth on her and the stress of her time in the dungeon, she looked peaceful, as though she could sense on some level that she was safe.

As safe as one could be when hunted by the most powerful man in all of Piefferburg and every last member of his Shadow Guard and the goblin army.

But he wasn't ready to think about that yet. Instead, he leaned his head back against the wall and closed his eyes.

AISLINN woke slowly, wrapped in warmth and softness. After a moment of disorientation, the memories came flooding back along with the ache and the iron sickness. She blinked, coming more fully awake, and her gaze focused on a large cream-colored spill of sunlight in the center of a ceiling with crown molding. This was not a dungeon. She pushed up, wincing in pain, and the blankets fell down around her waist. Expensive, soft blankets.

Gazing around at the room, she blinked again. The shaft of sunlight glinted in from an opening in the teal-colored curtains covering a huge window overlooking a wooded area.

No, this was definitely not the dungeon. *This* room was fit for the Rose Tower.

The modern and low bed she lay on sat in the center of a large bedroom. Floor-to-ceiling windows, all mostly covered with curtains, lined the walls. A doorway led to what appeared to be a spacious walk-in closet. Another doorway led to a bathroom. Her flesh itched at the possibility of a shower. A creek-stone fireplace took up most the wall across from the bed. The floor was wood, polished to a high shine and covered with throw rugs here and there. Modern furniture that matched the bed decorated the room. Everything was done in soothing shades of green.

And Gabriel Cionaodh Marcus Mac Braire was leaning against a wall, fast asleep.

Snarling, she lunged from the bed toward him, immediately collapsing to the floor. In its iron-sickened state, her body wouldn't cooperate with her heart's fondest wish that she make it across the room and strangle him for lying to her, duping her, and—almost—breaking her heart.

His eyes opened slowly, blearily focusing on her where she lay five feet in front of him.

Forcing herself up, she closed the distance between them and leapt on him. *"You,"* she rasped in her ruined voice. "You! You knew the Shadow King meant to kill me and you tried to lure me right into his arms." She snorted. "You did a great job, Gabriel. I fell for all your lies."

He forced her to the floor, where she kicked and flailed at him with all the energy she had—not much—and pinned her wrists to the floor on either side of her head. His gaze locked and held hers and for the first time she moved past her rage and saw him—*really* saw him. He was as dirty as she was, bruised, and he'd lost weight. He smelled like she did, too— like he'd been stuck in a dungeon, abused.

"I'm sorry. I didn't know he wanted to kill you," Gabriel said in a voice as raspy as hers. "I swear it. Please forgive me."

She went still, looking questioningly up into his eyes. "What do you mean you didn't know? You came to the Rose Tower knowing everything, knowing I was truly the Shadow King's bastard daughter and that he needed me to come to him of his own free will so he wouldn't violate the agreement he had with the Summer Queen. You knew!" She yelled the last two words at him. "You deceived me and lied to me, knowing the Shadow King planned to obliterate every single remnant of my being down to my soul! You knew all of it!"

He swore in Old Maejian, let her wrists free, and backed away. Hitting the wall, he slumped down and pushed a hand through his dirty, tangled hair. "I didn't know, Aislinn. Not all of it. I only knew my orders were to seduce you to the Black Tower. I never thought he meant to harm you."

She sat up. "Oh, so you only duped and lied to me to seduce me into reorganizing my entire life. When I arrived at the Black Tower chasing your fake love—*as you tried to get me to do*—what would you have told me? Get lost? My job is done? Okay, that's so much better."

He shook his head. "I'm sorry for what I did, Aislinn, but don't make the mistake of thinking I don't care about you."

"Care? About me?" She spat the words and leaned forward. "That would infer you are capable of feeling, incubus. I know you aren't."

He sighed and let his head fall back to rest against the wall.

Her gaze shifted from his gray face down his body. He wore no shirt, no shoes, only a loose pair of ripped black trousers. Dried, rust-colored blood marked him from head to toe. He was even filthier than she was and bore the telltale traces of iron sickness. It gave her pause. "What happened to you?"

He gave a bark of raw, mirthless laughter. "Once I found out that the Shadow King meant you harm, I objected. He threw me in the prison to break my will—or just to get me out of the way, maybe. My ho—friends broke me out and I, in turn, broke you from the dungeon. Remember? You saw my face right before Ronan's spell put you to sleep."

She fell silent. Yes, she remembered seeing his face, hearing the magick-laced spell. Swallowing hard, she struggled for a hold on her emotions. "Thank you for getting me out of there."

He said nothing, only continued to rest his head against the wall, his eyes closed. Finally he said, "Don't thank me, Aislinn. I was only righting a wrong I put in motion."

"Where are we?"

He tipped his head forward to look at her. "We're at the very edge of the *ceantar láir*, backed up to the Boundary Lands. The person who owned this house died recently and left no heirs. It belongs to the city of Piefferburg now. We should be undisturbed here for a while."

"We're in a dead person's house?"

He nodded. "We're in a dead person's house, thankful we aren't dead ourselves and planning ways to stay that way for the foreseeable future, yes?" He paused and swallowed, throat working. His pupils darkened a degree. "So, you're the Shadow King's daughter." It wasn't a question.

She nodded. "Apparently."

"Gods."

"Don't tell me you didn't know."

"I didn't know. He told me you were a long-lost relative. I didn't put it all together until I met him that day, when I'd returned to the Black after turning down the Summer Queen's invitation."

She rolled her eyes.

"It's true, Aislinn. I swear it." He swore again. "You look nothing like him except for the color of your hair."

"Why did he want to kill me? Does he consider me a—"

"Threat. Yes. I now know he's the one who killed his mother, your grandmother. Remember the story I told you about Brigid?" She nodded. "It wasn't her consort who killed her, it was her son. Aodh wanted her throne and wasn't willing to wait. Now he's paranoid that you'll try for his throne."

"He didn't just want to kill me. He wanted to destroy every single fiber of my being. Murder was not enough for him."

Gabriel nodded. "Because you're a necromancer."

"He didn't want me bugging him after he killed me." She snorted.

"I'm sure your grandmother is an ever-constant weight on his conscience."

"That man has no conscience."

"The Shadow King is fucking scared of you, Aislinn. You're the heir to the Unseelie Throne by right." He gave her a cold smile. "He should be afraid because you're powerful."

"I'm not." She shook her head. "I can't—" An agonized sound escaped her throat. "I'm *not* powerful, Gabriel. I'm a fluffy bit of Seelie Sídhe. That's all."

He moved so fast he made her jump. Grasping her chin in his hand, he forced her to look up at him. "You are a necromancer, Aislinn, and I am Lord of the Wild Hunt. We're a good fit, don't you think? Together we make one hell of a powerful team. And we better make a powerful team because we both have made the strongest of all possible enemies."

She sucked in a breath. "You're the Lord of the Wild Hunt?" It made sense now, the house he'd chosen. Of course he'd known of a recently "vacated" place to take her where she'd be safe. She ripped her hands from his and pushed away from him. "Do you have any other revelations to tell me?"

He had her flat on her back and pinned beneath him in less than a second. "I might have a few," he growled into her face.

"Get off me!"

"Not until you understand a couple of fundamental things. One, you're stuck with me, *princess*. Two, we better find a way to get along because the Shadow King wants you dead." He bared his teeth at her. "And that will happen only over my own lifeless body."

Aislinn went still, staring up at him. His gaze moved from her eyes to her lips and remained there. For a wild moment she wondered if he was going to kiss her. Then she wondered what she would do if he tried. After all, he'd misled her, lied to her, tried his best to seduce her to the Black Tower. But then he'd rescued her from the dungeons and vowed to sacrifice his life for hers. She wasn't quite sure how to feel about him at the moment. Gabriel was a living, breathing paradox.

His gaze skated downward and she became painfully aware of her clothing, or lack of. She was barefoot and dressed in a filmy, light shift that showed the press of her nipples and the curve of her breasts through the fabric. His eyes let her know that he saw all of that, too—and appreciated it.

Her heart thumped fast and her blood roared through her head as she fought her body's reaction to him. Her emotions might be in a tumult and her mind might want very much to be angry with him, but her body wanted him. There was no question of that.

Apparently he wanted her, too.

He gazed for another long moment at her lips, then pushed away from her and allowed her to sit up. He rocked back on his heels. "This house backs up to the Boundary Lands. There are woods on either side of us. We won't be disturbed by neighbors. I'm packing two bags with clothes, supplies, and weapons and putting them in easy reach in case we need to run. All right?"

She nodded.

"When you're more stable on your feet, I'll show you all the exits." He gestured toward the bathroom. "Take a shower. There's clothing in the drawers in here that I think will fit you. I'll fix us something to eat. I know you have to be as hungry as I am."

He did look hungry—lean, hungry, battered, and tired. If he was to be believed that was a result of his defense of her.

Her rage at him eased. He'd done her wrong, but he was doing his best to make it better. He could have just walked away.

She sat up and watched him warily.

He stood and nodded at her. "Are we agreed?"

"For now."

"I'll take that." He walked out of the room, leaving her with her thoughts.


AISLINN didn't care that she was squatting in a dead man's house and using a dead man's shower. All she cared about was the hot pounding of water on her back and how it eased the tension in her muscles and chased away the deep chill that had settled in the center of her bones. All she cared about was the slick tangle of her hair over her shoulders, now squeaky clean from rigorous shampooing.

In the cabinet below the sink she'd found small green boxes filled with palm-sized bars of scented soap. She used one of these soaps to lather her skin, rinse, repeat—washing away the stink of the dungeon, the smears of grime, the cling of dark magick, and the taint of dying things. She took it one step further, using a brand-new loofah she'd also found under the counter to exfoliate away an entire layer of gray, dead skin to reveal soft pink flesh beneath.

It was like being reborn.

After the water turned cold, she shut it off and got out, wrapping herself in a huge fluffy towel. The man who'd owned this place had enjoyed the finer things in life even though he'd been troop.

The scent of food being prepared wafted to her nose and nearly made her double over with hunger. At some point the empty gnawing sensation in her stomach had become integrated with her being—just another part of her existence, like pain or the promise of death. She nearly dropped the towel and ran to the kitchen to find the source of the smell . . . then she remembered who was preparing the meal.

She wiped her hand across the steamed-up mirror. Dark

smudges of exhaustion marked her under-eye areas. Her cheekbones were a bit more prominent than they'd been a week ago and her eyes held a hardness that hadn't been there before. The hardness was a thing to cultivate, to mold into something useful. She would need an edge, that bit of hardness, in order to go up against the Shadow King. The thought was terrifying, but if she wanted to live—and she did—that was exactly what she'd have to do.

The last week had changed her forever. Time would tell whether that change was for the good or for the bad.

After slathering some expensive and luscious lotion on her skin, drying her hair, and finding a pair of thin, soft jersey pants, a fluffy pair of white socks, and a white turtleneck sweater, she felt a bit more like herself. The week she'd spent in hellish limbo still clung to her mind and she couldn't shake it. It seemed like she'd been in that dungeon five years, not five days, but now, at least, she could remember a bit of the person she'd been before she'd made the decision to go to the Black Tower.

She'd feel even better once she got some food in her mouth. She could no longer avoid the ache in her stomach and needed to eat, even if it meant having to face the man in the kitchen. Touching walls and furniture to keep herself steady on her feet, she made her way to him.

He was standing at the stove, pushing something around in a pan with a wooden spoon. It smelled of perfectly roasted chicken and it made her mouth water. He'd taken a shower, too, and was dressed in a pair of loose black pants, no shoes and no shirt. His dark hair hung in damp tangled skeins down his back. For a wild moment her fingers curled to touch it, to take a comb and carefully untwist and untangle every last one.

She fisted her hands at her sides.

He turned at the sound of her feet on the tile and motioned at the round kitchen table that sat in a nearby alcove. A bay window looked out upon more trees. "Sit down. I'll give you a real meal. If they treated you like they treated me, you want one pretty bad. I've only had moldy bread and tepid water for the last week."

Yes, they'd only given her enough to make sure she didn't die before they could figure out a way to shred her soul.

She went to the table and sat, staring out the window at the edge of the Boundary Lands. She'd never seen them before. She'd never been very far from Piefferburg Square, truth be told. "How do you know they won't find us here?" she asked without looking at him.

He walked over and set a plate heaped with steaming chicken on a bed of rice and doused in some sort of sauce, roasted vegetables on the side. "I'm betting a lot on Ronan Quinn." He got his own plate and sat down next to her. He said a couple more things that she couldn't hear because her mouth was full of food and everything in her world was now focused on that event alone.

The flavors exploded against her taste buds. Never in her life had she tasted anything so fine. It was hot and filled with satisfying, nutritious goodness and her body absorbed it all like a drop of water in the desert. After five mouthfuls she could function again. She took a long drink of cold, pure water, closing her eyes and stifling a moan of pleasure.

"Ronan Quinn?" she finally asked.

"He gave me a spell that will prevent tracking. Said that he'd perfected one, a spell that is nearly impossible for any other mage to find a countermeasure for. I don't think they'll look for us here, in this house, since as the Lord of the Hunt I'm one of the few who even knows the former tenant has passed on. I wouldn't have brought you here if I didn't think it was safe. You can rest easy for now. You and I both have to recuperate from the iron sickness."

Yes, she could still feel the toll it had taken on her. She lacked energy and her muscles ached all of the time.

He took a bite, chewed, and swallowed. "Before we have to do what we have to do."

She pushed a bite of chicken around on her plate. "And what's that, do you think?" But of course she already knew.

"We live in a bubble here in Piefferburg. It's not like we can run off to Singapore. If we want to live, we have to confront that which doesn't want us to live."

"The Shadow King and the armies he commands."

He nodded and took another bite. Gesturing with his fork, he spoke around his mouthful. "So eat up. You're going to need your strength."

She slowly released the breath she'd been holding. "You really think we have any kind of a shot at defeating him?"

He grinned at her and winked. "I think we have no choice but to try."

"Try and die."

"Maybe. Probably."

"You're not cheering me up."

He stood and took his empty plate to the sink. She finished up her food in silence while he leaned against a counter and watched her. Crossing his arms over his chest, he said, "I'm a realist."

Yes, he was also a liar.

When she was done eating, she pushed her plate away and savored the feel of a full belly and a warm, clean body. The shower and food had done wonders.

Wiggling her toes in her soft socks, she sighed. "Why did you do it?" She stared out the bay window at the trees. "Why did you take such a huge risk for me? You were out of the prison, you could have disappeared. Walked away. You could have saved yourself. Instead, you chose to risk entering the dungeon, defeating the mages . . . for me." She looked at him. "Why?"

He walked to her and pulled her chair out to face him. Then he leaned down, bracing his hands on the armrests on either side, and bracketed her there. The clean soap scent of him teased her nose and a tendril of his still-damp hair brushed her cheek. "I did it because I felt responsible for you, Aislinn. I did you wrong, even if I didn't know the extent of my sins. I was ultimately the reason you came to the Black Tower, since without my intervention you never would've defected. I didn't want that karma on my soul."

He'd done it because he felt guilty. It had nothing to do with her at all and everything to do with him. Perhaps somewhere in her most secret self, Aislinn had been hoping for something else. What? Something romantic? Had she wanted him to declare his undying love for her? Maybe tell her he'd done it because he couldn't imagine living without her? She rolled her eyes. Danu, she was an idiot. Their entire relationship up until now had been based on lies.

How had she ever expected anything else from him? He'd probably never sustained a relationship with a woman in his life. Gabriel wasn't built for that. Love just wasn't in his nature.

And he was so beautiful. Almost too beautiful to bear. She could see how any woman would quickly come under his spell. Even without his magick, the man was lethal to any female within twenty feet of him. It didn't matter that he was arrogant and self-serving. None of that registered in the face of his perfectly shadowed jaw, the sculpt of his lips, and the ever-present dark erotic promise in his eyes.

She couldn't allow herself to fall victim to it. She had to remain strong if she was going to be forced to stay so close to him through this ordeal.

"Okay." Her breath shuddered out of her. "Again, thank you."

"And again . . ." He leaned in closer to her, making her breath catch. His lips just barely brushed hers and her heart thudded in her chest. Then he bared his teeth. "Don't thank the man who put you there just because he got you out."

"Don't flatter yourself, Gabriel. I didn't go to the Black Tower for you." He hadn't been the only reason, at least. "I went because I wanted to train my magick, to become useful, to have a goal in life other than shopping and attending balls. That's all. I went to better my life." She gave a harsh laugh. "To find out who I really am. How ironic."

He stared at her for a long moment before pushing up and away from her. "Well, you're going to get your chance."

"What do you mean?"

"You need to learn how to come into your own as a necromancer. Luckily, I'm just the man to help you do that."

"I'm glad you're so confident, but there's one problem with your plan."

"And that would be?"

"I left all my possessions back at the Black Tower and that means the Shadow King now has the book."

"Book? What book?"

# FIFTEEN

"THE book."

The words were spoken softly, in a male voice. Magick oozed in through the cell phone and entered Carina's ear like an airborne virus. Black and viscous, the druid's spell made her jerk and go still, forced her to hold the phone to her ear and not throw it across the room despite the fact every ounce of her will to live screamed at her to do just that.

"The book," she answered breathlessly, fear draining the blood from her fingers where she gripped the cell phone. "You gave me more time to find it. Thank you for that." Carina closed her eyes and plunged ahead. "I've searched everywhere for it. I even broke into Aislinn's safe. I've asked everyone and . . ."

"And?"

*Oh, sweet Danu, have mercy.* She opened her eyes, focusing on a framed picture of herself and Drem that sat on a nearby end table. "If she ever had it, it's gone. I believe she took it with her and she has it over there. In the Black Tower. Only . . ." She chewed her lip.

"What?"

"There's been a lot of activity in the Black lately. The Shadow Guard and the goblins have been swarming the square and the city, even coming close to the Rose. It started right after Aislinn went over there. I don't know for sure, but I think she may have been captured or killed. At the very least, I suspect some kind of trouble for her. If that's true, then it's possible the Shadow King has the book now."

If the Shadow King truly did have it, the Phaendir had no hope of recovering it. Either way, her job was done. Now she only waited for their judgment. She was so tired.

She jerked as an invisible worm entered her ear, making her fingers go numb around the cell phone. The earpiece glued itself to her, preventing her from throwing the phone across the room.

Silence.

The silence was colder and blacker than the thick spell weaving its way through her brain, sucking the fire from her synapses one by one. It even stole her panic. She knew she should be frightened. She'd failed. So she knew she should say something. Otherwise he might decide he didn't need her anymore.

"No. I can still help you," she whispered. "I can still— Spare Drem. *Please*."

The cell phone dropped from her hand and broke into spinning, fragmented pieces. Blood trickled from her ear as she collapsed sightlessly to her polished marble floor, her mind just as shattered.

"THAT book you're talking about, you said it has a dark red leather cover and vellum pages. It has a section in the back that can only be unlocked by fitting some object into a grooved area, sort of like a key."

She nodded at Gabriel.

He walked to the window and pushed a hand through his hair. His voice was flat, almost stunned. "You said you found it in your father's things after he died."

Aislinn stood from the couch, feeling shaky and weak, and walked over to stand next to him. "Yes." She chewed her thumbnail while she stared out the living room window at the Boundary Lands. Apparently the book was more than just a guide for necromancers.

"*Danu*. It must be the Book of Bindings. It's been lost for thousands of years. That book was written when the Phaendir and the fae were allied. It's the most complete book of spells known, a mixture of both fae and druid." He paused and drew a breath. "Aislinn, that book contains the spell that can break the warding around Piefferburg."

"I've heard of it. I just didn't know that's what I had." She supposed she should feel something, shocked and awed, maybe. She didn't. Maybe she was shocked and awed out right now. She was so tired. It was a miracle she could even remain on her feet.

"Who the hell was your father?"

She turned and looked at him solemnly.

"I mean your father, the man who raised you. Who was he?"

She shrugged. "I didn't think he was anyone special aside from having very pure Seelie Tuatha Dé blood. He had nearly no magick at all that I know of, capable of only a few weak illusions. He had little power, but was placed very highly in the Rose Tower because of his pedigree, which I now know I don't share."

"How did he die?"

She turned back to the window and said nothing for a moment. It was a horrible memory. She'd always been so close to him. Since her mother didn't really feel like a mother, when her father had died she'd felt orphaned. It was rather ironic, really.

"He was killed in Piefferburg Square one night while coming home from a late dinner with friends. Random act of violence."

"Maybe not so random."

She squeezed her eyes shut because the thought had occurred to her, too. Had the book been why her father had been killed? "I don't know. If someone killed him over the book, they never got it. There were no break-ins, no telltale signs someone was looking for it."

"If it was the Shadow King everything would be on the lowdown. He doesn't want trouble with the Summer Queen. If it was the Phaendir—"

She turned at that.

"—they have no interest in calling attention to themselves when dealing with any of the fae races. It's not in their best interests to stomp into Piefferburg. They'd come in on little cat paws. Secretly. Using threats and promises from the outside."

She blinked. "The Phaendir? Do you really think it's possible they killed my father?"

"More than possible."

"Tell me everything you know about this book." She took a seat on one of the soft armchairs because—wow—this revelation was full of shock and awe that couldn't be denied. She needed to sit down.

"The Book of Bindings contains the strongest spells ever created. Some say the very pages of the book are doused in magick. The Phaendir possessed it, but lost it a long time ago in their conflicts with the Tuatha Dé. The spot in the back is where a puzzle box fits, the *bosca fadbh*. Have you heard of it?"

"Of course. The *bosca fadbh*. It's the only object that might have the power to break the warding around Piefferburg. The only problem is that all three pieces of the *bosca fadbh* are in the human world."

"Not anymore. Your friend Ronan Quinn was hired to obtain one of the pieces, but he double-crossed the Phaendir and returned to Piefferburg with it, even though he knew he'd be killed by the Summer Queen."

She sucked in a sharp breath. *"That's* the artifact he stole?"

Gabriel nodded. "He gave it to the Summer Queen to save Bella's life, knowing the Summer Queen could do nothing with it since the other two pieces are unobtainable. No one knew the Phaendir's book was in Piefferburg. Everyone thought it was in the human world somewhere, lost like the pieces to the *bosca fadbh*. The book and the puzzle box are very old, Aislinn; they predate the trouble between the fae and the Phaendir. Once upon a time, thousands of years ago, we collaborated. That collaboration is the Phaendir's weakness if we get our hands on the book and the box." He stopped and smiled slowly. "And if it's true that the Shadow King has the book and if it's true that the Summer Queen has a piece of the box then we're halfway to defeating them."

She raised an eyebrow. "And the other two pieces of the *bosca fadbh*? They're in the human world, unattainable."

"Never say never, sweetness. Never give up hope."

Biting her tongue against lashing out at him for the 'sweetness,' she let her hand, propped on the armrest of her chair, swing wide. "How does this help us defeat the Shadow King?"

"It doesn't. Not in the short term, anyway. Once the Shadow King sees the book and opens it up, he'll know what it is and there will be no getting it back."

"The spell I need to call souls is in the book. I know because I called my father once with it."

"Do you remember the words you spoke?"

She bit her lower lip and concentrated, dredging up a memory that seemed like it had happened years ago. "Not all of them. I didn't know what I was saying the first time or that the words were important."

He walked to her. His long feet were bare and sank into the plush, deep, cream-colored carpeting covering the floor. "You don't need any spells to help you. If you're a true necromancer, the power to call souls is within you, inherent. You only need to tap into it. It's written into your DNA."

She must have looked doubtful because he leaned over her in the same way he'd done in the kitchen—hands on the armrests on either side of her. It should have made her feel pinned, trapped, but it only made her feel safe. Still, she backed up against the cushion behind her in an effort to get some distance. She couldn't help her attraction to him, but she could fight it tooth and claw.

"It's inside you, just like the power of the Wild Hunt is inside me," he said, staring hard at her as though his gaze alone could instill the belief into her head. "Can't you feel them talking to you sometimes? Murmuring in your head? Can't you sense the lost ones out there calling for you—for anyone—to pay attention to them? I may not be a necromancer. I may only be Lord of the Wild Hunt, but I can hear them. I can sense them. You must be able to feel them, too."

He spoke with such passion. Clearly he loved being Lord of the Wild Hunt. She never would have guessed he loved anything more than women and sex. He put on the façade of jaded courtier so well that he'd never given her a hint of the man who lay beneath the shallow pretense. There was much more to Gabriel than what he displayed.

And that made him even more deadly attractive to her.

*Remember how arrogant he is. Remember his self-centeredness. Remember that he lied to you in the Rose.*

*Remember he risked his life to save you.*

She cleared her throat and schooled her expression—not to mention the beating of her heart. "I can feel them."

"Good. That's the seed. It's already planted and, I'm sure, already budding. Now all we have to do is follow the stem and make it blossom."

He was looking at her lips again. He was also making birds and bees references. Her gaze found his lips. This was not going to work.

"Turn off the charm," she whispered, gripping the armrests.

"What?"

"Turn off whatever magick you use on women to make them sexually drawn to you."

His luscious lips curved in a cocky smile. Yes, *there* was the arrogance. "That's not how it works, Aislinn, and you know it. You're just looking for things to blame your attraction on."

He dipped his head before she could respond and caught her lips against his. She jerked back, but he followed her, pressing her head back against the cushion and slanting his mouth over hers with a groan in his throat. That groan made her think of naked bodies and silky skin, made her think of twisted sheets and fusing bodies. It made her wonder what it would be like if he kneed her thighs apart and slid his cock inside her. To what heights could a man like Gabriel take her in bed? A man like him, for whom sex was like breathing and with whom erotic promise was almost certainly fulfilled?

"Give it up. Stop fighting so hard," he whispered against her lips. "Give it up to me. Just *give in* to me, Aislinn." He nipped her lower lip and she shuddered with lust.

"Gabriel." She'd meant his name to come out strong and clear, meant for it to act as a warning and make him stop. Because she wasn't sure she could make him stop—wasn't sure she wanted him to stop. His name came out breathy instead.

He yanked her up in one smooth movement, flush against him. The breath hissed out of her and she knew she was well and truly lost to him. One more kiss and she'd be his. He dropped his head and rubbed his mouth over hers as though savoring the taste of her lips.

It sealed the deal.

Her nipples stabbed through the material of her sweater and her breathing began to quicken. She'd come so close to death in the dungeons of the Black Tower and now she tasted life—vibrant and erotic—on Gabriel's lips. He could make her feel flush with blood and vitality and chase away the death that had clung to her for the last week.

She went up on her toes and pushed her mouth against his, spearing her tongue into the hot recesses of his mouth. Pulling back a little she murmured, "Yes," against his lips.

He groaned in the back of his throat and picked her up. She wrapped her legs around his waist and kissed him as he carried her through the living room and into the bedroom. Dropping her gently, she fell into the tangle of sheets and blankets on the bed. He stood over her, looking down at her like she was the most gorgeous woman he'd ever laid eyes on—like she was the only one in the entire universe he wanted to make love to.

For now, she'd believe the lie. Right now she needed to believe it.

"Take your sweater off," he said.

She slipped it over her head and tossed it aside. Wearing no bra, her nipples tightened from the combination of cool air in the room and his hot, roving gaze. She leaned back against the pillows, her heart thudding.

Slowly, his gaze locked with hers, he unhooked the button of his pants, undid the zipper, and slid them over his hips. His cock was hard, long and wide and as beautiful as the rest of him—broad shoulders melting into a muscled expanse of chest leading to narrow hips and strong legs.

Taking a couple of steps forward, he came over to her and slid her pants and socks down and off, leaving her bare from the waist down. Sliding his hand over her outer thigh and up her hip, he held her gaze. Everything he wanted to do to her seemed to dwell in his eyes. Then he lowered his head to her breasts, licking and sucking at each hardened peak until she squirmed beneath him, her back arching.

His hand dipped between her thighs and stroked her softly until a small moan escaped her throat and she sank her teeth into her lower lip. His cock pressed into her thigh as he used his thumb to pet her clit, making it plump and pulse with need. Sliding two fingers deep within her sex, he thrust in and out just the way she wanted his cock, all the while either sucking one or the other of her nipples into his mouth or whispering sweet, dirty things to her.

"Gabriel, please," she whispered, her fingers tangling his hair and roving over all the skin he allowed her to touch. Not his cock; he angled away every time she got close.

He held her fast on a threshold of pleasure. Sexual need dominated her body and her mind, overriding all else. He could push her over the edge, give her the climax she craved, but he never gave in. It was like torture.

"Tell me you want to come, Aislinn. Tell me you want me to fuck you."

*Danu,* she'd say anything at this point. "I want to come. Gabriel, yes, please fuck me."

The fingers deep inside her unerringly found her G-spot and stroked it. At the same time, he rubbed her clit with his thumb, steady pressure that was just right. She came. Her climax washed over her like a tidal wave, stealing her thought, her words, even her breath. She gasped and her back arched, body shaking in gentle convulsions of absolute pleasure. The muscles of her sex pulsed around his still-pistoning fingers.

Just as the waves of her orgasm began to ebb away, he moved between her legs. With strong hands, he pushed her thighs apart and held them down, then lowered his mouth to her. She jerked in surprise at his sudden movement, but he held her fast, sucking her climax-sensitive clit between his lips. Slowly, softly, he coaxed her past that uncomfortable postorgasm point and into pleasure again.

He groaned and closed his eyes as though she was the sweetest thing he'd ever tasted and all her muscles relaxed. She melted back on the pillows, watching him. The erotic sight of his dark head between her thighs was almost enough to make her come again, but what he did next made it a certainty. He tongued and licked her very sensitive bundle of nerves until her climax ignited once more. Pleasure ripped through her body anew and she bucked against his wickedly skillful mouth in a second orgasm.

By the time he was through she lay boneless on the bed, sated beyond her imaginings. He leaned over her and kissed her deeply. She could taste only the faintest trace of herself on his tongue. She twined her arms around him and tried to pull him down on her. She wanted to feel him inside her, wanted to return the favor of the pleasure.

"No," he whispered against her lips. "Not yet, Aislinn. We have time for that later." He kissed her forehead. "You'd be surprised how healing a good orgasm can be. Sleep now."

Riding the gentle waves of utter sexual fulfillment, she did just that.

GABRIEL stared down at Aislinn, who slumbered beautiful and naked in a tangle of bedclothes. His gaze traveled for the millionth time over the creamy skin of her hip and stomach and the spread of her hair on the pillow. He'd spent most of the day next to her, just watching her while she rested.

She needed that rest. The iron sickness still weighed heavily on her, even more heavily than it had affected him. It was in her eyes and the way she moved. She needed sleep, good food, and lots of fluids for a couple of days so she could regain her strength.

In his opinion, she needed what he'd given her, too, needed that sexual release and the heavy, sated exhaustion that had come in its aftermath. His cock was still hard from giving it to her. She'd melted in his hands, given in so sweetly to the pleasure he'd offered and taken it so hungrily.

He wanted to give her more.

She shifted in her sleep and a tendril of her silver blond hair curled around a hard, rosy nipple. Gabriel reached out and brushed it away, dragging his finger slowly over that lovely peak and feeling every one of its hills and valleys. She moaned in her sleep and shifted, her legs parting so that he could glimpse the pout of her clit nestled in the silvery curls.

He couldn't taste her on his tongue anymore and he missed her flavor, so hot and sweet. It was easily addictive. His fingers curled as he fought the desire to stroke that small, pouting bud, and he wondered how hot and bothered he could make her in her sleep. She was gorgeous all of the time, but when she was aroused . . . then she became irresistible. Would she wake up moaning for him, spreading her thighs so he could sink his cock deep into her heat?

Placing his hand to the inside of her knee, he slowly moved upward. As he suspected, she opened like a flower for the sun. Unable to resist, he dragged his fingers over her heated sex, exploring her damp softness.

Before he did something he would regret—like wake her from the deep healing sleep she needed so badly—he rolled away from her, stood, and rubbed his hand over his face. Gazing back at her, he wrapped his hand around his aching cock and stroked from base to tip. He tipped his head back on a groan of frustration. She would be his in every sense of the word. He just needed to be patient. Aislinn didn't know it yet, but he planned to act out with her every one of the erotic acts that crowded his mind.

Once she was healed, she wouldn't know what hit her. Every free moment they had he planned to spend making her scream and moan with pleasure.

Oh, and one other thing—he wanted her heart, too.

Every inch of Aislinn Christiana Guinevere Finvarra, from her pretty little toes to the top of her gorgeous head, would be his by the time he was through.

And no one was taking her away from him.

# SIXTEEN

AISLINN woke and stretched, becoming immediately aware of the fact she was naked. A lingering arousal clung to her body even through the fatigue of waking from a deep sleep. That may have been the deepest and best sleep she'd ever had. The faint arousal made her feel like a warm kitten, cozy in its bed.

Then she remembered all that had happened in the past week.

Suddenly chilly, she rose, pulling a blanket from the bed and wrapping herself in it. Pushing a hand through her tangled hair, she glanced out the window. The sky had that grayish cast that marked either twilight or early dawn. She frowned, not sure which it was.

Walking through the doorway, her gaze lingered on the bags packed and ready on the floor by the exit of the room. She hoped they'd never need them, but it made her feel good that they were there. He'd packed them with a change of clothes for each of them, shoes, a little food and water . . . and some weapons. Gabriel had found a couple of charmed iron knives and clubs hidden away in a cupboard. They were illegal to possess in Piefferburg. Luckily for them, the former tenant hadn't cared.

As soon as she walked into the living room she noted the floor plan. Every time she came into the room she did that, reminding herself where the exits were. Gabriel had done well to select this place. The front of the house had an entry from the street, a snaky, sparsely inhabited, and numerously treed road. On the opposite side of the living room was a winding staircase that led to the smaller lower level and the patio doors that let out into the woods. Beyond the large window that showed such a beautiful scene of the Boundary Lands, small lights flickered and flitted—the tiniest of the nature fae.

Gabriel was in the living room, his big body stretched out on the couch. His eyes were closed and one arm was thrown back over his head. He was still shirt- and shoeless, wearing only a pair of jeans that rode low, exposing the jut of his hip. Her gaze traced over his washboard abs and the narrow trail of dark hair that went past the waistband of his jeans to the long, wide cock she'd seen but not yet touched.

Her hands tightened on the blanket she held around her as her gaze traveled to his hands. He'd given her the most powerful climaxes of her life with only his hands and lips. What could he do with his entire body?

"Morning." His voice came out a rasp.

Her gaze flew to his face. "So, it is morning."

"You slept for about fourteen hours."

"Really?"

"You needed the rest." He sat up and rubbed a hand over his face. "Do you feel better?"

She nodded. Actually, she felt worlds better than she had the day before.

"The dark smudges are gone from underneath your eyes and your color is healthier. You're healing well."

"You're so worried about me. You spent two weeks wrapped in charmed iron, longer than me." She shifted her weight to her other foot in the slightly uncomfortable silence. "Why did you sleep on the couch?"

He looked up at her with heavy-lidded eyes and slowly blinked. "Why? Did you miss me?"

"I'm just saying"—she swallowed hard—"you're recovering, too, and the couch is uncomfortable. You could have shared the bed with me."

"I didn't want to disturb you. You needed a deep, uninterrupted sleep." He paused and his eyes seemed to get darker. "Anyway, I couldn't stay in there and resist you. If I'd kept looking at your beautiful body while you slept, eventually I would have pulled you beneath me and teased you awake. And then, pretty Aislinn, you wouldn't have been sleeping anymore. You'd have been otherwise . . . occupied."

Her mouth went dry. "Oh."

"Today we need to work. I think you're ready for it."

"Work?"

The slight smile he wore faded. He nodded. "Showers. Coffee." He paused. "Souls."


"WHAT do you mean, you can't find them?" Aodh Críostóir Ruadhán O'Dubhuir, the man who had been the Shadow King of the Unseelie Court since before Columbus had sailed the seas, tried to keep his voice quiet. Every ounce of him wanted to turn and kill the messenger where he stood.

His crystal-topped fighting staff whirled in the air as he jumped up and twisted in midair, slashing at an imaginary enemy even as he pretended it was the messenger. The messenger, sensing his precarious tether on life, stepped away from the training ring and cleaved to the gray stone wall that surrounded it. Sensible man.

Aodh continued to practice, his fighting staff whipping in maneuvers with the sharp sound of air being sliced. His body moved freely, muscles bunching and stretching as he rotated on the balls of his bare feet and leapt occasionally into the air.

Gabriel had managed to escape his prison and steal the woman from his dungeon in the space of a few hours. It made him, as king, look incompetent—*stupid*. No one knew exactly what had happened because everyone—even his mages—had died before they'd woken from the sleeping spell they'd been put under. There were only two men in the Black Tower who could weave a spell like that one, Ronan and Niall Quinn, and they were both missing, along with Ronan's wife, Bella.

"We've got every guard to a man searching for them, my liege," said the messenger, his voice shaking. He probably understood that the mages, guards, and everyone else unlucky enough to have been in the dungeon and unfortunate enough to fall under Ronan's spell now wore bloody second smiles on their throats. The burning pyre had been enormous and hellishly hot that morning. He hoped that wherever Gabriel was, he smelled the burning flesh and shuddered at it.

Aodh came to a stop and stared incredulously at the messenger. Sweat poured down his face and chest, though he wasn't at all out of breath. "It's not like you're searching the entire world. They didn't fly to Australia. There are limits to Piefferburg. They can't have gone far." His hands tightened into fists at his sides, his knuckles going white around the fighting staff. "It shouldn't be difficult to find five people in a fishbowl."

He wanted Ronan, Bella, and Niall every bit as much as he wanted Gabriel and Aislinn. Bella might be the most important one. If he could get his hands on Bella, he would have the perfect leverage to use against his daughter. Aislinn was clearly a tender-hearted, sweet woman—a sucker for someone she loved. Surely she would sacrifice herself to save her dearest friend.

"The countermeasures used to thwart our tracking spells are formidable and most of your mages are dead. We have no one left who can break them."

He went very still and imagined that the tall, blond messenger was bleeding from his eyes. Yes, he'd look much better that way. The delicate Twyleth Teg was delivering messages from the captain of the Shadow Guard. It was a smart move on the captain's part since he was less likely to lose his temper with a messenger . . . unless that messenger dared to insult him. "Are you suggesting that I made a mistake?"

The man blinked and his mouth opened and closed a couple of times. "I would never presume to—"

"Are you saying that because I killed the mages who were in the dungeon—the ones who were supposed to keep their charge safe from all who meant to take her from me—I have somehow hindered the guards' efforts to locate Aislinn and Gabriel?"

"No, my lord—"

"You are dismissed."

The man practically ran out of the room. Aodh turned and exhaled slowly, trying to gain a handle on his temper. It had always been his Achilles' heel. He'd done a very good job of keeping his explosive, violent anger in control since the time the Black Tower had been constructed, but this situation with his bastard daughter had inflamed it.

One night's indiscretion had resulted in a child. He would never be so careless again.

Slowly, he moved the fighting staff in the air in front of him, breathing slowly in and out until his temper was better in check. Then he increased the pace of his maneuvers, the staff whipping faster and faster through the air in front of him.

Over the years he'd been careful not to father any children, though it happened from time to time. Generally, it was easy enough to take care of early on, when the babe was still in the cradle. The girl children were especially dangerous.

So Aislinn had come as a nasty surprise.

He'd met her mother in the square many years ago. It had been dark outside and the woman had been upset. She'd clearly been Seelie Sídhe and one of the purest blood, too. Irresistible to him. Forbidden fruit was so much sweeter. She'd sat there, her beautiful alabaster face turned to the moonlight, tears on her cheeks. The collar of her summer dress had dipped to show the smooth curve of her shoulder.

She'd been lovely, so pure and fragile, sitting there by the statue of Jules Piefferburg, so close to the Unseelie side of the square. It had been as though she'd been looking for trouble. Like she'd been tempting the shadows to reach out and swallow her whole.

He'd neither cared nor wondered why she'd been so upset and tempting the shadows, but she'd succeeded in the latter. He'd sat down near her and slowly seduced her with charming words, cajoling and luring her to his side of the square, just for a little while. Just for as long as it had taken to find an obliging pocket of night, to coax her skirt up and her panties down. He'd meant to come outside her, but she'd been so sweet and soft, and the loveliest, dirtiest things had fallen from her lush mouth while he fucked her.

At the time, he had worried about his slip and considered killing the woman right then and there, just to stave off possible problems in the future. But not even he could kill a woman he'd only just fucked. Not with his bare hands.

He hadn't known about Aislinn until many years later. Not until Aislinn's friend Bella had come to the Black Tower. She'd had no photos of her best friend, so she'd drawn some pictures instead. One day he'd caught a glimpse of these sketches and had immediately recognized his line. She didn't look like him much at all, save for the color of her hair, the mirror of his natural silver-blond. But in the face she looked exactly like his mother, his grandmother, and even his great-grandmother.

There had been no question.

So he'd deep-searched Bella's mind when she hadn't been paying attention and he'd learned Aislinn's deepest and darkest secret.

That was his magick—the kind that could kill. Sadly, murdering people with their own thoughts only worked on the weakest of minds, on babies and small children. Unfortunate, since it was a useful talent.

Aislinn hadn't known she was a necromancer, of course. She'd only known she was Unseelie, strongly so, stuck in the Seelie Court. But he'd known she was much more than she thought—knew it because his mother had been a necromancer, and his grandmother, and his great-grandmother.

Necromancers were powerful Unseelie and she was next in line for his throne. That was when he'd realized she could not live. In fact, it became his absolute obsession to kill her and not just kill her, but obliterate her. A difficult task, considering she resided in the Rose Tower and to take her by force would mean a war with the Summer Queen.

Enter Gabriel.

Aodh passed a hand over his tired face. That had been his mistake. He'd misjudged Gabriel Cionaodh Marcus Mac Braire. He'd thought the incubus totally cold in his heart and ruthless in his seduction of women, never allowing himself to grow close to them, never falling victim to such silly emotions like love or compassion. Yet somehow Aislinn had brought both of these to the surface in the Lord of the Wild Hunt.

And then all had been lost.

But it was only a temporary loss. He wasn't going to lose, ultimately. There was no way Aislinn and Gabriel could hide from him forever in the small bubble of Piefferburg. He would find them and destroy them both. He would flay every inch of their beings so that they couldn't even be together after death—Aislinn because he had to, Gabriel because he could.

In hindsight, he never should have sent the Lord of the Wild Hunt to her in the first place. Gabriel and Aislinn had too much in common, could help each other too much. But he'd never anticipated—never believed—Gabriel's icy heart could melt this way.

Never. And then it had.

He had to find them before Gabriel and Aislinn realized how powerful they were together, before they harnessed the strength within his daughter and mated it to Gabriel's skills. He was sure the possibilities were not lost on them. Together Aislinn and Gabriel could call and control an army that would flatten his forces. If they did that, he didn't have a prayer against them.

Aodh gave a battle cry that came from the center of his being and landed on his feet, yelling his anger to the room.

"IT'S rude to ignore a ghost."

Gabriel shook his head and laughed. "Like it's rude to summon a soul from the Netherworld?" They'd been "talking shop" for the last half hour. She seemed to love to discuss this topic, probably because this was the first time she'd ever been able to talk to someone who understood. "I don't think the ghosts care much one way or another."

She frowned at him. "Then clearly you haven't dealt with many ghosts."

He gave her a look. "I'm essentially what amounts to the grim reaper of the fae, Aislinn, I see them nearly every night. Most souls go with me, though. I don't leave many behind."

"What about the old woman who wanders the square when the moon is waning? Why did you leave her behind?"

"I can't make them go if they don't want to. Her name was Greta. She died during the waning moon and lived near the square. The night we came to collect her, she refused to leave her husband, but he has since moved away. She's searching for him."

"Did you ever go back and try to get her to come with you later?"

He sighed patiently. "I visit her at least once every couple of weeks. She always refuses to pass over. Believe me, I'm giving her many opportunities. Eventually, when she's ready, she'll join the hunt. Until then, she's not hurting anyone."

"What about the hobgoblin boy who wanders the alleys in the *ceantar láir*? He's so sad and confused."

"He was murdered. It was very violent. He thinks he's still alive and won't listen to reason."

She pursed her lips and folded her arms over her chest. "He wails every night. He's miserable and always refuses to talk to me even though I've snuck out of the Rose several times to go to him because his pull is so strong."

"Sometimes they need time to figure things out. Eventually

he'll come to understand that he's dead and better off leaving this place and moving on. You can't rush it, though. They do it in their own time. Sometimes they stay behind because they're not ready to say good-bye to a loved one yet, or sometimes they feel like they have a job they need to do before they pass over. I don't forget about them, Aislinn, not any of them. I can't. They pull at me, every single soul that doesn't cross over. It's a part of being the Lord of the Wild Hunt."

"Did you ever find his killer?"

The other job of the Wild Hunt was to mete out punishment to murderers. The hunt hounds sniffed out fae who had killed innocents in cold blood. The Wild Hunt swept the souls of those fae from their bodies so they wouldn't be left to endanger others. The justice was swift, clean, and never misplaced. Because the punishment was sanctioned by Danu and the gods, murder was a rare crime in Piefferburg. The only fae exempt from the Wild Hunt were those who killed in self-defense, in legitimate euthanasia . . . and the royals.

The royals and those under their orders could literally get away with murder.

He nodded solemnly, remembering that night. "It was an adult male hobgoblin. We took him only hours after he'd committed the crime. He resides with the sluagh now, as unforgiven dead." Eternally shackled in servitude to whomever had the power to use them. It was not an enviable fate. "My only regret was that it was too late to save the boy."

She studied him hard for several moments before speaking. "You actually sound as if you care."

"Of course I care. Why do you sound so surprised?"

"Because you—you—"

"What? Because I'm an incubus?"

Her gaze snapped to his and her jaw locked. "Because you didn't care very much about me in the Rose when you were lying and tempting me to the Black."

His mouth opened and closed. Sighing, he leaned back against the couch and closed his eyes. He couldn't deny that had been his original goal. "You're right. I made a mistake." He looked at her, right into her eyes so she could see he was telling the truth. "But by the time the week was over, I was a different person than the one who had arrived. You did that. You changed me, Aislinn."

Aislinn closed her mouth and looked away from him. Her foot jiggled in agitation, though her expression seemed sad. She was barefoot and had the cuff of her sweatpants hiked halfway up her calf. Her toenails were painted an alluring shade of red.

The man who had owned this house had been the kind who'd accepted his death. He'd been pretty talkative on the ride to the Netherworld. Apparently he'd once loved a woman so much that even after she'd left him, he kept her clothes because they retained her scent. Now Aislinn wore them. He suspected the deceased Sídhe, a friendly guy who'd died in a car accident, wouldn't mind.

That morning, they'd showered and then raided the kitchen. As both of them were still recovering from the iron sickness, they were ravenous. So they made eggs and bacon and washed it all down with coffee and orange juice. While they feasted, she'd talked animatedly about all the things she'd experienced growing up. Her face had flushed from the pleasure of sharing these things with someone who understood. Her eyes had shone and the words had poured forth in an excited tangle.

She seemed to have grown accustomed to the idea that she was only part Seelie and that, indeed, the Unseelie half of her was much stronger. Giving up the Rose Tower didn't seem to be much of an issue for her, even though she hadn't exactly had a warm welcome at the Black Tower.

They didn't talk about the Shadow King.

Several times during breakfast he'd nearly pulled her chair close to his, kissed her senseless, tumbled her to the floor, and pulled off her clothes piece by piece. It was Aislinn he wanted to feast on, not breakfast. He wanted nothing more than to lose himself in her lush curves and sink his cock into the warm, satiny heart of her.

But he had to restrain himself. Work needed to come first. And the odds, obviously, were against them.

"So how do we do this?" She raised her eyes to his. They were clear, the expression on her face determined.

He stood from where he lounged on the sofa. They'd ended up there while they finished their coffee. The morning had been idyllic. It was almost hard to remember they were on the run for their lives. He walked to the window and gazed out over the beauty of the Boundary Lands. "You have to find the power inside yourself, Aislinn. I can start you off. I can help you a bit, but, ultimately, it's all about you discovering what it is you were born to do."

Silence.

He turned and looked at her. "I can't call ordinary fae souls to me. I can't make them do my bidding. All I can do is feel them, find them, help them. You have more power than I do in this regard, but make no mistake—together we're a powerhouse." He paused. "I *can* call the sluagh and you can control them. With you guiding them—"

"The sluagh?" The blood had drained from her face.

"Don't fear them."

"The sluagh are dangerous. They're the restless ones, the darkest of the fae who have passed over. You told me Brigid, my grandmother, controlled them, but I guess I never realized until just now that . . . that means I can control them, too."

He nodded. "And the Shadow King is terrified of them, terrified you and I might set them loose on the Black Tower with orders to carry him away to the Netherworld. The ironic part is that he'll be destined to serve in the sluagh as punishment."

She stared at him for a long moment, then shifted her gaze out the window. Gabriel knew exactly what she was thinking. It was written all over her face. She was an exceptional woman, Aislinn Christiana Guinevere Finvarra.

"You don't think you can kill him, do you?" he asked softly. "Not even after what he was going to do to you."

"No." She swallowed hard. "No, I don't think I can. That sort of bodes ill for us both, don't you think?"

"I think it makes you a bigger, stronger person than the Shadow King. Much less a coward. I think it makes me respect you."

She shifted her gaze to his face and blinked. "I think it makes us both dead."

"Let's take this one step at a time, shall we? You have to walk before you run and commanding the sluagh is definitely running. Maybe you won't have to kill the Shadow King."

He could think of a few fates worse than death for him. Anyway, when it came down to it, he would be the one to kill the Shadow King if he meant Aislinn harm. Gabriel would protect Aislinn against any comers and not blink an eyelash at having to collect their souls afterward.

She let out a long, slow breath. "All right, so how do we begin?"

"I think we should start with your father." He walked over and sat beside her on the couch. "I think he has some questions to answer, don't you?"

She worried her lower lip between her teeth. "More than one."

"It's already inside you, Aislinn. The spell you found in the book worked the way it should, taking the ability from you without you even consciously wielding it. But you don't need the words to find the power. So close your eyes, relax your body, and breathe slowly in and out, evenly and deeply."

She settled back against the cushions and closed her eyes.

"That's it. That's right."

His voice was low and deep, like warm chocolate on a winter's day. It made goose bumps rise all over her body. The words entered the center of her and sank deep inside her womb, making her react in a sexual way. She pushed past the sexual reaction, strove for peace, and drifted awhile, hearing every little sound and feeling every little twitch and pain in her body until, finally, she pushed past all of that, too. Distractions gone, she went deeper, her limbs growing heavy and Gabriel's voice now lulling instead of exciting her.

"Concentrate on your father," Gabriel crooned. "Bring an image of his face into your mind."

She did, tears pricking her eyes. Grief rose in her throat and chest, that familiar heavy feeling drowning her. She took a deep breath, pushed past it. A presence began to pull her awareness to the left. Someone was standing there and it wasn't Gabriel. He was sitting on her right.

"Carina?" snapped Gabriel's voice.

# SEVENTEEN

AISLINN'S eyes popped open. Carina wavered there in front of them—a specter, a shade, a disembodied fae soul. Shock ripped through Aislinn as the implication hit her. Carina was dead. She sucked in a hard, fast breath, her hand flying to her mouth and her eyes widening.

"I know," said Carina with a sad smile. "It must be a stunner for you. It sure was for me, even though I should've expected it."

Aislinn stared at her friend for a long moment, her eyes filling with tears. The image of Carina swam and she swiped her hands over her eyes to clear them. "How? When?"

Her image flickered and nearly faded away. The tether that connected her to the Netherworld pulled taut for a moment, its yellow and silver light stretching thin.

Aislnn reached out. "No! Don't go!"

The tether snapped back fatter. "I don't have much control," Carina said, her voice sounding far away. "I can feel something pulling at me. I know I can't go to the Netherworld yet, but I'm waiting for something to come and take me there. It was hard for me to find you."

"The Wild Hunt," said Gabriel. "That's what she's feeling. Aislinn, command that she take corporeal form. She won't be able to deny your magick."

Aislinn glanced at him, disbelieving. It sounded far-fetched, but it was worth a shot. She looked back at Carina, stared at her, and said, "Take corporeal form." Something deep inside her tingled as she said it. Magick lacing through her words, perhaps?

Immediately Carina seemed to solidify, though she retained an indescribable air of etherealness that Carina had never possessed in life. A silvery aura seemed to cling to her. Carina looked down the length of her body in disbelief. "You're a necromancer."

Aislinn cut to the chase. "How and when did you die, Carina?" Tears choked her throat. Like most souls did, Carina looked younger than she had when she was alive.

Carina went stock-still for a moment. "I died yesterday." She paused. "I was murdered."

"Why are you here?" Gabriel asked. "The Wild Hunt should have delivered you to the Netherworld this morning."

"I refused to go with them. I had to see Aislinn before I left. To—to beg her forgiveness."

Aislinn jerked in surprise. "What? Why would you need my forgiveness? *Tell me who killed you, Carina.*" Tingles again. She hadn't meant to, but she'd just compelled Carina magickally to answer that last question.

"The Phaendir," she answered instantly.

"Why?" The query came from Gabriel and it was full of sharp suspicion. Aislinn shot him an annoyed look, but he didn't notice. He was too busy staring Carina down like she was the murderer instead of the victim.

Carina didn't answer.

Aislinn frowned, her gaze shifting back to Carina's apparition. Carina was eyeing Gabriel nervously. *"Why?"* Aislinn compelled her.

Carina's gaze jerked to hers. "Because I was helping them

watch you." Pause. "I had to do it or they'd kill Drem." Her words came out in a rush. "They told me to befriend you, to watch you, to search your apartment for some old book with a red leather cover, vellum pages, and a bunch of spells. I did it. I befriended you, but I could never get as close to you as Bella got. You would never spill all your secrets to me. I searched your apartment but I never found the book. I failed. And then you left the Rose Tower and I searched again. The book wasn't there and I told them you probably took it with you. They—"

"Murdered you," Gabriel answered. "Killed you using some long-distance spell from beyond the boundaries of Piefferburg."

Carina nodded and looked miserable. "They left Drem alive." She sighed heavily. "I'll miss him, but I'm grateful I'm the one they took."

"Oh, Carina." Aislinn's mind was awhirl. Carina had never truly been her friend. Their whole relationship had been a sham. The Phaendir had threatened her . . . *murdered* her, and all for something Aislinn had had in her possession. It was so much to get her mind around. The Phaendir knew about the book? About her father? They'd been watching her? And they'd killed Carina. It was all just a little too much on top of what was happening with the Shadow King. "It was the Book of Bindings they were looking for."

"You had the Book of Bindings?"

Aislinn nodded. "Why did you feel the need to come and see me?"

"I wanted to warn you. I needed to find a way to let you know that the Phaendir are interested in you. I never imagined you'd be able to talk to me. You're a necromancer, Aislinn!" She sucked in a breath. "You're Unseelie!"

Aislinn chewed the edge of her thumbnail, deep in thought. "Yes, I am."

"The Phaendir aren't interested in Aislinn. Not anymore," Gabriel broke in. "They must know by now that the Shadow King has the Book of Bindings. That's what they want."

Carina looked at him. "They're evil. *Evil*, Gabriel. Don't assume they're done with Aislinn yet. Protect her."

Gabriel gave Aislinn a long, hard look, a muscle in his jaw jumping. "At the moment I live and breathe for just that." Warmth flushed her body at the look in his eyes.

"How is Drem?" Aislinn asked, the question coming out in a rush.

"Grieving me." Carina's image flickered. "If you ever see him again, tell him I love him. I'm going to miss him so, so much."

"I will. I'm sorry, Carina," Aislinn whispered. How could she blame Carina for doing what she'd had to do to protect her loved one?

"No." Carina shook her silvery, ethereal head. "I'm the one who's sorry, Aislinn. Just watch your back. If you ever need me for anything, call me from the Netherworld. I'll do anything to make up for what I did to you. Now, please, let me go. I've said what I came to say and the pull toward the Wild Hunt is very strong now. Let me go so I can find a place to wait for them."

"Of course." Aislinn contemplated her for a moment longer and then whispered, "Good-bye, Carina. You're free."

Carina disappeared.

Gabriel and Aislinn both fell silent. After a moment, Gabriel moved over to her and cupped her chin, forcing her to turn and look at him. "Are you all right?"

She blinked. "I'm fine. I'm just processing a lot."

"Believe me, I wasn't expecting that, either." He pushed a hand through his hair. "I guess Carina found you before you had a chance to call your father."

The fact that Gabriel called him her father, as in real and true, endeared him to her. "I'm just having a little trouble with the fact that the Phaendir have been watching me, and that Carina was reporting on me to them."

"You've come closer than most to pure evil, but they're done with you. The Shadow King has the book and that's what they were after. They've got to be nervous now that the book is within the boundaries of Piefferburg and the Summer Queen has one of the pieces to the *bosca fadbh*."

"I hope you're right about them losing interest in me." She stood and realized her knees were shaking. Ridiculous, she told herself. She'd just spent a week in the Shadow King's dungeon. This news was nothing compared to that. "Maybe my father will be able to shed more light on the situation."

But she wasn't going to call him. Not just yet. She needed to digest this chunk of information before she bit off any more.

Gabriel stood and went for the small cart in the corner filled to bursting with bottles of clear and amber liquid and short glasses. "I need a drink."

"It's not even noon."

"I still need a drink." He poured some of the amber liquid into a glass and took a swallow and then refilled it. He turned. "Want some?"

*"It's not even noon,"* she repeated with emphasis.

He grinned. "Aislinn, the Shadow King and all his minions are searching every square inch of Piefferburg for you right now, you just compelled your first soul as a necromancer, and you found out the Phaendir have had their eye on you for years. Still think a social law like no drinking before noon is important?"

Wow. She really hadn't needed the recap.

She crossed the floor toward him. "You're right. Give me some of that."

She took the glass from him and his finger skated over her hand as she did, sending little tremors of need through her body. Bringing the glass to her lips, she took a long swallow. She didn't drink very often, but the sweet, harsh burn of the alcohol down her throat seemed somehow cleansing. Closing her eyes and grimacing, she took another long swallow of it, draining the glass. Warmth spread from her tongue to her throat to her stomach.

When she opened her eyes it was to find Gabriel staring at her, eyelids at half-mast.

"What are you looking at?"

"You're so fucking beautiful."

She gave a short laugh and gazed down into the empty glass. "I'm sure you say that to all the women you've tried to seduce."

He tilted her chin up so she was forced to look at him. "I am trying to seduce you, Aislinn, but I don't mean you're beautiful in the ordinary sense. You are beautiful inside and out, upside and down, straight into your soul."

Oh, he was good. He really sounded like he meant it. She nearly even believed him. In fact, there was a part of her that *needed* to believe him. Just for now anyway.

The look on his face made her mouth go dry. His eyes seemed to hold every single erotic thing he wanted to do to her.

And she wanted him to do every last one of them to her.

She wanted to lose herself in him, let him take her away to a place where none of the rest of this existed. Somewhere far from death and souls and fates she'd never bargained on. Away from the Book of Bindings, the Phaendir, the Shadow King, and the tangled web they wove.

He slipped his hand to the nape of her neck and very gently fisted his hand in her hair. It didn't hurt, but it did effectively keep her from moving. Then he wove his other arm around her waist, placing his opposite hand possessively on the small of her back.

The empty glass she held slipped from her fingers and thudded onto the carpeted floor.

"Do you remember what you told me you wanted me to do yesterday?" he asked silkily as his mouth descended slowly toward hers. He nipped her lower lip while holding her head in place. Her nipples tightened and her breath caught in her throat. "Remember what you asked me?"

"Yes," she breathed. "I remember all of it."

"You asked me to fuck you. Do you still want that?" His warm breath eased over her lips.

She nodded. "Right now, more than anything." Her voice had a tremor to it. Her body felt tight with need and she knew he would unravel that tightness inch by inch until there was nothing left of her but all-consuming lust and, eventually, only sated relaxation.

He used the grip he had on her head to angle her face to the side. His mouth came down over hers as he pulled her up against him and slipped his hand down the back of her pants. She gasped at the sensation of his fingers sliding along her bare skin. His tongue skated between her lips and branded hers. He tasted of brandy and man.

His hand slid over her rear and between her legs. A groan rolled out of him as he slipped his fingers over her hot sex, feeling how damp she was from just his words and kisses. "You're so sweet down here, Aislinn. So hot and so irresistibly gorgeous. I touched you while you slept yesterday." His lips brushed the edge of her chin.

"Yeah?" The word came out breathy and she could barely keep her eyes open. Lust made her feel warm and heavy.

"Yeah." He pulled her head to the side and she tried not to whimper as he traced the tip of his tongue over her skin. "I wanted to see if I could make you come in your sleep. I would've, too, if you hadn't needed your rest to heal."

She shivered under the power of his words and his touch, shuddered in pleasure that he would have mastery enough to make her come while she slept. She had no doubt he could do it.

His teeth grazed a sensitive part of her neck, just under her earlobe, and her fingers tightened on his shoulders where she gripped him. He pulled her head back, exposing the long column of her throat, and nibbled his way from her earlobe to her collarbone.

Her breath came faster now and her knees were growing weak. Her body had primed itself for him in every way possible—her nipples going tight and hard and her sex becoming slick. Between her legs, he stroked her again, dragging his fingers over her heated flesh and slowly and carefully driving her insane.

He drew her back toward the couch, pulling her shirt over her head and throwing it to the floor. She wore no bra and his gaze skated over her bare breasts with heated interest. She gave him her own interested perusal, over his tights abs, the wide, muscular expanse of his chest, and his broad shoulders. Then she reached out and undid the button of his pants, wanting to once again see his beautiful long, wide cock. Maybe this time she'd even get to touch it.

His hand covered hers and gently pulled it away. "All in good time. It's my turn first." Then he pushed her back down onto the couch. Off came her pants and he knelt between her spread legs, his gaze touching her bared sex as surely as his hand had done only a moment before.

"Beautiful," he murmured. Then he dipped his head and tasted her.

Her back arched as his hot mouth closed over her, tongue dragging over her folds. Eyes closed, he made a sound of ecstasy as he explored her. His tongue found her pouting clit and bathed it. He could probably feel it grow against his tongue as she became almost unbearably excited.

She squirmed under his mouth, watching his dark head move between her thighs. It was almost too much. She almost wanted to get away from the intensity of it. Her breath hitched and her nipples went hard as diamonds from the lust cruising through her veins. He didn't let her. With a small sound in his throat, he clamped his hands down on her inner thighs, holding her down and spread to him. His tongue aggressively lapped at her clit, practically forcing her to come.

Her body tensed and then exploded. This was no slow, torturous buildup and retreat, buildup and retreat. This time he brought her to climax fast and hard with his mouth. It wasn't a wave this time, it was a freight train. Her spine arched and she cried out, her body shuddering. Gabriel had the ability to completely override her brain with his touch. It was wonderful and frightening at the same time. All she could do was hold on and ride the power of it.

Before the ripples of pleasure completely ebbed, he pulled her to the thick carpet on the floor, pushed her to lie on her stomach. Bracing himself with a hand on the floor to either side of her waist, he half covered her back.

She heard the blessed sound of a zipper and the rustle of his jeans being pulled down enough for him to get his cock out. Sliding a hand beneath her pelvis, he yanked her hips up, fitting her against his midsection where she could feel the jut of his cock against her aching sex. The smooth head of his shaft slipped just into her entrance and she whimpered, going up on her hands and knees and pushing back against him, desperate for more of him.

He gave it to her. Thrusting his hips, he pushed inside her to the root of him. She was so wet from the climax he'd given her that he slid deep inside without any pain, despite his large size. Her back arched at the sensation of him filling her, stretching her muscles and overwhelming her.

He stayed that way for a moment, sunk deep into the heart of her, and groaned. He murmured her name, told her how she felt around his cock—hot, silky, and perfect. Then he began to move and she couldn't hear anything else he said. Her world became Gabriel thrusting inside her.

There was something animalistic and primal about the way he took her and it pushed every button she had. He pushed inside her to the hilt, withdrew and plunged within again, pulling a raw sound from her throat. Over and over. Harder and faster.

She braced her hands flat on the floor and wished for something to grip. Instead she curled her fingers into the thick carpeting. He drew his hand around to her front, between her thighs, and stroked her clit. Softly, he pushed it past that sensitive point of postclimax and straight back to swollen, aching need.

This was not a gentle lovemaking. He took from her, demanded of her, pushed her.

His body rocked against hers, completely dominating her. He shifted his angle and the head of his cock rubbed her G-spot on every inward thrust. She came again, this time more powerfully. Racking spasms of pleasure poured through her. Her muscles rippled and pulsed around his shaft and her body went limp. She collapsed to her stomach on the carpet and he came with her, still thrusting inside her. Behind her he groaned her name and she felt his cock jump.

He stilled, then rolled to the side, into the curve of her body. "I'm sorry," he breathed into her hair.

She forced her eyes open and her breathing to calm a bit. Gentle waves of residual orgasm still flirted with her body and made her sex tingle and pulse. "For what?"

"I had no control. I just needed you. I needed to fuck you. It was fast and hard, not gentle the way I intended."

She gave a low, throaty laugh of total sexual lethargy. "I think I like fast and hard."

"Good to know," he murmured, brushing her hair to the side and kissing her earlobe. He dipped his hand to her breast and toyed with her nipple, brushing it back and forth until it went hard and she shivered. "Very good to know, in fact."

"So, do you use magick when you make love or is the . . . goodness . . . just your innate incubusness?"

He gave a deep laugh and drew his hand down between her legs, where he stroked her gently and made her sigh. "Neither. My 'goodness' comes from age and experience, from learning a woman's body and paying attention to where she likes to be touched, just how hard and just how fast." His voice was a low silken rasp against her earlobe and his hand was weaving magick on her body no matter what he might say.

"Oh," she managed, even though her tongue had gone dry.

"The fact that I'm incubus registers with women, though; you've seen that. Women are naturally drawn to me. Well, most all of them. You were a notable exception."

"And the magick?"

"Mostly it's a myth. I can't sexually enslave anyone, Aislinn. I can only mildly addict them when I try, which I never do. It makes them needy and clingy. You don't have to fear me."

She realized with a jolt that she didn't. Never had. She had believed the stories of death-by-sex to be true and she'd never once even thought of the possibility he might use it on her.

Simply, she'd trusted him not to do it.

His fingers still played over her sex. She rested her head back against him and sighed. "What are you doing to me?"

He nuzzled her earlobe. "Going for number three."

She had no complaints.

After he'd brought her to a third orgasm, this one softer and easier than the others, there in his arms on the floor, she stared up at the ceiling and marveled at her body and at Gabriel. She'd had two climaxes while making love before, but never three, and she still felt ripe, lush, and aroused—ready for more. Gabriel could do amazing things to a woman's body and she suspected that—if she wasn't careful—he might be able to do amazing things to her heart as well.

It was dumb even to be thinking about that, since their futures looked bleak. Yet, she couldn't help but warn herself not to fall in too deep with Gabriel, a man who wasn't meant for just one woman. A man who'd lied to her for the first week she'd known him, who had deliberately tried to lure her from her home under false pretenses. Even though he'd saved her life in the aftermath, it didn't change the events of that first week. She needed to protect herself.

If they survived what was to come—and she had every intention of doing just that—and they got past all of this, if they went back to their lives, well, then Gabriel would surely break her heart.

The solution was simple, yet so very hard—she had to avoid giving her love to him. If she did, she was doomed.

# EIGHTEEN

THE image of Aislinn's father wavered in front of them for a moment and then solidified. The cord that attached him to the Netherworld shimmered in a riot of rainbow colors. Souls, as near as Gabriel could determine, were the basic, primal energy of the fae they had been while inhabiting a physical body. He didn't believe they existed in this form in the Netherworld. Gabriel believed they took the form of raw energy, in a sort of collective mass, awaiting rebirth.

Gabriel, like most fae, believed that life was a continuous circle. Without beginning and without end. All things died. All things passed away, but that didn't mean they passed out of being. All that passed away into the Netherworld eventually returned when its season came. Albeit in a new form.

Of course, he didn't know for certain. No one knew but the souls and they wouldn't talk about it. Anytime he'd asked, some force prevented them from revealing the truth, making their words come out soundless. Not even a necromancer could command information of that nature from them.

But now the energy that had formerly been Aislinn's father wavered in front of them, having taken the form that either they—Gabriel and Aislinn—most expected him to take. Or perhaps it was the form that Aislinn's father most associated with himself. No one knew.

A small noise escaped Aislinn. *"Papa."*

The word was broken and filled with longing. It made pain twist in Gabriel's stomach. Gods above, he'd never cared for a woman as much as he cared for this one.

Hells, he'd never cared for anyone more than he cared for her. It was beautiful and scared him shitless all in one go.

Her father's face softened. "I miss you, my daughter."

"But I'm not your daughter." She shook her head, her fists clenched in her lap. Her voice sounded accusing. "I'm not your biological daughter, am I, Papa?"

His face fell. "So, you know the truth. I had hoped to spare you from it. No, you were not my biological daughter." His voice sounded far away. "You were the child of my heart, a bond stronger than any genetic link."

Aislinn ducked her head and blinked rapidly. Gabriel's fingers curled as if to pull her close to his body, to comfort and protect her. He looked down at his hands, marveling at the impulse.

"You know you're not my biological daughter because you can do this." He encompassed his body with a sweep of his hand. "You are a necromancer and that ability doesn't come from my blood or your mother's blood."

"Did you know Mama had an affair?"

Her father nodded. "We'd had an argument the night it happened and she'd thrown her engagement ring at me. I took it and yelled that I was happy our engagement was off and would gladly accept the ring back. She ran off into the square crying. According to her, she was approached by a dark fae. To spite me, she let him seduce her. That was the night you were conceived. I loved your mother very much, Aislinn. We got back together, repaired the engagement. We never dreamed she'd conceived a child, since it was so against the odds." He smiled. "But she had. I embraced you

and accepted you as my own from the day we first discovered she was pregnant."

"That dark fae was the Shadow King, Papa."

He jerked a little in surprise. "The Shadow King. Well,
that explains the necromancy."

"Is that all you have to say? I'm Unseelie," Aislinn
breathed. "The bastard daughter of the king of them all!"

He smiled. "And look how beautifully you turned out."

Gabriel's opinion of Aislinn's father rose into the stratosphere. He displayed none of the snobbery that was so common among the Seelie toward the Unseelie. He just loved his
daughter, no matter what.

Aislinn shook her head. "So you hid the information from
me and from the Seelie Court."

His smile faded. "It was the best way we knew to keep
you safe."

"But *you* weren't safe, Papa, were you? Who killed you?"

His ethereal face grew ashen. "The Phaendir had me
killed in the square."

Aislinn dropped her head and a teardrop splashed into her
lap.

"They killed you for the Book of Bindings, didn't they?"
asked Gabriel.

His gaze never wavered from Aislinn. "I know you found
the book because you summoned me with the spell in your
apartment. I saw the book fall from your lap onto the floor. I
had hoped you'd never find it, but it seems all the danger I
ever wanted to help you avoid you've managed to find."

"I did find it," answered Aislinn. All the shakiness was
out of her voice now and it was clear and strong. "It was
under the floorboards in your bedroom, Papa. How did you
get that book?"

"It was handed down in my family. I don't know how
we first came to have it, but my father managed to bring it
with him when he was forced into Piefferburg. He handed
it down to me to keep and impressed upon me how critical
it was. I never let anyone know about it. I assume the
Phaendir must have tracked the book into my Seelie lineage,

however we gained possession of it, and followed the trail. They contacted me, demanding the book. When I failed to produce it, they killed me, thinking they could find it on their own. You found it first." He paused. "Get rid of it, Aislinn. Burn it. Do whatever you need to; just make sure the Phaendir never get it."

"The Shadow King has it now, Papa."

"How did he get it?"

Aislinn looked a hundred years older than she was for a moment. "Never mind that. It's a long story and it's not your concern."

"But—"

"I'm watching over your daughter," Gabriel interrupted. "She'll stay safe; I swear it on my soul." His words were strong and fierce and he felt them all the way through his body. Aislinn's face whipped toward him while he spoke, her lips parted slightly and her eyes wide.

Aislinn's father regarded him in silence for a long moment. "I believe that."

"As you should."

Her father strained as if listening to something far away that neither he nor Aislinn could hear. "I'm being called back, Aislinn."

She nodded and wiped at a tear track on her face. "May I hug you before you leave?"

"You must command me to take a corporeal shape. I can't do it on my own."

She did and he solidified. Aislinn rose and hugged her father, but he disappeared a few moments into their tender embrace, leaving Aislinn to stagger forward and then bring her hands up to cover her face. Gabriel stood and went to her, pulling her against his body.

She melted against him for only a moment and then pushed away. "Okay, what now?"

"Are you all right?"

"Yes." She swallowed hard and cleared her throat—clearly trying not to break down. "I miss him."

He nodded. "I understand. I've escorted people I care

about to the other side before. It's a"—he searched for the right words—"bittersweet honor."

"I was much closer to my father than to my mother."

"I gathered that."

"But my father is gone now and I learned a while back to deal with the grief. Anyway, I just received a huge gift. Not many people get to see their loved ones after they're gone. I feel grateful for this." She wiped away the last of the tears on her cheeks and looked up at him, her gray eyes turning the color of gunmetal. "Now, what's next?"

He considered her for a long moment. "The scary stuff is next, Aislinn. We're done with friends and family. Now we need to find weapons. Make a plan. Now we need to call the sluagh and you need to make them obey your will."

Her expression hardened. "Now it's time to attack dear old dad."

THE lights went off that evening. They'd been eating a dinner of salmon and roasted vegetables when their current living— or squatting—space was plunged into darkness.

"Piefferburg Electricity finally got around to shutting everything off." Gabriel laid his fork to the side of his plate. She could just make out his actions by the light of the moon spilling in through the window. "Damn."

"It was nice while we had it."

"I'll get some candles." Gabriel got up.

She sat, the reflection in the window showing candles flare up one by one in the living room behind her. When Gabriel didn't return, she cleaned up the table and walked in to meet him, leaning up against the archway separating the rooms.

He sat on the couch, one arm draped over an armrest. His dark hair hung long and loose around his shoulders and his chest was bare. The candlelight licked his skin the way she wanted to every time she saw him . . . especially when he had his shirt off.

"You didn't eat much." She swallowed against the dry

throat that always accompanied her view of his bare skin. When he didn't answer, she asked, "What are you doing?"

Shadows moved over his face and caught in his hair. "Thinking."

She crossed her arms over her chest. "About what?"

His head turned and his gaze fixed on her. "You."

"Uh. What were you thinking . . . about me?" She could only imagine. Probably things that ran along the same lines she'd been thinking. Heated bodies. Silken skin. Tangled legs. The press and rub of his chest against her breasts as he kneed her thighs apart and . . . "Never mind. Maybe I should"—she swallowed again—"go to bed. It's been a long day."

He rose and slowly crossed the floor toward her. "Bed sounds like a good idea. No lights. Not much else to do."

Uh-oh. Fifty alarm bells went off in her head even as her hormones did an Irish jig. She wanted to back up, retreat away from him. But if she did that, it would make her seem weak and she *wasn't* weak.

Anyway, Gabriel was a man who got what he wanted. If he wanted her, he'd just follow.

She put a hand out and touched his chest to stop his advance. Touching his bare skin was a mistake. He was warm and the muscles under his skin moved as he breathed. It made her think about smoothing her palm down over his nipple, over his stomach, and then lower. She wanted to touch his cock. She hadn't yet taken it in her hand, stroked him, made him sigh and moan. She craved that sort of sexual power over him, especially when he had so much power over her.

She brushed his skin once, twice. He smiled. She could just see it in the candlelight. It was the smile of a man who knew what he wanted, the smile of a man confident he would get it.

Forcing her fingers to still, she spoke again. Her voice was shaky. "I meant, I need to go to bed al—"

He dipped his head and caught her lips against his. Slowly, he brushed them back and forth, making her knees feel like they might buckle. A sexual cloud filled her mind.

This was dangerous. A moment from now and she'd be completely lost. She had to act before he pulled her under.

She pushed at him, rocking him back on his heels and moving those devastating lips away from hers. "This is not a good idea."

His mouth curved in a smile. "Why not?"

She couldn't exactly tell him the truth: *I need to keep my distance from you in case, by some miracle, we survive this because you'll take my heart, mash it into a bloody pulp, and then walk away.* Her mind searched for alternatives.

"I'm tired. It's been a long day." Oh, that was lame.

The laugh that rolled out of him was like leather, wood smoke, and chocolate. All things that gave her pause, made her stop and inhale, savoring the fragrance. "And I intend to make it a long, tiring night."

"Gabriel—"

He captured her wrists in his hand and pressed them upward, pinning them against the wall. His head dipped, his lips coming close to hers. "I want to immerse myself in you. I want to touch your body, kiss your breasts. I want to make you forget all this, the Shadow King, the sluagh, just for a little while. I want to make you forget everything but my breath across your skin and the skim of my lips on your inner thigh and maybe a little higher. I want to make you sigh, moan, call my name, and claw the sheets. *Aislinn*, let me."

A small puff of breath escaped her.

His lips brushed hers again and this time she didn't fight it. She pushed forward, pressing her mouth more firmly against his, craving a deeper taste of him.

He dragged his hands from her wrists down over her arms and then over her braless breasts through her shirt. Her nipples hardened against his palms and he made a low, appreciative sound in the back of his throat. "See? I knew you'd come around," he murmured against her lips.

"I have the force of an incubus seducing me. What chance do I have?"

"None, sweetness. You're all mine."

That was exactly what she was so terrified of. Yet she

couldn't push him away, no matter how loudly common sense was yelling at her.

He slipped his thumbs under the waistband of her pants and pushed down. They fell to her ankles, leaving her bare, since she had no underwear. Then he pushed her shirt up and left that part of her bare, too. His hands covered her breasts, teasing her nipples until they were diamond hard, until a rush of heat swept through her, centering between her legs.

Now she was well and truly lost.

Her fingers quested for and found the button fly of his jeans, the trail of his coarse dark hair brushing her knuckles. She undid the button and the zipper, reached in, and sought the prize she'd been longing to hold. Ah, heaven. At last.

He groaned and his head fell back as her fingers closed around his thick shaft. She used his foreskin to pump up and down. It was everything she'd imagined it would be—long, wide, and silken hard.

With one sweeping, powerful move, he lifted her, pinning her against the wall. She wound her legs around his waist and her arms around his neck as he ground his beautiful cock against her vulnerable, bare sex. This time it was her head that fell back, her groan of need that tore from her throat, her eyes that closed in surrender. His teeth nibbled at the skin of her arched neck, tongue stealing out to taste her from time to time.

"Gabriel, please," she breathed. She wanted to feel him inside her.

He ground his hips again, this time stimulating her clit. It made her move her pelvis like she was in heat. Gabriel was the only man in her life ever able to put her into this state of erotic longing. Her fingers twined in his hair as his mouth came down on hers. He consumed every gasp and sigh she made.

"Please, Gabriel," she murmured against his lips. Her sex was heated, needy. Her body had slipped into a place that bordered on mindlessness and all he'd done was whisper at her, stroke her breasts, and kiss her.

"Not here. Not up against the wall. Not hard and fast. Long and slow. This time I want to savor you."

Her answering groan was something between anticipation and disappointment. If he moved just a little, his gorgeous cock would slip inside her and sink deep. He could take her up against this wall. A few pumps and she would come, screaming his name, into the quiet house. Instead, he lifted her away.

Somehow they made it to the bed and somehow she ended up rolled beneath his big body, his hands roaming her heated flesh and his lips trailing the sensitive skin of her throat, limning her chin and then once again claiming her mouth.

She pushed his jeans down past his hips and helped him get them all the way off. Then his long, lean, muscled body was pressed flush up against her, the press of his hard cock against her leg. He shifted a little and his thigh rubbed against her sex, making her cry out. She reached for his cock, but he pulled her wrists up, pressed them against the mattress, and lowered his mouth to one nipple, exploring every single ridge and valley until she squirmed on the bed beneath him. Then he did the same to the other.

When he released her wrists, she searched again for his cock and found it. A ragged groan escaped his throat as she stroked him, trying to push him into skipping the foreplay and simply fucking her. Instead he rose and returned with two long silk ties. He'd had them ready somewhere, obviously intending to use them on her at some point. They'd simply been sitting in a drawer—handy for when he'd need them.

She regarded him warily. "Why?"

"These are so you don't make me come too soon, sweetness. Keep touching me that way and you'll get what you got before. On your knees, me behind you, hard and fast. I said I wanted it slow this time and I get what I want."

The silk ties slipped smooth and tight around her wrists. He secured the opposite ends to the metal feet of the bed. Her arms were up, her offending hands immobilized. He circled the bed, staring down at her like a wolf ready to devour his prey. Her heart beat out a rapid cadence, her breath coming fast. Her nipples were hard and supersensitive. Even the slight stir of air he made from his passing made them tighten further. Her sex was heated and swollen with need. This was sexual torture and he knew it—he meant for it to be that way. It was clear he had every intention of nearly driving her crazy before he gave her what she wanted.

"Spread your thighs," he commanded in his wood-smoke voice.

She allowed her knees to fall apart and cool air bathed her, that sensation alone drawing a ragged moan from her throat. He stopped at the bottom of the bed and let his gaze trace from her feet, up her inner thigh, and over her sex. She felt it like a physical touch. He knelt and his hand followed the same path, moving from her calf, agonizingly slowly over her inner thigh, to her sex. His fingers traced her folds, rubbing, exploring, and gathering moisture. He petted her clit, pulled so completely from its hood and pouting at him—begging for attention.

She moaned and moved on the mattress, pulling against the ties that held her in place.

"What do you want me to do to you?" he asked. He seemed so calm, so completely in control, but there was a slight tremor in his voice that let her know that was just an act. He was suffering as she was.

"You know what I want," she answered in a breathless voice.

He slipped a finger inside her and she jerked, trying not to move her hips but wanting to seek more contact. "So pretty," he murmured, his gaze fastened on his thrusting finger. He added a second, further stretching her muscles, and another low moan escaped her. "Do you want this? Don't be shy. Tell me."

"I want you, Gabriel. You."

His thrusts became a little faster. "Do you mean my cock?"

"Yes," she hissed. Her body was straining toward him as much as it could, her hips moving in time with his thrusts.

"You want me to fuck you."

"Yes."

He touched her clit with his opposite hand, pressing and rotating as he thrust his fingers in and out of her. Aislinn grabbed the ties that bound her as her body shuddered in release. The pent-up energy of the withheld climax burst over her, making low, animalistic sounds tear from her throat, making her spine bow.

Then he was there, his head between her thighs, lapping gently at her clit while her sex still trembled and pulsed around his fingers. With the flat of his tongue he brought her to climax again, using the tail end of the energy of the first. Her head tossed back and forth on the pillows as she whimpered under the force of it.

"Now, Gabriel," she gasped. "Don't make me wait any more."

He mounted her, guiding his cock into her sex, sinking in as deep as he could go. His hips met her inner thighs just as his gaze met hers. She gasped at the intimacy of it, having him in this position—face to face, hips to hips, chest to chest—instead of behind her.

"Aislinn," he murmured. Her name seemed filled with a meaning she could barely discern, layered, as it was, under so many blankets of lust and passion.

He levered up, sliding out of her to his crown, and then pushed back in, hilting within her and stretching her muscles so deliciously with his girth. She closed her eyes against the sensation of it. It was just what she wanted, just what she'd craved—to feel completely possessed and overwhelmed by him. Her fingers curled around the silken ties and gripped tight, hanging on for dear life as he thrust into her over and over.

Her hips rose and fell with the tempo he set, driving them both in a primal dance. His head fell to her breast and his lips covered her nipple as she came again, her body surrendering to his in a rush and a cry.

After he'd released himself, he stayed buried deep inside her and kissed her long and thoroughly. His tongue mated with hers over and over and she gave herself to it, despite the fact that kissing Gabriel was like conceding a part of her soul. Kissing him was too much like bliss and she couldn't deny herself the pleasure of it.

She wasn't kidding herself; she was falling in love with him. She'd started to do that way back in the Rose Tower. She wasn't the type of woman who could have sex with a man and not have feelings for him. Many of the fae could sleep around just for the erotic thrill of sex—and never lose a little bit of their heart to those they slept with.

Like Gabriel could.

Aislinn had never been that way. It was unavoidable—she was going to get hurt in the long run if they survived, but she could try to limit it as much as she could. And, if it came down to it, she would reject Gabriel before he had a chance to do it to her. At the very least she could do that much to protect herself. She was not going to go through what she'd gone through with Kendal.

Never, ever again.

For now, she would enjoy this man and the bounty he offered her. When staring death in the face, there wasn't much reason not to.

# NINETEEN

BELLA snuggled into Ronan's side, inhaling the scent of him and trying to relax. When Gabriel had been busy breaking Aislinn out of the dungeon, they'd been busy running, too. They'd known that as soon as the Shadow King discovered Aislinn was gone and how it had been done, he would know Niall and Ronan had helped.

Niall, like always, had gone his own way. She and Ronan had taken off for the Boundary Lands. They weren't able to be tracked, thanks to Ronan's perfection of countermeasures to block such spells. They figured the Shadow Guard and the goblin army would be dispatched immediately to go door-to-door and the Boundary Lands offered them the best chance of survival. They had some experience with this.

The wilding fae would either warn them of the approach of the guards or they would choose to do nothing at all. They were unpredictable that way. They'd gone to Aurora, one of the birch ladies, for shelter and she'd been more than willing to give them a small cabin in the woods to stay in. She could be trusted.

It felt familiar, except this time they were on the run from the Shadow King instead of the Summer Queen. They were running out of royals to piss off and she wasn't sure what would happen to them when this was all over. Ronan had explained the fact that together Aislinn and Gabriel could call and control the sluagh. It appeared there was a war brewing and if Aislinn and Gabriel could come together, they had a good chance of winning.

Maybe.

It depended on whether or not Aislinn had survived the dungeon. Bella's mind couldn't comprehend the possibility she may not have, so she'd immediately dismissed that.

It depended on Aislinn controlling the sluagh. Whether or not she would want to. Whether or not she *could*. It was hard to imagine her gentle friend commanding legions of unforgiven dead in a war against the Shadow King in a bid to take her place on the Unseelie Throne.

Bella shook her head a little at the strangeness of it all and nestled in closer to Ronan. How bizarre a turn of events their lives had taken.

There was no telling what would happen to them at the end of these unfolding events. Ultimately, she was willing to change her life drastically for Aislinn. If it meant her friend would survive, she and Ronan would live out the rest of their days hidden in the Boundary Lands, residing in this small birch-built cabin. She'd be happy anywhere, as long as she was with Ronan.

Ronan turned, pulled her into his arms, and kissed the top of her head.

"I thought you were sleeping," she murmured. Moonlight filtered in from the few windows in the cabin, leaching the light from the already pale birchwood floors and walls. The bed beneath them creaked with their movement.

"No." He exhaled long and slowly. "I feel something tonight. Something in the air."

"What do you mean?"

"Something's changed. It's different now. I don't know what."

"Something good or something bad?"

"Something good."

She lifted up to look at him. "I've thought up five million different curses for the Shadow King for what he did to Aislinn, but not a one of them have taken hold so far as I know."

He cupped her cheek. "Everything will turn out the way it's supposed to."

"I wish I shared your faith."

He leaned forward and kissed her lips. "I just feel like we'll be all right, no matter what."

She smiled and kissed him back.

And the door splintered open under the force of the Shadow Guards' boots.

Bella screamed in surprise and scrambled back, up against the headboard of the bed. Ronan leapt in front of her, trying to shield her from the guards and goblins that were pouring into the cabin. They lined up on either side of the bed as though waiting for something.

The Shadow King himself sauntered into the room, holding Aurora's arm. The ethereal birch lady who had given them shelter was paler than usual and obviously angry. Her normally calm blue eyes were a tumultuous ocean of hatred as she looked at her captor.

"Ronan, Bella," the Shadow King greeted with a cold smile. "So nice to find you here." He shook Aurora. "You thought going to her for help was a good move, but you failed completely to understand the nature of the wildings. Some of them are easily bribed for information. I just kept throwing money at the problem until an obliging Hu Hsien told me who was providing you shelter." He smiled again, showing sharp white teeth. "Nice try, though."

GABRIEL awoke on a long groan. In the moonlight, he could see Aislinn's light head near his hips, her lovely full lips moving up and down on him. It was a sight straight out of his fantasies. He dropped his head back and gritted his teeth, trying not to come instantly.

It seemed like some dam within Aislinn had finally given way since the last time they'd made love. She'd been so deliciously sweet and wanton when he'd tied her up and stroked her with his hand, moving her hips as if looking for something to fuck, pulling against the ties and making soft sounds of need. She was different in every way since the dungeon, a little more intense and with a slightly harder edge than she'd had before.

She would need it.

After they'd made love they'd taken a shower with the very last of the warm water in the heater. In the candlelight, their bodies had slid together, wet and soapy. Her hard pink nipples had peeked from between white bubbles, bubbles that had slipped down her abdomen and into her belly button and driven him crazy. She'd been shameless, her inhibitions gone, rubbing up against him like a cat in heat, and caressing his cock, which seemed like it never went soft in her presence. She'd begged him to fuck her again.

So he'd taken her up against the shower wall, his cock sliding in and out of the hot, soft clasp of her sex and rocking her against the wall with her legs around his waist, heels hooked at the small of his back. Then he'd dried her off, taken her back to their sex-rumpled bed with the silken ties still attached, and she'd run her hands over him, kissed him—never seeming sated.

Now this.

She'd woken him from a sound sleep, her lovely mouth wrapped around his cock. And she was trying to make sure he came fast and violently between her pretty lips.

"Aislinn." Her name rasped from his throat, his fingers curling in her hair. "Are you trying to make me insane?"

She didn't answer, only continued running the tip of her tongue up and down his length, sucking him down her throat to the base of him.

A ragged sound escaped him and he pulled her up, dragging her beneath him. He stuck his knee between her thighs, parted them, and sank his cock deep within her. His mouth came down on hers, hard—punishing her for putting him in a state of desperation for her, for taking sexual control away from him. She was the first woman ever to be able to do that.

Several pumps into her wet, silken heat and he came, groaning her name against her lips. "Bad girl," he murmured and he felt the mischievous curve of her lips against his mouth. She'd gotten exactly what she wanted from him, a loss of control.

But she hadn't come and that was not acceptable. His ultimate goal was to sear himself into her mind and onto her body sexually. He intended to make her his in every way, but if he died defending her, he wanted to make sure she never lay with another man again without thinking of him and the erotic pleasure he once gave her. In that way, at least, she would always be his. Maybe it was selfish, but he couldn't deny the need to do it—to mark her as his.

Still buried deep within her, he slid a hand under her lusciously curved rear and used his hold to leverage himself on her, up and down, rubbing himself against her clit until she moaned.

"Come for me, Aislinn. Come on, baby," he whispered. Her nipples hardened against his chest, he felt her body tense, and he knew he had her.

It wasn't long before her body gave itself to him in a sweet, soft release, her fingernails lightly scoring his shoulders and his name falling from her lips.

Then he tucked her body against his, covering her with himself as much as he could, and held her until they both fell asleep.


*GET out. They're coming.*

Aislinn gasped at the disembodied voice pulling her from the deep sleep she'd been in. She sat straight up, the blankets falling away from her nude body and the cool morning air bathing her breasts.

That had been a warning and she couldn't ignore it. "Gabriel!" She shook his shoulder. "Gabriel, wake up." He groaned.

She rolled out of bed and went for their clothes. As Gabriel sat up, she tossed his jeans at him. "Quick. They're coming." She yanked her jeans up over her hips.

Someone pounded on the door at the front of the house. She stilled, her gaze locked with his.

"Fuck." Gabriel bounded out of bed and pulled his jeans on while she jammed a shirt over her head and shoved her feet into her shoes. Together they ran to the doorway. Gabriel scooped the bags up from the floor.

The pounding sounded again. A loud male voice yelled, "Open up in the name of the Shadow King. Your house is to be searched for fugitives under an Unseelie Court edict." More pounding. "If you do not open the door, we have orders to break it down."

She ran toward the spiral staircase, but Gabriel just stood there, staring at the door. Halting near the stairs, she looked back at him. His pupils were large, every muscle in his big body tense. His jaw was locked and he seemed to be straining toward the Shadow Guard on the other side, as though holding himself back from rushing toward it. Her gaze skated down and she saw that he'd pulled a charmed iron club from the bag and he held it tight in one fist, skin protected by the leather-bound grip.

"No," she whispered harshly. "Not here, not now."

He didn't move.

She walked to him and moved his jaw, forcing him to look at her. Black hate overwhelmed his eyes. "I know it goes against your nature to run. I don't like it, either. But there are at least five Shadow Guards on the other side of that door." She paused, pressing her lips together. "You said you would protect me, Gabriel. Right now that means we have to get out of here and bring the battle to them when we're prepared."

He gave his head a tiny shake as though to clear it. His eyes bled from hatred back to the warmth she more commonly saw. She pulled him forward and he followed. They ran to the window that overlooked the Boundary Lands. Finding no Shadow Guards on the back side of the house, they made their way down the spiral staircase to the patio doors below.

Gabriel opened the door and they flew out into the trees and kept running. Together they jumped logs and dodged tree limbs, Aislinn's heart pounding.

In only a moment the Shadow Guards would break down the door and enter the house. They would discover the electricity was off and the evidence of squatters having been there— the burned-down candles, the freshly cleaned dishes in the sink. They'd be able to deduce quite easily that there was a high likelihood the squatters had been the fugitives they were looking for. They'd call in reinforcements, start searching the woods. They'd try to call in the magickal "bloodhounds," but thanks to Ronan that probably wouldn't work. All the same, this area would be swarming with Shadow Guards and goblins in a short time.

Nature spirits swirled around them, sensing the drama. The nature fae who lived in the Boundary Lands probably already knew who they were and why they were fleeing through their land. Unlike the troop, the nature fae mostly stayed out of court business.

"Wait." Gabriel stopped her by a fallen tree trunk and ripped open one of the bags. He pulled out a sweater and shoes for himself, an extra pullover for her against the chill in the air. He tossed the garment to her. "We need to go in the opposite direction."

Clutching the pullover, she leaned over, out of breath, and braced her hands on her thighs. "What? Why?"

"Deeper into the Boundary Lands is exactly the way they think we'll go. We need to go into Piefferburg City. They won't expect that and they won't be looking there."

"Are you crazy? Someone will recognize us. I bet *Faemous* has been playing our faces on a loop."

He shook his head. "No way. The Shadow King will be keeping this hush-hush. He'll have concocted some story about why his guards are searching houses, but I bet anything that story doesn't include you or me. If the troop knew he was trying to kill his blood daughter because she posed a threat to his throne, they would rise up against him and protect us. He wouldn't want the Summer Queen to know what he planned to do to you, either. He's only barely avoiding a war with her by the fact that you came to the Unseelie Court of your own free will. If it came out that you were coerced or influenced—"

"By you."

"By me, that would throw the legitimacy of your defection into shadow and there might be a war after all. The Summer Queen would use any excuse."

She looked further into the trees, searching around as though the right answer would fall from the sky. Somewhere above, a bird called. Her inclination was to stay hidden in the woods, not go back toward the violence. But then what? Set up a little cabin or tree house and blissfully live out the rest of their lives here in the Boundary Lands untouched by the Shadow King? No. Of course not. There was no running away from this. There was only meeting it head-on.

She swallowed hard, managed to catch her breath, and looked at him. "Okay. Let's go."

He nodded and tossed one of the bags with the weapons to her. "Arm yourself."

Fishing inside, she found a long charmed iron dagger in a leather sheath. She hooked the sheath to one of the belt loops of her jeans, so it hung at her hip—ready to grab when she needed it.

*When,* not if.

They took the long way around, seeing no nature fae but the small flitting lights of the littlest ones. They found a good place to sit and then waited until nightfall. Under cover of darkness, they would make the trek back into the city, back into Piefferburg. It was time to put an end to this.

Time to face her father.

They found a place to wait for the gloaming to fall. Spirits flitted around them and then away, but still no nature fae sought them out, yet flowers grew mysteriously quickly around them, twining around trees and snaking across the ground. She sat in a soft bed of leaves, eyes closed, waiting. Gabriel sat opposite her.

She opened her eyes. "Call one," she said, gazing into the branches of the trees above them. Sunlight dappled through the leaves, painting the ground in spots of gold.

"Call one?" He paused, understanding. "Call the sluagh."

She nodded, finding his gaze. "Not the whole army, please. Just one. Can you do that?"

"I can." He paused, looked up into the tree limbs, and then rubbed his chin. "You want to see if you can do it."

She drew a steady breath and looked down at the leaves at their feet, her jaw locking. "I've never been to Goblin Town or the *ceantar dubh*. Until a couple of weeks ago, I'd never even seen a creature like Barthe. I couldn't stop staring at him like some farmer who'd just come to the city for the first time. I don't know if I can command the sluagh and I need to find out."

"I've never called any of the sluagh before but I feel in my blood that I can do it." His voice was strong and sure and his eyes were clear and straightforward. "Don't you have that same assurance?"

She dragged the toe of her shoe through the dirt and looked up at him. "No."

"So you need to see one, command one, in order to find that confidence."

"It's better I find out now, don't you think? And better *one* that I can't control now than an *entire army* later, don't you think?" She paused, a sad smile twisting her lips. "That would be bad."

"Yeah, that would be bad."

"So, if I can't control it, how will we dispel it?"

"You mean, how can we ensure it won't escape and wreak havoc and mayhem all over Piefferburg right after it kills us?"

She swallowed hard. "Yes, exactly. That."

He grinned, showing a quick flash of white teeth. "I guess you'll just have to make sure it doesn't, necromancer. Ready?"

"No."

"Ready?"

"Oh, *Danu*, yes." She drew the dagger to make herself feel better, the thick leather grip heavy in her hand.

He muttered words in Old Maejian—way, way too fast for her taste.

And it appeared.

# TWENTY

———❧———

"RONAN!"

The word ripped from Bella's throat as she watched her husband fall. Charmed iron wrapped his arms, though that didn't faze him. He had immunity to charmed iron. It was the drug they'd just injected him with that worried her.

He collapsed and the goblins caught him, their thin, gray fingers gripping his arms and legs and hefting him on the Shadow King's command. On the way back from the Boundary Lands, they'd used her to keep him in line, threatening to harm her if Ronan tried anything.

Now they were back in the Black Tower, in the Shadow King's quarters, and the royal had decided the only way to keep Ronan from making trouble was if he was unconscious.

She watched, her heart lodged somewhere just behind her teeth, as they carried him into one of the bedrooms. Her throat worked and blood trickled where the Shadow King had cut her to ensure Ronan's cooperation. All Aodh had to do was threaten her and Ronan did whatever he wanted. Aodh had laughed as he'd commanded him, saying love had made him weak.

Ronan had done things, woven spells—laid traps.

"He'll be fine, Bella," purred the Shadow King.

He lounged on his couch, while Barthe gripped her arm. They'd left Aurora knocked out back in the cabin. Bella hoped the fragile woman was stronger than she appeared because the guard who'd hit her had backhanded her so hard she'd slid halfway across the floor.

"Do not speak to me," she ground out, her voice a low tremble of absolute rage.

He moved faster than she'd ever thought possible, coming to stand directly in front of her. His red-tipped hair swirled around his shoulders with the action and brushed her collarbones. "I am king of the Unseelie, *your* king. You'd best master that tongue in my presence or I'll cut it out."

She refused to look at him. Her jaw locked, she unfocused her eyes and gazed past him, lifting her chin.

"Tell me where they are and I'll spare your husband."

Even if she knew where Aislinn and Gabriel were and told him, he would never let Ronan live. Bella understood that cold, hard fact. Ronan was too much of a threat to him. So was Niall. "I don't know where they are. We left the Black Tower before Gabriel took Aislinn from the dungeon."

His fingers snapped out fast and hard, gripping her chin hard enough to bruise. Guiding her face up to his, he brought her eyes to focus on his face. She felt there was no resemblance between the Shadow King and Aislinn, not a breath. "And Niall? Don't tell me you don't know where he is, either?"

"I don't."

He pushed her to the side. She stumbled and fell to the floor, sprawled there, looking up at him with pure hatred on her face. He smiled down at her. "It's a good thing for you that you have some value to me. I can think of five different ways I'd like to flay the skin from your body right now."

Bella knew the kind of value she held for him.

She was bait for a trap and there wasn't anything she could do about it.


GABRIEL had requested the firstborn, the oldest, of the sluagh as a way to summon only one of them.

The creature oriented itself. Growled. Turned and fastened its eyes on each of them in turn. Appraising the male as the greater threat, he charged Gabriel.

All of this happened in the time it took for Gabriel to raise the charmed iron hatchet he'd taken from the weapons bag— a heartbeat.

*"Halt!"*

The sluagh stopped midcharge, so close to Gabriel he could scent the bone-dry dust of almost completely decayed flesh. His immediate gut reaction had been to slash with the hatchet. It sailed harmlessly through the creature's abdomen just as he'd presumed. If Aislinn hadn't commanded it to stop, his action would have been too little, too late.

It was gray and scaly, with a bulbous body like an ant's— puffed-out chest, minuscule waist, and a thicker pelvis region. Its arms and legs were thin, but wiry with muscle. The tattered remnants of decayed clothing hung from its bony shoulders and wrapped its starved, tiny waist. Its head was shaped like a gray peanut, with hollowed, deep-set eyes and a large, gaping maw with sharp, pointed teeth—a mouthful of fangs. In one narrow hand it gripped a machete.

Gabriel stared at its weapon and the teeth and claws, betting anything this creature would draw real blood with or without a necromancer to command it. It had no tether to the afterlife as other souls possessed and its privates hung small and shrunken between its spindly legs. It was hard to believe the thing had once been some kind of fae.

"Oh, sweet Danu," Aislinn breathed.

Gabriel still had a grip on the charmed iron hatchet even though he knew it wouldn't work against a sluagh because they were spirit. If Aislinn commanded it to take corporeal form and then lost control of it, he wasn't even sure if the blade would do anything to it then. After all, it was already dead.

"Take six steps backward, face me, and take corporeal form." Aislinn enunciated each word clearly and loudly. She'd leapt to her feet the moment it had popped into existence, her face chalk white and her hands—one of them gripping the dagger—fisted at her sides, bloodless. Aislinn looked fierce. She was probably frightened out of her mind but she'd taken charge to make this work.

And he was pretty grateful, too.

The sluagh did exactly what she'd demanded, though its face was contorted, as if it was trying to fight her commands and couldn't.

Aislinn blew out a long breath, clearly meant to steady herself. "Okay."

The sluagh's massive head swiveled toward her.

She considered it, chewing the edge of her thumbnail. "Can it speak?"

"I can speak," it answered, startling Aislinn back a step. Its voice was low and gravelly, obviously male, but it was also surprisingly intelligent sounding. It pronounced the words clearly and even had the edge of a British accent.

"Have you ever been commanded by a necromancer?"

"Yes," it growled, clearly unhappy with the fact.

"How many times?"

"Many times," it gritted out. "All times. I am the first of my kind."

"Tell me about any three necromancers who have commanded you."

"Baustia in the time before time began when the fae owned this earth and the humans were still living in caves, in a successful attempt to overthrow the sitting Shadow Queen. Caruagh Elisabeth Moore in the year 1123 in her efforts against the Phaendir. Brigid Fada Erinne O'Dubhuir in the year of 1325 when she set us upon the fae murderer Fallon Brodie who used a type of magick that concealed him from the justice of the Wild Hunt."

Gabriel, and Aislinn, too, undoubtedly, knew all these instances. Every time the sluagh were called, it went into the history books.

"And does the sluagh army obey as one?"

"Whatever you say, we can do nothing but obey. What you ask, we shall answer. What task you command, we shall perform. We are the necromancer's weapon, her right arm, provided she can call us through the veil from the Netherworld." He ground out the words, as though fighting not to say them.

"And what did you do to deserve this immortal fate?"

"I was a rapist and a murderer of my people. This servitude is my punishment."

"The Lord of the Wild Hunt will call you again. Next time he will call all of you and I will command you."

"And so we will come and obey."

"Return from where you came from, until I need you again."

The sluagh disappeared.

Aislinn stood staring at the empty spot where the sluagh had just been, her eyes wide and her lips parted a little. "Oh, Danu," she breathed. "I can command an army of forsaken dead."

"You can. And you can do it with a fierceness that makes my cock get hard."

That broke her stare. Her head whipped toward him and color—finally—suffused her cheeks. She gave a surprised laugh. "You never stop, do you?"

The smiled faded from his lips and he held her gaze steadily. "Not where you're concerned, Aislinn. I'll never stop where you're concerned."

She blinked and her lips parted a little in surprise. After a moment, she slid the dagger back into the sheath at her hip. Then she looked away, glancing up at the sky through the canopy of trees. "It's time we start into the city."

He nodded. "Let's go make history."

SOMEHOW, someway, Gideon had attracted the aid of an angel. Emily swiped cotton balls over his weals and Gideon endured the sting of the antiseptic with hardly an eyelash flutter. Her gentle hands slipped over his skin and he closed his eyes. It was an exquisite torture. Pleasure and pain made one. Labrai's gift to him for his duty and sacrifice.

"You are even more pious than Brother Maddoc," she murmured in a voice of reverence.

"I love my God and will suffer for Him."

"It's a beautiful thing, Brother Gideon," she said in the sort of shushed voice that one might use in a church.

But he didn't want her to think of him in terms of piousness, reverence, or godliness. He wanted an earthier type of appreciation from her.

Emily wasn't employed at the Phaendir headquarters just as Brother Maddoc's personal assistant; she was also a Worshipful Observer. The human group was composed of humans who respected—worshipped—the work the Phaendir did in keeping the evil of the fae races separated from the rest of the world. Many of them were women, and many of them occupied the beds of the brothers, as Gideon suspected Emily occupied Maddoc's.

He couldn't think about that without losing his temper.

"It's to show my devotion to the God who keeps us all safe from the wickedness loose in the world," he replied to her, his hand finding and fisting a pen on his desk. "I do it for you."

"I attend the Phaendir services on Tuesday nights. This last week Brother Maddoc preached about the punishment of the Phaendir through flogging, the attempt to keep at bay the faelike part of you." The back of her soft, warm hand brushed his shoulder and lingered a moment longer than was necessary. "I just want you to know there are humans who appreciate all you do for us."

Yes, but there were some, like the HFF, Humans for the Freedom of the Fae, who had no appreciation and actively worked against the Phaendir. And there were even more, the overwhelming majority, in fact, who simply didn't care one way or another. Those apathetic humans were a blight on all things holy, almost as bad as the fae themselves.

Emily leaned down and spoke near his ear as she tidied the cotton balls and antiseptic. "Perhaps one day you and I can attend services together."

It wasn't an offer to sleep with her, but it was enough to make his lips curl in a satisfied smile. If he could get to know her better through her piousness, maybe he could ride it all the way to her bed. And her body was one step closer to her heart. He wanted all of it. Gideon wanted Emily soul, heart, and body.

Apparently she was seeing something in him that she liked. If only he could make the rest of his plan come together—if he could only get that damn book—then she would be his. He felt it.

For decades he'd been angling to procure the Book of Bindings before Brother Maddoc could manage it. Gideon had schemed, betrayed, and concealed information, bringing him close to obtaining it before Maddoc even had a clue. Then the book had slipped from his fingers like water.

Gone.

She gathered her things and walked toward the door. Once there, she turned back and smiled shyly. "You never answered my question, Brother Gideon."

He blinked, coming out of the slight haze of fantasy that had captured him. "Yes! Yes, of course, I would love to do that sometime."

One more lingering, small smile and she was gone.

He stared at the empty doorway, making no move to cover his naked upper half. That little hint of interest from Emily had been exactly what he'd needed. He closed his eyes and gave thanks to Labrai.

He'd been losing faith that he could procure the Book of Bindings now that the Shadow King seemed to have it in his possession. Aodh was a powerful Unseelie Royal. If it had remained in possession of the Seelie fluff, the woman known as Aislinn Christiana Guinevere Finvarra, perhaps he would have had a chance.

That seemed impossible now, judging from the intelligence he'd gained from the Black Tower. As soon as the

Finvarra woman had arrived, she'd been taken into custody, and she had soon escaped somehow. Now no one truly knew what was going on, but the Shadow Guard and the goblin army were on the move, searching for her and others. Purportedly two of the most powerful Unseelie mages were involved, one of them Ronan Quinn, a man Gideon would personally enjoy disemboweling for thieving the piece of the *bosca fadbh* from the Phaendir.

Gideon would lay his ear closer to the ground in Piefferburg and try to glean what was happening with the Finvarra woman. If somehow he could help that bit of Seelie fluff to be victorious against the Shadow King, perhaps she would regain control of the Book of Bindings and he could get it from her.

He had the magicked patch in the warding around Piefferburg he could use if he needed it. He had the men to send, men who were loyal to him and would prefer to see his policies in place over Maddoc's. There was even a tunnel and trapdoor into the heart of the city, though it let out in a highly inconvenient area. The Phaendir weren't stupid. They'd built secret ways into Piefferburg when the detention area was being constructed, but the town had changed and evolved over their pathways throughout the centuries. Now the entryway was in the heart of Goblin Town. It was probably the worst possible place for it with the exception of the Black Tower.

*Still.*

He leaned forward, tapping his pen on his desk. Perhaps, indeed, there could yet be a way for him to gain all that was due him. All it might take was a little interference on his part.

And a big steel trap for the Seelie fluff.

THE crush of the commercial district on the outer limits of the *ceantar láir* around her, Aislinn stared at the big television screen broadcasting in the middle of one of the district's squares and blinked. She couldn't believe what she was seeing.

*Faemous* commentator Brian Bentley, with his blond human head and huge white teeth and cleft chin, dominated the screen. He was standing in front of the Black Tower on the dark side of Piefferburg Square, a sight that hadn't been seen since the goblins ate the *Faemous* crew assigned to cover the Unseelie five years before. He gave the camera a smug smile to remind everyone of that and began to speak.

*For the first time in years, the Shadow King has allowed* Faemous *access to the Black Tower, with his personal assurance that no one on the film crew will be harmed. Why? He has requested we cover the capture early this morning of Ronan Achaius Quinn and Bella Rhiannon Caliste Mac Lyr, two of the fugitives that have been at large this past week. Niall Daegan Riordan Quinn still remains at large.*

*As you will remember from our earlier coverage of this incident, Ronan Quinn and Bella Mac Lyr have once again gone against their royal. This is not the first time this pair has operated outside fae law, although this time it was the Shadow King instead of the Summer Queen. One wonders where the couple will find refuge after this latest dustup, having now alienated both royals.*

Bentley continued speaking, but that was all Aislinn heard. That was a message sent by the Shadow King through what passed as fae media and she had received it loud and clear. He had Bella and Ronan and he would kill them if she didn't turn herself in.

She could hear between the lines just fine.

"Come on," said Gabriel near her ear. "The Shadow Guard is coming this way." He yanked her arm, jerking her out of the stunned stare of horror she'd fallen into.

He led her around the corner and they started walking down it. Aislinn concentrated on putting one foot in front of the other, her mind in a nasty, dark tangle.

They walked until they crossed the border of the commercial district and were just inside the *ceantar dubh*, getting closer and closer to the Black Tower. They would keep to the alleys and the shadowy places until they reached their destination—an apartment that Aeric O'Malley, the famed

Unseelie blacksmith and Gabriel's friend, kept close to Pief-ferburg Square.

"We won't let anything happen to them," Gabriel said. "Remember, we have the sluagh to use as a weapon."

The icy shock slipped from her bones and hot rage poured into its place. "We need to act soon, sooner than we planned. There's no telling how he's keeping them. They could already be—"

"No. No way, Aislinn. He needs them alive. But he's keeping Bella in charmed iron at the very least. He's probably got Ronan trussed up some other way."

"But they could be—wait." She put a hand on Gabriel's arm to stop him. They halted in the middle of the dank alley. Somewhere on their left, water dripped. A shape moved in the shadows of the alley ahead of them. "Something's up there."

"We're in an alley in the *ceantar dubh*. I'd be surprised if there wasn't something up there."

"No. I don't mean a dark fae who lives here. I mean something's up there waiting for *us*. I just know it. I feel it."

He stared at her for a long moment as if searching for an explanation in the certainty of her voice. "Okay. And is this someone waiting to kill us or kiss us?"

"I'm not kissing your skanky ass." Niall stepped from the shadows ahead and gave Aislinn a long once-over. "Although I wouldn't mind kissing—"

"Niall, what the fuck are you doing jumping us in dark alleys," Gabriel yelled. "Do you know that your brother and his wife are in the Black Tower right now? The Shadow King got them."

"Yeah, I know. I told them to keep moving, but they went to ground instead. Trusted people they shouldn't." He shook his dark head. "Bad mistake."

"How did you find us?" Aislinn asked.

"I figured you'd be coming out of hiding to fight Aodh, so I set up a net around the Black Tower to tell me when you arrived." He grinned at the look on their faces. "Don't worry, my brother and I are the only mages left alive who can do that. Well, unless Aodh has enlisted the help of the

Piefferburg witch, but I find that unlikely. Priss hates Aodh's guts."

"Are you coming to help us?" Aislinn asked.

"I'm helping you in order to help my brother and his wife." He shrugged. "Also, I'd like to see Aodh taken down once and for all. The time of his reign has come to an end. I would much prefer to see a Shadow Queen on the throne of the Black Tower than a Shadow King for a while." He gave her a deep bow. "Sídhe princess. I hope you will be my next liege."

Aislinn's whole body jerked as she realized for the first time what removing the Shadow King from his throne would mean. She was the next in line for possession. She was, for all intents and purposes, overthrowing the royal of the Unseelie Court and putting herself in his place. No matter her reasons for doing so, that was the end result.

Gods, she'd never signed on for this. She'd never dreamed of this, never *wanted* it.

The ironic part was that she'd never have made a move for the Shadow King's throne if Aodh hadn't tried to kill her and threatened those she loved. By trying to avoid the fate he most feared, he'd brought it about.

Niall took another step into the light, leaving one half of his body in shadow. The one bright blue eye that Aislinn could see glittered coldly. "So call your crew, Lord of the Wild Hunt, and let's go take out the trash."

# TWENTY-ONE

AERIC had rented an apartment using cash and a false name during the last week. It was an anonymous place on an anonymous street in the border area between the *ceantar dubh* and the commercial district. A sticker on the door and a broken lock declared it had already been searched by the Shadow Guard. A sparse place, meant only for one person or maybe two, it had a single bedroom, one bath, and a small living room and kitchen. Today it fit six people and one dog.

The dog was a sleek black hound named Blix, a hunt hound, in fact. He'd come with Bran, who, according to Gabriel, had an affinity for animals. As far as Aislinn could tell, Bran seemed to get along better with four-footed living things than the two-footed variety. Though Bran had lost his furred friend early on when Blix had decided he liked Aislinn more. Lex, Bran's crow, stuck close, however, never leaving Bran's shoulder.

Now Aislinn sat on the floor of the bare living room, long gray skirt pooling around her ankles on the floor, while the others murmured in the kitchen. Melia had brought them both a change of clothes. Out in the kitchen, Gabriel spoke in that lighthearted, arrogant way he had, asking them how badly the Shadow King had questioned them about him. Now she knew there was much more under the surface of that carefree, rakish mask he wore. He was very concerned his friends had been in danger because of their connection to him, but he was trying not to show it.

"He questioned every woman who ever spent a night in your bed," Aelfdane said, a smile in his voice. "It took him a long time."

"Yeah, because fuck if that isn't almost every woman in the Black Tower," Aeric added.

Gabriel laughed. "That's not true. I only sleep with the pretty ones."

"Oh, really? Then how do you explain Aeria?" Melia chimed in.

"Beauty is in the eye of the beholder. Aeria has gorgeous eyes and a—"

"—nice pair of tits," Aeric finished for Gabriel.

Everyone laughed.

"Yes, well, we just want you back there and all returned to normal, so you can go back to your old ways," Melia finished.

His old ways. Yes. Aislinn was sure Gabriel wanted that, too.

She leaned her head back against the wall behind her and threaded her fingers through the hound's short hair. Tomorrow morning she would do all she could to ensure that happened. She wanted things back to normal for herself, too, whatever that new "normal" was going to be. As long as it wasn't dead, she'd be okay.

However, the likelihood of her—of any of them—still being alive by tomorrow evening was somewhat in question. Okay, a lot in question. But that was something none of them talked about. Positivity was the name of the game on the eve of one's death, apparently. She could see the allure.

They spent the day and evening planning for what would happen in the morning. By nightfall all of them had gone the way they'd come—one by one, cautiously, keeping to the shadows. At the window, she watched Bran ghosting away into the night with the odd Netherworld hound at his side and his crow like a smudge of charcoal perched on his shoulder. The moonlight silvered the pavement of the street and licked shadows up the sides of the nearby buildings.

She felt Gabriel more than heard him come to stand behind her. "Okay?"

Inhaling carefully, she took a moment to answer. "As okay as I can be on the eve we attempt to overthrow the Unseelie Court."

"Surreal, isn't it?"

"Unbelievable." She paused. "You're lucky to have such good friends."

"They're more than just friends; they're my family. I've been with them since whatever mystic powers chose me for the Wild Hunt."

She continued to stare out the window at the darkened street. Not a fae soul could be seen out there now. "How did it happen?"

He leaned down close to her back, a hand to each side of the windowsill, pinning her there, and spoke near her ear. "The previous Lord of the Wild Hunt died and his host disbanded. One night something—some force—pulled me from my sleep and compelled me to the top of the Black Tower. At the top were the others—Melia, Aelfdane, Aeric, and Bran. We just *knew* why we were there. I was the only one with the ability to call the Wild Hunt and the only one able to ride Abastor, the black horse who leads the others. Eventually, as my second in command, Aeric also developed the magick needed to call it down." He chuckled. "But Aeric still can't handle Abastor."

"Were Melia and Aelfdane already married when they were called to be a part of the Furious Host?"

"No. They fell in love as a result of being on the hunt together." He gave a low laugh and the sound in the darkness reminded her of fall wood smoke or the scent of a fine cigar. "They're an odd couple, I guess. She's so battle hardened and he's deceivingly fragile looking, as a male Twyleth Teg, but they're well suited and very happy with each other."

"I get Aeric O'Malley. He's very old, a blacksmith who can no longer craft the weaponry he used to in the old days. I remember the romantic story about him and his beautiful fiancé, Aileen. Emmaline Siobhan Keara Gallagher, the Summer Queen's assassin, killed Aileen out of jealousy and Aeric was heartbroken. He is strong, loyal, and brave. Bit of a temper. Good sense of humor. He respects you." She shook her head. "But I don't get Bran."

"Bran." He let out a slow breath. "He's in a different world most of the time. Quiet, dreamy. We think he's mostly wilding, probably only just this side of Unseelie. His power is with the animals and with birds. He doesn't talk just to hear his own voice. When he speaks it's to say something worth hearing. He's secretive, but I would trust him with my life."

"You *are* trusting him with your life."

"I am."

"If you trust him, I trust him."

He grasped her shoulders and turned her to face him. The shadows half concealed his expression, moonlight catching the other side in pale silver. He stared down at her for a moment before dipping his head and catching her lips against his.

She'd meant to push him away. She'd meant to tell him no if he tried this tonight. But now all her protests dried in her throat. At dawn she was bringing an army of unforgiven dead down on the head of the Unseelie Royal. By tomorrow at around brunch time, it was doubtful she'd even still be alive. Why not take this night and spend it in the kind of ecstasy she knew only Gabriel could give her? Saying no to him didn't make sense, not at this point.

She rose up on her toes and pushed back at him aggressively, her teeth nipping at his lower lip. He shuddered against her and yanked her up against his chest, his mouth slanting over hers. Forcing her lips apart, he slid his tongue within to dance against her tongue. Fisting handfuls of her skirt, he dragged the material upward, rubbing his palms against her outer thighs, then going higher.

He pushed her back, so she half sat on the windowsill, and yanked her underwear down. She helped him get them off her legs as her fingers quested and found the button and zipper of his jeans. She stroked his length as soon as it was in her hand, and he groaned. She couldn't wait to have it inside her.

"Wait. No, no," he murmured, cupping her face in his hands and forcing her to look at him. "I want you slower than this, better."

She nipped his lower lip again. "We have all night." She laughed a little against his mouth. "What? Did you think you'd sleep tonight? I won't be able to." Her fingers danced along the underside of his cock. "Might as well have something to do."

"Bad girl."

"Apparently I'm the worst. Just ask the Shadow King."

"No." He shook his head and nipped her throat in almost a punishing way. "No, we're not going to talk about him. His name doesn't cross your lips again tonight." He smiled and kissed her, a sweet drag of his mouth over hers. "Anyway, I can think of better uses for those lips."

She thrust her hips forward and found the slick head of his cock. He slid inside her and her head fell back on a moan as he pushed deep within. Kissing the arch of her throat, he moved inside her, taking away the horror of the upcoming battle and the uncertainty that dawn would bring.

"THEY'RE here." The words slid like ice down the back of Aislinn's throat. Her fingers curled into the silky fur of the hound that stood waist-high beside her. Blix was an ever-present fixture this morning.

She could feel the sluagh a moment before they appeared in the square. The chill of them touched the back of her neck and slid beneath her shirt. The sluagh winked into existence before her, a shimmering gray army of unforgiven dead.

Each of them held a weapon. Some fisted hammers, some swords; others wielded scythes. No matter the weapon they gripped, all of them struck fear into the hearts of those few who could view them in their noncorporeal form. She was glad this was happening now, in the early predawn hours, before the city was filled with onlookers.

A split second after they appeared, Aislinn commanded them before they could act of their own volition. "*Sluagh, obey me*. Stand still and do not move until I order it." She raised her arm and her voice boomed out of her, shivers of magick rocking her on her feet.

The sluagh went stock-still at her command. Even the slight rustle of moving bodies stopped.

She took a careful breath and touched Blix at her side for support. Her other hand gripped the charmed iron dagger Gabriel had given her. The twisted leather grip felt good in her hand. "Sluagh, take corporeal form."

A subtle sound, something like the faint creaking of leather, filled the air and the sluagh were corporeal. Making them corporeal meant everyone could see them instead of just herself, Gabriel, and the Furious Host. A murmured hush rose like a wave in the square interspersed with a few surprised screams.

"Oh, fuck," breathed Niall on her other side.

Behind them, in the Black Tower, the inhabitants had begun to stir. Shouting and pounding feet, all coming closer. Alarm at the sight in the square. The sluagh seemed to frighten even the goblins.

"Aislinn," said Gabriel. "I would hurry if I were you. The goblins are on their way."

Yes, Shadow King would have ordered them to the square already. "Legion of unforgiven dead, sluagh, hear my commands. You will hunt down the royal of the Unseelie Court, Aodh Críostóir Ruadhán O'Dubhuir. Once you find him, you will return from whence you came . . . taking Aodh Críostóir Ruadhán O'Dubhuir with you. Anyone who raises a hand against you, you have permission to battle. Otherwise, you will raise your hand to no one, harm no one, as you execute my wish." She paused, hearing the approaching horde behind her.

The doors of the Black Tower opened; men and monsters poured through.

*"Aislinn,"* Gabriel said again, his voice full of warning.

"Move, sluagh, go! Carry out my order!" she yelled.

Gabriel yanked her to the side, sweeping her out of the way just as the first wave of Shadow Guard and goblin combatants washed forth from the Black Tower into the square. The black hound bounded alongside her and Gabriel. On their other side were Melia, Aelfdane, Aeric, Bran, and Niall. Overhead Lex flew in a wide circle over the square. From a distance away, in the gray early morning murk, the two sides—the sluagh and the forces commanded by the Black Tower—collided.

The sluagh were merciless and efficient. Killing machines. That was how Aislinn knew they would win. The Black Tower didn't stand a chance against this army of immortal unforgiven dead. Not against all-too-mortal goblins and men.

Aislinn wanted to turn her face away from it, but she was ultimately responsible for it. Therefore she needed to watch. She needed to see every one of the Shadow King's supporters fall in their defense of him, every drop of blood spilled. She needed to see every goblin life lost, goblins who didn't fight of their own free will, but because they were enslaved by the Shadow Amulet and compelled by the Unseelie Royal's will.

She had set this into motion and she needed to see and take responsibility for it all.

"Come on," said Gabriel. "We've got to use this chaos to slip into the Black Tower."

"Here come the goblins," Aeric yelled. "Straight at us."

"Hells!" Niall answered, watching in horror with the rest of them as the horde of goblins—released on the populace by the Shadow King, no doubt—poured in among the sluagh and fought them for the highest horror honors.

The sluagh and the goblins were controlled by Aislinn

and the Shadow King respectively. The difference was that
Aislinn had instructed the sluagh not to harm innocents. She
was certain the Shadow King had given no such order to the
goblins.

A seven-foot-tall powerie with his bald head dyed bloodred
attacked Aelfdane, swinging a club at his head, which he
ducked and missed by a hair. Melia screamed and attacked with
a blast that sent the powerie careening backward. Melia was
one of the only Unseelie fae able to use her magick that way,
luckily enough for her husband.

That drew attention to them and the next attack came
from a goblin to their right. The gibbering creature flew at
Aislinn. Gabriel knocked the goblin to the side with a heavy
fist, preventing it from slamming into her and sinking its
teeth into her flesh. Of course the goblins were gunning for
her in the melee, under orders from their liege. Gabriel followed up, beating it back away from her with a vicious
vengeance she'd never seen in him before.

Then it seemed as if the entire goblin army attacked them at
once. Gabriel gave a battle roar, Aeric, Melia, Aelfdane, and
Bran right beside him, all ready for bloodshed. Aislinn had
never even pulled someone's hair. She stood for a breathless,
stricken moment, wide-eyed and allowing Gabriel to defend
her, before her survival instinct kicked in, full force.

Two goblins came for her at once. Blix, the black hunt
hound, leapt toward the throat of one, and she brought her
dagger up fast and hard. It struck the creature's midsection,
gushing hot blood down her hand. The goblin dropped to the
cobblestone at her feet. She stared down at him for a moment
in shock, the dagger hanging limply from her fingers.

But then another was on her, and another. Soon Aislinn
was wielding the blade like it was a third appendage. Dis-
connected from her mind, her body fought from primal
instinct—*she wanted to survive*. Her body twisted, the dagger slashed and her booted feet kicked.

Long claws tore her shirt, drawing blood on her stomach
and thighs. One of them raked her upper arm with its teeth,
rending shallow, jagged marks through her flesh.

"We have to get out of here. They're coming for Aislinn. There's too many of them," yelled Aeric over the din. He pivoted on his heel and engaged another attacking goblin.

*"Tae marjian sa glas elle bea!"* Gabriel yelled at the sky in Old Maejian.

Immediately wind swooshed down around them and the full Wild Hunt host was there. Gabriel threw himself up onto the back of the rippling black horse that had to be Abastor and pulled her up astride. Aeric mounted an enormous chestnut quarter horse. Melia and Aelfdane bounded up on a white Arabian and Niall and Bran both took huge bays. Then they were all in the air just as a goblin hand full of sharp claws breezed past her leg.

She clung to the horse and to Gabriel, staring down at the horde below them. It spilled across Piefferburg Square, almost to the statue in the center. It swarmed into the Black Tower and throughout and around it, into the alleys and streets of the *ceantar dubh*. The sluagh looked as if they were pushing inside the building in a concerted effort—a deadly arrow pointing to her prey. That meant the Shadow King was inside. Per her directive, the sluagh would flow to his presence like a river to the ocean. She was sure it wouldn't be that easy, though. The Shadow King had to be expecting this and he'd have something up his sleeve.

Right now they just needed to get to Bella and Ronan. They'd deal with the rest when they got to it.

The Wild Hunt set down on the top of the Black Tower and Gabriel slid off the mystical Wild Hunt horse, Abastor, pulling her down after him.

Carina shimmered into view just as the rest of them were dismounting.

Before they'd entered the square and Gabriel had called the sluagh, Aislinn had summoned Carina, remembering what she'd said about wanting to make amends. Aislinn had requested that Carina go to the Black Tower in noncorporeal form, locate Bella and Ronan, and return with information.

"Did you find them?" asked Aislinn.

Niall looked at her like she was crazy and Aislinn remembered that he was the only one who couldn't see spirits. To him it looked like she was talking to air.

Carina nodded. "They're being kept in the Shadow King's quarters. Ronan has been drugged and is unconscious. Bella is well enough, but cuffed in charmed iron and very frightened for Ronan. The Shadow King is with them. I think he's waiting for you." She paused. "Be careful, Aislinn. There's magick at the door, a kind of impassable boundary."

"We will." She smiled. "I forgive you, Carina."

Carina let out a long, slow breath and seemed to become almost physically lighter, which was an odd impression to have, considering Carina wasn't physical at all. "Thank you."

"Now go and do whatever it is you do over there. I wish you could tell me."

A smile flickered across her face. "I wish I could, too. Good-bye."

And she was gone. This time forever.

When Aislinn turned, the horses and hounds were gone and the host and Niall were all looking at her for instruction. "I know where we need to go and we better hurry. The goblins will be on the move." She paused, looking at each of them in turn. "Thank you for doing this, for risking everything to throw in with me this way. I just want to say that I never intended for this to happen. But now that it has, I appreciate your support."

Aeric stepped forward. "We couldn't stand aside knowing what the Shadow King has done to his mother, to you, to the former Lord of the Wild Hunt and undoubtedly many others. We may be Unseelie, but that doesn't mean we support the cruel and vicious. As far as we're concerned, you're the rightful holder of the Shadow Throne."

She shivered as she always did when the full impact of the day's events—if they were successful—fully hit her.

"Now, come on," said Gabriel. "We need to move."

# TWENTY-TWO

THE sluagh had already swarmed around the door of the Shadow King's apartment. Dead goblins lay on the floor at their feet.

"Carina said there was a kind of warding," Aislinn said, watching the sluagh milling restlessly in the hallway, unable to enter and carry out her commands.

"Yes." Aelfdane reached out and touched the outside wall of the apartment. He closed his eyes for a moment. "He's got some kind of barrier up against the sluagh. They can't enter."

Niall ran his hand along the wall. "If you get me in there, I can probably break it. Any mage worth his salt could. That's probably why he's got Ronan out cold."

"I can take care of that." Gabriel kicked the door open and immediately a volley of heavy magick crashed through the air in cloying waves toward them. They all hit the floor. The sluagh tried to surge through the open doorway, but failed to push through.

Beside her, Niall muttered something in Old Maejian. The waves of power relented, but the sluagh still couldn't pass. He'd broken Aodh's assault, but hadn't broken the barrier.

"Niall, you always ruin my fun," said the Shadow King. His cool, calm voice shivered through Aislinn.

Aislinn raised her head from under Gabriel's protective arm and glanced up to see the Shadow King standing in the center of the foyer with Bella in his grasp. She was bound by charmed iron cuffs, wrists in front of her, as Carina had said. She was also gagged and blindfolded. Blood trickled down the pale skin of her throat from the curved knife that the Shadow King was pressing to her flesh. Bella didn't slump or cower and she didn't whimper. She stood straight and tall. If Aislinn were going to name what emotion Bella's body language broadcast, she would say it was anger.

Aislinn leapt to her feet. "Release her!" The others also rose.

Barthe lurked in the corner, half hidden in the shadows behind his liege. Ronan was nowhere in sight and that made her heart skip a beat. Carina had said he was all right and she had to hope that was true.

The Shadow King gave her a withering look. "I'm not a sluagh to do your bidding, daughter."

She shuddered. "Don't call me that." Cautiously, she picked her way past the sluagh and entered the room to stand a distance away from the Shadow King in the large foyer of his apartment. Gabriel and the others were right behind her.

He poked Bella's throat with the knife, making her head jerk to get away from it. "You're hardly in a position to dictate to me. I'll call you what I choose."

"There are five hundred sluagh just waiting to get in here and take you away with them, *father*. I think you're the one unable to dictate terms."

"In order for the sluagh to get in, Niall would have to break the barriers, and considering it was *Ronan* who constructed them, I find that eventuality unlikely. What? You look confused. Yes, Ronan built the barriers that are keeping me safe. It's amazing what a man will agree to if you threaten the woman he loves enough." He poked the tip of the blade against Bella's throat and her blood welled. Bella inhaled sharply through her nose. Her throat was a bloody mess of shallow wounds.

"Stop it!"

He grinned, showing teeth. "No." He pushed the tip in farther and Bella's body tensed. "Here's the deal, daughter of mine. I want to do an exchange, you for Bella. You will die by this blade right now, but your soul will live on. You can haunt me until the end of my days. Bella and Ronan will leave here to live out the rest of their very long lives. The sluagh will dissipate with your death and all this silliness will come to an end." He paused. "If you don't agree, you will watch Bella die right now. There's no way Niall will be able to break the barriers in time to save her. Understand? What's your answer?"

She didn't believe him.

In order to keep the Shadow Throne safe, all of those involved in this mess would have to die. He wouldn't trust any of them not to make trouble down the line. No, this wasn't as easy as simply giving up her life for Bella's. She wasn't naïve enough to believe that. More like, once she was dead and the sluagh were gone, the king would order the goblins to rip the rest of them to shreds.

Beside her, Niall muttered in an endless stream of Old Maejian interspersed with curses when he failed to break down what his brother had erected.

"Where's Ronan?" she asked.

"Safe," Aodh barked. "Stop stalling for time."

"I never wanted your throne, Aodh," she growled at him. "If you had left me alone, ignorant of my unfortunate biological parentage, I would have continued on, lived out my life, and none of this would be happening right now."

"I couldn't take that chance. Now toss that dagger aside and come to me."

She gripped the leather handle of her weapon tighter.

"Make your decision." He dug the blade into Bella's neck and started to cut. Bella's scream, muffled by the gag she wore, sliced through Aislinn.

She dropped the dagger to the foyer floor with a clatter and held up her hands. "All right!"

Gabriel pulled her against his body. "No."

"I have to." She pushed him away and took a step toward Aodh, glancing back and meeting Niall's eyes. The mage was still muttering like mad. He shook his head, indicating he was no closer to breaking the barrier. They needed the sluagh desperately.

"On one condition," said Gabriel, stepping forward. "I want to accompany her and aid in making the exchange."

The royal barked out a laugh. "Do you think I'm an idiot? I haven't remained the Shadow King for over five hundred years without considering every angle. Stay back and don't move. Disobey and Bella dies."

Aislinn took slow, measured steps toward Aodh, hoping Niall might be able to perform some kind of last-minute miracle. Closer and closer she inched. In an abrupt move, the Shadow King thrust Bella to the side—she tripped and fell to the floor—and grabbed Aislinn, pressing the knife to her throat.

Bella ripped the gag from her throat and the blindfold from her eyes. "Aislinn, don't do this."

"Too late," the Shadow King snarled. "Already done."

Malice overcame Bella's beautiful face. "I have cursed you and cursed you, Aodh. I've brought all the dark magick I have to call down on your head. There's no way you're leaving this room alive."

He laughed. "I think you overestimate your powers, pretty."

"No, she's right. You're dead," said Gabriel. His voice was made of menace and his fists were at his sides, bloodless. "Harm Aislinn and I'll rip you apart. We all will. No matter what, you're not leaving this room alive."

"Wrong. She dies, the sluagh disappear, and you're all goblin food. *The end*."

The blade sank into her skin and she winced, even though she'd given herself a pep talk about being brave. Pain lanced through her and hot blood welled, trickling down her skin.

*"Aislinn,"* said Gabriel. So much emotion was embedded in the utterance of her name that she could almost imagine he loved her. She met his gaze and held it, wanting his face to be the last one she saw.

"Aeric the Blacksmith, don't you find it ironic that I'm going to kill her with a charmed blade forged by you?" Aodh said with a note of pure joy in his voice. He thought he'd won . . . and maybe he had.

"Only half as ironic as when Gabriel hacks you to pieces with this one." Aeric tossed his bloodied battle-ax to Gabriel.

Holding weapons in each hand, smeared with blood, and with a brutal expression on his face, Gabriel looked ready to take on the Shadow King and the whole goblin army by himself.

"I'm going to cut deep," Aodh whispered into her ear. "Through tendon and muscle. I'm going to do it slow so your boyfriend can watch. I'm going to slice right through your windpipe all the way back to your neck bone if I can. It would make me happy to nearly decapitate you."

The knife bit deeper.

*Ah, Danu, she didn't want to die. Not yet.* Aislinn threw chance to the wind and cast a wish into the Netherworld. "Papa!"

The Shadow King stilled the knife at her throat, perhaps confused by the emotion-laced entreaty she'd yelled loud enough to carry to the Netherworld.

Her father shimmered into view right in front of them. The confusion on his face swiftly turned to absolute rage as he took in the scene. Normally no spirit but the sluagh could affect the physical environment. *Normally.* A spirit who'd amassed enough emotion could throw things, kick things, destroy things, and could even kill.

Aislinn was banking on the strength of her papa's love.

All the events smashed together so fast it was as if they happened at the same time.

"Corporeal!" she yelled.

Her father went corporeal, yanked the Shadow King's arm away from her throat, and then winked out of existence.

Aislinn brought her elbow back hard into Aodh's solar plexus. The knife flew from his hand and slid across the floor under an armoire.

Then Gabriel was on him. They battled, Aodh kicking both weapons from Gabriel's hands. Gabriel backhanded him and Aodh stumbled. Gabriel leapt on him, pushing him onto the floor, punching him over and over as if he could kill him with his bare hands. Aislinn crab-walked backward in the face of Gabriel's all-consuming rage, then slumped down, her fingers going to the wounds on her throat.

Bella uneasily scrambled to her side, her wrists still cuffed in front of her. "Are you all right?"

Aislinn nodded, touching her throat. "Go! Go to Ronan."

Bella kissed her temple and awkwardly stood, then raced to one of the back bedrooms of the apartment.

"Goblins, to me!" the Shadow King yelled just before Gabriel punched him again.

Oh, that was not good.

Almost immediately, goblins found a way past the sluagh and streamed into the room. Niall and the host turned and hefted their weapons, cutting down the flow of gibbering monsters as they poured through the doorway.

Barthe ambled toward Gabriel, growling low in his throat. Aislinn spotted the Shadow King's fighting staff in the corner, the long, cool length of polished wood and smooth crystal knob glowing with possibility. She leapt to her feet, grabbed it, and swung at Barthe with everything she had. It hit the creature's stomach and made him *oof*, but it didn't stop him. He just yanked it from her hands and tossed it aside, then picked Gabriel up with a low growl and tossed him after it.

Gabriel fell heavily to the floor, slid, grabbed the fighting stick, and jumped back up to his feet, just as the Shadow King rose from the floor—his nose and mouth bloodied from Gabriel's fists.

Barthe tried to stalk past him toward Gabriel, but the Shadow King put a hand to his pet's chest. "No. I want Gabriel." He jerked a chin toward Aislinn. "Take care of her," he finished, as though she was just an afterthought and not the purpose of the entire kerfuffle.

And an afterthought she would be in only moments.

Barthe advanced on her just as the Shadow King sprang at Gabriel. She edged her way backward into the living room, casting her gaze about for some kind of weapon to use on the Unseelie creature. If she couldn't find anything, she was a goner.

"Aislinn!" Gabriel called right before the Shadow King's foot smashed into the side of his head, making him *oof* and stagger to the side. Before Aodh attacked again, he tossed her dagger. He must have scooped it from the floor where she'd dropped it.

She caught the weapon and turned toward Barthe, brandishing the blood-covered edge of the blade. It only made Barthe emit a low gravelly sound that might have been a laugh. The creature came closer, moving slowly and smiling to reveal sharp white teeth. He knew she was trapped and no match for him.

Behind Barthe, she watched Gabriel recover and engage the Shadow King again. They were a flurry of arms, fists, legs, and feet. They fought each other like they'd done it before, maybe in a practice ring. Now it was deadly serious. Blow for blow, the Shadow King tried to push Gabriel toward the fighting near the door—within reach of the goblins—while Gabriel tried to push the Shadow King away. They were matched well, each anticipating and blocking the other's moves. A former friendship gone violent.

Barthe gave another low laugh that raised all the hair on the back of her neck. She edged her way around a chair. He was stalking her and enjoying the hell out of it.

By the doorway, Niall yelled out a stream of Old Maejian as he and the host slashed and cut through the goblins that spilled through the doorway. Something around her in the air trembled, pulsed. Niall excitedly yelled out another stream.

Tremble. Pulse.

Then nothing.

Niall gave a loud bellow of anger and attacked the goblins

with a new vengeance. At the same time, Gabriel landed a good kick to the Shadow King's head that sent him sprawling.

And that was when Barthe rushed her.

She'd been in the process of inching around the couch in the living room. With a swiftness and agility she'd never expected the lumbering creature to possess, he leapt over the obstacle separating them, grabbed her by the throat with one huge, hairy hand, and sent her crashing down onto the coffee table.

Immediately she plunged her dagger hilt-deep into his side. Barthe roared in pain, his back arching and his head snapping back, but he didn't let go of her throat. She tried to pull the blade free and stab him again, but the creature's hide was too thick. The weapon seemed cemented in his flesh.

Letting go of the blood-slick grip of the dagger, Aislinn clawed at the thick fingers around her throat. Terror poured through her, made her icy and still. Her airway cut off, she gasped for breath and flailed against the enormous strength of the beast pinning her down.

*She was going to die*.

The thought cut through the frenzied panic that consumed her. If she couldn't find a way to release herself from Barthe's grip *now*, she was dead.

Blindly she groped for something—anything—on the coffee table to use as a weapon. Her fingers closed around an object that felt like a rock or maybe a paperweight and she smashed it against Barthe's head with every ounce of strength she possessed.

Barthe grunted and rolled away, falling to the floor. Dragging precious mouthfuls of air into her lungs and coughing, she pushed up, touching her ravaged throat. Barthe growled at her, his lips peeling back away from his teeth. Then Bella was there, behind Barthe. Her cuffs were gone and she had an iron fire poker in her hands, which she hefted over her head and brought down against his skull over and over until the creature lay still.

"Bella!" Aislinn whispered through her ravaged throat, rising shakily to her feet.

Bella dropped the fire poker, stepped over Barthe, and enveloped Aislinn in her arms. "Aislinn," she whispered through her tears. "Danu, you scared me."

Something around them popped, snapped, and then exploded, making Aislinn's ears ring. The sound of the battle at the doorway intensified and the sluagh poured in. Niall slumped against a wall, streaked with goblin blood, now finally at ease after breaking the barrier.

Still half embracing Bella, Aislinn's gaze met the Shadow King's across the room. Her eyes were narrow and as cold as she could make them. His eyes, wide, set in an angry face, revealed the fear he felt at the approach of the sluagh.

"Good-bye, father," she whispered a moment before the sluagh descended on him, covering him over and forcing him down and out of sight, like a pack of wild dogs devouring prey. Then the sluagh were gone.

The Shadow King lay still and pale on the marble floor of the foyer, his soul ripped away.

"A little help!" yelled Aeric at the door. They were still fighting the goblins with all they had and now lacked the aid of the sluagh to thin the ranks.

The amulet that had been only a tattoo on the Shadow King's skin before had now manifested as a physical object to lie around his neck. Gabriel reached down, yanked the amulet from the Shadow King's throat, and tossed it across the room at Aislinn.

As she caught it, he bowed deeply. "My queen."

A shiver of dread went through her, but she would deal with that in a moment or so. She slipped the heavy chain over her head and felt the cold weight of the amulet settle against her skin. It adhered to her and sank into her flesh slowly, the metal weight dissolving into her skin and becoming part of her. The jewelry definitely hadn't rejected her. Her gorge rose, bitter at the back of her throat. Bella grabbed her hand to steady her as the tattoo of the amulet imprinted into her flesh, in tones of silver and black.

A moment later, magick poured through her, making her limbs tingle and giving her body a momentary sensation of levity. She gasped at the alien power curling through her, but pushed her reaction to the oddness away. There was no time for self-indulgence now.

"Goblins, cease battle immediately." The words came out as loud as she could broadcast them. She had no idea how to command the goblins. She could only hope it was inherent, like her ability to order the sluagh, given to her by the power of the Shadow Amulet.

Oh, gods, she now commanded the sluagh and the goblins. The full impact of those truths hit her like a punch to the solar plexus.

The goblins all stopped fighting. The sounds of battle died away, leaving only the moaning of the injured and dying.

The host all dropped their weapons, sighed, and slumped with relief. All of them were covered in blood and goblin gore, but none of them seemed to have sustained major injury. Since they'd been defending a small opening, they'd had the advantage over the goblins. Many of the monsters lay dead on the floor of the foyer, unable to mount an effective attack while battling their way past the sluagh in the corridor and then trying to force their way into the room.

Aislinn gazed down at the dead and dying goblins, sadness filling her heart.

The sluagh were commanded and enslaved because it was their punishment, prescribed by whatever forces ruled the Netherworld. They'd committed terrible crimes during their lives and now paid the price for their actions. The Shadow King had now joined their ranks. But the goblins, ugly and naturally vicious though they were, were innocents. Commanded to fight by the power of the Shadow King—or Shadow Queen—they had no choice but to risk their lives and, in some cases, die. Aodh would never have even thought about the rights of the goblins. They had just been a tool to him, a way to keep his throne safe from all comers.

And that was Aislinn's first clue that she was in trouble as the new royal of the Unseelie Court.

Aislinn brushed the tattoo of the amulet, wishing she'd thrown it into the fire instead of putting it on. She didn't want this, didn't want this responsibility. "Goblins, collect your dead and injured. Take them home. Your fighting here is finished." Her voice was heavy, sad. The goblins immediately moved to do her bidding.

"You're the best person for this job because you don't want it." Gabriel's voice. He'd come to stand near her. His gaze searched hers. Blood and sweat marked him from head to toe. His clothing was ripped and his chest still heaved from the battle. "Don't you see that, Aislinn?"

How could he know what she'd been thinking? Was her expression really that transparent?

"He's right," said Bella. "You'll rule this court in the way it should be ruled."

Aislinn shook her head. "No. I'm not ruthless enough. I'm not tough enough to hold this throne. I should pick another to rule and give up the amulet." She wasn't exactly sure how to do that short of dying, but there had to be a way.

*"No!"* Aeric roared from near the doorway, his massive chest heaving with passion. He crossed the floor swiftly toward her. *"You* are the rightful heir to the throne. You have the blood, not to mention the amulet. If you even hint to the Unseelie that you're uncertain of your rule or that you want to hand off power to someone else, we'll have an all-out war and you won't be able to stop that one with a few well-chosen commands. Many people will die. I remember the fae wars of the 1600s. No one wants to relive those."

He was right. She knew he was right. It was important for her to take control of the throne as was her right as the biological daughter of the former king. For a while she'd been a bastard Unseelie princess.

But now she was a queen.

Aislinn gasped, remembering. "Ronan!" Her gaze flew to Bella.

Bella glanced at a doorway to the bedroom she'd run into earlier. "He's okay, just drugged up. He's falling in and out of awareness right now. It will take some time for it to wear off." She gave a tight smile. "He's going to be mad he missed the fight."

Aislinn reached out and traced the side of one of the wounds on Bella's throat. "I don't think that's what he'll be angry about."

Bella took her hand and squeezed. "We'll be here to help you. All of us in this room." Her gaze touched everyone. "You can trust us to support you."

"I don't want this," she said softly, lowering her hand, "but what I want has become irrelevant."

"Now you're starting to think like a queen," said Gabriel.

Her gaze rose and met his. He smiled sadly at her and she had another odd impression that he really cared about her. Or was it perhaps her newfound status as queen he cared about?

The words Kendal had screamed at her the day he'd dumped her in front of the Seelie court filled her mind. *I never loved you. I only used you.*

*No.* She shook her head and blinked. Those thoughts needed to give way to more pressing concerns. She was a queen now and personal concerns needed to take a backseat.

Aislinn blinked and brushed her fingers over the tattoo of the amulet. It was now a part of her being, and it felt heavier by the moment.

# TWENTY-THREE

GABRIEL reached out and brushed his finger over the tooled red leather cover of the Book of Bindings. He'd found it in the dungeon, still in Aislinn's suitcase, secreted away on a musty shelf. Apparently Aodh had never even known what he'd had.

He'd delivered it to Aislinn, now fully ensconced as the new Shadow Queen, in her quarters.

After the battle in the Shadow King's apartment, he and the host had carried out the Shadow King's body for all to see. Aislinn had steeled herself, straightened her spine, and forced all trace of uncertainty and dread from her body language and walked beside them out into the square wearing the tattooed amulet proudly on her skin, revealed to all by the torn and bloodied neckline of her clothing.

The action had clearly proclaimed to all who saw them that the power had been passed from one royal to another. The word had passed quickly, like wildfire, through the Black Tower. They had a new queen; she wore the amulet, and she possessed O'Dubhuir blood.

All of them had bent their knee to her, every last Unseelie in the shadowed part of Piefferburg Square, and Aislinn had barely flinched.

A week had now passed and Aislinn was still settling into her new role. To all but those closest to her, she exuded a countenance of perfect control and power. Only those nearest her sometimes saw her mask slip or glimpsed how her hands trembled. She seemed miserable under the burden of her new status.

Gabriel ached for her—ached that the weight on her slim shoulders was so heavy to bear. Wished he could take it from her and transfer it to someone else.

But he'd settle for a smile.

Or a moan of pleasure.

He'd given her room to breathe. He hadn't pushed her in any way, only offered himself to her in whatever supportive role she wanted to place him in. But he wanted her. He missed the scent of her skin and its silky softness. He wanted to part her thighs and slide deep within her, to regain some of the closeness they'd shared when they'd been on the run.

Now she sat on her couch and studied the book on the table before her. She'd rejected the Shadow King's apartment and instead taken slightly more modest accommodations on the other side of the tower. She was dressed regally because it was required of her. Today she wore all red—a perfectly cut crimson gown with a full skirt and a plunging neckline. As she breathed, her breasts heaved gently against the tight confines of the bodice and made him crazy with need. His fingers curled to touch her, to slide under the material and stroke her nipples until she moaned his name.

But he wasn't pushing her.

He settled back against the cushions and forced himself to relax. All he wanted was to jump her, but that was not what she needed right now. And if her cool demeanor toward him was any indication, it was not what she wanted, either. She would come to him when she was ready, when she needed him as much as he needed her.

She pulled the book toward her and set it in her lap. "Thank you for bringing it to me."

He inclined his head. "You have the book and the Summer Queen has one of the pieces of the *bosca fadbh*. If we can manage to locate the other two pieces, we may have a shot at breaking the hold the Phaendir have on Piefferburg. We're closer now than at any time in Piefferburg's history to breaking free."

"I am aware."

His eyebrows rose at the icy tone of her voice. "And?"

"And I'm considering our options. I have my first meeting with the Summer Queen soon. I'll take her temperature on the issue at that time. I don't know what lay between her and the Shadow King, but all that is done now. Along with it may go some of the hostility between our courts."

"You and she have your own issues."

"Of course. It's no secret to her that I defected from the Rose Tower to come to the Black. That will have her nose out of joint, but I don't know how badly. I need to confer with her and see where we stand." She fisted her hands in her lap.

He glanced from her lap to her face. "Are you nervous about meeting with the Summer Queen?"

She lifted her chin and locked her jaw for a moment before answering. "I wouldn't admit it if I was."

"You don't have to put on a show for me, Aislinn. You can just be yourself."

She stood, holding the book close to her chest. "Are we done here?"

He cocked his head to the side. "Aislinn, what's wrong?"

"Nothing's wrong. It's just that I have a lot to do. I need to prepare for my meeting with the Summer Queen."

"All right." He stood and walked to the foyer. She followed. When they reached the door, he turned to her and closed the distance between them. Her swift intake of breath sounded panicky and she took a step back from him. "If you ever need me, call. I am yours, Aislinn, body and soul. Please remember that. *Remember me.*"

"Are you saying that as my subject or as my lover?"

"Both."

She blinked slowly and hugged the book to her as if for protection. "We aren't lovers anymore, Gabriel. We were thrown together under extreme circumstances. I appreciate your help and your sacrifices, but the ordeal is done."

"Aislinn?"

She paused, drew a breath, looked him in the eye. "And so are we."

AISLINN met the Summer Queen on neutral ground. The Summer Queen would not set foot in the Black Tower, so then neither could the Shadow Queen enter the Rose Tower, just from a standpoint of pride. Aislinn didn't really understand it, but it was the dance she was forced to dance. Thank Danu for Hinkley, who was advising her on proper etiquette.

She'd always assumed the royals communicated only through messenger fae, but now she learned there was a meeting room they sometimes used in one of the buildings that edged Piefferburg Square. Piefferburg Financial traded stocks in the world securities markets. The fae were separate, but equal, in many ways and Piefferburg boasted some of the most profitable companies in the United States. Many humans coveted products made by fae hands, including elderberry wine and woven rugs.

Piefferburg Financial's building was one of the most richly appointed in the city. The boardroom, where she and the Summer Queen met, had a shiny marble floor, with high, elaborately carved tray ceilings with gold leaf. The long, large room reminded Aislinn a lot of the throne room in the Rose Tower. The Summer Queen was probably fairly comfortable here.

Score one point to Caoilainn Elspeth Muirgheal. Aislinn had declined to enter the Rose Tower and yet the Summer Queen had managed to find a room that looked just like home anyway.

The Summer Queen sat at the end of the long table, a row

of windows that overlooked the square to her left. The Imperial Guard, bedecked in their signature gold and rose, stood in a row behind her.

The Seelie Royal was dressed in heavy lavender and gold brocade. Her old-fashioned skirts spilled down in a train that draped to the side of the chair and lay in an artfully arranged sweep of rich fabric on the floor. Her pale hair was arranged in a complicated knot on the top of her head. Heavy gold jewelry glittered at her ears and winked from the hollow of her slim, white throat.

As befitting her station as the Shadow Queen, Aislinn had also dressed elaborately. It was expected of her. She had dressed in bloodred velvet and silk. Her Victorian gown was fitted at the waist and pushed her small breasts to overflowing at the top with the help of a tight corset. The collar of the dress flared and ruffled at her nape, leading down to a silk bodice of a paler shade of red. Her skirts stopped above her knees in the front, revealing black thigh-high button-up boots, also with a Victorian feel. The skirt hung long in the back, giving her a train that was just as lengthy, but less voluminous than the Summer Queen's. Ruby jewels glittered at her ears. Having the vibrant tattoo of the amulet for throat ornamentation, she'd forgone a necklace.

Her hair had been left long and natural, although the silver blond tips had been dipped in red, as was the tradition for the royal of the Unseelie Court. She'd opted to steer clear of the fading multihued effect the former king had sported, just to avoid being reminded of him every time she looked in a mirror. She'd destroyed the fighting staff he'd always carried.

Hooking her hair behind her ear, she approached the Summer Queen with a row of her own Shadow Guard—in their colors of silver and black—walking behind her. She would use the goblin army much more sparingly than her predecessor. One of the men pulled out a chair and she sat down, the guard sweeping her train to the side and settling it on the floor with a flourish before going to stand behind her.

Score point number two to Caoilainn Elspeth Muirgheal.

She was sitting at the head of the table and Aislinn had been forced to sit at her left hand. Aislinn was sure it was clear to all present just how green she was at being a queen. She should have dictated where they met and she should have arrived there far earlier to take cherry placement.

The Summer Queen smiled slightly. "Aislinn. You're the last person I thought I would ever greet as the Shadow Queen of the Unseelie Court."

"I aim to surprise . . . even me. However, I *am* the rightful descendant of Aodh Críostóir Ruadhán O'Dubhuir and have inherited the throne by blood."

"And might."

"I had no choice. I either called the sluagh or suffered the deaths of nine innocent people, myself included."

"Indeed. You definitely have a backbone, Aislinn." Her slight smile faded. "Now why did you desire a meeting with me?"

A guard came up on Aislinn's right side with the book. "I am in possession of the Book of Bindings and you possess one of the pieces of the *bosca fadbh*. We need to discuss potential possibilities."

The Summer Queen's face went pale at the sight of the book that the guard had placed in Aislinn's hands. She tore her gaze from it and centered it on Aislinn's face with effort. She recovered from her slight slip of shock with ease, her face settling back into its implacable mask. "How did you get that?"

"I inherited it from my father."

A stricken look passed over the Summer Queen's face like a fast-moving storm, then was gone. "The Shadow King had this?"

Aislinn shook her head. "No, not him."

The Summer Queen shifted slightly in her chair. "You not only have the book, you have Ronan and Niall Quinn. They are the best mages of either court. If anyone can help us obtain the final two pieces of the *bosca fadbh*, it's them."

Inwardly Aislinn let out a long, slow breath. She'd used the word *us*. That meant she was on board with working together.

"That implies you think it's possible."

The Summer Queen shook her head. "I don't. Not really." She raised an eyebrow. "Yet hope springs eternal. Is the faery tale of freedom the only reason you asked me here?"

Aislinn lifted her chin. "And to take your measure."

The Summer Queen had a relaxed look on her face, but her eyes were keen. "The courts will always be at odds, Aislinn. Like the day and the night, there's only a little common ground, a bit of twilight made from mingling light. Freedom for the inhabitants of Piefferburg, for our people, is our common ground, our twilight. Revenge against the Phaendir, on that much the courts can agree, yes? So while I may not be inviting you to tea very often, you can count on my assistance in any matter regarding the Book of Bindings or the pieces of the *bosca fadbh*."

"Would you have made the same offer to the Shadow King?"

"When I banished Ronan Quinn from the Rose Tower, I did just that." She stood and one of the guards gathered her train. "Is that all?"

Aislinn also stood. "That's all."

The Summer Queen inclined her head. "I bid you welcome to the twin throne of the fae. May your reign be peaceful and lengthy."

Aislinn also inclined her head, clutching the book to her chest. "Thank you."

With a rustle of brocade skirts, the Summer Queen was gone. After she'd left, Aislinn walked to the window and looked out over the inhabitants of the square. It was noon on a workday and fae hurried over the cobblestone area on their way to lunch or to run errands.

The Summer Queen had been friendlier and more cooperative than Aislinn had imagined she would be and she hadn't mentioned—not once—the fact that Aislinn had rejected the Rose in favor of the Black before she'd discovered her dubious biological parentage.

But there'd been a look on her face and a note in her voice that Aislinn didn't trust. The Summer Queen had said all the right words, but Aislinn had a niggling feeling that she didn't like that the Shadow Royal—whoever that may be— was in possession of the Book of Bindings.

Unless she was being paranoid, and she didn't think she was, perhaps she needed to be wary not only of the Phaendir, but of the Summer Queen, too.

AISLINN walked along the corridor late at night, unable to fall asleep. Sleeping had been a problem since her meeting with the Summer Queen, but Aislinn couldn't put her finger on an exact reason. Most likely it was the result of the stress of her position—suddenly becoming a queen hadn't been an easy transition to make.

Or maybe it was because she missed Gabriel.

She loved him. She had no doubt on that score. Silly, stupid woman that she was, she'd fallen head over heels for yet another man she couldn't trust. Only this time the man had the potential not only to injure her heart—as Kendal had done—but to completely annihilate it. It was better that she distanced herself now, no matter how much it hurt. In the long run she was saving herself some blood loss.

Yet she missed the scent of him and the rough brush of his unshaven chin along her skin. She missed the sound of his voice and the steadiness of his presence, the protection she always felt when he was near.

But it was in Gabriel's nature to seduce and bind women to him and then let them go without care for their hearts. Everyone expected him to go back to his old ways, as Melia had put it. No one would ever, *ever* expect a man like Gabriel to commit to one woman out of love. That he wanted—or seemed to want, anyway—to continue this relationship with her was suspect.

Was he like Kendal? Only wanting to be with her because of what her station could do for him? By all accounts Gabriel had been close to the Shadow King, had been placed very highly in the Black Tower. Perhaps he didn't want to lose that.

Of course, Gabriel had contributed greatly to the Shadow King's demise. He'd risked his life for her, done the right thing by fighting his royal. He could have turned on her, could have betrayed her. He could have stood by and done nothing while the Shadow King had stolen her soul . . . and he hadn't.

But how much of the reason he'd intervened could be attributed to guilt?

No, she'd done the right thing.

Even if it was breaking her heart to do it.

She reached out and ran her fingertips along the smooth, cool black marble wall of the corridor she walked through. The oil of her finger pads left smudges; her fingerprints marking this place. A few weeks ago she never could've imagined walking through these halls as if she owned them, could never have imagined feeling contentment at the fact she now, in a way, claimed them as her own.

Now that the Shadow King was gone, she felt very at home within these walls. There was a far greater sense of acceptance here, a sort of more open feeling about the building and the people in it. Oh, yes, one needed to watch one's step. Monsters dwelt in this place. Red caps, joint-eaters, phookas, alps, and more. Dark magick abounded. Yet, oddly, it was more comfortable to her than the starched, shallow hallways of the Rose Tower.

She finally felt like she belonged.

The Book of Bindings was hidden away, secreted magickally by Ronan and Niall, who were both on her committee of advisers. Gabriel and his host were also on it. She might not trust Gabriel with her heart, but she trusted him with her politics and, ultimately, with her life.

Gabriel was a good man. He simply wasn't a man built for love. Not a man built for her.

She stopped short in the middle of the hallway as the man in question appeared from the shadows at the end of the corridor. Somewhere in the distance, laughter boomed, chatter swelled and then fell away to silence. The Black Tower never slept. There were always fae up and roaming around even as late as this, though the late hours were quieter than the day-lit ones.

Aislinn was momentarily arrested by the sight of him, long and lean, his body half hidden in shadow. They hadn't spoken since she'd told him she didn't want him romantically anymore. Every time they'd seen each other since then, they'd had others around them, and she'd been avoiding him otherwise.

Avoiding exactly this situation.

Suddenly she regretted leaving her room to take this walk.

He walked toward her slowly and she fought the urge to flee. She wasn't sure she could remain composed if he was angry at being rejected, and she didn't want to hear what he might have to say to her.

She swallowed hard as he approached. His handsome features were set as rigid as chiseled stone, his dark brows drawn up. His dark blue eyes weren't cold and angry as she'd expected; they were hot and filled with confusion and pain. His long dark hair was unbound and shifted around his shoulders. He hadn't shaved today and the too-long growth shadowed his face.

Aislinn cleared her throat and set her hand flat against the wall of the corridor as if trying to draw strength from the building itself. "Gabriel—"

"Aislinn, I love you." The words came out angry, accusatory.

Her breath stopped in her throat and shock stole through her. "What did you say?" she managed to push out in a whisper.

"You heard me. I love you. I've loved you since the Rose Tower. I couldn't let the Shadow King have you because by that point you were mine. Mine to protect. Mine to love. I should have told you sooner."

She glanced away, blinking away sudden tears. These were the last words she'd been expecting him to utter. Was this a game or did he really mean it? She shook her head. "Gabriel, I don't know what to say to you."

He closed the distance between them, grasped her wrist,

and dragged her up against his chest. "You say what you feel, Aislinn. You stare into my eyes and tell me how you feel. I dare you to look at me and tell me you don't love me. Do it."

She raised her gaze to his and he held it firm, challenging her.

*"Do it."*

She opened her mouth to lie, and then closed it, looking down.

"I thought as much. Then say it, tell me you love me back. I know you do. I can feel it. Tell me."

Aislinn said nothing, did nothing. She couldn't speak. All she could do was hang on while her world listed to the side like a ship about to sink.

He made a frustrated sound and turned her face-first toward the wall. Her breasts, the part that spilled from the top of her gown, pushed up by a corset, pressed up against the cold marble. She gasped and closed her eyes. Overwhelmed by tumultuous emotion, tears slipped down her cheeks.

He leaned in behind her. "Aislinn, don't you think you can leave me. You're mine. I know it and so do you. I love you and you love me, too." His words shivered through her, spoken close to her ear. She was helpless against him, craving his touch and drowning in the words he spoke and in the possessive way he spoke them. *"I need you."*

# TWENTY-FOUR

GABRIEL lifted her heavy skirts, up past the tops of her thigh-high stockings, and, pushing aside the panel of her panties, quested between her legs to find the evidence of her arousal. Making an appreciative sound in the back of his throat, she knew he found it.

"Tell me to stop," he growled into her ear. He pushed a finger deep inside her, then two, thrusting in and out. "If you don't want me to fuck you right here, right now, tell me to stop." His voice shook like he was groping for control and couldn't find any.

Her breath shuddered out of her as her body reacted to his touch and the sound of his voice, to the sensation of his fingers pushing in and out of her so slowly.

"Don't stop," she murmured. "Danu, please, don't stop."

He let out a harsh breath that touched her shoulder and made her shiver. Then he grasped the side of her panties and yanked them down to her knees.

He unzipped his jeans, forced her thighs apart, and pushed his cock hard and deep into her sex, rocking her up against the wall. His hand stole between her thighs from the front, bunching her skirts up. Finding her clit, he stroked it over and over as he levered his body up and down, thrusting inside her. He took her like an animal up against the wall, forcing an orgasm from her body.

When she came she had to bite her knuckles against her cries, not wanting to draw attention. He came deep inside her with a groan and her name spilling from his lips.

He replaced her panties, lowered her skirts, and turned her toward him. His fingers were hard as he guided her face up toward his. "You're mine, Aislinn. Never forget that. I will wait for you, but don't expect me to be patient or well mannered while I do it."

Then he turned and walked away.

*AISLINN, you must give us the Book of Bindings.*

Aislinn came awake with a shudder and the sensation of icy fingertips tracing down her spine. The breathy, ominous voice still echoed in her head, laced with a malice that clung to her. It compelled her to want to give the book up to the speaker.

For the briefest of moments, that was all she wanted in the whole world.

*Irrational.* Her lip curled.

The glow of the fireplace filled the room, the wood snapping and popping. The apartment was otherwise quiet and she felt no presence, alive or otherwise, in the room. No soul that she could perceive.

It had been a dream and she'd caught only the tail end of it. Yet it hadn't been an ordinary dream. This one had been filled with malice and maybe even threaded with . . . magick. She frowned. Was that possible?

Of course that was a dumb question to ask, when she'd called up an army of the unforgiven dead to fight the Shadow King on her behalf. Judging from that, anything was possible.

She shivered and slipped from between the red silk sheets and sapphire blue comforter. Everything in her new bedroom was in contrasting jewel tones, while the elegant living room was in shades of gray—from dark to dove to nearly white.

Her nightgown stuck to her body, clammy from the dream, so she went to the fireplace opposite her bed to warm herself and chase away the last of the nightmare. It wasn't very cold outside, but she far preferred the light of a fire at night if she could get it, so she'd had Hinkley order fires for her every evening. She knelt on the heap of pillows on the floor before the hearth and reached her hands out toward the flames.

Those flames reminded her of Gabriel. And reaching out to him so he could warm her was exactly what she desired. She wanted him and he would come to her if she asked.

Because *he loved her*.

The words still made her shiver when she remembered how he'd said them, how he'd annihilated any doubt she'd had in her mind about what he felt for her. Kendal had told her that he'd loved her, too—*but not like that*, not with emotion infusing every syllable, not with that look in his eyes. And Kendal's words had never made her feel the way Gabriel's did—soft, hot, vulnerable, and achy . . . and so filled up, so complete.

Like anything could happen to her but everything would be okay. Like his love provided her with a shield, made her bulletproof.

He'd told her he needed her. And she needed him. Especially right now.

Every instinct she had screamed at her that she shouldn't be alone tonight. Every fiber of her body yelled for Gabriel's presence. She'd wasted enough time on her fears; now it was time to embrace the man who'd told her he loved her so vehemently and truthfully.

If she got hurt in the end, then she did. That human saying was true—it was better to have loved and lost than never to have loved at all. Even if letting Gabriel break her heart would slice her open emotionally from chin to gut. It was worth it to her to take a gamble.

What she felt for him was worth the risk.

The phone sat on the table near the hearth. She took it from its cradle and dialed his number.

"Gabriel?" she said when he picked up and sleepily murmured hello. Then all of a sudden her words left her and she couldn't say anything more without dissolving into pathetic tears.

The soft rush of his breath filled the quiet space that separated them. "I'll be right there."

Moments later he was at her door. She opened it and immediately said, "I love you, too." The words were spoken loud and clear and there was no taking them back once she'd uttered them. For better or for worse, they were true.

He crossed the threshold and embraced her, lifting her up and burying his nose in her hair. He kicked the door closed with his foot. "I won't hurt you, Aislinn. All I want is to love you," he murmured into the curve of her shoulder.

She shivered against him and let out a long, shaky breath of relief.

She retreated into the darkened apartment, back to the firelit bedroom. He followed her to the bed. The glow of the fire licked at only half his face. "Is that why you called me here? To tell me that?" he asked.

She pressed herself against the length of his body and breathed in the delicious scent of him, that quintessential combination of his cologne, soap, and the added ingredient of man that was uniquely his. "I woke up and wanted you with me. The need to see you and touch you was nearly overwhelming, like an empty space inside me I needed to fill."

He took her hand and kissed her palm softly and slowly. The action warmed her more than the fire ever could and chased away the last clinging vestiges of the nightmare. "That's what I've felt every single night since you pushed me away."

She ducked her head. "You betrayed me once. And Kendal—"

"I get it, but I'm not Kendal." There was a note of anger in his voice. "I'm a lot of things, especially before I fell in

love with you. You were right to be cautious about me at
first, but I'm not Kendal."

"I know that."

He pressed her down onto the mattress and covered her
body with his. His knee slipped between her thighs. "I know
I don't have the best track record with women, but *you've*
got me, Aislinn, body and soul. I've never felt this way for
anyone before. It has nothing to do with your station as
Shadow Queen. If anything, I wish I could take that weight
from you. I just love you, every part of you, any way I can
get you." He kissed her forehead, then trailed down slowly to
kiss her eyelids, the tip of her nose, and her lips as he murmured, "Every hope you have, every fear, every inch of you
from the top of your head to your toes, and every inch of
your soul besides."

She relaxed into the blankets and the mattress, feeling
bolstered by the support and strength that Gabriel gave her.
A little of the tension of her new position eased. "I gave you
my heart long ago, back when I thought it was the dumbest
thing for me to do."

"You can't control who you fall in love with, it just hap-
pens. I promise to take care of your heart."

"And I will take care of yours."

"You already have. You made it come to life again." He
paused, looking toward the fire. "There are things you should
know about me, Aislinn. Things I should have told you a
long time ago, but the circumstances never gave me an opportunity."

She sat up a little. "What?"

"Right after Piefferburg was created, times were hard.
Many fae—most fae—were suffering from Watt syndrome
and the other effects of the Great Sweep. I was young at the
time and after my mother died, I was alone. I had no money,
no way to feed myself." He swallowed and waited a heartbeat before continuing. "But I was attractive and I was half
incubus."

Her throat went dry as she made the logical leap. *Danu,*

*no*. The horrors he must have endured as a child and the humiliations. Her heart ached for him, for the boy he'd been and all he'd had to go through to survive.

"I—"

She leaned forward, enveloped him in her arms, and kissed him. "I understand," she murmured against his lips. "You did what you had to do. I love you, Gabriel. I love you no matter what. I only wish I could turn back time and make things different for you."

He kissed her. "It was a long time ago. I healed the worst of those wounds years ago, but you just stitched up the last of them."

She ducked her head and smiled into his shoulder, his words warming her through.

"Why did you wake up? It's early in the morning."

The dream came rushing back to her, stealing her warmth and making her smile fade. "I had a dream, Gabriel, like no dream I've ever had before. It compelled me to give up the Book of Bindings, but to whom I'm not sure. It was menacing and almost seemed laced with some kind of malevolent magick." She glanced up at him. "That's impossible, isn't it? I've never heard of such a thing before."

Quiet reigned for several moments, his body rigid against hers. "We'll ask Ronan and Niall about it in the morning. If anyone will know, they will."

She kissed his collarbone, wanting to relax the alert stiffness in his body, wanting to lose herself in him and forget the dream.

He lowered his head, the fire snapping and crackling in the background. His lips brushed hers and she pressed upward for a firmer contact. He covered her mouth with his and kissed her deeply, his tongue stealing within to brush up against her tongue.

She moaned against his lips and moved her body, shifting her thighs so she could wrap her legs around his waist. His hand slipped from her waist, over her hip, to her rear, where he cupped one cheek and ground himself against her.

Then they leisurely undressed each other, revealing silken skin to the gentle, fire-warmed air. Sighs escaping them became moans of pleasure and then soft entreaties for more. Finally he slipped between her thighs and then deep within her, becoming one with her, and they showed each other with their bodies that the words they'd just spoken were true.

GABRIEL awoke naked and tangled in the silken sheets of Aislinn's bed. It was the only place he wanted to be. The remnants of the fire no longer warmed the room and early morning sunlight peeked in from around the edges of the heavy sapphire-colored curtains covering the window that overlooked Piefferburg Square.

Contentment filled him as he rolled over. Aislinn's scent from her pillow filled his nose. Finally, she was his.

All the stars seemed aligned suddenly. All was right with the world.

He reached for her, the memory of how her body had felt the previous night still fresh in his mind—her soft skin and the velvet clasp of her sex around his cock, her hot mouth and the mesh of her tongue with his. His name falling from her lips mingling with the sweet sound of her orgasms.

His hand slid against the opposite side of the bed, brushing the cool sheets. Aislinn had already gotten up.

Gabriel raised his head and glanced at the now-dead fire in the fireplace and the bright, multicolored furniture in the room. Aislinn wasn't anywhere within eyesight. The kitchen or bathroom maybe? He sat up, letting the slick sheets fall to his waist, and pushed a hand through his long, tangled hair. The whole apartment felt empty.

"Aislinn?" he called, but got no answer.

Now alarmed, he tossed the blankets back and rose from the bed. He searched the apartment, not finding her. When he returned to the bedroom, that was when he spotted the piece of gray paper stuck to the fireplace mantel.

He ripped it off and read it.

*Give us the book and you get your queen back.*
*Tell the masses and she dies.*
*The Grand Temple in the Goblin Town. Five p.m.*

He'd been here when they'd taken her. He'd been right next to her and it had happened anyway. Now she was in danger—again—and he'd done nothing to prevent it.

Gabriel crushed the note in his hand, heart pounding, and got dressed.

# TWENTY-FIVE

———

RONAN drummed his fingers on the table in Aislinn's living room and Gabriel knew he was concerned. He'd known Ronan Quinn a long time, since long before he'd defected from the Black Tower for the Rose in pursuit of Bella. The look on Ronan's face, combined with the drumming fingers, meant it was bad.

Gabriel clenched his jaw. Rage had begun to burn low in his belly when he'd found the note and it wouldn't be extinguished until he had her back in his arms. "Just tell us, Ronan," he ground out.

Bella shifted next to Melia. Both women glanced up at him at his tone.

Ronan sighed. "There's only one thing it could be if there really was some kind of magick in that dream that disturbed Aislinn."

"The Phaendir." That came from Melia, who uttered it matter-of-factly.

Ronan gave a curt nod.

Gabriel paced back and forth in front of the couch. "They

want the book, of course, and they know Aislinn has it hidden. I wonder if they're pulling the same shit with the Summer Queen to get the piece of the *bosca fadbh*."

"They've been after the book for a long time, Gabriel. They don't like that we have it within the borders of Piefferburg," Melia answered. "The piece is valuable, too, but it's worthless without the Book of Bindings. That book holds the key to everything. If they can get that and destroy it, well, then the fae are shit out of luck."

"They're afraid because we have two of the four necessary pieces," murmured Bella. "They're worried we might actually manage to break the warding."

Melia spoke vehemently. "Maybe they're right to be concerned." She pressed her lips into a firm line. "They can't have the book, Gabriel. No matter what. This is bigger than Aislinn's life. You know she would agree."

Gabriel turned on Melia with a growl in his throat. Nothing was more important than Aislinn's life, *nothing*. Yet once he parsed through his gut response, he knew she was right. The majority of the inhabitants of Piefferburg yearned for freedom and they deserved it. Aislinn would agree and she would gladly die to give it to them.

But he wouldn't let her die to obtain it. Not for any price.

He stared at Melia as these thoughts crowded his head and he worked on an answer to his quandary. She shrank back into the cushions at the look on his face. "We won't give them the Book of Bindings," Gabriel said finally, "but fuck if we're letting them have Aislinn, either."

"On that we can all agree," said Bella. "I'm not willing to sacrifice Aislinn's life, either, Gabriel."

"We'll have to be careful of everyone we bring into the planning, even the rest of the host. Even my brother," said Ronan. "It's difficult for the Phaendir to enlist help this side of the borders, but it's not impossible. When they twist any fae to their side, they do it with the threat of death over their heads—theirs or someone they love."

"Yes." Gabriel remembered Carina. She'd done what she'd done to protect her husband, Drem, and died when she'd failed to please the Phaendir. She probably would've been killed even if she'd been successful in her mission. "No one outside our circle can know anything about our plans."

Ronan nodded. "Agreed."

"Melia and Bella, can you cover for the queen today?" They were Aislinn's court aides and were trained to take on issues when the queen was indisposed.

Bella nodded. "As far as the Black will know, Aislinn is ill."

"Then I'll get everyone else together and we'll start laying our plans. We're bringing Aislinn home tonight."

THEY hadn't bothered with a gag.

They didn't need to. All they had to do was clamp charmed iron handcuffs around her wrists and that prevented her from filling her mouth with the words and magick that would bring the goblin army to her defense. Her arms were wrenched behind her back, twisted viciously. It had hurt at first, but the pain had faded to numbness and now she couldn't feel them at all.

Why they'd plopped her down right in the heart of Goblin Town remained a mystery to her. All she had to do was free her wrists, which would free her tongue and her magick, call for aid, and the Phaendir that held her would be hors d'oeuvres. There had to be a reason they'd selected this location, but try as hard as she could, she was unable to untangle the mystery.

Maybe they were just that arrogant. She supposed perhaps they had a right to feel that way. After all, they had successfully imprisoned all the fae races for over 350 years.

And it would take a miracle for her to get these cuffs off.

Still dressed in her thin nightgown and still barefoot, she sat in the pulpit of the Grand Temple at the foot of a huge carved jade statue of the goblins' primary goddess, Orna. She watched the black-robed figures of the Phaendir—they hadn't introduced themselves, but she had no doubt that was who they were—walk the premises. They'd taken over the building and closed it up. Who knew what they'd done with the goblin priests and their attendants?

All the windows of the temple were shut, the shutters drawn, all the doors locked. They'd even snuffed the candles on the tables lining the sides of the temple that the goblins came to light when they prayed to their gods—much different deities than the rest of the fae worshipped.

The minor deities were honored with statues that writhed and shifted on pedestals all along the edges of the temple, bespelled to modify and transform continually. The gritty sound of ever-shifting stone was the only filler for the silence. The only light that penetrated the murk in the temple came through the pale red-tinted glass panels near the top of the arched ceilings.

Daylight shifted lazily as the sun moved across the sky and Aislinn mostly spent her time watching dust motes dance through the air, when she wasn't stabbing looks to kill at the Phaendir or planning ways to defeat or escape them without her magick.

Twice now they'd caught her trying to escape out the back of the temple. So now she'd been assigned one solitary druid to guard her, while they'd stationed more at the doors of the building that led out into the alleys of Goblin Town. They hadn't hit her, hadn't hurt her except for twisting her arms behind her back to get the cuffs on. They never spoke to her. They were silent, strong wraiths, united and unswerving in their purpose.

Of course, she had no illusions about her fate.

If they got what they wanted, they would probably let her go. They didn't need to sow discord with the fae, who were, for all intents and purposes, under their thumbs so thoroughly as to be completely helpless. One little Unseelie queen meant nothing to the Phaendir. As long as they got the Book of Bindings, they would let the fae keep their Unseelie queen and their silly, harmless customs. Hatred burned up bile from the back of her throat.

But they would never get the book.

Gabriel wouldn't give it to them. *He couldn't.* He knew

this issue transcended his love for her, transcended even her life. If he turned the book over to the Phaendir, they would destroy it. If they destroyed it, all hope the fae had of getting out of Piefferburg would die. She would never forgive Gabriel for that and he knew it.

Her people wanted out of Piefferburg.

Looking at the arrogant, black-cowled tyrants that held her now, fury ignited and raged in her stomach, racing through her veins and keeping her warm in the chilly room. Now, more than ever in her life, she wanted them defeated. She wanted revenge.

Freedom for the fae.

She wanted her hands filled with weapons or her mouth filled with magick and her immediate surroundings bursting with legions of unforgiven dead and goblins. She wanted to defeat these men who oppressed them and made them feel so much weaker than they were. But all she had were bare feet and a filmy nightgown that barely covered her icy skin, charmed iron against her wrists, and her magick stoppered up inside her by a supernatural plug. Even the tattoo burned into her flesh seemed dull and faded where she could see it on her chest.

The only weapons she had at her disposal now were her mouth, her mind, and her cunning.

"Why do you hate us so much?" she asked the man who guarded her.

His black-cowled head turned toward her and all she saw was blackness. "I'm not here to have a conversation with you. I'm here to guard you and, perhaps, execute you." His voice was flat, but human sounding. Emotionless. That was no good. She needed him worked up.

"They'll never hand over the Book of Bindings, which I'm certain is what you've asked them for. Therefore, I'm a dead woman. Can't you honor a dead queen's last request and talk to her?"

He only stared out over the expanse of pews that filled the temple.

"You must be really worried about the fae breaking free,

right?" she goaded quietly, her red-tipped hair shifting over her shoulders as she gazed up at the druid. "I mean, you're going to such extremes to get the Book of Bindings. This must be the first time you've dared to enter the city. After all, you must know that if you're found out, you'll be ripped from limb to limb and, at least in this part of town, eaten. Odd that you chose Goblin Town as the place to make your stand."

"Don't presume you know our intentions or our purposes."

Oh, there had been a note of anger in his response. Now she was getting somewhere.

"Well, all I can do is presume, since the Phaendir aren't exactly forthcoming. I know my history, of course. I know about the grudge you bear the fae." She tipped her head to the side and affected a light, innocent tone. "Is it because we snubbed you? We smacked you down and humiliated you, didn't we? Considered you less than ourselves? Especially the Seelie Tuatha Dé Danann. Of course, they have snobbery down to an art form." Interesting how she could say "they" and not even care she wasn't a part of them. "The Unseelie or the troop would've accepted you, but you were too good for them. I'm Unseelie, but on this issue I think I agree with the Seelie."

"You have no comprehension of what you speak," the man ground out.

"Oh, is that not it? Well, if it's not some sort of revenge for being rejected, then it must be flat-out fear. Are you doing this because you fear us?" She paused. "But, I guess you should. *Now*," she tacked on carelessly.

The druid rounded on her. "Fear? Revenge over a shallow social slight? Some event in ancient history that none of us remember anymore? Is that what you think? You think the Phaendir are afraid of you, child? We trapped you here. *We* did that. While you're here, we can do anything to you we want. We could convince the human government you're a threat and have you all exterminated. Cleanse your filthy races off the face of the earth. I would watch my tongue if I were you, queen, and be happy we haven't killed you yet."

"You're lying. You don't have that much control. You got

lucky when you trapped us, but you know that the fae are more powerful than you. After all, the Phaendir resorted to a bunch of cheap tricks to get us in here, didn't they?"

"Cheap tricks?" He took a couple of steps toward her and the action made his hood fall back. He was a man, just a man. There was no monster in the blackness. No ugly creature. Flesh and blood and a paunch around the gut. He was a middle-aged, balding man with brown eyes and thin lips. Euphoria filled her. They were defeatable.

"You heard me."

"Faith. Righteousness. Cleanliness. Duty. Think on those words for a while and maybe you'll get a clue." His face came down so close to hers that his utterances moved the hair around her face. She smelled his lunch on his breath. He bared his teeth. "There are those men in the Phaendir who would wipe you all off the face of the Earth and be done with this stinking prison completely. Think on the name Gideon and fear it."

Her mouth snapped shut.

"Conlon!"

The man stepped back and whooshed his hood back over his head at the voice of reprimand ringing across the pews.

# TWENTY-SIX

THE stench of the marketplace filled Gabriel's nose and he tried to black out the knowledge of what he smelled. It wasn't often the rest of the fae races visited Goblin Town and the goblin diet was one reason why.

They had just finished one of the three major holiday festivals they had each year. They didn't celebrate Yule, Imbolc, Beltane, Samhain, and the rest like the other fae. Instead they had Yarlog, Lugoc, and Warmok festivals to mark the passing of the seasons. They'd just finished with Lugoc, which marked the world's entrance into spring. A wind-tattered banner had half fallen into the street in front of them and goblins hurried to and fro, treading it to dirty shreds.

He passed the mouth of the street that contained the goblin market from which emanated the stench. No sticky sweet fruits were for sale there, like the Christina Rossetti poem described. It was flesh, mostly dead, but some still living to be dined upon in dubious circumstances. Small shops lined the crammed and dirty streets.

The goblins' population had exploded since the Great Sweep, but Goblin Town hadn't been able to expand, making it overcrowded. Even though Piefferburg City comprised only a small part of the Piefferburg Detention Compound, the goblins showed no inclination to move to the country. The district was hemmed in on two sides by the *ceantar dubh* and the *ceantar láir* with clear borders marking each. The goblins chose not to mix with the other fae, for the most part.

Behind Gabriel walked his host—Melia, Aelfdane, Aeric, and Bran. On either side of him walked Ronan and Niall. They were all dressed for battle and ready with their most powerful magick. Dominating the entire cobblestone street, they stopped traffic and turned heads.

Gabriel didn't notice much but the road in front of him, the one that would bring them to the Grand Temple and to Aislinn, but he did see the goblins stopping on the sidewalk to stare. The women, dressed in bright colors and carrying bags of food home to their many children, dropped their clawed, bony arms at their sides and watched them pass. Some of them formed clumps and whispered and pointed. Behind them gathered a clutch of goblins, following them toward the temple, which was exactly what they wanted.

The Unseelie Tuatha Dé Sídhe were almost never seen in Goblin Town; the Seelie Sídhe, never. The trooping fae didn't venture here and the goblins most certainly never saw the wildings. They had to be wondering why they were being visited by outsiders now.

In the note, the Phaendir had said Gabriel couldn't tell the masses. Undoubtedly they would know via magickal means if he did. This was his way of getting around that. He wouldn't breathe a word to the masses of the Phaendir's presence, but nothing had been said about the masses coming of their own volition. Leading goblins to them this way wouldn't violate the order.

Of all the places to orchestrate a meeting, Goblin Town wasn't the brightest idea they'd ever had. Yet Gabriel could have tried this same thing in any part of Piefferburg with the same result. Even the gentle wilding fae who lived in the Boundary Lands would be happy to have some druids to rip apart.

He wondered how the Phaendir had gotten in. The main entrance to Piefferburg was watched carefully by the fae and every entrant was reported to both the Rose and Black towers. It was possible the Phaendir had hidden in a shipment of supplies, but every vehicle was thoroughly searched twice, once by the Phaendir on the outside and once by the fae on the inside.

No matter how they'd gained entry, it was clear the Phaendir were desperate to get their hands on the Book of Bindings. Undoubtedly these druids they'd sent were expendable. They had to know they'd never get out alive. Of that Gabriel was sure.

He wasn't sure if Aislinn would get out of this alive, either.

So, as they walked down the street, Gabriel's heavy black boots falling on the littered cobblestones and his long dark coat flapping behind him, they gathered the army that Aislinn couldn't call and brought them along for the ride . . . right into the laps of the Phaendir.

He had no doubt the goblins would thank him for the tasty meal.

The Book of Bindings was still in its secret place. The decision to leave it still churned in Gabriel's stomach—fear of losing Aislinn, fear she was already lost. It fueled his rage. Fire arched through his veins, hotter with every step he took toward the cathedral he could see in the distance.

When they were about two blocks away, his host fanned out and disappeared into the side streets, leaving him with the mages and the ever-growing legion of curious goblins behind them.

They halted one block away from the cathedral, waiting. One heartbeat. Two. Three. Gabriel's fingers itched for action.

Four. Five . . .

Wordlessly, he looked at Ronan and Niall each in turn

and nodded at them. They walked toward the front doors of the church, magick gathering around them.

Gabriel called Abastor. The horse swooped down from the Netherworld, and he jumped astride, sailing up past the gasping goblins, just as Ronan and Niall burst the front doors of the church from their hinges. If his host had done their job, the druids inside would soon be surrounded from the back, thanks to a secret entrance revealed to them by the Black Tower's goblin liaison.

The Phaendir were stupid to fight them in their own territory.

Abastor's hooves hit the red-tinted glass at the top of the church, shattering it. Gabriel's objective was one thing—find and protect Aislinn. Inside was chaos—the Phaendir fighting the host and the mages in bursts of magick and mayhem.

AISLINN leaned against the wall at the feet of the goddess and waited. Glancing up at the pale red windows at the top of the temple, she could judge that it was almost five. Conlon stood near her, silent and still. Like her, he waited. She hadn't been able to get him to speak after he'd been reprimanded by his peers.

Moments later, the doors to the temple blew open in an explosion of magick she recognized. After the smoke cleared, Ronan and Niall stood framed in the remnants.

Battle broke out all over the church.

So this was how it would go.

Leaning on one side, she lashed out with her feet, hitting Conlon in the back of the knees and crashing him to the ground. Before he had a chance to react, she kicked again, into the blackness of his hood. Soft cartilage cracked against the arch of her bare foot. He grunted and cradled his face, his hood falling back. Pulling his hands away, she saw she'd broken his nose. Blood streamed over his mouth and down his chin.

"Bitch," he growled. He raised his hand, chanting in some language she didn't know, and magick blasted into her.

Pain blossomed through her body, quickly fading to numbness. Her back arched and she screamed.

She had to hold on. Had to hold on for Gabriel. She dredged up every ounce of willpower in her body to fight the magick seeping into her body and trying to steal her life. The last thing she saw before the world went black was Gabriel on Abastor, descending from the sky like some avenging angel.

But it was too late.

The next time he saw her, he would be reaping her.

THERE was Aislinn, on the floor at the foot of the goddess Orna, her skin pallid, arms twisted cruelly behind her back, silent, too still. Red-tipped hair in a tangle over her face.

Goblins rushed in to fill the church and found the hooded Phaendir. Magick exploded around Gabriel as his horse touched down in the row of pews, filling his nose with the scent of sulfur, the scent of the Phaendir's power.

The magick and the fighting didn't touch him as he slid from the back of Abastor and closed the distance between himself and Aislinn's too-still and fallen form. Time somehow seemed to slow to a crawl around him.

A Phaendir, his hood ripped back to reveal a middle-aged portly man, leapt to block his path. Blood smeared his nose, mouth and chin. "We told you we'd kill her," he snarled.

Gabriel punched him.

The crunch of the bones in the man's face was satisfying, but he had no time to enjoy it. He pushed aside the druid's fallen body, raced to Aislinn and knelt. Cold, empty grief filled him as he lifted her limp body into his lap. Studying her eyes, he looked for the rise and fall of her chest. He found nothing.

No breath. No heartbeat. She was cold and too pale to still be living.

Gabriel hugged her to him and buried his nose in her hair. "No," he ordered her. "Don't leave me, Aislinn. Not now. Not when I've just found you."

They'd been through so much—the attack of the Shadow King and the overthrow of the Black Tower—she couldn't die now, not when she'd survived all the rest.

His world couldn't *be* without her.

He closed his eyes and buried his face in the curve of her neck, unwilling to look around him in case her spirit stood nearby. He wasn't ready for that. Never would be.

# TWENTY-SEVEN

"PHAENDIR were dumped outside the gates of Piefferburg, Gideon. All men known to follow you and your unorthodox ideas about where the Phaendir should go in its policies. They've been gnawed on." He paused. "By goblins."

Gideon had taken a stance of full contrition, nose to the ground in front of Brother Maddoc, shirt ripped open and pulled down to show his scarred and lacerated back as a mark of piety. He could not deny any of it. He'd been caught. "I ask for your mercy and leniency, brother."

Maddoc's boots stepped around him, softly displacing dirt and grass. All of the Phaendir and all their human employees had assembled on the lawn for his public censure. Even Emily. Gideon's cheeks burned with humiliation.

"I have been merciful with you, Brother Gideon," Maddoc intoned loudly so all could hear. "I have been more than lenient with your ideas that run so counter to mine. I have kept you in your high position because so many agreed with you and I wanted to respect their beliefs. Men like the ones you used like tools this day, as though they were disposable." The boots halted in front of him. "In a secret mission you conducted by yourself, sacrificing the lives of good Phaendir. Tell me, Brother Gideon, what price should you pay for these high crimes?"

"What I did, I did in the name of Labrai."

*"And how do you think Labrai feels about the needless disposal of Phaendir lives?"* The words roared out of Maddoc with a forcefulness that Gideon had forgotten he possessed. "How do you think He feels about secret agendas and missions? How do think He feels about conniving, deceitful, upwardly mobile Phaendir? How do you think He feels about losing important ancient Phaendir artifacts that could endanger all we hold precious?"

Gideon lifted his nose from the ground. His gaze touched a concerned-looking Emily and instantly refocused on Brother Maddoc. "I am so very sorry for what I have done," he intoned, trying his best to appear miserable and contrite. "I know it was wrong. Please, let me live so that I may serve you and Labrai another day."

A silence stretched. Gideon's back clenched. His neck twinged.

"You are demoted, Brother Gideon, a full four places down the power structure," Brother Maddoc said finally. "And you will take a public lashing for your sins."

Gideon rested his head on the ground once more and closed his eyes in relief. He wasn't surprised the weak Brother Maddoc had allowed him to live, but he was relieved to hear the verdict out loud. He might be demoted and humiliated, but he still had his life. If air still filled his lungs, he would not stop in his quest to gain Brother Maddoc's seat.

Maddoc should kill him. If he was a smarter man, he would.

Even though Gideon had failed in his quest to obtain the Book of Bindings, eventually he would see his agenda take the lead in Phaendir policy making.

Then he would see the extermination of every fae-blooded thing in Piefferburg.

First, unfortunately, he would have to start with his brothers. That was clear enough. It was time to take his gloves off and get his hands dirty. A full four places down the power structure? Pity the men above him.

Pity Brother Maddoc.

Men gripped his clothing, shredding the fabric and leaving him naked on the ground. The creaking leather sound of a whip being unfurled behind him filled the air and made him shiver with anticipation. The first lash snapped against his flesh and his body arched backward in shock and pain, hot blood welling. Sweet, delicious, *beautiful* agony followed.

The crowd made a collective gasp of horror, but no one would guess it was a smile on his face and not a grimace.

His will would be done.


"I'M sorry, Gabriel."

"I don't want to hear that." His voice was harsh, hard—filled with grief. "I want to hear that you can bring her back."

Ronan smiled sadly. "I'm a powerful mage, but I'm not all-powerful. Issues of life and death lie in Danu's realm alone."

Aislinn lay on the bed in her chambers, her skin pale against the ruby coverlet they'd only recently made love beneath. The amulet tattoo, though dull, still marked her skin. It meant she was still alive, although only barely. In his numb state back at the temple, he'd failed to grasp that fact as a sign of life.

The doctors could only detect the slightest breath in her body and her skin was ashen, her eyes closed. The illness she suffered was magickal in nature so not even medical means could help her now. Only magickal countermeasures, and there were none. Aislinn was on her own.

"A weaker person would have died by now," murmured Niall, coming to gaze down at her. "She's fighting. As long as she's fighting it, there's hope."

The battle at the temple was done and all the Phaendir who'd dared cross the line into Piefferburg were dead and had been delivered past the main gates of Piefferburg on a truck and dumped unceremoniously. *Faemous* had loved that. The Book of Bindings was still safe. Word of what had happened at the Grand Temple had spread fast—the second upheaval in the city in less than a week.

The fae races were riled. Volatile. You could feel the pulsing energy of it on the streets.

Perhaps now more than ever, with the exception of the years after the Great Sweep, the fae wanted blood for what had been done to them.

News of the fate of the Unseelie Royal had also spread. Many had been by to pay their respects. Her apartment and the corridor beyond were littered with flowers, candles, and other trinkets of well wishes. Even the Summer Queen had sent a bouquet.

Aislinn lingered in some place where he couldn't go. Not here in the land of the living and not in the Netherworld. She existed somewhere in the middle, suspended by the magick of the druids that had done its best to kill her. He couldn't go there and save her. This time there was no summoning Abastor, no descent into the unknown to rescue her. This time there was nothing he could do. She was all alone.

And it killed him.

If he could fall into the magick that held her captive, he would let it swallow him whole. If he could swim through the murk that held her so close to death and free her, he would plunge into it. He would let it take him instead and leave her living, breathing, laughing, and free to love.

"Since she had no children, we will have to consider a list of candidates for the Shadow Amulet," said Hinckley from where he stood near the door.

Gabriel turned and speared him with a look so black and poisonous that Hinckley stumbled in his haste to leave the room.

Turning back to Aislinn, Gabriel stared down, his gaze tracing over her prone form for the millionth time since they'd carried her back from Goblin Town. He hadn't changed his clothes yet and the residual stink of sulfur from the druids' power still clung to him, competing with the scent of flowers in the room.

"Leave me alone with her." His voice sounded raspy and broken to his own ears.

Ronan nodded and herded the others in the room out.

Gabriel crawled onto the bed and pulled Aislinn's limp body against him. Her skin was cold and her lips were blue. He molded her to him and kissed her cheek, her neck, anywhere he could press lips to flesh.

"I love you, Aislinn," he murmured. "I haven't loved anyone since I was a child. I thought I'd forgotten how to love or maybe that I wasn't capable of it. Then I met you." His voice broke on the words and he fought to maintain control. "I can't lose you."

The offering candles guttered in their holders, casting flickering shadows over the walls until they eventually spent themselves completely.

Eventually, morning dawned. Roseate fingers inched their way over furniture and floor, giving the room a merry lightness that didn't reach inside his heart. Gabriel closed his eyes and held her, willing his spirit to somehow enter her and help to free her from the trap she was caught in. He tried to project himself into her, fall into her. Immerse himself in her troubled waters, join with the injured portion of her mind and body and yank her away from whatever magickal forces had its claws sunk so deep.

But his magick was only of two things—sex and death.

Not life.

"Fight it. Come back to me." He pushed up and stared down at her. "Do you hear me, Aislinn? *Fight it!* You're mine, remember? You're not death's, not yet. You won't belong to the Netherworld for many years, not until long after we've had kids and watched them grow up. Not until long after we've grown old together."

But she didn't move, didn't make any indication she heard his plea.

Gabriel dipped his head and fought the grief rising up from the depths, trying to choke him. "Don't leave me."

* * *

AISLINN pulled at the hands that held her down, the moaning, reaching arms of those in the Netherworld who wanted to drag her down into unfathomable depths.

"You're ours," they whispered.

"Stop fighting," they growled.

"Let go and it will all be over," they crooned. "So easy . . ."

Her body and mind were exhausted and every time she managed to extricate herself from one grasping bunch of hands, another group of them latched on to some other part of her body and the battle began again.

All she wanted was to sleep, to give up and let go . . . just like they said. But distantly, she understood that if she went to sleep, it would be the sleep of death.

Someone far away called her name, told her to fight, told her she was his—not death's. Death. Were those the hands that pulled at her? *Fight it. Come back to me.* The voice was familiar, someone she loved.

Gabriel.

She remembered what he looked like, could recall the stroke of his hands on her flesh and the brush of his lips on the nape of her neck. The scent of him teased her nose, a distant memory she wanted to wrap around her like a soft, warm blanket. The look in his eyes when he was aroused. The sound of his voice, his laughter.

She strained toward the memory of Gabriel and away from the grasping hands. Calling up an image of the man she loved, she fell into it, used it as an anchor.

*Don't leave me.*

No, she didn't want to leave him. She needed to fight. She wasn't theirs, these hands that grasped and pulled at her. She was Gabriel's love. He'd told her so. She *wanted* to be his.

And she was, heart, body, and soul.

Strength renewed, Aislinn fought with a renewed will. She pulled and kicked and fought and twisted, yelling back at the moaning voices that they couldn't have her. She was already claimed. Claimed by life and by love.

An image rose up. Gabriel stood behind a sheet of shimmering silver, like a smooth mirror or the surface of a lake. He reached through the barrier that separated them, entreating her to take hold. She grasped for that lifeline and held on, used it as leverage against the sticky pull of the dark on her other side.

Light glimmered. The hands fell away.

More light.

Her eyelids opening.

Morning light.

Warmth beside her.

Despite the ache of her body and the fatigue that permeated every part of her, she turned her head to meet Gabriel's face, his eyes closed and anguish clear on his handsome visage.

"Gabriel," she croaked.

His eyes opened, widened. His hands cupped her cheeks softly, as though afraid she might break or disappear. His face filled with emotion that needed no words to express. He dipped his head, his lips pressing against hers, long and lingeringly.

"I thought I'd lost you," he whispered against her mouth.

Aislinn smiled, basking in the perfect warmth of the home his arms made and knowing she was exactly where she should be. "Never. I'm yours."

# TWENTY-EIGHT

AISLINN stood on the top of the Black Tower at dusk still wearing her wedding dress, a bloodred and cream affair, accompanied by dripping ruby jewelry that would rival any outfit of the Summer Queen's. Her hair was gathered and twisted at the back of her head, the red tips fanning out in an arc at the top and secured by a silver and black crown.

Her new husband stood beside her, now a king. The Unseelie Court had never had both a Shadow King and Shadow Queen and the inhabitants had been celebrating since the morning wedding ceremony.

Once, long ago, marriage had been unheard of in fae culture. However, human culture had leached into theirs and marriages had become common. But not for the royals. Sometimes the court royals had taken consorts, but they'd never trusted anyone enough to share full power.

As soon as she'd recovered, there'd been no question that she would marry Gabriel. They belonged to each other, belonged together, and would rule side by side.

The ceremony had been beautiful, but it hadn't been because of the decorations in the main gathering hall, the expensive food and drink that had followed, or even the joy and celebration of the Unseelie. Honestly, she'd hardly seen any of that. She'd only seen Gabriel's face.

His vows had echoed through her mind all day.

He'd spoken the words in Old Maejian first, weaving the spell between them—magick knitting the halves of their souls into one. Now wherever her soul went, his would follow. Then he'd spoken them in English.

I give you my blood, bone, and breath.
I give you my soul and the spirit it rides in.
Should you be discarded by others, I will cherish you.
Should danger come, I will give my life to protect you.
Should your honor be lost, in mine I will cloak you.
Should you become sick, I will heal you.
Should you be lost, I will find you.
Ask me never to leave you. Stop me not from following after you.
Where you go, I will go. Not even death shall part us.
I am yours.

She'd been surprised he'd used the Joining Vows, the traditional mating vows of the Tuatha Dé. No one used them anymore because of the magick involved. They bound souls together, making two halves one whole. When one of them died, the other would follow. Conversely, because the Shadow Amulet made her immortal, so now was Gabriel. As he'd pledged himself to her, the magick-laced vows had wrapped around her, held her close, and let her know that Gabriel's love was pure, genuine, and strong.

Not that she'd doubted it.

She said them back immediately, happy tears streaming down her face.

Gabriel took her hand and they stood in an easy, contented silence, surveying the scene below them. They'd been able to slip away at the end of the day, leaving the others to continue the party, which she was sure would last well into the night.

Dusk rose on the horizon. Shades of orange and yellow gave way to dark blue, purple, and gray. Slowly the day slipped away, giving over rule to the dark.

The city still seemed to seethe and pulse after the populace had discovered the Phaendir had dared to step foot on Piefferburg soil. The old hurts and anger at their imprisonment, long since settled and cooled since the Great Sweep and Piefferburg's beginnings, had been stirred up.

Maybe her near death had been a good thing. It was a rage they could use.

The book was safely hidden away and the Summer Queen had one of the pieces to the *bosca fadbh*. They needed two other pieces. It seemed impossible, but it was already impossible they should be in possession of half of what they needed to break free.

Clearly anything could happen. In the days ahead, Aislinn was pretty sure lots of things would.

She laid her head on her husband's shoulder and watched the day give up its last gasp of light and give way to the mysterious and powerful dark.

Dear readers,
curious where Piefferburg is located?

Visit my website for an interactive map:

www.anyabast.com

# GLOSSARY

**Abastor** The mystic black stallion that leads the Wild Hunt.

**Black Tower** A large building on one end of Piefferburg Square that is constructed of black quartz. This is the home of the Unseelie Court.

**Book of Bindings** Book created when the Phaendir and the fae were allied. The most complete book of spells known. Contains the spell that can break the warding around Piefferburg.

*bosca fadbh* Puzzle box consisting of three interlocking pieces. Once was an object owned by both the Phaendir and the fae, back when they weren't enemies. When all three pieces are united, it forms a key to unlock part of the Book of Bindings.

**Boundary Lands** The area where the wilding fae live.

*ceantar dubh* Dark district. This is the neighborhood directly buttressing the Black Tower.

*ceantar láir* Middle district. Fae "suburbia," it also borders a mostly commercial area of downtown Piefferburg where the troop live and work.

**charmed iron** Iron spelled to take away a fae's magick when it touches the skin. Used in prisons as handcuffs and by the Imperial and Shadow guards, it's illegal for the general fae population to possess it. Charmed iron weapons were a major reason the fae lost in the war against the Milesians and Phaendir in ancient Ireland.

**Danu** The primary goddess of the Tuatha Dé Danann, both Seelie and Unseelie. Also followed by some other fae races. Danu is accompanied by a small pantheon of lesser gods.

**Furious Host** Those who follow the Lord of the Wild Hunt every night to collect the souls of the fae who have died and help to ferry them to the Netherworld.

**Goblin Town** The area of Piefferburg City where the goblins, a fae race with customs that differ greatly from the other types of fae, live.

**Great Sweep** When the Phaendir, allied with the human race, hunted down, trapped, and imprisoned all known fae and contained them in Piefferburg.

**Humans for the Freedom of the Fae (HFF)** An organization of humans working for equal fae rights and the destruction of Piefferburg.

**iron sickness** The illness that occurs when charmed iron is pressed against the flesh of a fae for an extended period of time, eventually fatal.

**Joining Vows** Ancient, magick-laced vows that twine two souls together. Not often used in modern fae society because of the commitment involved.

**Jules Piefferburg** Original human architect of Piefferburg. The statue honoring him in Piefferburg Square is made of charmed iron and can't be taken down, so the fae constantly dishonor it in other ways, like dressing it up disrespectfully or throwing food at it.

**Labrai** The god the Phaendir follow.

**Netherworld** Where the fae go after they die.

**Old Maejian** The original tongue of the fae. It's a dead language to all except those who are serious about practicing magick.

**Orna** The primary goddess of the goblins. Accompanied by many lesser gods.

**Phaendir ("fane-dear")** A race of druids whose origins remain murky. The common belief of the fae is that their own genetic line sprang from the Phaendir. The Phaendir believe they've always been a separate—superior—race. Once allied with the fae, the Phaendir are now their mortal enemies.

**Piefferburg ("fife-er-berg") Square** Large cobblestone square with a statue of Jules Piefferburg in the center and the Rose and Black towers on either end.

**Rose Tower** Made of rose quartz, this building sits at one end of Piefferburg Square and houses the Seelie Court.

**Seelie ("seal-ee")** A highly selective fae ruling class, the Seelie allow only the Tuatha Dé Danann Sídhe into their ranks. Members must have a direct bloodline to the original ruling Seelie of ancient Ireland and their magick must be light and pretty.

**Shadow Amulet** The one who wears the amulet holds the Shadow Throne, though the amulet might reject someone without the proper bloodline. It sinks into the wearer's body, imbuing him or her with power and immortality, leaving only a tattoo on the skin to mark its physical presence.

**Shadow Royal** Holder of the Unseelie Throne.

**Sídhe ("shee")** Another name for the Tuatha Dé Danann (Irish) fae, both Seelie and Unseelie.

**Summer Ring** Like the Shadow Amulet of the Unseelie Royal, this piece of jewelry imbues the wearer with great power and immortality. It also sinks into the skin, leaving only a tattoo, and may reject the wearer at will. This ring determines who holds the Seelie Throne.

**Summer Royal** Holder of the Seelie Throne.

**trooping fae** Also called the troop, those fae who are not a part of either court and are not wilding or water fae.

**Tuatha Dé Danann ("thoo-a-haw day dah-nawn")** The most ancient of all races on earth, the fae. They were evolved and sophisticated when humans still lived in caves. Came to Ireland in the ancient times and overthrew the native people. The Seelie Tuatha Dé ruled the other fae races. When the Milesians (a tribe of humans in ancient Ireland) allied with the Phaendir and defeated the fae, the fae had to agree to go underground. They disappeared from all human knowledge, becoming myth.

**Twyleth Teg ("till-eg tay")** Welsh faeries. They're rare and live across the social spectrum.

**Unseelie ("UN-seal-ee")** A fae ruling class, the Unseelie will take anyone who comes to them with dark magick, but the true definition of an Unseelie fae is one whose magick can draw blood or kill.

**water fae** Those fae who live in the large water areas of Piefferburg. They stay out of the city of Piefferburg and out of court politics and life.

**Watt syndrome** Illness that befell all the fae races during the height of the race wars. The sickness decimated the fae population, outed them to the humans, and ultimately caused their downfall, weakening them to the point that the Phaendir could gather and trap them in Piefferburg. Some think the syndrome was biological warfare perpetrated by the Phaendir.

**Wild Hunt** Comprising mystic horses and hounds and a small group of fae known as the Furious Host, led by the Lord of the Wild Hunt, the hunt gathers the souls of all the fae who have died every night and ferries them to the Netherworld. The identities of the Unseelie fae who make up the Wild Hunt are kept secret.

**wilding fae** Nature fae. Like the water fae, they stay away from Piefferburg proper, choosing to live in the Boundary Lands.

**Worshipful Observers** Steadfast human supporters of the work the Phaendir does to keep the fae races separate from the rest of the world.

Turn the page for a preview of
the next paranormal romance from Anya Bast

# CRUEL ENCHANTMENT

Coming September 2010 from Berkley Sensation!

*EMMALINE Siobhan Keara Gallagher.*

*Clang. Clang. Clang.* The shock of hammer to hot iron reverberated up his arm and through his shoulders. As Aeric shaped the hunk of iron into a charmed blade, her name beat a staccato rhythm in his mind.

He glanced up at the portrait of Aileen, the one he kept in his forge as a reminder, and his hammer came down harder. It wasn't every night the fire of vengeance burned so hot and so hard in him. Over three hundred and sixty years had passed since the Summer Queen's assassin had murdered his love.

*Emmaline Siobhan Keara Gallagher.*

He'd had plenty of time to move past his loss. Yet his rage burned bright tonight, as if it had happened three days ago instead of three hundred years. It was almost as if the object of his vengeance was close by, or thinking about him. Perhaps, as he'd imagined for so many years, he shared a psychic connection with her.

One born of cruel and violent intention.

He was certain that if the power of his thoughts truly did penetrate her mind, she had nightmares about him. If she ever thought his name, it was with a shudder and a chill.

If Aeric knew what she really looked like, he would envision her face with every impact of his hammer. Instead, he only brought her essence to mind while forging weapons others would wield to kill, maim, and bring misery. If he could name them all, he would call them *Emmaline*.

It was the least he could do, but he wanted to do so much more. Maybe one day he would get the chance, though odds were against him. He was stuck in Piefferburg while she roamed free outside its barriers. Aileen was far from him, too, lost to the shadowy Netherworld.

He tossed the hammer aside. Sweat trickling down his bare chest and into his belly button, he turned with the red-hot length of charmed iron in a pair of tongs and dunked it into a tub of cold water, making the iron spit and steam. As he worked the metal, his magick pulled out of him in a long, thin thread, imbuing the weapon with the ability to extract a fae's power and cause illness.

Aeric O'Malley was the Blacksmith, the only fae in the world who could create weapons of charmed iron. His father had once also possessed the same magick, but he'd been badly affected by Watt syndrome at the time of the Great Sweep. These days he wasn't fit for the forge, leaving the family tradition to Aeric.

Creating these weapons every night was his ritual, one he had kept secret from all who knew him. His forge was hidden in the back of his apartment, deep at the base of the Black Tower. The former Shadow King, Aodh Críostóir Ruadhán O'Dubhuir, had been the only one who'd known about his illicit work; he'd been the one to set him up in it.

Now the Unseelie had a shadow queen instead of a king. She was a good queen, but one who was still finding her footing in the Black Tower. Queen Aislinn might not look kindly on the fact the Blacksmith was still producing weapons that could be used on his own people. Queen

Aislinn wasn't as . . . *practical* as her foul biological father had been.

He pulled off his thick gloves and, with a groan of fatigue, wiped the back of his arm across his sweat-soaked forehead. The iron called to him at all hours of the day and night. Even after he had done his sacred duty riding in the Wild Hunt every night, the forge summoned him before dawn. He spent most nights fulfilling orders for illegal weaponry, or sometimes just making it because he had to, because his fae blood called him to do it. As long as his magick held out, he created.

The walls of his iron world glinted silver and deadly with the products of his labor, and in the middle of it all hung Aileen's portrait, the one he'd painted with his own hands so he never forgot what she looked like.

So he never forgot.

Despite the heat and grime of the room, her portrait was still pristine. Angel-pale and golden-beautiful, she hung on the wall and gazed down at him with eyes of green—green as the grass of the country she'd died in.

His fingers curled, remembering the softness of her skin and how her silky hair had slipped over his palms and mouth. His gaze caught and lingered on the shape of her mouth. Not that he needed to commit the way she looked to memory. He remembered Aileen Arabella Edmé McIlvernock. His fiancée had looked like an angel, walked like one, thought like one . . . and made love like one. Maybe she hadn't been an angel in all ways—no, definitely not—but his memory never snagged on those jagged places. There was no point in remembering the dark, only the light. And there was no forgetting her. He never would.

Nor would he ever forget her murderer.

Emmaline had managed to escape the Great Sweep and probably Watt syndrome, too. He couldn't know for sure; he just suspected. His gut simply told him she was out there in the world somewhere and he lived for the day he would find her. She'd taken his soul apart the day she'd killed Aileen and he'd never been able to put it completely back together again.

It was only fair he should be able to take Emmaline's soul apart in return. Slowly. Piece by bloody piece.

The chances she'd walk through the gates of Piefferburg and into the web of pain that awaited her was infinitesimal, but tonight, as Aeric gazed at the portrait of Aileen, he hoped for a miracle.

Danu help Emmaline if she ever did cross that threshold into Piefferburg. He'd be waiting.


THE fae checked in, but they never checked out. It was a fae roach motel. Did she really want to cross that threshold and possibly end up a squashed bug? No, of course not. Problem was, she had no choice.

Emmaline Siobhan Keara Gallagher stared at the outer gates of Piefferburg. Was she really ready to take this risk? After all she'd done, all the years and energy she'd committed to the cause, she still shuddered at the thought of going in there for fear she may never come out.

She stared at the hazy warding that guarded the fae from the human world, set a few inches out from a tall, thick brick wall. The wall didn't go all the way around Piefferburg, since the detention compound—*resettlement area* was the more PC term—was enormous and the borders included not only marshlands, where a wall could not be built, but the ocean, too. It was the Phaendir's warding that kept the fae imprisoned, not that thick wall. That was there only for the eyes of humans. An almost organic thing, the warding existed in a subconscious, hive portion of the Phaendir's collective mind—fueled by their breath, thoughts, magick, and, most of all, by their very strong belief system.

That warding was unbreakable.

"Emily?"

She jumped, startled. Emmaline turned at the name the Phaendir knew her by, something close enough to her real name to make it comfortable. Well, as comfortable as she could be while undercover in a nest of her mortal enemies. That didn't exactly make every day a picnic.

Schooling her expression and double-checking her glamour—she was paranoid about keeping it in place—she turned with a forced smile. "Brother Gideon, you frightened me."

His thin lips pursed and he smoothed his thinning brown hair over his head, favoring her with a glance that anyone who didn't know him would call nervous. Emmaline, of all people, knew better. Gideon was confident, dangerous. The face he presented to the world was one calculated to make people underestimate him.

Brother Gideon was average in every way possible—medium brown hair, average height and build, unremarkable brown eyes, weak chin, receding hairline. A person walking by him on the street would glance at him and immediately dismiss him as nonthreatening. In reality, Brother Gideon was the most menacing of all the Phaendir, a black mamba in a cave filled with rattlers. While you were busy overlooking and underestimating him, he'd be busy killing you. That's what made him extradangerous.

It was no secret that Gideon was nursing a crush on her. She'd been carefully fostering that crush for quite some time now, using it as an effective tool. It wasn't a pleasant or easy thing, having a man as vicious as Brother Gideon admiring her. It was, however, a useful thing. Useful to the HFF—Humans for the Freedom of the Fae—an organization to which she'd dedicated her life.

"I'm sorry, Emily," he replied in his very average light tenor of a voice. "I didn't mean to startle you. I just saw you standing out here and wanted to see you off."

A little over a year ago, Brother Gideon had attempted a coup. He'd tried to obtain the Book of Bindings before Brother Maddoc, the leader of the Phaendir, could do it. Emmaline speculated it had been a move to take over Maddoc's place. Brother Gideon strove very hard to implement his much bloodier agenda for dealing with the fae.

Luckily Brother Gideon had been caught and punished by being demoted four places in the Phaendir power structure. But Maddoc should have killed Gideon. During the last year, two of the Phaendir who occupied spots above Gideon had met their ends in freak, horrific accidents. Not one being could prove Gideon had anything to do with the deaths.

But Emmaline had no doubt that Gideon wasn't done yet. Maddoc needed to watch his back.

The prospect of having Gideon leading the Phaendir made her mission more critical. It even made her fingers itch for her old crossbow, and it took a hell of a lot for that to happen. If anyone needed a quarrel through the throat, it was Brother Gideon.

She forced a smile. "And I'm so glad you did."

"Are you sure you're ready for this?"

"I may be human, but in my heart, I'm Phaendir. I live to serve."

Gideon smiled and she fought the urge to vomit on her hiking boots.

She looked away from him, up at the hazy warding. Gideon thought she was human and a human wouldn't be able to see the warding, so she motioned to the wall. "It's immense and so . . . strong." She made sure she glanced at Gideon with a shy smile as she said the last. "It's a beautiful thing, this place the Phaendir have created to keep us safe." She used the reverent tone of the Worshipful Observer that Gideon believed she was.

Gideon came to stand near her and clasped his thin, pale hands in front of him. "Labrai wills it so." He paused. "As he wills your entry into Piefferburg and your eventual success. You're a woman with a strong, stable character. It can be no other way."

She wanted to laugh. *A strong, stable character.* Right. Her characters were so layered even she had trouble parsing them. She was a fae HFF member currently undercover as a human Worshipful Observer who was soon going undercover as a member of the *Faemous* film crew in order to mine information for the Phaendir while actually working a mission for the HFF.

Yeah. Not confusing at all.

It was an event that would ironically blow *all* her covers, bringing her back to what she really was. A free fae.

As if she wasn't already bewildered enough.

Danu and all the gods, why was she going into Piefferburg of her own free will? She swallowed hard. *The Blacksmith* was in there. She had nightmares about coming face-to-face with him often enough to warrant a prescription for Xanax.

And hell, she was *seeking him out*. He was the only one who could help the HFF at this point. How crazy was that? He wanted to kill her . . . maybe. Probably.

Maybe.

It had been so long—over three hundred and sixty years—since the night she'd killed Aileen Arabella Edmé McIlvernock. She didn't even know if Aeric had survived Watt syndrome, though she hoped he had. If he hadn't survived, and if there was no other fae who could forge a charmed iron key, they were all doomed. She knew Aeric's father also had the talent, but he'd been one of the first fae to come down with Watt syndrome. At the time she'd left Ireland, he'd been very ill and was not expected to live.

But she felt it in her blood that Aeric O'Malley had survived. She could feel him in there, within the boundaries of Piefferburg. Almost as if he was waiting for her. She shivered. That couldn't be possible of course; it was only her vivid imagination.

And he wasn't the only one who might be thirsting for her blood. Once upon a time, when she'd been the Summer Queen's greatest weapon in the Seelie war against the Unseelie, she'd burned some bridges. Many, many bridges. There were those in the Black Tower who would love to cross the charred ruins of those bridges . . . to strangle her.

*Danu*, she hoped her glamour was strong enough to fool the Blacksmith. If the illusion slipped, if he found out who she really was, her life was as good as gone. If *any* of the Unseelie found out who she was . . .

Or if the Summer Queen found out . . .

Or Lars, the Summer Queen's barely leashed pit bull . . .

Emmaline shuddered. Once she was in Piefferburg, she didn't plan to go to the Rose Tower at all. It was straight to the Black in heavy glamour. There was no way she was going anywhere near the woman who'd screwed up her life so much and, via Lars, planted nightmares in her subconscious that put the ones she had about the Blacksmith to shame.

Gods, why was she doing this again? Oh, right, because she was the only one who could. *Damn it*.

"Emily? Are you nervous?"

She blinked and glanced at Gideon, pulling herself back from the muck of her thoughts. For a moment, she groped for something plausible to respond with. "Well, a little. I've heard the stories about the goblins." Humans were terrified of goblins, though, as a fae she didn't swallow the boogyman tales. There were other races that were much more terrifying. "I saw the bodies of the Phaendir you sent in after the Book—"

He waved his hand, not wanting to take that conversational road. The men he'd sent into Piefferburg after the Book of Bindings had come out gnawed on. "You'll be fine. You're going to the Seelie Court, to the Rose Tower. They're much more hospitable to humans than the Unseelie. No goblins there, only the tamer breed of hobgoblin. They're servants, mostly."

She smiled. "I know I'll be fine. You would never let me come to harm, would you, Brother Gideon?"

He smiled at her and she suppressed another shudder. There was lust in his eyes—a thing no woman wanted directed at her. "Never."

"Anyway, like I said, I'm ready to sacrifice my life for the cause of the Phaendir."

"Emily." Gideon took her hands in his. His skin was papery-feeling, dry. On his wrists, she could feel the start of the scars that marked his arms, chest, and back. Brother Gideon flagellated himself every day in name of Labrai, though Emmaline had long suspected he enjoyed the floggings with his wicked cat-o'-nine-tails. "But I am not willing to sacrifice your life, Emily. Not for anything." He blinked watery brown eyes.

"Oh, Gideon," she said in a practiced, slightly breathy voice. "Your piousness is already so attractive and to know you actually care about me as a person is so . . . moving."

She didn't melt against him or bat her eyelashes, but she did stare adoringly into his eyes.

"Shhh, I understand. I only hope that one day—"

"Brother Gideon? Emily?"

Gideon gritted his teeth for a moment. His face—just for a heartbeat—made the transformation from medium to monster. Veins stood out in his forehead and neck. His skin went pale and his eyes bulged. He dropped her hands and moved away from her, his natural, unassuming visage back in place in a matter of seconds. Just the glimpse of Gideon's true self was enough to leave Emmaline shaky, a reaction that luckily worked for this particular situation.

The tension in the air ratcheted upward between the two men. Power struggles within the structure of the group seemed to permeate all their interactions. Then, of course, there was the carefully orchestrated charade she'd been performing for Gideon to make things worse—making Gideon believe she was sleeping with his arch enemy.

As undercover HFF, it was her job to throw wrenches into the best of the Phaendir's machines and she was good at her job.

"Are you ready?" asked Brother Maddoc with a warm smile. Brother Maddoc was annoyingly likable considering he was Phaendir. With him, you got what you saw on the surface. Trouble was, he hated the fae. Not as much as Gideon hated the fae, but enough to want to keep them imprisoned forever.

Her smile flickered. "No."

Maddoc laughed and pulled her against him for a hug. "Don't worry, you're all set up. They're expecting you at the Rose Tower as the newest addition to the *Faemous* crew. Just go in like you're a real anchor and start snooping around for information about the *bosca fadbh*. I don't think I need to impress upon you how important a job this is, Emily."

Except it wasn't her real job. She wasn't going to step foot in the Rose Tower.

She knew all about the *bosca fadbh* and information about the valuable puzzle key would be found nowhere near the Seelie Court. The HFF had found clues to the second piece in records buried in a room of an ancient castle in Ireland. The piece she was trying to get was halfway around the world, off the coast of Atlit, Israel. It sucked that the only man capable of helping the HFF get that piece was stuck in Piefferburg.

She laid her head on Maddoc's shoulder, an action that made Gideon shuffle his feet and cough as he tried to conceal his irritation and jealousy. "I won't let you down, Brother Maddoc."

"I know." He smiled and kissed her temple. "Now go. They're ready to let you in."

She turned toward the heavy wrought iron gates that separated Piefferburg and most of the world's fae from the fragile human world. The huge doors opened with a groan and all the heavy protocol that went with the admission of individuals began. On this side of the gate things were monitored by the Phaendir. On the other side of the gate, all deliveries or people passing through were carefully inspected by the fae and all arrivals reported to both towers.

Of course neither side trusted the other. The fae exerted what little control they had by checking to make sure no Phaendir entered—some had tried, all had been brutally killed. The Phaendir, of course, would not allow any fae to leave. Humans could come and go at their own peril. Not many did. Only the very brave and the very stupid dared cross into the land of the fae.

Or the very desperate. That would be her.

Glancing back at Gideon and Maddoc and shooting them a look of uncertainty she didn't have to feign, she stepped past the gates.

Surely the Blacksmith wouldn't recognize her under her powerful glamour. Surely she would be safe from his wrath. If she could fool all of the Phaendir, she could fool one fae. Even if somehow he did recognize her, hundreds of years had passed since that unfortunate day and her errand was of monumental importance to the fae.

Surely this would turn out all right.